New York Nights

Book One in the Virex Trilogy

Eric Brown

The right of Eric Brown to be identified as the author of this work
has been asserted by him in accordance with the
Copyright, Designs and Patents Act 1988.

This edition published in Great Britain in 2001 by

Gollancz
An imprint of Orion Publishing Group
Orion House, 5 Upper St Martin's Lane, London WC2H 9EA

A CIP catalogue record for this book is available
from the British Library

ISBN 1 85798 782 9

Typeset by SetSystems Ltd, Saffron Walden, Essex
Printed in Great Britain by
Clays Ltd, St Ives plc

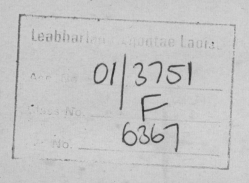

This novel is dedicated to
Sandra Sogas Romeu
with all my love –
*Els somnis més bonics també es poden
convertir en realitat!*

New York City
Winter 2040

One

That night was like a thousand others he'd woken to in El Barrio, but looking back Halliday realised that it marked the beginning of what he would come to see as the darkest period of his life.

The alarm went off at ten. He blinked himself awake, his breath pluming in the icy air of the moon-lit loft. Kim lay beside him, her warmth tempting him to doze for another hour. The thought of what work Barney might have on file moved him to abandon the sanctuary of the futon and cross the loft to the bathroom, shivering in the sub-zero chill.

He showered, relishing the jet of hot water. As he stood below the drier, looking through the open door along the length of the loft, he noticed that Kim had rearranged the furniture yet again. The Salvation Army couch and threadbare armchair now faced the wall-window that overlooked the back alley.

Last week, intuiting a look from him as he tried to find the coatstand, she had wrestled him to the bed and pinioned his arms with her knees, jet hair falling around her serene oval face. 'I've known you how long now, Mr Halliday?'

'Seems like ten years.'

She slapped him, hard. 'Not even ten months, Hal. And in that time, what's happened?'

In ten months, his partnership with Barney had prospered: they never seemed to go more than a day or two

1

without another case coming in, and their success rate in solving commissions was higher than ever. Halliday put it down to coincidence, or that psychologically he was feeling better for having this beautiful Chinese sprite enter his life like a miniature whirlwind and blow away his old apathy and desperation. He was feeling better in himself, and he was working harder: therefore, he was solving more cases.

'I see this place, Hal . . .' Kim had gestured around at the loft, 'and I think negative energy, sick room, bad chi. I think, things need to change around here. So I rearrange things. And lo, your luck changes – you get more work, more dollars.'

Halliday heard a squeal from the loft. He finished dressing and stepped from the bathroom. Kim was dancing around the room like a naked dervish, long hair falling to her child-slim waist. She pulled on underwear, minimal panties and bra, managing in the process to stare at him with massive eyes. 'I told you to set the alarm for eight, Hal!'

'When? You never said a thing!'

'I get in at noon, you wake, I say, Set alarm for eight, Hal. You say, Hokay.'

He barely remembered her sneaking under the thermal beside him. 'I was dead to the world . . .'

'You answered!'

'In my sleep!'

She cursed him in Mandarin, hopping on one leg as she forced the other into a pair of jeans.

Halliday found his jacket and pulled the zip to his chin, shutting out the cold. 'Anyway, why did you want to be out by eight?'

'Work to do, Hal. Stalls to organise. Busy night.'

'You could delegate.'

Briefly, she stopped dressing and stared at him, shaking

2

her head. 'Delegate' was a word that had yet to enter her vocabulary. Kim Long owned a dozen Chinese roadside food-stalls in the area, and Halliday had once calculated that she worked at least fourteen hours a day, every day. When he protested that he only ever met her in bed, she always went out of her way to make time for him – she'd take him to a restaurant, or a holo-drama, gestures to placate his dissatisfaction. Then, in a day or two, she'd be back to her gruelling work routine and they'd hardly go out together until the next time he moved himself to mention the fact.

'Can't trust other people to do what you should do yourself, Hal,' she told him. 'Gotta make them dollars. I'm a busy girl.'

He didn't know whether to be amazed by her materialism, or sickened. She'd arrived from Singapore at the age of fifteen, following the Malaysian invasion ten years ago, penniless after her father's restaurant had been confiscated by the Communists. She'd taught herself English, bought herself a microwave and a patch in a side-street, and slowly built up a thriving fast food business.

He paused by the door. 'Kim, why don't you just slow down, take it easy? Enjoy yourself.'

In moonboots and chunky climbing jacket, she widened her eyes at his apostasy. 'I enjoy my work, Mr Halliday. If you enjoyed your work, you'd be happier person.'

She ran into the bathroom.

He almost let that one go, then thought about it.

'Hey, that isn't fair. My work's different.' He moved to the bathroom, kicked open the red-painted door with his boot, and leaned against the woodwork. 'I spend hours looking for people . . . and sometimes I find them, sometimes I find corpses. And sometimes I find nothing at all . . . which can be even worse.'

She squatted on the john, jeans shackling her ankles,

3

and pissed. 'Well, I like my work!' she shouted. 'I like what I do! Don't blame me for that, Hal!'

'I'm not blaming you, I'm just . . .' He trailed off. He sometimes wondered why he bothered arguing. He'd never change her.

She was a creature of extremes. She combined a feminine gentleness, an almost obsessive desire to please him on the rare occasions they were together, with a fierce, driven determination to get her own way in matters where finance and business were concerned. On the street, he'd seen her giving instructions to her managers, letting go with a rapid-fire burst of Mandarin that sounded like the high notes of a xylophone played by a madman. The depth of her rage often alarmed him.

He'd once accused her of possessing a split personality.

She'd snorted, 'Please don't give me none of that Freudian bullshit, Mr Halliday! You never heard of yin and yang?'

Now he sketched a wave. 'I'm outta here.'

'Hal, if you don't like your work, why do you do it?'

He pushed himself from the jamb. I sometimes wonder, he thought to himself. 'See you later, Kim.'

As he left the loft, she called after him, 'And remember to be back by . . .' but the rest was lost as he closed the door. He wondered what she was talking about: he recalled no arrangement to meet her at whatever time.

He made his way down the steps to the office on the second floor, descending into the welcome, starch-laden heat that rose from the Chinese laundry.

A light was on behind the pebbled glass. He pushed open the door. The office was a long, narrow room with a mould-coloured carpet and nicotine-stained walls. A desk stood at the far end, before the window that looked out on a rusty fire escape. Most of the right-hand wall comprised a big screen, in twelve sections, the bottom right square defective for as long as Halliday could remember. The door opposite the wallscreen gave onto the bedroom where Barney slept nights. A fan clanked on the ceiling, stirring the soggy heat. A portable fire puttered beside the desk. The warmth was a relief after the arctic temperature of the loft.

Barney sat with his outstretched legs lodged on the desk, a mug of coffee balanced on the hummock of his belly. As ever, the smouldering butt of a fat cigar was pegged into the side of his mouth.

Halliday had once asked him if he'd ever thought of giving up his cigars, on health grounds. But Barney had just laughed and said, 'Part of the clichéd image, Hal. What kind of private dick would I be without my cheap stogie? Anyway, I'm addicted.'

He was regarding the screen of the desk-com past the V of his slippered feet. Halliday guessed that his partner hadn't ventured very far from the office today.

'I'm bushed, Hal,' Barney rumbled. 'The graveyard shift's yours.'

Halliday poured himself a coffee and sat on the battered chesterfield by the window, warming himself before the heater. 'Anything new?'

'Just those on file,' Barney said, 'and what Jeff sent along last week.'

Every so often Jeff Simmons, over at the NYPD, sent them old cases that the police had failed to solve. They paid Halliday and Barney two hundred dollars per file to take over the clerical work; if they happened to close the case, they were given a bonus. It was donkey work, often futile, but it paid the overheads.

Halliday often thought back to how he'd started in this line of business, and wondered why he continued. He'd been posted to Missing Persons, under Jeff Simmons, when he worked for the NYPD ten years ago. Barney was his

5

partner at MP and, along with Simmons, they got along well and made a good team. Eight years ago Barney had quit the force and set up his own agency, specialising in missing persons. Five years ago, after the death of his wife, Barney had approached Halliday with an offer: join me and do the legwork for more than you're bringing in down the precinct, and in five years you'll be a partner.

At the time, Halliday had been sickened by the grinding routine, the never-ending paper pushing of police work. The extra pay and the promise that Barney would handle the clerical side of things had swung it. He'd joined Barney and they'd done okay; they charged by the hour and demanded a bonus if they located the missing person, and their success rate hovered around the fifty per cent mark, which was not a bad average in the business.

'I'll leave you with the file,' Barney said. 'I'll work on the Lubanski case tomorrow, after I've been downtown.'

Halliday gave him a quizzical look.

'Last day of the course, Hal,' Barney reminded him.

He nodded. 'Look, I haven't said anything so far, okay?'

'You got a problem?'

He wondered whether it was because Barney's application made him appear lazy. For the past month, Barney had been paying a private tutor to fill him in on the technical aspects of virtual reality. As far as Halliday was concerned, this was going to be just another nine-day wonder that swept America and died a quick death. But, then, he'd thought the same thing about holo-drama.

Halliday stared into his coffee. 'You think we'll need it in this line of work? The way you're talking, people will be quitting the real world for VR like some crazy sci-fi holo-drama.' He gave Barney a look. 'You think we'll be having to go in after them to get them out?'

Barney was shaking his head. 'Not as things stand. There's a limit to how long you can stay jellytanked, for

6

safety reasons. It'll be a decade before you can remain under for any serious length of time.'

'How long's "serious"? Weeks?'

Barney shrugged. 'Some people are saying we'll be able to live in VR indefinitely. But that probably won't be in my lifetime.'

Halliday smiled. He envisaged a depopulated New York, great hangars stacked with tanks each containing a floating, dreaming human being.

'In the meantime,' Barney went on, 'I want to keep my finger on the pulse. If it's happening out there, and might affect my line of business, then Barney Kluger's interested.'

Halliday smiled and took a long swallow of coffee. That's what he secretly admired about his boss. Barney was what – over sixty now? He ran a third-rate detection agency in a run-down district of El Barrio, his wife was six years dead and he wasn't in the best of health himself – and yet he was still up for the fight. He reminded Halliday of an ageing, punch-drunk boxer who didn't understand the meaning of the word defeat.

Knuckles rapped on glass, and the door at the far end of the room swung open. Kim leaned through, her scarlet moonboots and primrose padded jacket a rude intrusion of colour into the drab, smoke-hazed office. In her fur-lined hat, she looked like an Eskimo.

'Hal, did you hear me? I said be back here for ten, okay?' She sketched a wave. 'Hi, Barney.'

'Hi yourself, sweetheart. How's trade?'

She stuck out her bottom lip. Sometimes the simple expressions of her unlined, almost unformed face gave her the appearance of a child. 'Up and down, Barney.'

'You should be in the elevator business, kid.' It was a line Halliday had heard many times before. Dutifully, Kim rolled her eyes.

'What's happening at ten?' Halliday asked.

7

'Hal always complains,' Kim said, addressing Barney. 'He says I never go out with him, says we never go places. Big surprise tomorrow, Hal. Don't be late.'

Before he could question her, she pulled the door shut and ran down the stairs.

'Big surprise. She knows how I hate surprises.'

Barney grunted. 'You complain you never get out, and when she arranges something, what do you do? Complain. Listen, Hal. Lighten up. She's the best thing that ever happened to you.'

'You think?'

'I know, buddy. A year ago you were one sad, miserable bastard, believe me. I had to share this dump with you.'

'That bad?'

'That bad.' Barney laughed. 'Sometimes I think you don't realise how lucky you are.'

Halliday shrugged. 'I don't know . . .' He considered how simple all relationships seemed to an observer looking in from the outside.

'Hal, do you love the kid?'

Halliday laughed. 'Love? Jesus Christ, what's love?'

'You know, that simple human emotion, care for another human being, lust mixed with affection. The need for each other's company.'

'Yeah, all those things . . . But I don't know if they add up to love.'

Barney shrugged. 'Hal, trouble with you is you can't see a good thing when it lands in your lap.' He paused, his eyes seeing something long gone, and Halliday wondered if he was going to start another riff about him and Estelle.

He smiled to himself. He wanted to tell Barney that you couldn't judge one relationship against another. Every couple was different, made up of complex psychological imponderables. And anyway, things were different back then, thirty years ago. For a start, men and women mar-

8

ried, supposedly – amazingly – for life. Halliday never looked further into the future than the next week.

Perhaps, he thought, it was because he saw so little of Kim that they were still together. Then he chastised himself for such cynicism and wondered what surprise Kim had in store for him tomorrow.

Barney stretched his arms above his head and gave a giant yawn. 'I'm turning in, Hal. See you in the morning.'

He eased himself from his swivel chair, hardly any taller standing up than sitting down, all thickset, thrusting torso, beer-belly and bandy legs. He closed the bedroom door behind him and a minute later Halliday heard the beat of the shower and Barney's baritone rendition of some doleful Irish lament.

He slipped into the swivel chair and accessed the desk-com. He scrolled through the half dozen existing cases, familiarity filling him with frustration.

He was about to check a lead on one of the commissions – a businessman missing for the past month with a stash of company funds – when he saw a flashing star next to a name, denoting a new case. He wondered why Barney hadn't mentioned it and read quickly through the notes his boss had made the day before.

A woman called Carrie Villeux had come to the office on Monday morning, to report the disappearance of her lover, Sissi Nigeria. (Dykes – Barney had typed in his notes – which might account for the patriotic, back-to-my-roots name-change. Wonder why Villeux hasn't changed her name to Quebec?) Nigeria had left the apartment for work one morning and had never been seen again. She'd failed to arrive at the offices of Cyber-Tech, where she worked as a computer technician. Villeux had left it a couple of days before calling the police, who had investigated and found nothing.

Halliday patched the com-recording of the meeting

through the wallscreen and watched a tall, severely hand-some woman in an expensive silver raincoat, her shaven skull tattooed with mandalas in the latest display of lesbian chic. She outlined the facts of the case in a steady French-accented voice, but beneath the sophisticated exterior Halliday could tell that the woman was more than a little concerned about the safety of her lover.

She had brought a pix of Sissi Nigeria with her: a strikingly beautiful black woman with a shaven head and high, angled cheekbones.

Halliday smiled to himself as he remembered his sister's anger at his chauvinist labelling. 'The subjectification of any woman as beautiful is just another bigoted, male-centric criterion employed to label and demean woman-kind . . .' or something like that. The thought of Sue provoked a slew of painful memories. He glanced back at the screen, read Villeux's address: Solano Building, Greenwich Village.

He knew why Barney had failed to mention the case. There was not much to go on. So Nigeria had taken off for a week, absented herself from work and not told her lover where she was headed . . . But Villeux had agreed to pay five hundred dollars an hour for the agency to try to locate her lover, and that was incentive enough for Halliday.

In the contact notes appended to the case file, Halliday read that Villeux would be at home most nights after seven. On Thursday and Friday she spent her evenings at the Scumbar, East Village.

He tapped her home code into the keyboard and waited out the ringing tone for a couple of minutes. He considered whether to leave it until she was home, or brave the hostility of Scumbar in the hope of finding her. She had left an entry-card for the bar with Barney, another reason why Barney had not followed up the commission. The thought of Barney Kluger squaring his shoulders before the portals of a lesbian-separatist enclave like the Scumbar was as improbable as it was comic.

He located the card in a desk drawer and slipped it into his hip pocket. He left a note for Barney on the desk-com, then locked the door and made his way down the stairs to Barney's battered Ford.

Two

Frost covered the sidewalk with a treacherous, glittery film. Halliday turned up his collar and glanced into the night sky. For the first time in weeks, the cloud cover brooding over the city had cleared, revealing a bright scatter of scintillating stars. The cold gripped at his exposed flesh, burning. He ducked into the Ford, which started at the second attempt, and edged out into the street.

Pungent clouds of steam hung above the food-stalls lining the sidewalk, colourful with red, white and blue polycarbon awnings. Small knots of people congregated before each stall, stamping their feet as they awaited their orders. The food-stalls were open night and day and constantly busy, catering for the shift-workers from the nearby factories and warehouses, refugees and the occasional insomniac. There were perhaps fifty stalls on either side of the street, serving a variety of Oriental cuisine – Vietnamese, Korean, Thai, Chinese – and Kim owned about ten of them, with one or two outlying stalls a block away. The night air was filled with a cacophony of strident voices, and the distant wail of patrolling police drones.

He turned onto East 106th Street towards Park Avenue. He passed down streets lined with tents, polycarbon boxes and any other container that could be pressed into service as a makeshift home. Some families were without even the luxury of cover: they camped out in the open, huddled around spitting braziers or flickering gas stoves. The arrival of refugees from the south had begun five years ago, with a steady trickle of refugees moving into the City following the Raleigh meltdown. The terrorist attacks on the other nuclear power stations at Memphis, Knoxville and Norfolk had displaced millions: not every refugee from the radiation-stricken areas had headed for New York – many had migrated south, to New Orleans and Florida – but the majority had come north, and the city, over-populated before the influx, was bursting at the seams. Last year had seen riots in New Jersey, street-fights between refugees and angry locals, and entire tracts of tenement housing had been put to the torch. As a consequence; these once densely populated, middle-income districts were strictly no-go, the haunt of gangs and, Halliday had heard rumoured, refugees irradiated in the blow-ups who had fallen through the welfare safety-net instituted by the Government after the first meltdowns.

The damned thing was, he reflected, that the change had happened so gradually he found it hard to recall a time when New York had not resembled some run-down, Third World capital city. The authorities claimed they were working to solve the homeless problem, of course, but nothing ever seemed to improve. The poor still starved on the streets and daily more refugees poured into the city.

And Halliday had the job of locating missing persons among a population of some thirty million. It was like trying to find the proverbial needle in a scrapyard. The miracle was that he sometimes succeeded.

While the sidewalks were packed with the homeless, the streets themselves were quiet; he counted only half a dozen other vehicles on the road at any one time. That was another change that had hit the citizens of New York. Two years ago the Arab Union had increased the price of oil in anticipation of falling yields, and consequently the cost of fuel had had gone up some five hundred per cent. Gas now cost almost fifty dollars a gallon. Most people left their cars at home and used public transport; Halliday and Barney used the Ford sparingly, usually at night when coaches ran infrequently.

He eased the Ford past a knot of sleeping refugees which had spilled onto the road, turned onto Park Avenue and headed downtown, passing a row of buildings adorned with the latest holographic façades. He knew they were not what they seemed because last week he'd seen engineers covering the front of these buildings with arrays of holo-capillaries. At the flick of a switch they changed from dull brownstones to whatever architectural wonder their owners desired. For the most part they were tastefully decorated in the style of Victorian town houses, with honey-coloured columns and ornate cornices. Halliday had seen other, more ostentatious, examples of architectural extravagance: miniature versions of the Taj Mahal, the occasional pyramid concealing nothing more than a general store.

He had thought that the last thing in holographic wizardry had been the long-range persona projections favoured by business-people and the rich. He'd never considered the possibility of cosmetically-enhanced buildings. He wondered what the next holographic advance might herald . . . if the technology was not superseded, as Barney was forever forecasting, by virtual reality.

He was considering what Barney had said earlier about virtual reality when he saw, in the distance, the city's first VR Bar, or rather the holographic advertisement alerting citizens to the recently opened wonderland. Projected out above the intersection with East 72nd Street was a scene of tropical luxury: a golden beach enclosing an azure lagoon. A rolling header stretching between the buildings made the crass proclamation: Cold? Come in and feel the sun!

Halliday slowed as he passed the Bar. It was the old Paradiso, he saw; a holo-drama cinema that had closed down last year. He recalled Barney's words, and wondered if this was a sign of things to come.

The sidewalk outside the Bar was packed with a two-abreast queue of citizens stretching back for a block. From time to time they shuffled forward minimally, and Halliday calculated that they must have been waiting for hours. Despite his earlier scepticism, his curiosity was piqued. If the experience really was as authentic as Barney had claimed, if you could enjoy ersatz sunlight in the middle of winter without being able to tell it from the real thing, then perhaps it was worth the price of a ticket. But that was another consideration: how much were they charging? He'd tackle Barney on that one in the morning. He accelerated past the Bar, heading south.

The Scumbar occupied a narrow side-alley off Christopher Street, a crimson neon in the shape of a double-bladed axe glowing in the darkness above a closed doorway. Halliday left the Ford on 7th Avenue and hurried along the street, chivvied by a wind that seemed to have come fresh off the tundra. The alley itself was lined with a dozen huddled figures wrapped in thin blankets, each one extending a hand into the icy air. 'Dollar, man. Gimme a dollar!'

Ahead, the occasional dark-garbed figure approached the door of the Scumbar, showed a card at the grille and slipped inside.

When he reached the door he raised the card Villeux had given Barney. He waited, hunched against the cold, expecting to be told to take a hike. Perhaps a minute later, to his surprise, the door opened a fraction, and he turned sideways and slipped through into warmth and darkness. He was met by an adenoid-pinching chemical reek and the blinding glare of a flashlight in his face. Then something like the claw of a mechanical tree-planter gripped his upper arm, causing him to gasp. 'What do you want?'

15

'I have a damned card,' he gasped.

The claw relaxed, minimally. 'This way.' He was pushed sideways and almost lost his footing. Another door opened into a tiny side room, this one so brightly illuminated with fluorescents that the glare was like a supernova. He covered his eyes, blinking. The chemical reek intensified. When his vision adjusted he saw that the room was occupied by two women in dark suits. One sat behind a desk and the other, improbably, sat cross-legged on top of an antique safe.

They were inhaling spin from aerosol canisters.

The claw released its grip and Halliday almost gasped with relief. He looked around: his captor was smiling, sweetly. She looked about twelve, and as innocent as a schoolgirl, but her right hand winked silver with a steel metacarpal brace.

Behind the desk, the hatchet-faced dyke with a shock of blonde hair was staring at him. He wondered if the malice in her expression was drug-induced, or a manifestation of her political bias.

'What do you want?' she asked, punctuating the question with a long draught of spin. Ecstasy showed, briefly, in her glacier-blue eyes.

'I have a card. I arranged to meet Carrie Villeux here.'

The woman held out a hand. 'The card.'

Halliday handed it over. The woman stared at the silver rectangle, looked up at him. 'Where did you get it?'

'I told you – Carrie Villeux.'

'What do you want with her?'

How much should he tell her? He wondered how favourably disposed she was towards private investigators. 'She came to my office yesterday. Her lover's missing – Sissi Nigeria. I'm trying to locate her.'

The woman looked disbelieving. 'Why would she use your agency?'

'She obviously heard that I'm good,' he said.

The woman perched on the safe spoke – and Halliday didn't understand a word. Some private Sapphic lingo?

'My sister says, how do we know you didn't attack Carrie and take the card?'

Paranoid, addled with spin, or just plain stupid?

'Steal a card to gain admittance to this place? Why the hell would I do that?'

The two women conferred, the words meaningless but their tone angry.

'Look,' he interrupted. 'I'm a friend, okay? Carrie trusted me and gave me the card. I'm on your side. Just let me into the club and talk to Carrie.'

Hatchet-face stared at him and inhaled more spin.

He tried the trump card, knowing that he might be making a big mistake. 'Do you know Sue . . . Susanna Halliday?'

'How do you know her?' Hatchet-face asked.

'She's my sister. Note the family resemblance? Dark curly hair, cleft chin?'

They had always got along okay as kids, but when Sue hit adolescence and discovered things about herself, their relationship had deteriorated. About five or six years ago, with no explanation, Sue had stopped answering his calls, moved from the Solano Building without leaving a forwarding address.

Now Hatchet-face spoke to Claws, who took his arm again, his time with the little girl pinkies of her left hand. She smiled again, so innocently. 'I'll show you around, Mr Halliday.' She giggled. 'It's a jungle in there and you'll need a bodyguard.'

Before he left the room, Hatchet-face said, 'Watch yourself, Halliday. Some of us aren't so forgiving.' She stared at him. 'Remember that.'

He passed into the darkness of the foyer, the woman's words echoing uneasily in his head. The little girl took the fingers of his right hand and led him through a swing door.

'Told you it was a jungle in here, Mr Halliday. Stick close to me and you'll be okay, okay?'

The Scumbar was an old holographic theatre, and playing tonight was a scene from some sylvan epic: holo-projectors beamed an optical illusion of trees for as far as the eye could see. They were fair projections, but discernible as fakes by the slight fuzziness of image at their peripheries. Mood music played, synthesised with appropriate bird song, and in the clearings between the tree trunks couples moved in rhythm to the beat.

They edged past dancers, his presence earning stares ranging from curious to overtly hostile. He was glad of the half-light which made his presence less conspicuous, but even so he felt uneasy.

She led him to a circular bar done out like someone's idea of a jungle hut, with bamboo palisades and a straw roof. He hitched himself onto a high stool. 'Care for a drink?'

'Thanks. Beer. Brazilian, if you're buying.'

The black-suited barmaid stared at him without expression.

Halliday ordered two Caribas and the barmaid uncapped the bottles and slid them along the bar. 'That'll be forty.'

He tried not to show any reaction to the robbery. He peeled off four notes and left them on the bar. The kid grabbed a bottle in her steel claw and suckled. Halliday sipped his beer and assessed the dancers. There were a lot of fashionably-shaven skulls bobbing in the twilight, and it seemed that the body voluptuous was back in vogue; the cycle had turned and the Earth Mother soma-type was all the rage, at least among the clients at the Scumbar.

'I don't see Carrie Villeux,' he said, scanning the dancers.

Claws pulled her furled tongue from the bottle and

peered. 'She must be around somewhere, Mr Halliday. She always arrives at ten. Wait here, I'll see if I can find her.'

Arms swinging to the music, the girl skanked across the dance floor, earning smiles from the dancers. Halliday found himself wondering if her mother knew where she spent her Friday nights. He smiled to himself. What had Sue accused him of? 'A conditioned tendency to traditional bourgeois values?' He supposed, being brought up by a father schooled in the military, that was to be expected.

The girl tapped and tugged at the occasional dancer, then stood on tiptoe and shouted into proffered ears. The women glanced at Halliday, frowned and shook their heads. The girl moved off, out of sight behind a spray of ferns.

Self-consciously, Halliday up-ended his Caribas and tried to appear as if he were enjoying the music. Two minutes later, the girl emerged through the trees, wiping imaginary sweat from her brow.

'Carrie hasn't shown yet. She was due in at ten. Some of her friends are at the next bar. You can buy me another drink, Mr Halliday.'

This time he ignored her hand and followed her through the trees. They arrived at another bar, identical to the first, where another crowd of dancers swayed to the same beat.

'Two Caribas, Terri,' Claws said. 'My boyfriend's paying.'

Halliday laid out another forty, writing it off to expenses, and finished his first beer. He found a stool and watched the dancers. Clearly, his assumption about what soma-types were in vogue had been premature; the women who had staked out this territory had nothing in common with their Earth Mother sisters across the way. They were, to a woman, slim, even angular, and a few had even had their breasts excised, low-cut shirts revealing the white sickle scars of the fashionable mutilation.

As he watched, a woman as tall and ebony as a Masai

19

warrior disengaged herself from the dance and approached. Whereas Halliday had climbed onto the high stool, she lowered herself onto the neighbouring stool and crossed her long, trousered legs. She wore a double-breasted pin-stripe jacket and, as she leaned forward for a drink and the lapels of her suit buckled, Halliday saw that she'd opted for the radical mastectomy statement.

'Hi, I'm Kia,' she purred. 'Kia Johansen.'

'Halliday.' He showed her his card. 'I'm looking for Nigeria. Will Carrie Villeux be in later?'

'She's usually here by now, honey.' She had the exagger-ated camp femininity of a transsexual drag queen, and Halliday wondered if lesbians pretending to be men pre-tending to be women was the latest fashion in counter-cultural chic.

Kia was shaven-skulled, and the contours of her bony cranium would have been a phrenologist's delight. Only when he stared, taken aback, did he see the inlaid beading of a silver implant circumnavigating her skull. A lead worked its way into her tiny right ear. He wondered if she really was rigged with a neural implant, or if the device was just a clever cosmetic simulation.

'We're all very concerned about Nigeria,' she said, laying fingers like cheroots on his forearm. 'Do say you'll be able to find her.'

'You're a good friend of hers?'

'One of the best. I mean, we were lovers many moons ago, but that's quite another story. Ain't that right, Missy?'

'Tell me about it, Kia,' the girl smiled.

Halliday said, 'Did you notice anything amiss in her attitude before she disappeared? She wasn't acting strangely at all?'

Kia lifted her head to the swaying holo-branches over-head and shrilled a high laugh. 'Man, it'd be odd if she

20

wasn't acting strangely.' Kia shook her head. 'No, she was just the same old dependable fun-loving Sissi as always.'

Halliday took a long swallow of beer. 'Is it like Carrie not to show when she'd arrange to come here?'

Kia regarded him, frowning. 'You know, hon, that is worrying. Long as I been coming here Friday nights, Carrie's shown. You don't think . . .?'

'I don't think anything, yet.'

'But it's after twelve now, honey. I'm getting worried.' She considered, staring at him. 'Look, I have a spare pass-card to Sissi's apartment, in case of emergencies. We could always drop by.'

Halliday sighed. 'I'll call her. She's probably had an early night.' He slipped his hand-com from his inside pocket, linked with the desk-com back at the office and down-loaded Carrie Villeux's code. Seconds later he was listening to the pulse of the ringing tone.

He gave it two minutes, Kia watching him all the while with eyes as big as golf balls. He shook his head and pocketed the com. 'No reply.'

'I'm worried. We have to go over. What do you think, Missy?'

Claws bit her tongue, considering. 'If it were a friend of mine . . .' She nodded. 'Yeah, I'd go on round.'

'That settles it. You can come if you want to, Halliday. I'm gone.'

Kia rose from the stool and stared down at him, ulti-matum in her expression. Halliday sighed. 'I have a car. I'll drive. Solano Buildings, right?'

'You know where that is?'

'I know where it is.' The thought of going back there, after so long, filled him with a vague sense of disquiet. It would be strange to enter the building with no intention of calling in on his sister.

Missy-with-claws escorted them back through the rain-forest. They pushed through the swing doors and into the darkened foyer.

The outside door opened, admitting a blast of icy air. As Kia shivered theatrically and Halliday followed, Missy tapped his back. 'Forgotten something, Mr Halliday?'

He turned. She was smiling her saccharine sweet smile of a schoolgirl temptress. She held one hand – her left, unaugmented hand – behind her back.

He patted the pocket where he kept his wallet, but it was still there.

He slipped his hand into his jacket, but the automatic no longer nestled against his ribs.

He'd never felt a thing . . .

'Very clever, Missy. If you don't mind . . .' He held out a hand.

She twisted her lips in a quick smirk of victory and dropped the pistol onto his palm. 'I'd be more careful with it in future, Mr Halliday. You never know when you might need to use it. A man should never be separated from his weapon. Even I know that.'

'You're too old for your own good, Missy.'

'Eleven in May,' she said.

'I'll send you a card,' he promised. 'A word of advice; just make sure your mom doesn't find out where you spend your free time, okay?'

Missy covered her pretty mouth with the steel claw. 'Mr Halliday, the lady behind the desk *is* my mom.'

She was still laughing as she slammed the door on him. He shook his head and began walking.

Kia was halfway down the street, arguing with a refugee demanding dollars. She turned to Halliday. 'What's the big delay, honey?'

Halliday hurried along the alley, away from the beggars,

22

and showed her to the car. He started the engine and drove across town to Greenwich Village. The Solano Building was a drab-looking brownstone overlooking Washington Square. He found a parking space beneath the trees and followed Kia up the front steps.

'Keep your distance, man. I mean, nothing personal, but if anyone sees us together, hey, then my rep is just shot to pieces.'

He looked at the pin-striped lesbian giantess. '*Your* reputation?' he muttered. He paused to allow her to get ahead, then followed her into the building at a distance.

The interior was just as drab and depressing as he recalled, the walls daubed the sickly pea-green of a psychiatric institute circa 1900. Years ago, Sue had rented a room on the top floor, with a view over the square to the university buildings. Halliday recalled the ancient lift, the ammoniacal stench of urine that made each ride a test of endurance. They would be spared the experience this time: Kia led him down a long ground-floor corridor to a steel-plate door. She slipped a card from her breast pocket and, a second later, pushed open the door and stepped inside.

'Carrie! You in here, hon?'

The automatic lighting came on and brightened, revealing a room more in keeping with the centre-spread of some interior decorating magazine than anything Halliday associated with the Solano Building. He recalled that both Villeux and Nigeria were professionals, Villeux in fashion design, Nigeria in computing – and they obviously had excess earnings to lavish on décor and furnishings. The open-plan lounge/dining room was decorated in cream, with plush Norwegian furniture and artificially-nurtured fur rugs. Psychedelic holograms cycled through gaudy phases on each wall, giving Halliday the unsteady sensation of being aboard a seaborne vessel.

Kia moved from room to room, calling Carrie's name. Halliday crossed the lounge to a glass display stand of holo-cubes. He picked one up and it began to play.

He watched Carrie Villeux and Sissi Nigeria stroll along a boardwalk, arm in arm. They waved, then faced each other and kissed. Halliday noticed that in this holo Nigeria's skull, like Kia Johansen's, was adorned with the silver inlay of a neural implant, though whether cosmetic or actual it was impossible to say.

Kia appeared in a doorway, almost as tall as the opening itself. She leaned against the woodwork, looking shocked. 'Halliday. In here . . .'

He hurried across the lounge, sure that Kia had found a body. She stepped aside. 'This is Sissi's room. Look . . .'

As he crossed the threshold, the sharp stench of burned-out circuitry hit him. He looked around a room decorated in black. Kia was pointing to a bank of what might have been computer consoles, stacked against the far wall.

'What is it?' Halliday asked.

'Sissi's deck. She did a lot of work from home.'

Halliday counted half a dozen flatscreens, three touch-pads and a headset. He'd only ever read about headsets: they were the latest thing, state-of-the-art neural interfaces still at the design stage.

'Impressive,' he said.

Only when he looked closer did he apprehend the cause of Kia's concern. The consoles of the stacked deck were fused, input ports blackened and charred. That explained the reek. He ran a hand across the melted surface of the deck. It was cold, not that this told him much.

Kia was shaking her head. 'Sissi loves her deck, Halliday. She lives for it.'

'What was her job, exactly?' he asked, and immediately regretted employing the past tense.

Kai seemed not to notice. 'She's a systems expert for

Cyber-Tech: she works on logic analogues and data recombination.'

Halliday nodded, as if he understood what she was talking about. 'You're familiar with the jargon.'

'Ought to be, sweetie. I work for Mantoni VR.'

He gestured at the fused consoles. 'Any idea what happened here?'

She was shaking her head. 'Looks like it's been deliberately sabotaged. I mean, no systems malfunction could do all this damage, not to every single port.'

Halliday looked around the room, and through the door to the lounge. 'The rest of the place seems pretty well intact. You think someone came in especially to do this?'

'Hey, you're the expert. You tell me.'

'I deal in missing persons. I wouldn't call myself an expert.' He paused. 'Could there be any reason why Nigeria might have done this herself?'

'Sissi? Wreck her deck? No way, man. No *way*.'

Halliday looked around the room. A personal data system stood beside the bed, the stack finished in matte black to match the room's colour scheme. He picked up a tray of write-to needles and slipped it into the pocket of his jacket. If Sissi Nigeria kept a recorded diary, then the needles might contain relevant information.

'I don't like it, Halliday. First Sissi goes missing, and then Carrie doesn't show.'

'You know if they had enemies?'

'Sissi and Carrie? They were loved by their sisters, hon. They didn't have enemies.'

'Not even outside the community?'

'They didn't mix *outside* the community.'

'Did they do drugs?'

She shook her head, vehement. 'Not even spin.'

Halliday sighed. 'There's not much more we can do, then. The police know of Nigeria's disappearance. I

wouldn't worry that much about Carrie not showing up.'
He looked around the room. 'I'll go through the place now,
see if I can come across anything.'

He moved back to the lounge. He was wondering where
to start when the lighting went out. 'Kia, what the
hell . . .?'

'Hey, I didn't . . .' she began.

Only the holograms on the wall, pulsing purple, provided the slightest illumination. In the twilight, with the
holograms twisting and distorting his perceptions, he felt
his sense of balance go awry. Later, he wondered if this
was the intended effect, or merely incidental. He reached
out for the wall to steady himself, but instead fell to his
knees. Now the holograms seemed to be moving beyond
the confines of what he had taken to be their frames,
amorphous shapes of purple and green crawling up the
wall and across the ceiling, totally disorienting him.

Nearby, Kia cried out. 'What's happening, man? Get me
outta here!'

'Where the hell is the door?' Halliday cried.

He was on the floor, trying to pick himself up. It was all
he could do to rise to his knees. Some tiny, rational part of
his mind was telling him that the disorienting effect could
not be caused merely by the visual distortion – and at that
instant he became aware of the subliminal tone strumming
through the air, less an actual sound than a note intuited
physically, a fluttery terrifying pulse in his solar plexus,
tuned to affect his sense of balance. Subsonics, he told
himself, and the realisation of what was being used to
disable him filled him with fear. This was not merely some
lighting malfunction, then: he and Kia were being targeted.
He felt an instant nausea as the subsonics took effect, tried
to hold onto the contents of his stomach.

He attempted to crawl across the floor towards where he

guessed the door might be. A sound crashed through the room: the opening and shutting of the steel door. The sound came from behind him, so he was heading in the wrong direction. He turned and peered into the purple twilight. He thought he saw a dark figure move across the floating shape of a hologram. At the same time he heard Kia cry out, 'This way, Halliday!' A second later he heard the front door open and Kia call, 'Come on!'

It was all he could do to pull himself along on all fours, never mind get to his feet and run for the door. He retched, dribbling a thin bile, grateful that he hadn't eaten for hours. He heard movement, footsteps. Panic expanded in his chest like an exploding coronary. He reached for his automatic and managed to pull it free from his jacket. Still on the floor, twisted awkwardly on his side, he extended the gun and gripped the butt with both hands, trying to steady his aim.

He would fire to miss, and frighten off whoever it was. His senses swimming, he looked around desperately for any sign of the shadowy figure. He thought he saw it again, ghostly before a hologram. He touched something with his elbow, the dark shape of the Norwegian sofa. He rolled behind its bulk, putting it between him and the spectral figure.

He tried to control his breathing, calm himself. It was a long time since his combat training with the police force. He remembered nothing, his mind blanked by the passage of years and the situation he found himself in. Perhaps anything he had picked up, he told himself, he would recall instinctively, when the attack came. At least he was armed. The weight of his automatic in his grip reassured him, helped to calm his nerves. Then another wave of nausea swamped him. He fought it, attempted to remain conscious.

He heard something, the soft, careful contact of a footfall on parquet. He braced himself, moved the automatic to the approximate direction of the sound.

The silence stretched, each fraction of a second calibrated by the beat of his heart. A sudden thought struck him, frightening in its implications. How was his stalker managing to counteract the disorienting effects of the subsonics and the dizzying visuals? Who the hell was out there?

He changed his mind about firing to miss.

Something hissed through the air, slicing the silence. He saw a line of silver light fall like a flashing sword. The sofa seemed to part, fall into two even halves, exposing him. Halliday kicked across the floor, towards a lighted rectangle he took to be a window. If he could throw something weighty through the glass, follow it out . . .

Footsteps again, pattering towards him. Another hiss – and a nearby wall unit collapsed, spilling ornaments and *objets d'art* across his prostrate body. Something heavy thumped him in the gut, winding him. He stifled a cry and reached out, locating the object, some kind of sculpture. He gripped it with his free hand, turned and swung the solid mass into the air towards the illuminated rectangle. If Sissi Nigeria had replaced the glass with reinforced plastex . . .

It was his last thought before the sculpture crashed through the window and shards of glass rained around him. Ice-cold air invaded the room. He pulled himself to his knees, hanging onto the sill like a survivor to the gunwale of a lifeboat. He took a breath and launched himself, rolling over the ledge.

Something prevented his escape, and Halliday felt panic clutch his throat. He tried to cry out. He turned, aware of the grip on his jacket. In the light of a street lamp he saw his assailant.

It was a man, perhaps his own height and age, a Latino with cruel eyes and a deep scar running in an arc from his temple to the corner of his mouth. Halliday experienced a bizarre surge of hope and relief, now that the shadowy figure had a face, an identity. His attacker was suddenly human, and vulnerable.

The man lifted his right hand, and Halliday saw the small silver sickle-shape of a cutter. He grabbed his wrist, smashed it in one motion against the woodwork. The expression of determined cruelty on the face of his attacker hardly flickered, but the cutter dropped and skittered across the parquet. Halliday raised his automatic, held it point-blank to the scarred face, and before he could consider what he was doing he pulled the trigger.

He flinched, pre-empting the recoil and splatter of brains, but the hammer clicked on an empty chamber. He tried again, with the same result, and before panic took him he swung a wild upper-cut, connecting with the guy's jaw. He heard his assailant grunt. He rolled through the window, his shoulder hitting the ground with a painful thud. He righted himself, sobered by the sudden cold, and ran. He was in a darkened alleyway, a canyon between the row of brownstones and a three-storey building. As he ran, he checked his automatic. The ammunition clip had been removed.

Missy . . .

He was still dizzy and uncoordinated from the effects of the subsonics and his legs seemed on the verge of buckling with every step. He chanced a quick look over his shoulder. There was no sign of the Latino. Was it too much to hope that his lucky punch had laid the guy out? He inhaled cold air, lungs burning. When he looked back again, his assailant was jumping through the window, reduced once more to the anonymity of a darkened shadow.

He increased his pace, sprinting now. He considered the

probable range of the guy's cutter, and the flesh of his back crawled at the thought of the sudden impact. Ahead was a turning, a narrow defile between buildings. He turned the corner at pace, caroming off the far wall and almost losing his footing. He ran on, and then stopped. Fear prickled his scalp and he experienced a sudden cold sweat.

He was in a dead-end alley. He faced the impasse of a red-brick wall. He looked around. There were doors, but they were padlocked; there were even windows, but they in turn were fronted by thick iron bars. He felt a sudden icy dread, and the image of his father came to him unbidden. He was shaking his head in wordless disappointment. The memory was as fresh as if it had happened yesterday, not twenty years ago when Halliday had swung and missed a third strike.

He turned, expecting the Latino to show at any second. To his right, zigzagging up the wall of the building, was a rusted fire escape. Halliday ran to it and jumped, catching the lower rung. The muscles of his arms ached in protest. For a second he hung, before summoning the strength from somewhere to reach for the next rung and haul himself up. It seemed to take an age of agonising grabs before his legs made contact with the first rung. He gripped the side-rail and ran, two steps at a time. As he took each turn he looked down, along the length of the alley. He was near the top of the building when he saw the Latino come to a halt at the end of the alley. They guy pulled something from his belt and turned down the alley, proceeding with caution.

Halliday stepped from the fire escape. He was on a flat concrete roof, silvered by moonlight, empty but for satellite dishes and microwave boosters. It sprawled away from him like a football field and offered little in the way of cover. He could run, but he couldn't hide, nor jump from this building to the next. He judged the distances between

30

neighbouring roofs to be in the region of five metres. He scanned the perimeter of the roof for any sign of another fire escape, but saw nothing.

Below, he heard the sound of footsteps on the fire escape. He took off, running to the nearest satellite dish. It was set at an angle of forty-five degrees, and facing the direction of the fire escape. He decided that to use the first dish as cover might be too obvious. He sprinted across the roof to where half a dozen dishes regarded the heavens. He grabbed one and tipped it back to give his boots more purchase on the lower rim, then took hold of the antenna and hauled himself aboard like some desperate wind-surfer.

A rivet was missing from the seam of the dish, and if Halliday lowered his head and squinted through the hole he could make out the expanse of the roof and the distant shape of the fire escape.

He wondered if the Latino would be stupid enough not to realise that the dishes were the only possible hiding places. If he checked them, or took no chances and either cut them or pumped them full of bullets one by one . . .

Only then did Halliday wonder why the guy wanted him dead, and what if anything linked the Latino to the disappearance of Sissi Nigeria.

His ankles ached and his hands, where they gripped the freezing metal of the antenna, felt as if they were being cut open with razor blades. He held on with one hand, warming the other under his armpit. He peered through the rivet hole in the dish and sighted the fire escape.

The Latino appeared. The top of his head showed slowly, cautiously, followed by his raised right hand bearing a weapon. When he saw that the immediate vicinity was clear, he stepped from the fire escape and crouched, taking in the length and breadth of the rooftop, assessing the possibilities. Halliday felt his mouth run dry. If he survived this, *when* he survived this, he'd have a hell of a tale to tell

31

Barney and Kim. He was aware of the laboured thudding of his heart, and his breath sounded loud enough to give away his position.

As Halliday watched, he felt his stomach turn and he was almost physically sick. The Latino walked towards the first satellite dish, the one facing the fire escape, and seemed to consider its potential as a place of concealment. He evidently decided that they offered perfect cover, slipped the revolver he was holding into his belt, removed the cutter and aimed at the dish. A vector of silver laser light illuminated the darkness. It sliced through the metal, and the upper half of the dish slipped to the roof with a crash. Christ, but if he did that to every one . . .

The Latino moved to the next dish, cutting a slash through the metal. He approached the stand of dishes where Halliday was concealed. He sliced the first dish from a range of two metres, approached the next. Halliday tried to think fast, work out what to do now. If he showed himself, he was dead meat. And if he stayed where he was . . .

The Latino cut another dish, and Halliday saw how he might survive the encounter. The dish protecting him was one of three in a line, each one arranged behind the other, like spoons. To get an angle on Halliday's dish, the gun-man would be forced to come close . . . close enough, perhaps, for Halliday to leap out and surprise him.

He readied himself, took the automatic from his pocket to use as a cudgel. The Latino halved the first dish of the three with a protracted squeal of torn metal and moved on to the next. He was perhaps two metres away. If Halliday waited until he was about to slice his own dish, it might be too late to act. He'd dive out when he was slicing the second dish, try to catch him off guard.

The Latino raised his cutter, fired. The line of silver light lanced out, cleaving the dish through its diameter. As soon

32

as he ceased firing and was lowering the weapon, Halliday dived.

He touched the ground once and leapt, hitting the Latino in the midriff and sending him sprawling. He dived again, falling across the guy's chest, and pinioned his cutter hand to the floor. He smashed at the hand with the butt of his automatic, breaking bones, until the fingers released their grip and the cutter fell away. Halliday dashed it across the rooftop, only now feeling a heady elation surge through him at the thought that, after all, he might survive. He reached for the guy's belt, found the revolver and flung it as far as he could. His captive was struggling, attempting to reach Halliday's face and gouge with his undamaged hand.

Halliday raised his automatic high above his head and brought it down with force, smashing the guy's cheekbone.

Nothing, Halliday told himself later, nothing at all could have prepared him for what he saw then. At first he thought he was hallucinating, that the adrenalin of the chase and fight had affected his vision.

The Latino's face underwent a rapid transformation. The very flesh seemed to flicker, lose its definition and shape. For a fraction of a second the face became one completely different, an almost subliminal flash of someone else, too rapid for Halliday to say whether it was a man's or woman's, young or old. Then the face was the Latino's again, before once more flickering and changing, and this time the change stayed for seconds. A pretty-faced blonde woman stared up at him – though the eyes, he thought, the eyes were just as cruel as the Latino's. The sight filled Halliday with fear greater than that he had experienced at any time during the chase, a fear of the inexplicable.

He cried out and rolled away, staggered to his feet and ran. He meant to head for the fire escape, but he was disoriented and got it wrong. He was heading in the opposite direction. He stopped, almost weeping now, turned. The Latino . . . or whatever the hell he was . . . climbed slowly to his feet, staggering, his damaged hand cradled across his chest. He saw Halliday and lurched towards him. In appearance he was the Latino again, though there was something nebulous, almost undefined, about the cast of the features – as if they were attempting to return to their original guise, but could not quite make it.

Halliday turned, ran, and stopped quickly. He was at the edge of the building. He turned and faced the Latino. Christ, but the euphoria he'd experienced just seconds ago tasted sour now. He knew he had to fight, but the prospect of facing again something that he could neither explain nor understand filled him with irrational fear. The Latino approached, crouched, ready for Halliday should he try to run for it.

'Who the hell are you?' Halliday shouted.

The Latino just stared, his refusal to speak almost as eerie as his earlier metamorphosis.

He caught Halliday by surprise. He had not expected the Latino to attack, dive at him. He yelled out as his assailant launched himself and hit him in the midriff.

Halliday felt himself topple backwards, experienced that sudden, fraction-of-a-second apprehension that there was nothing, nothing at all he could do to stop himself.

A sickening lurch.

Oh, Christ . . .

And he was falling. It happened too fast for him to understand that he was dead, that he could not survive a fall from a height of twenty, thirty metres, but the knowledge of his failure swept through him like a wave. Geared to think only of survival, his animal brain was denied any option, and howled at the fact of its extinction.

Then he hit something, something soft. He seemed to

bounce, roll, pain shooting through his torso and limbs, but not terminal pain. He was tumbling down a pile of something, and only later did he work out what had saved his life: garbage, bagged in polycarbon-weave sacks and awaiting the next collection.

He dropped again, a short distance this time. He yelled as he was deposited from the piled garbage. He struck the ground with a breathtaking impact. He tried to climb to his feet, but succeeded only in rolling onto his back. He lay moaning, barely conscious, staring up at the bright scatter of stars. Something warm was trickling into his eyes, which he realised must be blood. He found himself wondering how he might die – from loss of blood, or from exposure to the sub-zero temperature? – before he finally, blissfully, passed out.

Three

Anna Ellischild finished the last scene of the holoscript and emailed the pages to her producer over at Tidemann's Holo-Productions.

She ordered the TrueVoc program to shut down, pushed her swivel chair away from the desk and stretched, yawning. At Christmas, *Sapphic Island* had been a hit in holo-auditoriums all across the country, and Tidemann's had offered her a new, improved contract for a further six episodes. She'd dictated the second series in record time, around three hours per script, and told herself that three hours was probably too long to be spending on such shit.

The screen chimed and her producer, Felicity, smiled out, waving fingers. 'Just read the last scene, Anna. Loved it. Liked the conflict. Great cliffhanger. Sasha is developing into a wonderful character. A true heroine for our time.' She drew breath. 'But what did you think about the sex scene?'

Here it comes, Anna thought. The old 'love it, sweetie, but . . .' proviso.

She remembered Felicity's response to reading the very first script of *Sapphire Island* – as it was then – a year ago. 'Absolutely loved the script, Anna. But don't you think the title lacks a little . . . I don't know, specificity?'

It had become a joke amongst Anna's writer friends. 'Don't you think this scene lacks a little . . . *specificity*?'

Anna had responded with, 'Do you mean it needs to be less subtle? How about *Raging Dykes on Dildo Party Island*?'

Her producer had blown her a sweet kiss. 'Think not, Anna. How about *Sapphic Island*?'

Which was almost as bad as her joke title. But she who pays the ferrywoman ... *Sapphic Island* it had become. And, to Felicity's credit, she'd allowed Anna a pretty free rein with the script.

Perhaps only about fifty per cent of her original work was altered in production ...

Now Anna lodged her legs on the swivel chair and hugged her shins, staring at Felicity from between her knees. 'The sex scene?' she said. 'Well, I was deliberately keeping it low-key. This is the fifth episode, after all. We don't want to pre-empt the orgy in episode six.'

Sometimes she had to stop herself from laughing when taking part in script conferences with Felicity and the other luvvies over at Tidemann's.

Felicity was saying, 'But surely in this situation, Sasha would demand cunnilingus from Amanda and Jo – we should explicitly intimate that it's going on, even if the cameras don't dwell . . .'

How, Anna thought, does one 'explicitly intimate' anything?

'Felicity, Sasha doesn't even care for Jo. She's only invited her around to ingratiate herself in order to get the job.'

'In that case how about rewriting the earlier scene where Sasha approaches Jo for the job? How about sexing it up a little? That's it! Sasha fancies Jo as well as Amanda, and the last scene brings them together and Sasha gets the job. How does that sound?'

It sounded lousy. Felicity had obviously not followed the character's motivations through the earlier episodes ... But what the hell? She was being paid a hundred thousand dollars per episode, and the crap was appearing under a pseudonym. So what had she to lose?

She nodded. 'You might have something there. It'd certainly end episode five with a bang.'

Felicity smiled. 'Thought you'd like it. Okay, leave it with you? Need the rewrite by tomorrow early, okay?'

Anna nodded. She could do the work in fifteen minutes. 'It'll be with you tonight.'

'Terrific, sweetie. See you!' She waved fingers again and was gone.

Sighing, Anna stood and found her headphone and mic. She slipped the unit around her neck and walked to the window. 'TrueVoc, on.' She waited a few seconds. '*Sapphic Island*, episode five, scene fifteen. Cut lines . . .' She approached the screen and peered at the text. 'Cut lines five through to thirty. Replace with the following . . .'

She moved from the study to the lounge, dictating. She rented a big apartment in East Village, four big second-floor rooms overlooking Tompkins Square. She'd moved here late last year, after *Sapphic Island* took off, and was already beginning to feel guilty. For how many years had she lived in a tiny bedsit in the Bronx, practically starving while she wrote novel after novel which were met with the standard publishers' rejection: We thought this work showed great artistry and intelligence. However, we would find it hard to market in the current cultural climate . . .

Two years ago, on the advice of a friend in the holo-business, she'd developed the idea of a drama set on a holiday island catering for lesbians. Some dyke in production had liked the treatment and commissioned Anna to do a pilot episode. The original one hour holo-drama had gone down well, and she'd been commissioned to write six more.

She'd started the project with high ideals. She had intended the series to explore the psychology and sociology of alternative women, but done with a light touch so as not to alienate the mainstream audience. Felicity had greeted each draft with exaggerated enthusiasm . . . and then asked for a few minor changes. The *Sapphic Island* that showed to rave reviews at Christmas bore little resemblance to the original *Sapphire Island*. Come the second series, Anna had known exactly what Felicity required, and had hacked out the episodes in record time.

Each script contained about as much work as a page of her serious novels, and earned her about ten times as much as the elusive advance on a literary novel . . . each of which took her a year to write.

She finished the scene, reworked the dialogue to include the added oral sex, and emailed it off to Felicity. The irony was, Felicity was a tight-assed little straight who'd never even kissed a dyke, never mind experienced the pleasures of a woman going down on her.

Anna quit the apartment before the producer could get back to her.

It was a day rare for January, a bright blue sky, brittle sunlight, frost underfoot. She huddled into her coat and tried to shut out the ever-present noise of the city. It seemed impossible for New Yorkers to conduct a conversation without shouting: every few metres she passed people arguing and beggars calling for dollars. The piercing whine of road drills was a constant background effect, interspersed with snatches of mood-music belting at full volume from stores and private apartments.

She considered taking a train, then had second thoughts. The subway was unpleasantly crowded these days: a combination of refugees making the platforms their temporary homes and more city dwellers than ever using the rail system.

She made for Broadway, where she'd hail a cab and make the short journey to the Mantoni Tower, where Kia worked.

The sidewalks were busy with pedestrians and encamped

refugee families, while the streets were relatively clear of traffic. A few electric buses shuttled back and forth. Cop cars and taxis still patrolled, along with the occasional vehicle owned by richer citizens. Personally, she thought the oil crisis no bad thing – it made New York habitable again; the streets were no longer death traps and the air was getting cleaner by the day. She had to smile at the conditioned citizens, though: they still kept to the side-walks and crossed at the crossings, as if the old jaywalking proscriptions still held. Anna took great delight in walking across wherever she wanted. Late at night you could wander right down the middle of some streets in perfect safety.

She caught a cab and looked forward to meeting Kia. They'd missed each other last night. Kia had gone along to the Scumbar, while Anna had dined with a few writer friends in Chinatown. Kia had come home in the early hours, and was up early to start work before Anna awoke.

She'd met Kia Johansen in the Scumbar about a year ago, and at first Anna had no reason to assume that it wasn't going to be just another brief sexual encounter that would fade, after the first week of passion, to friendship. Anna had no more desire for monogamy than most of the women she knew. She was happy to live alone and reward herself with the occasional brief affair. Then she met Kia, and after a couple of days during which they rarely left the bed, Anna knew that this was going to be different. She was wary at first: Kia likewise had no plans to settle into a serious relationship, and Anna was loath to be the first to suggest that this might grow into something more than just a brief, passion-filled fling.

Mutually, they had sought each other's company. After a month of seeing each other every day, it was Kia who suggested that Anna move in with her. Kia had lived in a tiny apartment in West Village, hardly big enough for her alone, never mind Anna as well. Anna had been in the process of moving into the roomy second-floor suite in East Village, and it seemed sensible that Kia should move in with her.

It had been the first time that she had lived with anyone in eight years, and despite her own doubts – and the counsel of friends who forecast a quick separation – it seemed to work. Anna had found in Kia someone who understood her, who cared and sympathised. She loved Kia for her headstrong eccentricity, a mad exterior that concealed a serious sensibility she divulged only to those she trusted.

The affair had lasted almost a year now, far longer than she or any of her friends thought likely, and as far as Anna was concerned it could go on forever.

She paid the driver, stepped from the cab and pushed her way across the crowded sidewalk. She left the noise of the street behind her as she stepped through the sliding glass entrance of the towering jet-black obelisk, the head-quarters of Mantoni Entertainment.

She took the elevator to the thirty-fifth floor and remembered to affix her security pass to the lapel of her jacket.

Kia was a technician in Mantoni's virtual reality development section. At the end of a long day, she would start to tell Anna what had gone wrong during that shift, in a language that might as well have been Swahili to Anna. Mantoni, Cyber-Tech and a couple of other companies had been in a race for the past couple of years to develop the first, and finest, VR experience for a public ready and eager to spend its dollars on yet another outlet of entertainment. Kia had often told Anna that it was not enough to be the first on the market: what was the advantage of being first if your product was only second-best? Just before Christmas Mantoni's rivals, Cyber-Tech, had opened a couple of virtual reality bars in Manhattan. Kia had admitted that the Cyber-Tech experience was good, but it could be bettered. The public could be offered not only a greater verisimilitude when within VR itself but also a wider range of sites and venues.

Anna was cleared by a security guard outside the double doors of the research chamber and waved through. She had asked Kia to get her a security pass so that she could do a little research for the last novel she had written. One of the minor characters worked in VR, and for the sake of authenticity Anna thought she'd better take a closer look at the industry. She had found the atmosphere in the chamber, and the work going on there, fascinating in itself, and had often made the excuse of research to drop by and meet Kia at the end of a working day.

The chamber was an interior room and had no windows; far from appearing enclosed and claustrophobic, the chamber had the air of an open piazza. This was achieved by the placement, at intervals around the walls, of big flatscreens relaying vibrant images of strange landscapes and other worlds. A semi-circle of computer work-stations faced the screens, and a dozen casually-dressed scientists and technicians bent over the terminals or consulted with each other in hurried, frantic exchanges.

Anna looked around for Kia, but there was no sign of her at any of the work-stations. Then she saw the jellytank. It stood between the work-stations and the flatscreens, raised on a plinth of steps like some kind of ceremonial coffin, lying in state.

Kia was in the tank.

She was naked, and the sight of her long, brown body, on display to whoever cared to look, filled Anna with a ridiculous sense of jealousy. She told herself that the scientists here had more to think about than the desirability of the naked body of her lover.

She fetched a coffee from a machine on the wall, found

a seat at the back of the chamber and settled herself to watch what was going on.

Anna had wanted to experience VR when Cyber-Tech opened the first parlour on Madison Avenue a month ago, but out of a sense of loyalty to Kia she had never mentioned it to her lover. Mantoni had opened their own parlour a few days ago, and Anna planned to visit it with Kia over the weekend. She had read dozens of articles about the latest technological wonder to sweep the land, and wondered if she was letting herself in for a disappointment. All the hype surrounding VR suggested that the experience was indistinguishable from real life, but Anna remained to be convinced.

In the jellytank, Kia's long limbs were connected to leads which climbed through the jelly and over the sides of the tank. A sheaf of wires were jacked into her neural-interface, and they rose from her head like a shock of dreadlocks.

On the largest flatscreen, immediately behind the jellytank, Anna watched Kia stroll through a fantasyland of rolling green hillocks, like a version of Heaven as Monet might have painted it. She was garbed in a simple blue smock, striking against her ebony flesh, and from time to time spoke, evidently reporting on what she was witnessing.

Anna could hear Kia's voice issuing from the nearest work-station. The techs were listening intently to what she was saying, adjusting their computers accordingly.

'We have great tone in all the foreground representations here,' she reported. 'I'm happy with the analogue-sequencing. There's still some background interference – check on the sub-routine in the G3x file.'

Anna listened, smiling, and felt a strange sense of vicarious pride at the thought of Kia, her Kia, at the very forefront of this cutting edge technology.

43

Six months ago, she had been upset and concerned when Kia told her that she was going to have a neural implant inserted in her skull. To Anna it seemed like some grotesque Frankensteinian surgery, and that Mantoni were merely using her as a living tool. Kia told her that she was being primitive and reactionary, and patiently explained the process step by step, and the reason for it.

Kia would be the first person to work for Mantoni to be implanted, though two scientists working for Cyber-Tech had undergone the surgery. One of these people was Sissi Nigeria, and Kia had enlisted Sissi to convince Anna that the process was a hundred per cent fool-proof and safe. Reluctantly, Anna had allowed herself to be won over.

The implant would allow Kia to be more successful at her job, would make the task of programming the Mantoni virtual reality that much easier and faster. Kia had talked to Nigeria, had looked into the science of nano-cerebral interfaces, researched the hardware and software that would be used, and was eager to have the surgery.

To Anna's relief, the woman who had emerged from the eight-hour operation was the same extrovert she had known before the cut. The only difference was that she no longer sported a magnificent mane of jet locks. She was shaveskull now, her bald head inlaid with an intricate array of silver spars and access ports. Anna often caught her lover posing before the wall-mirror back at the apartment, admiring the coruscating inlay as if it were the latest and most exclusive fashion accessory.

'Are you picking up any interference on One?' Kia asked now. 'There seems to be some kind of signal loss. Check that, will you, Rodriguez?'

Rodriguez, a small woman wired up to a computer with a mic and headphones, stared at a screen in a work-station and spoke hurriedly into her receiver. She looked up and gestured to a tall silver-haired guy at the far side of the chamber.

'Bob, are you reading that? It isn't a programming anomaly, is it? Carol, you're responsible for the sub-system in the glade site. Tell me it isn't a programming error.'

A woman looked up from her work-station. 'Check. It's no error, Maria. I've never seen anything like . . .'

Anna sensed tension in the air. In the sudden silence, techs glanced at each other, looked uncomfortable.

A technician at the far side of the chamber looked up and called, 'I'm picking up an anomaly in the glade site. Check the sub-routine. There's something in there.'

'Christ!' Rodriguez said. 'It's a security breach! I thought the dammed system was closed, Bob! What the hell's going on?'

Bob said, 'It's no anomaly, Maria. There's definitely something going on in there.'

'What have we got here?' Rodriguez called to all the techs. 'I want an answer in one minute. Viral program, some lone hacker, system glitch? I want answers, fast!'

Anna felt her palms begin to sweat, frustrated that she didn't understand a fraction of what was going on.

She looked back at the flatscreen. In the virtual world, Kia was kneeling in the grass, staring into the distance with a quizzical expression.

'Rodriguez, Bob . . .' Kia said, 'I have a visual sighting of something that shouldn't be here, dammit. Can someone tell me what the fuck's happening?'

Anna stood up suddenly, spilling her coffee across the table-top.

It happened so suddenly that Anna doubted the evidence of her eyes. She was staring at the flatscreen, at her lover kneeling in the grass. On the horizon, she made out a tiny speck, no more than an irregularity. In a fraction of

45

a second it grew, expanded – and Anna told herself that she had seen some kind of animal, perhaps a bison or a buffalo, but seemingly made from some silver metal. It charged towards the wallscreen, and Anna heard Kia scream and dive from its path, and then vanish as she exited the site.

In the jellytank, Kia was struggling into a sitting position, tearing the electrodes from her limbs and yanking the jacks from her cranial interface. She rose to her full height like some black Venus rising from a gelatinous ocean, strings of jelly adhering to her slim limbs and lithe body as if in an attempt to draw her back into the tank.

She was quickly surrounded by techs. Someone passed her a robe and, like an imperious diva displeased with audience reaction, she pulled it around her and swept from the chamber towards a small side room.

Anna hurried after her. Maria Rodriguez was already with Kia in the changing room. 'I want to know what the fuck was going on!' Kia shouted. She stepped into a shower cubicle and slammed the screen shut behind her. 'Who the hell was responsible for that?'

Rodriguez pulled a face at Anna. 'Are you okay, Kia?'

'I'm fine, no thanks to you. What the hell was it?'

Rodriguez looked pained. She glanced at Anna and spread her hands. 'We're investigating. Bob suspects infiltration, some kind of invasion.'

'An invasion?' Kia shook her head. 'Not the Virex brigade?'

'We don't know. We're not sure. We think they might have introduced a virus . . .'

'A *virus*?' Kia echoed. 'Christ, how did that happen? I thought we were secure.' She switched on the drier. Through the stippled glass door of the cubicle, Anna watched the nebulous shape of her lover's tall body.

'We are secure,' Rodriguez began. 'I mean, we were

46

secure. Give me a couple of hours and we'll work out exactly what went wrong. I'd like to check your implant, Kia.'

'You can do that in the morning,' Kia said. 'That's me for the day. Did I see Anna in there?'

'I'm here, Kia,' Anna said.

Kia looked over the door of the cubicle and crossed her eyes at Anna. 'Please take me away from this place, *ma chérie*; whisk me away to a magical coffee-shop.'

'Are you sure you're okay?'

'Sure I'm sure. Quit the mothering bit, okay? All I need is a black coffee and pleasant conversation.'

'See you tomorrow, Kia,' Rodriguez said. She quickly left the room and closed the door behind her.

Kia stepped from the drier, statuesque without clothes. They embraced, and her head hardly reached the sickle scars of Kia's double mastectomy. In the early days of their relationship, perhaps as worried as Anna that what was going on between them was no more than mere lust, Kia had joked that the only place they were really compatible was in bed. Some time later, a year into the relationship, Anna liked to remind Kia of what she had said, shaming her.

Kia dressed quickly in pink leggings, four lace smocks and her multi-coloured knitted coat.

'Let's go for that coffee, girl.'

They left the changing room and hurried across the chamber. The techs were gathered around the work-stations, talking animatedly. Maria Rodriguez looked up, opened her mouth to speak, and thought better of it. As Anna followed Kia through the door, she couldn't help feeling a childish thrill of having stolen the best girl at the party.

They drove in Kia's beat-up purple Cadillac to a coffee-shop off Broadway that served lattes made in heaven. Kia

47

collapsed at a window table while Anna ordered at the counter. She carried the tray across the room.

'What happened in there, Kia?' she asked. She recalled something Kia had said. 'Who are the Virex brigade?'

'Only some nutcase Luddite group opposed to the development of virtual reality, is all. They try to hack in from time to time, disrupt the system.'

Kia shook her head in frustration. She was undoubtedly the most striking woman on the New York scene. Anna tried not to set much store by appearance, but she found Kia's beauty breathtaking: the long Kenyan face, blade-sharp cheekbones, lips as full as overstuffed cushions. The silver spars of the implant, which circumnavigated her skull like some bizarre orthopaedic brace, only served to emphasise her natural good looks.

'It should've been a routine system check, girl. The site was closed. There was no way, no *way*, that Virex could've got a virus in there.'

'Then what?'

'Tell you what – some lazy bastard fucked up bad and won't admit to it.'

Anna sipped her coffee. 'I . . . when you were in the tank, I saw something in the site with you.'

'The silver thing? The silver buffalo?' Kia shook her head. 'It came straight for me. I felt something in here.' She raised a long-fingered hand and touched her interface. 'Of course, it all goes on in here: the representation of the buffalo was just the analogue for some code.'

Anna smiled and shook her head. She was lost already. She reached out and touched Kia's hand. 'The main thing is that you're okay, okay? What are we doing tonight?'

Kia smiled. 'First, I sleep. Then we'll hit the town. Dine somewhere romantic, just the two of us, and after that . . . we'll decide then, okay?'

Anna sipped her coffee. 'What happened last night? The usual crowd at the Scumbar?'

Kia's eyes clouded, as if at a worrying thought. She placed a long white cigarette between her amazing lips, blew a billow of smoke. 'You heard about Sissi?'

She'd been working on the scripts for the past few days. She was out of circulation, behind on the gossip.

'She's dumped Carrie?' she asked.

Beside their own relationship, Sissi's and Carrie's monogamy was the only long-standing 'marriage' on the scene.

'No, girl. Sissi disappeared about a week ago. She just up and vanished. One day she's around, and the next – gone. Then yesterday, Carrie goes missing.'

Anna shrugged. 'So they've gone away somewhere.'

'Without telling friends? I have the card for their apartment, remember? I look out for them when they go on vacation.'

Anna thought about it. 'So, a week ago Sissi goes away. Yesterday, Carrie decides to visit friends. She'll probably be back today, you wait.'

Kia angled her cigarette, contemplated its glowing tip. She looked through the smoke at Anna, as if considering whether to tell her something.

'Something happened last night, something weird.'

'You had too much to drink, right?'

Kia shook her head. 'I'm in the Scumbar and this private detective shows up, looking for Sissi. According to him, he's been hired by Carrie. I told him that Carrie hasn't shown.'

Anna looked at her. 'A private detective looking for Sissi? What was his name?'

Kia screwed her lips askew, thinking. 'Hal, something like that.'

Hal . . . How long had it been since she'd last seen her

brother? Four years, five? Anna had gone through a diffi-cult period in her early twenties, a period of sloughing off who she had been, unloading the anger and becoming a different person. She had even stopped calling herself Sue, preferring Anna instead.

Around that time, her relationship with Hal had gone bad. He reminded her too much of their father, and rather than endure the fraught meetings which had always ended in her railing at her brother's conditioned assumptions, she had decided not to see him again. She had moved from her apartment in the Solano Building and not both-ered to give him her new address.

She remembered Hal from her early teenage years, before she had come to understand who and what she was: they had been close then. She had been brighter than him, and he more experienced than her, and despite the seven-year age difference they had shared an easy and trusting equality.

She wondered what he might be like now. Perhaps it was time to contact him again. She had become a different person over the past five years, less bitter and more toler-ant. She smiled to herself.

Kia looked at her. 'What? You know this guy or something?'

'Was he short, with dark curly hair?'

'That's the guy.' Kia looked dubious. 'You know him?'

'I told you about my brother – the private eye. That's Hal.'

'God! Now you come to mention it . . . there was a family resemblance. Hey, no wonder I kinda liked the guy. He was gentle, you know, soft-spoken. He wasn't full of shit. Kinda quiet, calm.'

'What happened?'

'Well, seeing as how he's looking for friends, working for

50

us sisters, I said I'll take him back to Solano and let him look over the apartment. So we go.'

Anna nodded. 'And?'

'And we're in there about five minutes when the lights go out. Then things start getting weird. I can hardly stand up. There's a ringing in my ears. I hear the door open, someone come in. I crawl to the door, manage to get away, but before I do, I see this figure in black, holding a weapon of some kind. So I run and call the cops – and about an hour later they decide to show up. When we get back to the apartment, place is one hell of a mess, all the furniture's been sliced, I mean cut up, and the window's smashed.'

Anna felt her pulse quicken. 'What happened to Hal?'

Kia shook her head. 'Don't worry. No sign of him, no blood, no body parts. I reckon he got out through the window, managed to escape.'

'What did the police do?'

'What do you think, girl? They took a statement, photographed the place. Said they'd put someone on the case. I'll believe that when I see it. Too many of those damned tin-pot drones around these days, and not enough flesh-and-blood cops.'

'What's going on, Kia?'

'Search me, girl.'

'You don't think . . .' she began. 'You don't think this guy with the cutter had anything to do with Sissi and Nigeria's . . . with their disappearance?'

'Like I said, Anna, search me. Whole thing's so shitful weird . . .' She paused. 'Hey, don't fret. I'm sure Sissi and Carrie are okay.'

Anna glanced at Kia. She wanted to say that she wasn't so sure, but stopped herself.

They finished their coffee and drove home. The sun had

51

gone down behind the skyscrapers, creating a cold, dark interregnum that was neither day nor night. Anna looked out at the anonymous blanket-shrouded figures of the homeless, settling down for another cold night.

Five minutes later she jumped from the car and ran up the steps to her apartment. The lounge received them with its hospitable warmth.

While Kia changed, Anna checked her email. There were half a dozen messages awaiting her. Three were from friends, inviting Anna and Kia out tonight. One was from Felicity: she thought the rewrite was just terrific. Another was from a demented dyke in Ohio who just loved *Sapphic Island* and wanted to look Anna up if she ever made it to the Big Apple.

The last message was from the editor of a literary press, who had very much enjoyed reading the manuscript of her latest novel, but who in the 'present publishing climate didn't think it was quite the right type of novel to engage the public's imagination,' etc. et cetera . . . .

And that was from the editor of a supposed literary publishing house.

She accessed the file containing the manuscript of her novel in progress. The first draft was almost finished: she had a short epilogue to complete, and then she could begin the leisurely process of the re-write. She skimmed the last few pages, liked what she read, and wondered what she had to do to make the breakthrough.

She didn't want to be remembered as the pseudonymous hack writer of *Sapphic Island*. She told herself she was better than that.

The wallscreen chimed with an incoming. She accepted the call and sprawled on the sofa as the screen flared into life.

She sat up, startled. Carrie Villeux stared out at her. She

was sitting in an armchair in what looked like a hotel bedroom, one long leg cocked over the arm.

'Anna, I've been trying to contact you all afternoon.'

'Carrie. Where are you? We've been worried.' She considered what Kia had told her about the guy with the cutter. 'Carrie, is Sissi okay?'

Carrie was perhaps forty, her thin, tanned face made even longer by her shaven skull, patterned with tattoos. She wore stylish cords, a black bolero jacket, and looked stunning.

'I need to talk, Anna. I . . . I need to talk to someone who understands people. We'll meet somewhere. I'll call tomorrow and we'll arrange a meeting . . .'

'Carrie, where's Sissi?'

Carrie hesitated. 'I'm with her in a hotel.' She spoke with a distinct Quebecois accent. 'She was gone for five days, then yesterday she called me up and said that she needed to see me.'

Anna shook her head. 'What's going on, Carrie?'

'I don't know. I met Sissi in the hotel, but she was acting very strange. It wasn't drugs,' she said, as if to dispel the notion. 'I don't know what was wrong with her. It was as if she didn't know me. She sometimes goes out for a few hours, but in disguise. Then she comes back and everything is normal, she's herself again, and everything's fine for a few hours.' She hesitated. 'You understand people, Anna. I need to see you, tell you about what's been happening.'

Anna shrugged. 'I'll do what I can.'

Carrie looked pained. 'Sissi claims that people are after her, that she needs to hide – which is why she wears the disguises.'

'It sounds as though she needs help,' Anna said. Psychiatric help, she thought to herself.

Carrie looked up suddenly, stared off-screen. 'She's coming back. I'll call you later, okay?'

'Fine,' Anna began, but Carrie had already cut the connection.

It seemed almost as if Carrie was afraid of her lover.

She moved to the kitchen and fixed herself a coffee. Kia was still changing. She carried the coffee back to the lounge, stared through the window, and waited for Kia to emerge from the bedroom, disturbed by the thought of what might be happening to Sissi Nigeria.

Four

At eight that morning Barney Kluger found Halliday's note on the desk-com: Looking into the Nigeria case, Barney – gone to the Scumbar. Be back around eight.

Barney fixed himself a coffee and lowered his bulk into the swivel chair. The chair was getting to be a tight fit these days. He'd been on a diet the past three months, cut out all the pastrami on rye he'd become addicted to over the years. The Ukrainian wheat beer they served along at Olga's, though, was harder to kick. Maybe if he could cut his daily consumption by a couple of bottles . . . 'You've got the circulation of a stone, Barney,' Doc Symes had warned him. 'Don't know how your heart keeps on going. Lose some weight, okay?'

Well, he'd done his best, shed half a stone in twelve weeks, but his waistline didn't seem to be getting any thinner. Maybe he'd invest in a new swivel.

He wiped Hal's note from the screen, called up the case file and sat back with his coffee. He'd look through his notes on a few cases for an hour, before heading downtown for his appointment at Mantoni Entertainments.

He was pleased to see that Hal had taken the Nigeria case. He hadn't fancied it himself, and not only because it would have meant him asking questions where he wasn't welcome. He'd had a hunch about the situation as soon as Villeux had walked in and told her story the other day. So her lover was missing and Villeux was concerned, but Barney had seen it all before: the girls had had a tiff, fallen out, Nigeria had gone back to stay with some old lover for a period of cooling off. In a few days she'd be back, and when Barney's bill came in at five hundred dollars per hour, Carrie Villeux would wish she hadn't bothered hiring his services.

He had to hand it to Hal, he had a hide as thick as a rhino's. Barney had no qualms about showing his face in some of the gambling dives in the area – at least, he hadn't a few years ago, when he'd been a bit younger, a little leaner – but the thought of asking questions around the Scumbar did not appeal.

He'd made a good move five years ago when he'd invited Hal to join him at the agency. They got on fine from their police days down at the Department. It was not long after Estelle's death, and the thought of running the agency alone had filled him with despair. When Estelle was alive, he'd had someone he could bring his troubles home to, someone he could talk to about a case. The months after her death had been hard. Looking back, he wondered how he'd seen them through. The cases came in, and he'd put his head down and worked hard. Some cases he solved and others he didn't, and the usual proportion ended up as suicides or murder victims. So soon after losing his wife of almost thirty-five years, the succession of tragic stories wore him down, and it was either quit the agency, sell it for peanuts, or get someone else in to shoulder some of the workload.

One day he'd bumped into Hal out on patrol, and the guy had looked as down as Barney felt. His long-term affair with an old girlfriend was through – she'd chucked him out, Barney gathered – and the file work was getting him down, so Barney made him the offer. Hal had said he'd think about it, get back to him by the end of the week, and what did you know, but a day later Barney got a call and Hal said that if the offer was still on, he'd take it.

Kluger and Halliday, Private Detectives: Missing Persons A Speciality. It had a certain ring.

Barney glanced at his watch. It was eight-thirty, and while Hal was usually punctual from his days with the force, he had been known to be half an hour late before. Even so, it was unlike Hal not to call him and explain what was happening.

He tapped Hal's code into the desk-com and waited. There was no reply . . . Barney smiled to himself. Hal was probably in Olga's, warming himself with a coffee, his com turned off.

A year ago, business had been going through a bad patch. The cases hadn't been coming in, and those that had had been bummers, bad earners that had lasted barely a day or two. Hal had seemed pretty low, though it was hard to tell with Hal: he wasn't the kind of guy to open up with his emotions and spill his heart out. He hadn't had a woman, so far as Barney was aware, for years. He was beginning to get that haunted, introverted look in his eyes that Barney recognised from his dealings with no-hopers and terminal sociopaths.

Barney started noticing this kid around the place, ten months or so ago. Tiny Chinese girl, slim as a broom, cute-faced, always running upstairs to the loft with Chinese take-outs. So Barney, knowing how Hal would never get round to saying anything if he wasn't asked, had delayed him as he was about to go out on a case, and said, 'Hey, Hal, notice you're eating a little Chinese these days . . .'

Hal had opened his mouth to say something, closed it again and just stared at Barney, nonplussed. Finally he'd said, 'Trust Barney, Manhattan's finest private detective.'

'What's her name, Hal?'

So Hal had told Barney about her. He was still at that stage with the girl where he didn't believe his luck – she had just stepped into his life and demanded that he love

57

her – a tall order for someone as distant as Hal. He'd seen him change over the months, though, come in some small degree to reciprocate the affection that Kim Long lavished on him. Not that it was all sweetness and light. The kid had a temper like a Chinese dragon and could go off like a firecracker, to mix metaphors. Then Hal would go quiet, tend to lie low, and spend a few hours with Barney at Olga's, sampling the whole range of wheat beers imported from the Ukraine.

Barney had got to know Kim over the weeks after she moved in, saw that beneath the cutesy exterior she was a shrewd businesswoman. She knew how to turn a quick profit and was on top of all the latest scams. Barney had listened to her about savings and investment, but he drew the line one day when she came into the office, took a long look around the place, snub nose turned up in distaste, and declared that the room was losing energy like a stuck pig loses blood and needed some changes. He'd complimented her on her imagery and said that he was perfectly happy with the office as it was, thank you. She tut-tutted and said that if he remained sitting at the desk with his back to the window, along with a dozen other things he was doing wrong, then he'd have a week of bad luck – and hell, if they didn't have a week of bad luck. They lost a case to a competitor; a customer left the country owing them a couple of grand; his sciatica had gotten worse . . .

So the next time she showed her smug little grin around the door, he called her in and said, 'About this . . . this sheng-phooey malarkey, Kim . . . run it past me again.'

And he'd moved the desk and the chesterfield as she instructed, more with amusement than a belief that it might affect anything. He'd hung a picture of the sunset on the south wall and positioned a vase of dried flowers in the south-east corner of the room. Kim had painted the office door green and placed a fern on a stand just outside the door, to counter the bad yin rushing up the straight staircase. She'd advised him to keep a pet, preferably a cat, but Barney had never had a pet in his life, and he was damned if he was going to start now. He did agree to keep the loo seat down in the bathroom, though, and to move his bed into the corner of his room.

Kim had told him that it might take a few days for the good chi to start flowing, and Barney had looked at her as if she had lost her marbles.

But gradually, over the course of the next week, things began to change for the better. Lucrative contracts came in; they solved cases they'd struggled with for weeks – and even his sciatica cleared up. Barney told himself that the sudden success of the business was due mostly to Hal's renewed enthusiasm for life. Over the weeks he'd watched Hal lose his apathy, begin to enjoy his life and work again.

The transformation of his partner soon made Barney realise something that he'd tried to push to the back of his mind for a long time. Despite it being almost six years since Estelle's death, and despite thinking he'd managed to get over the worst of the grief, the simple fact was that he still missed her like hell.

It was a combination of many things, not just the obvious. Hal had spent a lot of time with Kim in the early days; they ate out frequently, went to the holo-dramas, once or twice went skiing upstate. Barney missed doing the big things with Estelle, but it was the smaller details that he missed, too; the things which, when he noticed them pass between Hal and Kim, made him wish, with a kind of hopeless envy, that Estelle were still with him: the glances, the quick touches they assumed no one else noticed, the phrases and sayings that meant so much to each other.

Christ, but he still missed her, and her absence was like an open wound.

He hadn't seen anyone else since her death: that wasn't the solution. Other women were pale imitations of Estelle. Whenever he met women through the business, he was forever comparing them with his wife, and finding them lacking. They had been together for thirty-five years, ever since New Year's Eve, 2000. They'd met at a party to see in the New Year, the new century, the new millennium – he twenty years old, Estelle just seventeen – and while he never claimed that it had been love at first sight, there had been an attraction, and they had seen each other for a year before getting married. He'd been a rookie cop, she a secretary for a legal firm, and they'd lived in a tiny, damp, and dirty walk-up in Brooklyn, and it had been the happiest time in all his twenty-one years.

And their marriage had survived. They'd had their rocky moments. They'd never had children, and at first this forced them apart, until they reconciled themselves to the fact of childlessness, and found comfort in each other. Estelle had been special, the kindest woman he had ever known, quiet and gentle and without a bad word to say about anyone. Christ knew what she'd seen in him, who, he told himself, possessed the reverse of all these qualities. She'd laughed when he'd told her this, said that he was so stuck on playing the tough-guy cop ever to admit to being human, and who knows perhaps she was right.

Thirty-five years . . .

She'd died of kidney failure six years ago come March, after a year of illness during which she had been assured that she would get a transplant in time . . . But the nuclear power station in Georgia had suffered meltdown, and the refugees had flooded into New York. The health service had been stretched beyond its means, and the week Estelle fell acutely ill coincided with an intake of radiation burn victims at St Vincent's. The search for a donor kidney for Estelle was given low priority, and she had died in his arms in the early hours of a cold Sunday morning.

Another reason, he told himself, that he gave Hal the graveyard shift. Those cold, quiet hours before dawn just cut him up.

He glanced at his watch. It was after nine and Hal hadn't showed. Again Barney tapped Hal's code into the desk-com and listened to the ring tone. No reply.

Frowning, he shut the link.

A month ago Barney had run into an executive he knew in Mantoni Entertainments. He'd worked as a bodyguard for the executive, as well as for some of the company's most beautiful actresses, on and off over the years when business at the agency was slack. So he and this guy had downed a few beers for old times' sake, and three beers became six, and Barney had started to run off at the mouth. He told the guy about Estelle, and how much he missed her.

Couple of days later, the guy calls Barney at the office.

'About what we were discussing the other day. I have just the thing, Barney . . .'

'No introductions, pal. I'm past it.'

'No, nothing like that, Barney. Trust me on this one, won't you? Hear me out . . .'

So Barney heard him out, and liked what he heard, and every week for the past couple of months he'd been having regular sessions with the guy and his team at the swish Mantoni headquarters in Manhattan.

He left a note on the screen for Hal, saying he'd be back around one, then grabbed his coat and locked the door. He'd take a taxi downtown. Hal had taken the Ford last night – something of a luxury, these days, which they'd probably review at the end of the month.

He stepped out into the bright winter sunlight, ignoring

the crowds on the sidewalk and the cries of the stall-holders. He hailed a cab, then sat back as it carried him towards his appointment with the tech-heads at Mantoni Entertainments.

He recalled what he'd told Hal about VR last night, and the story he'd spun him these past few weeks about need-ing to be up in the latest technology, to keep abreast of the times. Hal was no mug, and he must've been wondering where all these supposed VR courses were leading. In a way, Barney felt guilty for stringing Hal along. But he couldn't bring himself to tell him the truth. As the cab pulled onto Broadway, easing through the crowds of refu-gees spilling onto the street, he wondered what he feared by telling Hal what was going on with Mantoni Entertain-ments; it wasn't Hal's ridicule, because he wasn't that sort of guy. Perhaps he was reluctant to confide in his partner because something within him, deep down, didn't think what he was doing was quite right.

The headquarters of Mantoni Entertainments occupied every floor of a fifty-storey skyscraper whose sheer win-dowed façade reflected the blue sky like some flawless virtual reality interface.

Sergio Mantoni, the millionaire chairman of Mantoni Entertainments, had begun as a producer of popular holo-dramas and over the course of a decade had built a world-wide empire spanning every facet of the entertainment industry. Now, not to be left behind, his company was at the scientific forefront of VR research and development. Barney, in his own way – and for a certain consideration – was doing his little bit to help the company. It was this consideration, the means of his payment, that niggled at his conscience.

He climbed from the cab and crossed the sidewalk. He was taking the first of the dozen steps to the sliding glass doors when someone, emerging from the building, called his name.

'Barney? Barney Kluger?'

He looked up. A vision of all that was perfect in the female sex posed on the top step, one hand stylishly holding a large white hat to her head. She wore a fitted sable dress like midnight made in Paris and her legs, as ever, were sensational.

'Barney, it is you!' She walked down the steps towards him.

Barney was aware of the gawpers on the sidewalk, staring as if they'd seen an angel descend.

Vanessa Artois was among the greatest holo-drama actresses of all time and certainly, in Barney's humble opinion, the best-looking. He had worked as her body-guard for a few months seven or eight years ago, in which time he'd come to know the star pretty well – realised that, behind the glamour, life at the top was not all St Tropez and champagne.

'Vanessa . . . Well, if this isn't a turn up. Must be what, seven years? You're still as beautiful as ever.'

She stepped onto the sidewalk before him, and he had to crane his neck to look up into the sophisticated angles of her face, wrapped about in a raven fall of hair.

'You're looking well yourself, Barney.'

'Give me a break. I'm feeling my age.' He climbed three steps and faced her, eye to eye. 'So how's it going, kid? Still in the holo-dramas?'

'You don't keep up?' Artois gave an affected pout of disappointment.

'You know me, no time to enjoy myself with the dramas.'

'Actually,' Artois said, 'the next big thing is virtual reality. I'm angling for a career shift, trying to make it big in VR.'

'You still with Mantoni?'

'If you mean am I still under contract, why yes I am. If you mean . . .' she spread fingers across her perfect throat, '. . . are we *romantically* attached, well, between you and me, I'm trying to get out of that deal, too.'

'Piece of advice from an old man, kid – hire a good lawyer and get rid of him.'

He'd never liked Sergio Mantoni. The man was an arrogant bastard who considered the stars in his employ as little more than pawns to be manipulated in a global game of business politics. The way he'd treated Artois in the past would have had a dog-owner imprisoned, Barney felt. He'd seen enough while working for Mantoni to make him consider the possibility of setting up an accidental exit for the millionaire tycoon. The irony was that he was now in the pay of the bastard . . .

'Still in the same business, Barney?' she asked.

'Missing persons a speciality. Got myself a partner, a younger guy to do the leg work; one of the best. You ever need anyone finding, Vanessa, look me up.'

He gave her one of his cards and she scrunched up her nose in an actressy smile. 'You know, I might just do that, Barney,' she said, slipping the card into a tiny purse.

A stretch limo as long as a bus eased into the kerb. ''Fraid that's for me, Barney. Say hi to Estelle for me, you hear?'

And with a quick wave of fingers she was gone before Barney could tell her that Estelle had been dead for more than five years.

He watched her cut a swathe through the gawping pedestrians and ease herself with estimable poise into the limo. He felt like running after her, explaining that Estelle was dead.

He lifted a hand as the limousine coasted away from the sidewalk, Artois invisible behind the tinted glass.

For all he'd admired Vanessa Artois, and not just her

good looks but her straightforward personality, some part of him had always felt sorry for her. He remembered telling her the story of how he and Estelle had been happily married for so long, and couldn't forget the look of sadness that had entered her eyes.

He walked into the building and took the elevator up to the R&D suite on the twenty-fifth floor.

Lew was standing by a flatscreen with four technicians when Barney walked in.

'How goes it, bud?' Lew said.

'I'm fine, fine. Any progress?'

Lew nodded. 'Those parameters we were worried about last week – everything's okay on that front. We've been running a mock-up for the past two days.'

'You mean . . .?'

Lew nodded. 'We're ready when you are.'

'Christ . . . This is a surprise. I figured another two weeks, more. Didn't think it'd be ready so soon.'

For the past month he'd been learning about the technical aspects of virtual reality, if only secondhand by kibitzing on what the technicians were doing while he hovered in the background, and the little that Lew divulged. The business was in the throes of rapid development, and companies were paranoid about competitors gaining an advantage, no matter how small. In consequence, secrecy was the watchword.

The team of scientists and technicians headed by Lew Kramer was working on the creation of artificial personalities within the world of virtual reality, constructs based on real-life individuals. Lew wanted to construct a site within Mantoni VR, inhabited by the great and famous from, to begin with, the history of the twenty-first century – and this was where Barney came in.

'If you'd like to get ready,' Lew said now.

Barney nodded, his thoughts in a swirl. For so long it

65

had been something which had always been a few weeks away, as glitch followed hitch in the system, and the delays piled up. At times, Barney had thought that VR might be nothing more than a fantasy, destined to come to nothing, in order to make his disappointment bearable. Oddly, when Lew assured him that it was ongoing, he had been beset by doubt, questioning himself as to whether what he had volunteered for was right.

Now it was time to see if what Lew and his team had developed was as authentic as the executive had claimed it would be. He crossed the room to the booth in the corner, his heart pounding with excitement and apprehension. He undressed and hung his clothes in a locker. A technician came and assisted him with the electrodes and facemask.

Every Friday morning for the past three weeks he'd entered virtual reality via a jellytank, a not-too-pleasant procedure resulting in án extraordinarily pleasant experience. The reality of the sites he'd entered, and the fidelity of his experiences within them, had literally left him breathless. On these occasions he had been merely a guinea-pig, reporting back to Lew and the techs on the success or otherwise of their programming. He'd met a few famous politicians in VR, a holo-drama actress or two . . .

This time, it would be the meeting he had been anticipating for so long.

Barney stepped into the jellytank, his skin crawling in reaction to the sensation of the viscous fluid as it sealed itself around his body. The goo, Lew had once explained to him, was an anaesthetic suspension which facilitated the process of tactile sensory deprivation.

Barney sat down and, at a signal from the tech, lay back.

He floated. He felt the jelly go to work on his flesh, deadening all sensation.

For a disconcerting second, before his mind adjusted to the fact, he found himself standing upright. He was initially amazed by the sudden shift of perspective from horizontal to the vertical.

At first he was blind, and then he could see. His vision was flooded with colour and sunlight. The reality of the world around him, the authenticity of his place in it, made him gasp in awe. He could not help but raise a hand to his face, trace its contours, and then stare about him in wonder.

He had never before visited this site. He was standing in the garden of a sprawling villa, on a lawn surrounded by flowers. The sun shone in a perfectly blue sky and the air was filled with the fragrance of the blooms.

He looked down, at the younger version of his own body that Lew had programmed for him.

Then he turned around, almost in desperation, searching for her.

He moved, his heart beating rapidly, towards a flower-entwined bower at the far end of the lawn.

Many aspects of what he was doing here with Lew and the others had worried him. How would he cope, psychologically? Was he being true to the memory of Estelle or was he in some way being unfaithful?

The seat on the bower was empty. He turned, disappointed . . . and then he saw her.

His heart hammered. He felt dizzy. He reached out a hand, opened his mouth to say something, but no words came.

She walked towards him across the lawn, smiling . . . and all he could do was stare.

'There you are, Barney,' Estelle said. 'I've been looking all over for you. Isn't it beautiful?'

He nodded 'It is,' he murmured to himself. 'It is beautiful.'

He had never expected her to be this convincing, this lifelike, when he had supplied Lew with the videos of his wife, the tapes of her singing, the still shots of her he'd taken over the years, even the samples of her clothing and perfume he had saved since her death.

'It's so good to see you, Barney,' she said. 'You're looking well.'

The sound of her voice brought tears to his eyes. It was Estelle, as he recalled her from all those years ago. She was perhaps forty, at the height of her bloom, a slim blonde woman with a tanned, smiling face, aged with lines of experience that, if anything, enhanced her allure.

He had been worried that the sight of her might bring back to him the fact of what he had lost, but the reality was such that, for all he knew the Estelle before him to be a complex technological ghost, he could only feel joy that she no longer existed merely in his memories.

He asked his wife, wherever she might be, to forgive him his weakness.

He reached out, then hesitated. Surely, he told himself, surely she cannot feel as real, as warm and alive, as the original Estelle. He was loath to touch her hand, which rose now to his, for fear of having his illusion cruelly shattered.

And then she took his hand in hers, and he felt the warmth, the strength of her fingers, as they enclosed his and drew him to her.

'Come inside, Barney,' Estelle said. 'I've so much to show you!'

Barney put an arm around her shoulders and, buoyed with elation, walked with her towards the villa.

Five

Meeting Kia in the Scumbar rainforest . . . The fused consoles . . . The terror and disorientation he experienced in the darkened room . . . The chase along the alley, across the rooftop . . . *The man with the changing face!*

Halliday lay on his back, blinking up at the bright sunlight above him.

After a period of being unable to remember anything at all about the night before, the memories came crashing in. He went through his recollections of the events of the evening. Everything made sense – at least, a kind of sense – until his encounter with the Latino, and then he was seized with a residue of the terror that had shaken him last night.

The last thought he could recall, before losing consciousness, was that either the cold, or the loss of blood, would surely kill him. Well, he had survived. He had not bled to death, and the garbage bags piled around him had kept the worst of the cold from his body.

Experimentally, he moved his limbs. He lifted first his right arm, and then his left. They seemed to be functioning perfectly well, and he felt no pain. He flexed his legs, and they too seemed to be working as well as ever. He sat up, or rather tried to, and immediately regretted the attempt as a throb of pain pulsed through his head.

He lifted a hand and touched his left temple, and his fingers came away sticky with congealing blood.

He rolled onto his side, carefully, and then onto his

stomach, and from there manoeuvred himself onto all fours. He hung his head, closing his eyes against the pain. He took a deep breath and stood slowly. The alley seemed to sway around him, but miraculously the pain had abated. It was there, nagging him like a constant headache, but no longer was it a debilitating, stabbing migraine.

The sun was high in the clear blue sky. He looked at his watch. It was almost midday. He recalled Kim's reminder to be back by ten. He'd be in trouble when he returned, and Kim was quite a sight when she worked on her anger.

He wondered if his excuse would be sufficient to defuse her rage.

His thoughts returned to the Latino with the changing face. Had the Latino assumed that the fall had killed him, and not bothered to check? Or had he, too, passed out? Halliday recalled bringing the butt of his gun down on the face. The guy had managed to get up and attack him one last time, but he had been unsteady on his feet. Perhaps, right now, he was on the rooftop, recuperating. The thought moved Halliday to set off along the alley in the direction of the square where he'd parked the Ford last night.

As he turned the corner and passed the row of brownstones where Sissi Nigeria had her apartment, a part of him wanted to finish the job he had started last night, go through Nigeria's personal items for any clue as to what might be responsible for the woman's disappearance, the fused consoles, and the Latino's pursuit and attack. But another part of him, spurred by fear, wanted nothing more than to put distance between himself and the scene of the attack. Later, he told himself, when he'd discussed the case with Barney, and maybe Jeff Simmons over at the Department. Maybe then he'd go back and investigate.

The thought of the Latino made him reach for his

automatic. His body-holster was empty. He recalled clubbing the guy in the face, and after that he had no idea what had happened to the weapon. It might still be on the rooftop, or in the alleyway . . . He was half-tempted to go back and look for it, but instinctive fear prevailed. What was a gun, compared to his safety? Barney had an armoury of the damned things.

He crossed the street, climbed into the Ford and started the engine. He drove around the square, relieved to be getting away, and headed uptown, passing crowds of Saturday morning shoppers and the ever-present hordes of homeless men, women and children.

Five minutes later he passed the VR Bar on Park Avenue, the hologram advertising the wonders of the tropical beach washed to a wan pastel shade in the bright sunlight. People were still lining up around the block; if anything, the queue was longer now than it had been the night before. Halliday gripped the wheel, something very like exultation at having survived, tempered by a fading fear, sluicing through him.

He parked outside the Chinese laundry. The aroma of cooking meat drifted from the food-stalls lining the street and reminded him that he hadn't eaten for what seemed like ages. He climbed out and crossed the busy sidewalk with his head down to avoid questions from the stall-holders about his bloody face. The ground-floor laundry was in full swing, snorting steam from the entrance and noisy with the chomp and snap of the presses, as if they had a dragon captive on the premises. He hurried up the staircase, hoping to avoid Barney until he'd showered and attended to the cuts and bruises. The office door was open, and as Halliday ducked past and climbed the first of the steps to the loft, Barney called out, 'Hey, Hal! That you? Hal, where the hell've you been?'

Halliday stopped, considered ignoring the call and continuing up the steps, but Barney would know that something was wrong and follow him up.

He turned and stepped into the office.

'Christ, but is Kim one angry . . .' Barney looked up, and stopped when he saw Halliday.

He was rocking back in his chair, his short legs propped on the table, and he almost spilled himself in his haste to stand up. He hurried around the desk, pulling the cigar butt from his mouth and peering at Halliday's head.

'Jesus, Hal, what the hell have you been doing? Sit down. Christ, you look terrible.'

'I'll be fine. Don't worry.'

Barney almost pushed him onto the chesterfield. 'Stay there. I'll get something for that.' He moved to the adjoining bedroom and emerged with a first-aid kit.

'Barney, I'll be fine. All I need is a shower.'

'Shut it and tip your head back. How the hell did this happen?'

'It's a long story, Barney.'

'I've got all the time in the world.'

As Barney cleaned the wound with antiseptic, Halliday went through the events of the night before, detail by minute detail, omitting nothing.

Every couple of days they went through the case they were working on, point by point, going back over details that might at first have seemed trivial, cross-checking facts, bouncing ideas and speculations off each other until the topic was exhausted and they had a clearer picture of the case.

When Halliday got to the rooftop encounter with the Latino, he paused. He was gripped by the knowledge, as if for the first time, that someone had tried to kill him. Out there, someone had wanted him dead . . . might very well still want him dead.

'I need a coffee.'

'Sure. I'll fix it.' Barney poured a mug of strong Colombian roast from the percolator. He passed it to Halliday and sat next to him on the chesterfield, peering at the cut.

'It looks okay. Nasty, but not that deep. I could get Doc Symes to . . .'

'Forget it. I'll be fine.'

Barney ignited the butt of his cigar. 'So, we're on the roof. What happened then?'

Halliday thought back to the fight on the rooftop. He remembered bringing his gun down, hard, into the guy's face. 'So I hit him, in the face, and then the damnedest thing . . .' he stopped.

'Go on.'

'You won't believe this, Barney.'

'Try me.'

Halliday shrugged. 'I don't know if I believe it myself.' He looked at Barney and laughed. 'The guy's face . . . it changed. I mean, one second he was a guy, Puerto Rican, maybe Cuban, and then I hit him and his face changed. He was a girl, a blonde.' His right hand was trembling, and he gripped his thigh to stop it.

Barney's expression was unreadable. 'So what happened then?'

Halliday recounted his flight to the edge of the building, his fear. 'Then the guy – he was back to the Latino, then – the guy launched himself at me, knocked me over the edge.'

Barney stared. 'You fell from the top of a three-storey building?'

'Landed on a pile of garbage sacks, fell to the ground and hit my head. I blacked out. Next thing I know, it's midday.'

Barney was shaking his head. He took the butt from his mouth, gave it a good long inspection, and then glanced up at Halliday. 'I'd say you're the damned luckiest son of a bitch in Manhattan, Hal. No, make that New York State.'

Halliday laughed, nervously. 'Don't you think I know it? The number of times I might've bought it last night . . .'

Barney moved to his swivel chair and tapped the keyboard. 'I'll get through to Jeff, see if he can get someone good on the case. Now that there's a potential killer involved, they might be more interested. I'll get Jeff to send the case file while I'm at it.'

The desk-com flared and Barney spoke with a receptionist.

'Lieutenant Simmons is in a briefing at the moment, Mr Kluger.'

'Get him to call me back when he's through.' He cut the connection and looked at Halliday. 'You say Carrie Villeux wasn't around last night?'

'Her friends were concerned. She'd arrange to meet them at the Scumbar last night at ten – she hadn't missed a Friday night in years. When she didn't show, I went to the Solano Building with a woman called Kia Johansen.'

'This dyke, you say she got away when the Latino came in?'

Halliday nodded. 'I think so. She was closer to the door. I'm sure she got out before he started firing.'

'We need to question her about last night, her relationship with Villeux and Nigeria,' Barney said. 'You say you found a fused com-console. Anything else? No signs of forced entry, burglary?'

Halliday shook his head. 'Not that I noticed, but I hardly had time to check before the lights went out and the fun started.'

Barney tipped back his seat. 'Any thoughts?'

'I want to get an expert to look at the console. I'd like to find out what Nigeria was working on.'

'I'll get Jeff to sort that out,' Barney said. He paused and looked at Halliday. 'About this guy, what you saw. You don't think . . .'

'What? That I was seeing things?' He regarded the dregs of his coffee. 'Look, right now, I want to believe that – it's a good explanation. I'd be happier if I had hallucinated the damned thing.' He shook his head. 'But, Barney, it happened. I saw it. It was no hallucination. The guy changed appearance before my eyes and it frightened me.'

Barney nodded, withholding judgement. He's being kind, Halliday thought, he obviously thinks I lost it last night.

He looked up, sensing someone else in the office.

Kim stood against the doorframe. 'What frightened you, Hal?' she said, glaring at him. 'The thought of getting home late, is that it?'

Oddly enough, the sight of her, bundled in her padded primrose jacket, pretty oval face framed by the fur of her hat, filled Halliday with a sudden surge of affection.

He savoured the tight, angry line of her lips, knowing that soon her rage would turn to concern. It would make a change from her anger, which could simmer on for days.

'Sweetheart,' Barney said. 'Hal was attacked last night. He's lucky to be alive.'

Halliday saw her expression change. She absorbed what Barney had said, took a second to readjust her thoughts away from the desire to shout at him. Her eyes widened and she hurried across to where he lay on the chesterfield, sat next to him and grasped his hand. She saw the cut at his temple and her fingers found his cheek.

'What happened, Hal? Who did this?'

He gave her a shortened version of the events, playing down the danger. She listened, biting her bottom lip in a gesture of ill-contained fear, like a child being told a scary story.

Her eyes had always fascinated and beguiled Halliday, their size, the width of the flattened space between them. Now, filled and filmed with tears, they shone with the lustre of rain-washed jet.

She was going over what he'd said, frowning. 'I heard you say something – the guy changed, and it frightened you?'

Halliday glanced at Barney, who merely shrugged.

'When we were fighting. I hit him and the guy's face changed. For a second or two he . . . he looked like a woman. I know, it's crazy.' He stopped at the sight of Kim's expression.

She was shaking her head. She looked as scared as he had felt last night. 'Hal, I believe you.' Her hands squeezed his fingers. 'I know what you saw.'

'You do?' Would she never cease to amaze him?

'Shape-shifter,' she whispered. 'Evil spirit.'

Barney raised his eyebrows and shuttled his cigar from one side of his mouth to the other, loving this.

Deadpan, Halliday repeated, 'Evil spirit?'

She nodded, serious. 'A terrible evil spirit. In Singapore, we know about shape-shifters. They possess people, force them to do what they don't want to do. They change their appearances so they can do these things. They give them superhuman strength.'

Halliday smiled. He cupped her cheek. 'Kim, this guy wasn't that strong. I managed to disarm him.'

'You were lucky!' The tears spilled now, rolling down her cheeks, and Halliday felt guilty for his show of gentle ridicule.

'Hal,' she said, 'please leave this case! Evil spirits, they never give up. You anger them, they follow you and never let you go. In the end, evil spirits get what they want. Just leave this case, hokay?'

She looked from Halliday to Barney, as if for support.

'I'm sure there's some rational explanation, sweetheart,' Barney said. 'No need to go getting yourself worked up.'

Kim looked exasperated. 'There's every need! You don't know how evil shape-shifters are!'

Halliday reached out and thumbed the tears from her cheeks. 'I'll stay off the case, if that's what you want, Kim. We'll let the cops deal with it.'

She hugged him, and the feel of her body in his arms persuaded him that the lie had been worthwhile.

She pulled away. 'Do you feel like going out, Hal? Big surprise, remember?'

'I'll get a quick shower and change. Where we going?'

She smiled radiantly. 'Surprise means secret, Hal. You'll find out when you get there, hokay?'

The screen chimed, and the receptionist at police headquarters stared out at Barney. 'Lieutenant Simmons online,' she said. 'I'll put you through.'

Kim squeezed Halliday's hand. 'I'll go and change.'

'I'll be up in a minute.' He watched her run from the office.

Barney said, 'You meant what you told her about dropping the . . .?'

Halliday raised a finger to his lips and whispered, 'What do you think, Barney?'

The screen flared and Jeff Simmons stared out. 'Barney, Hal. Good to see you both. How can I help?'

'It's the Sissi Nigeria case, Jeff. Your reference . . .' Barney dropped a screen menu and read off the reference number.

Jeff Simmons was a massive silver-haired Irish-American in his late fifties, thirty years in the force and nearing retirement age. He was softly-spoken and unruffled; in the ten years Halliday had known Simmons, he'd never heard him panic or raise his voice, never seen him move with undue haste. His reasoned, thoughtful approach to problems inspired confidence.

Now he nodded. 'I know the case, Barney. Carrie Villeux came by about a week ago . . .' He glanced off-screen at another com. 'I put Fernandez on the case. I'll send you his report. He came up with nothing much.'

Barney smiled. 'That's probably why Villeux came to us – she said you weren't getting anywhere.'

'That's right, but we had a call last night.'

'Tell me about it,' Barney said. 'Hal was there.' Barney briefed Simmons on the events of the night before.

Simmons leaned back in his seat and listened, massaging his fleshy cheeks with a big hand. He looked from the screen at Hal. 'This Latino guy, you said you saw him change?'

Halliday leaned forward on the chesterfield. 'I know it's hard to believe, Jeff. I didn't believe it at the time, and now I'm beginning to wonder . . .'

'Describe it to me. I mean, exactly what happened. Barney says you hit the guy?'

Halliday nodded. 'Brought my automatic down on his right cheek. Pretty sure I smashed the bone.'

'And only then did he change appearance.'

'That's right.'

'Jesus Christ,' Jeff said under his breath, leaning back in his seat and stretching.

'I know, I know. Like I said, I'm beginning to doubt it myself.'

Jeff was shaking his head. 'It isn't that, Hal. I believe you.'

'You do?' Halliday glanced at Barney.

'I wish I wasn't hearing this,' Jeff said.

Barney reached out and adjusted the screen slightly, staring in at the cop. 'What is it?'

Jeff chewed his lip. 'I thought they weren't out there. I'd heard about them, of course.'

For a crazy second, Halliday thought that the usually sane, dependable Jeff Simmons was about to come out with some spiel about evil shape-shifting spirits. He expected it from Kim: her past, the workings of her mind, was an exotic mystery to him. To hear the same talk from Simmons would have seriously undermined Halliday's view of the universe as a rational and logical system.

'Ever heard of shoes?' Jeff asked now.

'Sure,' Barney got in before Halliday. 'I even got a few pairs myself.'

'Still the same old comedian,' Jeff said. 'No, you wear these shoes, but not on your feet. It's an acronym, C-H-U.'

'Will you please explain what the hell you're talking about, Lieutenant?' Barney said.

'Chus, or Capillary Hologram Units. It's a fine net of holographic fibre optics. I'd heard some of the big software companies were experimenting with them. Frankly, I was hoping they'd bomb. I was frightened of what might happen if they ever got out there.'

'You mean,' Halliday said. 'This guy was wearing a chu, like a mask?'

Jeff nodded. 'It's a kind of elasticated hood which fits over the head. It can be programmed to emit a number of separate identities, different faces. When you hit this guy, it caused a dysfunction in the programming, hence the quick change.'

'Jesus Christ. So . . .' Halliday followed the consequences of what Jeff was saying. 'So even the guy's original appearance as a Latino, even that might've been a disguise?'

'That's right. Just another projected persona. See why I hoped these things would never hit the streets?'

'But they're expensive, right?' Barney said. 'I mean, you can't pick these things up at your local electrical goods store?'

'They're state of the art now, Barney. But you know how these things go. Within a year, two, every petty criminal in New York state'll be packing one.'

Barney was shaking his head. 'It won't make our job any easier. Imagine trying to trace someone who has a chu and doesn't want to be found.'

Halliday sat back on the chesterfield. The explanation was, despite the potential criminal consequences of the devices, personally reassuring. It stilled that tiny, superstitious voice that had nagged him with the possibility that what he'd experienced last night could not be rationally explained.

Then he considered Kim, and how truly he did not know her. What must the world seem like to someone with an unshakeable belief in spirits and the occult?

Not for the first time the contradictions that made up Kim Long amazed him. To all appearances she was a materialistic, twenty-first-century woman, with a veneer of sophistication and a sharp business brain. Under the surface, however, she had more in common with the long line of her ancestors stretching back into the mysterious mists of dynastic China and beyond.

Jeff Simmons was saying, 'I'll step up the investigation. We'll go through the building and question people acquainted with Nigeria and Villeux.'

'It'd help if we could trace where the chu came from,' Barney said.

'You bet. I'll work on it, see if any of the big companies know anything. I'll contact the industrial espionage team. They might know of leaks.' He nodded. 'Barney, Hal. I'll be in touch as soon as I learn anything.'

The connection died.

Barney smiled. 'Hey, you weren't going crazy, Hal.'

'It's good to know.' He paused, considering. 'Why do you think that guy wanted me dead, Barney?'

His partner shrugged, uncomfortable. 'You were snooping around the Nigeria case,' he said. He shook his head and looked at Hal. 'You don't think there's any way this guy could trace you?'

Halliday felt a sudden nauseating fear at the thought. 'No, no . . . I don't think so. He didn't know me from Adam, and anyway he left me for dead, didn't he?'

Barney changed the subject. 'Hey, are you going to tell Kim about the chu, or do you want me to break the news?'

Halliday stood up and stretched. 'You know something? She wouldn't believe me if I did tell her. She'd find the thought of evil spirits easier to believe in than capillary hologram units.'

He left Barney and made his way up to the loft. Kim was selecting a dress, holding it up against her body and looking at herself in the mirror, frowning.

Halliday showered, the hot water easing the aches and pains from tired muscles. When he stepped from the drier and crossed the loft to the closet where he hung his clothes, Kim was still trying to decide what to wear. She stood naked before a long rail of dresses and skirts, lower lip caught between her teeth, a picture of indecision. It forever amazed him that she could spend so long wondering what to wear, and then still regret her decision once the choice was made. No doubt his sister would have something to say about his lack of empathy.

'What kind of place are you taking me to, Kim? Formal or informal?'

She wore a distracted air. 'What? Oh, it doesn't matter.'

He looked at her, slim as a boy, tiny breasts the only sign of fat on her well-defined ribcage, her stomach scooped and incurving.

He laughed. 'What do you mean, it doesn't matter?'

'It doesn't matter what we wear, Hal. We can go naked if we like.'

He grabbed black jeans and a white shirt and dressed quickly. He approached her from behind and entrapped her in his arms. 'Sometimes I wonder which planet you're inhabiting, Kim.'

He released her and she made her choice, a short red dress and a long black coat, matching the fall of her jet hair. She dressed distractedly, her gaze seemingly focused miles away.

At last she said, 'Hal . . .?'

He was watching her. 'What is it?'

'Why do you think the shape-shifter wanted to kill you?'

He sighed. To explain what Jeff had told him would only frustrate and antagonise her. 'Probably because I trespassed on its territory,' he said, 'and it didn't like it.'

She buttoned her coat right up to her chin and regarded him seriously. 'Promise me you won't go near that place again, Hal. Say you won't.'

'I'll promise, if you promise to cheer up.'

With the forefingers of each hand she pushed up the corners of her mouth. 'Thut butter?'

He hugged her. 'Twenty-five going on twelve,' he said.

Outside, he grabbed an order of spare ribs and french fries from one of Kim's stalls. A radio was playing full blast, and between the music Halliday heard a snatch of news. The war between Thailand and China had escalated; the fledgling European colony on Mars was expanding. He thought of life on Mars, people going about their everyday lives on another planet, and found it hard to believe.

They ate as they motored downtown in the Ford. Kim drove, even though it entailed her having to take off her coat and fold it into a cushion in order for her to see through the windshield. He watched her as she turned onto Park Avenue.

'Now are you going to tell me where we're going?'

Thin-lipped with concentration, she gave him a swift glance. 'Be patient.'

'Give me a clue. Have I been there before?'

She shook her head. 'Nope.'

'I've never been there before? Not ice hockey? Skyball?' He slipped a french fry into her mouth.

'You hate sport,' she said, chewing.

'Have *you* been there before?'

'Nope again.' She looked at him. 'I gave you a big clue before, when I said we could go naked if we liked.'

He raised his eyebrows. 'I thought you were kidding.'

'No kidding, Hal.'

He thought of the sex clubs that had opened recently around Battery Park. 'Christ, not a sex club, Kim? If you think for one minute . . .'

She turned to him and gave a serene little smile. 'Not a sex club, but we can make love where we're going if we like.'

'So it's a private place? We'll be alone?'

'Not necessarily. There'll be other people there.'

'Kim, for Christ's sake . . . Put me out of my misery!'

She turned off Broadway onto Fulton Street and approached the towering twin monoliths of the World Trade Centre. Two minutes later she pulled into the kerb before a row of holographically-enhanced buildings, their usually bright façades washed out in the winter sunlight. In places, where the sun caught the original windows of the building beneath, the holographic projection flickered like a ghostly double-exposure.

'Here we are, Hal.'

He peered out. 'Where? I don't see anything.'

'There.' She pointed to a line of people on the sidewalk. He followed the queue to its origin.

'Christ,' he said, 'a VR Bar.'

She was peering at him expectantly. 'Well? What do you think?'

He tried to summon the requisite enthusiasm. 'It's . . . Well, we'll be queuing for ages.'

She pulled a golden envelope from the pocket of her folded coat and waved it in front of his face. 'I know the manager. He gave me complimentary tickets. We can walk straight in.'

He was tired, and the last thing he wanted was to immerse himself in a vat of jelly and experience the dubious delights of some spurious reality.

'I've been working hard lately,' Kim said. 'All work, no play. I've been neglecting you, Hal. This is my little present.'

He leaned forward and kissed her. 'Can't wait,' he said.

The foyer of the Bar was done out like the lobby of an expensive hotel, with thick pile carpet, potted ferns – artificial, Halliday noted – and bronze-framed mirrors. The scrolling legend above the reception desk said: Welcome to the Cyber-Tech VR Bar, TriBeCa.

Kim presented the tickets at the desk, and a minute later a smiling, blue-uniformed woman appeared through a pair of swing doors. She reminded Halliday of an air hostess.

'If you'd care to follow me this way,' she said, indicating the double doors. 'Is this your first visit to a VR Bar?'

Kim nodded, as wide-eyed as a child at the fair. Halliday felt her fingers squeeze his in excitement. They were escorted into a long room furnished in the fashion of the foyer, with ersatz palms and a blue carpet patterned with the intertwined CT logo of the corporation. Customers sat around on sofas and loungers, reading company magazines and brochures.

The chamber was flanked with a series of mock-timber doors, giving access to the VR booths. Their hostess ushered them across the room and swung open a door. 'Just follow the instruction on the programming screen. If you need any assistance, don't hesitate to press the call panel.'

They stepped inside and the door closed behind them. Halliday stared around him. 'Good God, what now?'

They were in a room the size of a hotel bathroom, white-tiled and brightly illuminated. A shower unit stood in one corner, but in pride of place in the centre of the floor were what appeared to be two large aquaria filled with a liquid substance the same colour as honey.

Kim was already reading the instructions from a wall-screen. She tapped the screen, summoning menus. 'Hal, come here. Look, these are all the options.'

He joined her. 'First, all the realms we can visit: over fifty different venues.'

Halliday stared at a succession of alluring panoramas, from what looked like the landscape of another planet to more recognisably terrestrial locations, mountain scenes, deserts, rolling grassland. Another menu listed dozens of historical options. Ancient Greece, Egypt, the South America of the Incas . . .

Kim touched the screen. 'This is the persona menu. Look, you just type in here the type of body you want, height, age, coloration, even sex.'

'You mean, you can appear as someone else in there?'

'That's what it says. Or you can take the default option and appear as yourself. Even then, you can change whatever you want about your appearance.'

'I think I'll go as I am,' he said.

Kim frowned. 'I don't know . . . I might try another body. How would you like to make love to a tall, shapely blonde, Hal?'

He laughed. 'You mean I could commit infidelity in there?'

'Well, you'd be making love to another body, but underneath it would still be me.'

He shook his head. 'I can't believe it'd be anything like the real thing.'

'According to the publicity, it's hard to tell the difference.'

'Go as yourself, Kim. I want to share the experience with you, not you in disguise.'

'Not even if I'm built like some holo-drama beauty queen?' she asked, watching him slyly.

The thought obscurely worried him. 'Especially if you're some holo-drama queen,' he said. 'You're perfect as you are.'

'Hokay,' she said, tapping the screen. 'And I've selected you to go as yourself.'

'How does the program know what we look like?'

Kim pointed to four cameras mounted in the corners of the booth. 'And dress?' she said. 'There's a default blue gown. We can choose from a menu of other clothing, or we can wear what we have on now.'

'That'll suit me.' He looked at her. 'I just hope you aren't going to take all day deciding . . .'

She punched him. 'So . . . where do you want to go to, Hal?'

'Surprise me.'

She tapped the screen again. 'It's all set. All we have to do is undress, attach the leads and put the facemasks on.'

They moved to the tanks and undressed, stowing their clothes in wall-units. They attached what might have been electrode leads to their arms and legs, and then slipped the faceplates over their heads. Halliday felt air-ducts locate his nose and mouth, tickling him. He looked at the tank, unsure now that the time had come to immerse himself.

He glanced across at Kim, naked but for the ludicrous facemask and leads.

'You don't know how bizarre we look,' he said, his voice muffled.

'Are you ready?' Kim said, as if from a great distance.

He watched her as she straddled the side of the tank and stood up to her thighs in the amber liquid. Demurely, she sat down and waved fingers at him.

He climbed awkwardly into his own tank, thinking that a distinct design improvement would be to have the tanks set flush with the floor, like bathing pools.

The fluid was viscous, and surprisingly warm. It oozed up around his legs, quite unlike anything he had ever experienced before. He sat down, then lay back so that only his head was above the surface. In the other tank, Kim had totally submerged herself. Wondering what to expect, Halliday did the same, feeling the jelly seal around him. He floated free, a specimen preserved in amber, and over a period of perhaps ten seconds he was aware of gradually losing contact with his senses. He could hear nothing, and the visor of his faceplate was darkened. Then all tactile sensation deserted him. For a second he seemed to be floating, disembodied, in absolute darkness.

Then, it was as if he had been reborn. His senses were flooded with an explosion of awareness, and for the very first time Halliday experienced life in virtual reality.

He had never really believed the claims Barney had made for the verisimilitude of the technology. He had expected to experience something along the lines of an improved holo-drama, to look out from the point of view of some clunking, robot-like version of himself, the movements and sensory awareness sloppy and imprecise.

What struck him in a sudden rush was the absolute reality of the world he was viewing, and of his place in it.

He was standing on an outcropping of rock, a warm breeze playing against his face, staring out across parkland towards an almost-familiar cityscape scintillating beneath a bright summer sun.

He looked down at his body, at the clothes he had worn

back in the real world. He touched his left hand, felt its warmth, its reality. He flexed his fingers. He reached up and touched his face, felt the stubble on his jaw, the ticking pulse at his throat. He found the absolute fidelity of the experience somehow frightening. Had he not known, intellectually, that he was in a jellytank, he would have been convinced that this was the real world, somehow altered.

He looked out over the city. Buildings soared into a blue sky, towering over the few skyscrapers that still remained. The new buildings seemed to be extruded from some diaphanous substance, like glass blown and elongated. He made out darting specks in the sky, which resolved themselves into air-cars. Higher still, he saw the great mammoth shape of a spaceship, moving through the air with stately, colossal grace. People hurried though the streets below, and the park was full of citizens strolling, roller-blading, jogging. The scene was at once familiar and strange, all the more bizarre for his knowing that it did not actually exist.

'What do you think, Hal?'

He turned. Kim stood beside him, radiant in her short red dress. Her jet hair fell sheer to the small of her back, almost iridescent in the sunlight.

He gestured feebly. 'Where are we?'

'This is New York sixty years from now,' she said. He could see that she was as amazed as he was by the experience. 'A programmer's vision of the year 2100.'

He stared at Kim, could not take his eyes off her. She was the woman he knew, but somehow altered. He reached out, almost experimentally, as if he expected her to vanish before his eyes, and took her hand. He felt the warmth of her fingers squeeze his as she smiled with excitement.

'What do you think of the new me?' she asked.

She had increased the size of her breasts, swelled the

curve of her hips – only slightly, but enough to make Halliday desire the original Kim.

She had often said that she wished she was different, wished that she had the body of a real woman, though Halliday had told her that she was beautiful as she was. Well, now she did have a more voluptuous body, but he didn't intend to spoil her fun and tell her that he thought the change almost gross.

He reached out and took her in his arms, feeling her weight, her warmth, against him. Good God, when he inhaled he could even smell her distinctive Kim-scent, soap, shampoo, warm skin, the subtle underlay of steamed noodles.

He laughed.

She pulled away. 'What?'

'I can't believe it,' he said. 'I just can't believe how damned real this is. I owe Barney an apology.'

'I never thought it would be this good, Hal. Must admit.'

He touched her face, then his own. 'How the hell do they do it? I mean, I'm wearing that damned mask. How can I feel my face?'

She reached up and touched her small chin, her broad nose. She laughed. 'I don't know, Hal. I'm no technician. Perhaps it's magical.'

He smiled. 'I thought there'd be rough edges, glitches.' He looked around at this futuristic Central Park.

She laughed. 'This is just the start, Hal. Come on.' She took his hand and tugged him down the hill.

He marvelled at the sensation of walking, the movement of his body, the stretch of his muscles and sinews, as he strode across the grass towards a curving path.

'Where are we going, Kim?'

'I read about it in the brochure,' she said. 'This way.'

They walked to Bethesda Terrace, two people in a crowd

of weekend strollers enjoying the open air and sunlight. He looked around at the towering city on all four sides.

'I think I've spotted where they've got it wrong,' he said.

'Trust you!'

He stopped and pointed at the futuristic city. 'Do you think New York will look like this in fifty years? The future is never as slick and shiny and new as films and books make out. It's always much as it is now, but grimier.'

Kim laughed and punched him with the heel of her hand. 'That's what I love about you, Mr Halliday. Always look on dark side.'

'I'm not criticising the programmers, though. Who'd want to escape one shitty New York just to find themselves in another?'

She looked past him, serious. 'Maybe future won't be so bad, Hal. Maybe things will get better.'

He reached out and pulled her to him, kissed the top of her head. 'Yeah, maybe you're right,' he said.

They crossed the piazza to where half a dozen small, separate crowds were gathered. Each knot of twenty or so people was congregated around a short, hexagonal column, each facet displaying a different scene. Over the heads of one crowd, Halliday made out a section of sky in one scene, mountains in another.

'This is it, Hal,' Kim said.

'What?' he asked her.

She shook her head. 'Wait and see.'

They joined a gathering. Kim made no move to push to the front to view the columnar displays. He frowned at her and shrugged. 'What now?'

She was enjoying his confusion. 'We just wait,' she said.

Oddly, the people around him were moving forward, as if in a queue that was being slowly absorbed. He stepped forward with Kim. The crowd was only three deep now, and he wondered where everyone had vanished to. He looked at Kim again, but she wore a tight-lipped smile and was giving nothing away. Behind him, more people had joined the gathering. He turned to the front and watched the couple before him move around the column, pointing at the glowing scenes and talking in whispers. They made their decision and approached the facet of the column displaying a desert scene. As Halliday watched, the couple stepped into the image, moved from the reality of Central Park and walked across the desert towards an oasis.

Kim tugged his hand. 'Our turn.' She led him around the hexagonal column, from one scene to the next: fabulous cities, rural landscapes, alien vistas . . . Every ten seconds the scene on each facet switched, providing a staggering choice of locales.

'Where do you want to go, Hal?'

He shook his head. 'I don't know . . . You choose.'

'Hokay.' She pursed her lips. 'How about there?'

A picture of tropical paradise, a calm lagoon, a crescent of sand, rolling greenery. He nodded. 'After you.'

Kim approached the portal, hesitated and stepped through. She was instantly transported onto the beach. The transition from his point of view seemed to remove her from him, imprison her in a distant, unreal world. She turned and waved at him from the picture postcard paradise.

Halliday stepped forward, paused, and then passed through the portal as if stepping from one room to the next. Instantly, warm sunlight beat down on his skin, a gentle salt breeze blew; he heard the rasp of cicadas and the sound of Kim's delighted laughter as she watched his expression of amazement.

He walked with her along the beach, then turned. The interface between this world and that of Central Park hung in the air above the sand, like a detail from a painting by Dali. As he watched, the scene changed. 'How do we get back?' he began.

'If we want to, we just wait till the park cycles round again. Or we can go to another location.'

'How do we get back to the VR Bar?'

'Our ticket entitles us to one hour. After that, we'll be returned to the tank.' She lifted her hand. 'If we want to leave before that, we just touch the red spot on the back of our hands.'

He glanced down at the crimson circle located at the base of his index finger. 'So we only have one hour?' He tried to keep the disappointment from his voice.

She laughed at him. 'And you were the one who told Barney you didn't like the idea of VR!'

He shrugged. 'So I was wrong. I admit it. I think Barney should thank you for converting me.'

She ran off along the beach, stopped suddenly and began pulling off her clothes. She kicked off her shoes, bent her arms around her back to reach the fastener of her dress.

'What if someone . . .' he began.

'There's no one here, Hal! We have the whole beach to ourselves! Come for a swim!'

She pushed the dress down the length of her body, unhooked her bra, allowing her enlarged breasts to spill free. She removed her panties, cast them aside and skipped into the lagoon.

Halliday watched her go, affected by her nakedness despite the changes to her body. He glanced back at the portal in the distance. They were still alone.

Quickly, he undressed. He dropped his clothes beside Kim's and joined her in the water. She had waded out until it covered her knees, and now turned to watch his approach.

They faced each other, a metre apart. He looked down at his body and smiled in bewilderment. 'How the hell did the programme know what it looked like?' he asked.

Kim smirked. 'They were filming you when you undressed, remember?'

He was pleased to see that she had not augmented her womanly attributes with the addition of body hair. She was staring at him.

'What?' he said. 'Do you wish it was bigger?'

She shook her head, wordless. In the real world, arousal often rendered her unable to articulate her thoughts in English, and while making love she would cry aloud in Mandarin. His pulse quickening, he stepped forward and fell to his knees in the shallows. She threw her right leg over his shoulder and he coaxed her lips apart with his tongue and found the pink slick pearl of her clitoris, holding her thighs as she bucked slowly, rhythmically.

He ate her until the sound of her Chinese cries almost brought him to climax, and then moved up her body. Kissing her belly, her unfamiliar breasts. They passed, lips and tongue crashing briefly, in a kind of frantic, inarticulate language of desire, and she moved down his body and he hung his head as his heart pounded. She took him in her perfect teeth, her head sideways, and bit his length, some gentle wild beast tearing at the kill.

And suddenly she gave up and swam away towards the shore. On all fours she crawled into the shallows, sprawled on her belly with her legs apart, and looked over her shoulder at him, her eyes beseeching. He almost ran at her. His fingers found her perfect bottom and parted the lips, and she reached through her legs, grasping him and guiding him home.

They lay on the beach, later, pressed together. He stroked her hair and stared down into her eyes. He wanted to ask her, irrationally, if here in this technological wonderland she still believed in spirits, but at the same time he had no desire to spoil the perfection of the moment.

She propped herself up on one elbow, lodged her chin on his chest. 'Hour's almost up,' she said.

'How do you know?' he asked sleepily.

She raised her hand in the air. He saw that the disc at the base of her index finger now showed only a sliver of red, like the sun eclipsed.

'When the dot is all white, goodbye virtual reality.'

He sat up and reached for his clothes.

Still propped on her elbow, she gazed up lazily at him and laughed. 'Come back here, silly. No need to get dressed!'

He smiled. Old habits died hard. He lay back down, fitted himself to the shape of her body and closed his eyes.

At first, he thought that it was an effect of the transition from the beach back to the tank and wondered why he had not experienced a similar sensation upon immersion. Something seemed to explode inside his head. He was aware of a silver flash in his mind's eye, a fleeting recollection that vanished at once but left in its place a stabbing, painful melancholy, like a lifetime's depression distilled and experienced in an instant. He sat up, crying out, expecting to find himself back in the jellytank.

He was still on the beach and he glimpsed, fleeting, elusive, the distant image of a little girl improbably walking on the water of the lagoon. In a twinkling, she turned and looked at him over her shoulder, and then she was gone.

'Hal?' Kim was sitting up, concern on her face. 'Hal, what is it?'

He could hardly speak for the melancholy that echoed in his head. As he took in the beach scene, Kim staring at him, the feeling abated, but something told him that it would remain for a long time, haunting him, like grief recalled.

'Nothing. It's okay. I thought I saw something. It's nothing.'

She was rubbing his back, repeating soothing sounds, when suddenly he was no longer on the beach. His vision blanked, and the sun no longer warmed his skin. He was back in the tank, enclosed in the viscous jelly. He sat up, the ecstasy of his love-making with Kim usurped, eclipsed by whatever had happened to him in the final seconds on the tropical beach.

He climbed to his feet, forcing his way through the heavy clinging jelly, and stepped unsteadily from the tank. As he stood, the goo drained from the tank, to be cleaned in readiness for the next customer.

Halliday removed the facemask and the leads. Kim was already out, her slim body streaked with jelly. She hurried round to him and touched his arm. 'Hal, what happened to you in there? Are you okay?'

He smiled through his fear. 'I'm fine, honest. It was nothing.' In a bid to convince her, he pulled her to him. 'It was wonderful, Kim.' He kissed her forehead. 'Thank you.'

They showered, soaping the clinging jelly from their bodies. Once or twice Kim caught his gaze and half-smiled, as if awaiting some signal that he wanted her, but the strange experience on the beach had emptied him of desire. He felt suddenly, bone-achingly tired.

They stood beneath the drier, then dressed quietly and left the VR Bar. Halliday drove home through a Manhattan made shabby in comparison to the programmer's futuristic version of the city. It was almost four, and as they sped north the first flurry of snow eddied down through the gathering twilight. Beside him, Kim shivered, found his hand and squeezed.

The office light was off when they got back: Barney was out, for which Halliday was grateful. He was dead beat and a bull session with Barney was the last thing he needed. He followed Kim up to the loft, sat on the futon and wearily removed his jeans and shirt. He set the alarm for midnight, the start of another shift.

Kim stood before him and undressed. She was watching him, an unreadable expression on her face. Usually they undressed seated on the bed, their backs to each other, and met naked beneath the warmth of the thermal blanket. Something in Kim's attitude now registered her unease.

She stepped from the pool of the red dress around her ankles, quickly divested herself of her panties and bra. She stood before him in the cold air of the loft, shivering, something almost childishly pathetic in her need to prove herself to him.

She stared.

'What?' he asked, at last.

'Do you like me, Hal?' she asked.

'Like you?' He almost laughed. 'Of course I like you.'

'I mean . . . I mean, do you like me as much as the other . . .' She stopped, her eyes downcast. 'As much as the other me?'

'Oh, Christ.' He reached out, snared her legs, and pulled her to him. She came in a reluctant shuffle. He hugged her legs and lay his head against her thigh. 'Kim, I love you, okay?'

He felt something fall onto his back, quick and warm, a tear.

'But . . . but it's never been as good as it was on the beach, Hal. We were perfect!'

He looked up the length of her body at her tear-stained cheeks. 'Kim, it's been as good as that in the past . . . it's been as good as that for me.'

She laughed through her tears. 'You're just saying that,' she murmured. 'You like my improved body better.'

He almost told her that she could think what she wanted, that words were useless, that she would disbelieve whatever he told her anyway.

He calmed his sudden anger and buried his head in her crotch.

'I think you're perfect,' he whispered. 'I love you as you are. I don't want anyone else, not even a different version of you.'

He almost laughed as he listened to what he was saying, as he tried to persuade her not to be jealous of her virtual alter ego.

He felt her shaking. It was an indication of how variable he knew her moods to be that he could not tell, now, whether she was laughing or crying. He looked up.

She was crying.

'Christ, Kim . . .'

Her words were almost inarticulate. 'You didn't choose me,' she sobbed.

'What?'

'I said, you didn't choose me! I just walked into your life, decided I loved you. You didn't choose me, you accepted me.' She paused, then sobbed, 'So how can I be perfect for you?'

He worked to quell his anger again. 'Kim, I had a choice once I knew you, whether to stay with you or not. Can't you understand that? I'm here, aren't I? You're still here? What's your problem?'

She shook her head, would not, or could not, answer him. He had lost count of the number of times over the past six months that she had tried to explain why he did not love her. He wondered why she insisted on these tortuous inquisitions, why she did not instead allow the simple fact of his presence, his actions, to stand in lieu of words.

He pulled her down without protest and rolled her into bed, drew the thermal over them and held her. He turned out the light and stroked her back until her small, hic-coughing sobs ceased and eventually she fell asleep.

Ten months ago, Kim had turned up out of the blue. He'd met her at his favourite food-stall. He was ordering sweet and sour chicken, noodles and rice. A small woman, her Oriental features almost martially severe, jet slant eyes set above arrowhead cheekbones, watched him from behind the counter. Halliday had seen her before; she never seemed to be working, just casting imperious glances up and down the stalls that lined the gutter. Halliday had figured her for the big-shot owner of these cut-price eateries.

'You regular customer, mister?'

'Every day for the past, hell . . . five years, at a guess.'

The young woman looked him up and down, a swift glance that seemed to assess him and make some impulsive decision. She spoke rapidly to the boy serving Halliday, all glottal stops and elasticated whining vowel sounds.

'This meal's on me, mister.' She packed the take-out herself. 'You run detective agency, yes?'

Halliday nodded. 'Word gets around.'

'Never met detective before,' she said. 'Never seen detec-tive agency.' Her expression was unreadable.

Halliday took his chance. 'Why don't I show you around?'

'Hokay, why not?'

He ushered her across the street to the three-storey walk-up. On the second floor, he opened the office door. Bar-ney's snores reverberated from the adjoining bedroom. 'This is the headquarters, such as it is,' he said.

She sniffed and gave the room a swift glance. In retrospect, he knew she was assessing the room's negative energy, already making plans to move the desk.

'My place is up there,' he said, indicating the loft. 'How about a coffee?'

She had accepted, and they had sat and talked, shared the take-out. She told him about her flight from Singapore ten years earlier, her start in America. As she talked, she lost some of her imperious severity, became human. When she smiled, he thought, she was even beautiful.

She had said goodbye and quickly left, as summarily as she had introduced herself, saying that she was busy-busy. He had watched her go with amazement, shaking his head. He had looked out for her on the street for a week after that, without a single sighting, and then one night before he was due to start work he was roused from sleep by an insistent tapping on the door of the loft. When he answered, she walked straight in, bearing food, and after they had eaten the meal – Kim telling him a long, involved story about venal wholesalers – she had paused, staring at him with that unnerving, assessing look, before quickly undressing and wrestling him to the futon.

Now, as he lay on his back and stared up at the skylight, he knew that for all the intimacies they had shared in the ten months they had been together, in spite of the many hours of traded history and confessions, the workings of her tortured psychology was a complete mystery to him. He did not know Kim Long, and her neurosis frightened him.

He was awoken, later, by a nightmare. He sat up, sweating. He could not recall the contents of the dream, but now a familiar, stabbing sensation of melancholy pierced his consciousness. It faded, leaving the same faint after-echo of depression ringing in his head.

He turned, quickly. Across the loft, before the door, he made out a faint shape. He had no doubt that she was real, that he was not hallucinating. He rolled out of bed, moved across the room. Already she was through the door: a quick twist of slim body and she was gone. He snatched open the door, stared. She was running down the stairs, and as he watched, a cry frozen on his lips, she turned her pale face over her shoulder and smiled up at him.

He reached out. 'Eloise . . .?' and, as he said her name, the vision faded and he was alone.

He had no idea how long he remained at the top of the stairs in the freezing cold, leaning against the wall and staring into space. The cold finally moved him to return to the loft. It was almost eleven-thirty. Kim was sleeping peacefully. He found his clothes and dressed, then made his way down to the office.

He turned the heater up to full, brewed himself a strong coffee, and sat in the swivel chair before the noisily humming desk-com.

He tapped the keyboard. It was a long time since he'd bothered to contact his father. How long, now? Five years, more? So long, anyway, that he could hardly recall the details, except that it must have ended, as it always did, in an impasse of silence and the mutual inability to express sentiments of any real meaning at all.

He listened to the ringing tone. His father would still be up. Halliday's liking for the night was one of the few things, thankfully, that he had inherited from his father.

It was a full minute before his call was answered. The screen remained blank, however; only a querulous voice greeted him. 'Who is it?'

Halliday cleared his throat. 'It's me, Dad. Hal. I . . . I just thought I'd call. I need to talk.'

'Christ, it's been ten years and then you call at damned near midnight.'

He wanted to correct him. Six years at the most, and it was not yet eleven-thirty.

'I'm sorry. I knew you'd be up. I was working, and . . .'

'I was reading, Hal. You know I don't like to be interrupted when I'm reading.'

Halliday paused. A part of him wanted simply to cut the connection. 'Aren't you going to open the visual link?'

He heard a sigh. A pause. Then the screen flickered and showed a thin-faced, steel-haired man in his seventies, sitting severely upright as if the maintenance of posture was the sole guarantee of increased longevity.

'What do you want, Hal?'

He stared at the old man. 'Have you seen Sue lately? Has she been in contact?'

'Sue? I haven't seen her for years. Is she still . . .?' He stopped himself, as if belatedly realising the stupidity of the question. Instead he said, 'Neither of you has bothered to call for years, never mind visit.'

Little wonder, Halliday thought. You were so eager to get rid of us, and before that to demean us, our choices, our endeavours.

'Dad, I want to talk about Eloise.'

Something closed in the old man's face: the grudging willingness there had been to grant his only son a few minutes of his precious time was suddenly withdrawn.

'If that's what you called me for, I'll sign off.'

'No! Please . . . I need to know what happened.'

'You can't understand how painful I find the episode, Hal, or you wouldn't have bothered calling. Goodbye.' He reached forward, quickly, and cut the connection.

Halliday sat back in the chair, staring at the dead screen. He found his coffee and held it in both hands. He wondered whether to try and contact Sue, and smiled to himself. What a beautiful irony it was that he was in the business of locating missing persons, and every time he had tried to find his sister during the past five years or so he had drawn a blank. Perhaps, he thought, something in his subconscious had not allowed him to try hard enough.

He pulled the keyboard towards him, opened a new file, and began the official report for Jeff Simmons on the events of the night before.

Six

Barney woke late, showered, then stood in the doorway of his bedroom and stared into the office.

The only changes he'd made to the place over the years was to move the furniture here and there, on Kim's instructions. The carpet had come with the office when he began renting eight years ago, mould-green and threadbare and probably as old as the century. The walls were stained with the smoke of his cigars, and could use a coat of paint. In general, the place had the run-down appearance of the manager's office in a fifty-dollar flop-house.

He'd always rationalised his disinclination to get the place decorated with the argument that, if customers used a detective agency in El Barrio, then they were unlikely to be put off by the appearance of the office. But the area was moving up-market. Some of the tenements nearby had been redeveloped, knocked into expensive apartments for work-from-home executives in the computer industry. Maybe, when this case was through, he'd talk to Hal about getting the room fixed up, see what he felt.

He made himself a coffee, then had a better thought. What the hell, he'd shown discipline over the past week, kept off the beers and watched his diet. He needed a proper breakfast. He'd go to Olga's, take some needles with him and work on the ancient machine Olga kept behind the bar.

He took a copy of the report Hal had made, the diaries

103

of Sissi Nigeria – and the needle Lew had given him when he'd emerged, dazed, from the jellytank yesterday.

He locked the office and walked along the block. Olga's was a cellar bar with the finest stock of imported beers in the district. Barney ordered a Ukrainian wheat, a ham on rye with gherkin, and hauled the old Sony to his booth beneath the street-level window. The bar was warm after the chill outside; a TV in the corner relayed a west coast ballgame, the sound turned low. He thought again about going to the expense of having the office redecorated – he'd see what Hal thought about moving the business to Olga's back room.

For the next couple of hours he scrolled through Sissi Nigeria's diaries, coming to some understanding of who the woman was, but none at all as to what might have happened to her. She was some kind of high-flying technician working for Cyber-Tech, one of Mantoni Entertainment's rivals in the VR business. She mentioned her work in passing, and then not so much her work as her colleagues. The diaries were taken up with detailed and graphic accounts of her affairs with the various women she picked up at the Scumbar, as well as her life with her live-in, as Nigeria called Carrie Villeux. It was a lifestyle alien to Barney's old-fashioned sensibilities, but who the hell was he to knock it? There had to be advantages to sharing love, and sex, with more than one person. Christ, it was all very well being with one person for all your adult life, but it was hell when they were no longer around. He shut out that line of thought, took a long swallow of beer and started into his sandwich.

He read through Hal's report as he ate. It was as exhaustive as ever, filled with details that might have no bearing on the case, but then again might prove vital. Barney recalled thinking the other day that the case would come to nothing, a lover's row ending in Nigeria's walking out

104

for a few days. But the diaries made no mention of any argument with Villeux, and what had happened to Hal the night before last indicated that something serious was going down.

Trouble was, they were getting nowhere fast. There were no leads, no clues as to what had happened to Nigeria, why her console at the apartment was fused, why the Latino had wanted Hal dead. They needed a break, some information from someone that might open up an avenue of inquiry. Later, he'd go down to Greenwich, poke about the Solano place, talk to people there and see if he could come up with something.

He came to the end of Hal's report and ordered another beer. He finished the sandwich, thought about another one. He showed willpower. If he limited himself to one, and a couple of beers, he could do breakfast here again tomorrow. He lit up the butt of his cigar and sorted through the needles he'd brought with him.

Only the one from Lew remained.

He'd been surprised, on emerging from the jellytank yesterday, when Lew passed him the needle. 'Thought you might like this as a keepsake of your first meeting in VR,' he'd said.

Barney had taken the needle. 'You were watching?'

'Only to the point where you entered the villa.'

So Barney had taken the needle, troubled by the thought that, no doubt, a copy of what had passed between Estelle and himself existed somewhere on Mantoni files.

Now, almost reluctantly, he slipped the needle into the port of the Sony and waited apprehensively for the image to appear on the screen. He wondered what Hal would say if he knew that his cynical, hard-bitten partner was meeting Estelle's ghost in virtual reality. Would he understand that after so many years he needed someone and that some computer-generated simulacrum of Estelle was better than any real woman, who anyway never lived up to his memory of Estelle? Perhaps Hal would have said that he needed to get out and meet more women, and try not to make the inevitable comparison . . . and perhaps Barney agreed, which was why he felt guilty.

But, dammit, his experience in VR yesterday had been so damned wonderful.

The needle kicked in, and the screen was flooded with colour. The bountiful garden, the blurred haze of flowers, sunlight, the emerald lawn. The viewpoint angle – what would have been the camera angle, if a camera had recorded this – seemed to be from the villa, looking down the length of the garden. Barney watched himself appear on the lawn in an instant, a slimmer, younger version of himself. He walked towards the bower as he recalled doing, and then turned to face the villa. He hurried forward, almost stumbling, and reached out.

Estelle walked from the villa and into view, seeming to glow with vitality, an ersatz life invented by the technicians at Mantoni, but which had seemed wholly real to Barney yesterday. They touched hands, and now Barney recalled the warmth of her skin. He watched them walk into the villa, the viewpoint following them into a front room, where they sat and talked.

At least as amazing as the physical reality of his wife was her psychological similarity to the woman he had loved for thirty-five years. Over a period of four weeks, Lew and his team had compiled a comprehensive dossier of Estelle's personality, her views, preferences, passions and pet-hatreds. Lew had questioned Barney about his marriage, cataloguing his recollection of events: with this information he had invested the ersatz Estelle with a memory of their time together.

They had talked for an hour, and it was as if he had

been transported back in time. This was the Estelle he recalled from almost twenty years ago. He could detect no flaw, no glitch or error, either physically or in her personality. He had told himself again and again that this was not a real person, not his wife, but the evidence of his senses overruled his knowledge of the fact.

Something had made him ask, 'Where are we, Estelle? Do you know?'

She had stared at him. 'Of course – don't you remember? It was your idea to move to California, Barney!'

And he had marvelled at Lew's ingenuity. He had often talked with Estelle of leaving New York and moving west, and ten years ago they almost had. But Estelle had gained a promotion in her job and they'd decided to remain.

Now, he was experiencing the virtual reality of what might have happened, had they moved.

'We'll spend our retirement walking along the beach,' Estelle had said, 'dining at expensive restaurants . . .'

He had not intended for the meeting to escalate into intimacy. It was enough that they be together, share their memories. But something, the look in her eyes, had made it inevitable.

Now he watched as the younger version of himself reached for Estelle. They kissed, and she took him by the hand and led him up the stairs and into the bedroom. Now Barney recalled the feelings he had experienced as they fell onto the bed and came together, like the very first time, all over again.

He quickly halted the program. It was enough that the events of the following hour lived on in his memory.

When he'd emerged from the jellytank, Lew had told him that as payment for his time, for allowing the team to reproduce Estelle in VR, he would be allowed one hour a week with her in their Californian retreat.

He told himself that he was not abandoning reality,

merely that this was another form of entertainment, that he would be a happier person because of it . . . He could hardly wait until his next session in the jellytank.

The door opened, admitting a cold wind, and foorsteps clattered on the stairs. Barney looked up. Casey, the pale scrawny refugee Kim employed on one of her stalls, swung around the corner of his booth, swaddled in the soiled pink climbing jacket Kim had cast off months ago.

'You got customers, Barney. They asked me if I knew where Kluger and Halliday's was. Two big mean-looking guys in a swish car, parked outside the laundry.'

Barney returned the Sony to the bar, slipped Casey five dollars and followed her up to the street. The car was the latest model Lincoln, a big maroon Delta, and Barney made out two heavies inside. He climbed the stairs to the office and settled himself behind the desk.

He didn't like the look of the guys in the Lincoln. Something about the combination – two rough-looking dudes in an expensive Delta – turned his thoughts to petty criminals made good, thugs into extortion and pro- tection rackets. He found himself wishing that Hal was around.

The desk-com flared, and the dollar sign in the top right corner began to flash. The screen showed the staircase leading up to the office. The two guys walked up the stairs as if they meant business, one behind the other because they were too wide to walk side by side.

One guy was short and white, built like a wrestler, with a crew-cut and a face that had taken constant punishment over the years, and had come back for more. The second guy was tall and black, and just as mean-looking.

The white guy rapped on the pebbled glass and pushed open the door without waiting to be invited . . . and at that second the screen decided to go belly up. The image of the heavies advancing down the room flickered and died. Barney reached out and switched off the screen, hoping that the malfunction wouldn't affect the computer's recording of the meeting.

He was reassured by the weight of his automatic, nestling beneath his jacket.

He remained seated, staring at the men as they stood before the desk. The black guy seated himself and crossed his legs, smiling at Barney in silence.

The white guy remained standing, unsmiling.

'Barney Kluger. How can I be of assistance, gentlemen?'

He looked from the white guy to the black, who widened his smile and gestured at his standing partner. 'Mr Culaski does the talking,' he said, breathing on a couple of chunky gold rings the size of knuckledusters.

Barney nodded. 'So, Mr Culaski . . .?'

The white guy stared at Barney. 'How long have you been in this line of business, Mr Kluger?' His voice was like his face, ugly and well used.

Barney played along. This was not going to be your regular consultation, he knew. There was a canister of freeze in the bottom drawer of the desk . . . but would he be quick enough to get to it if things turned nasty?

'Let's think about this,' he said. 'The old brain, you know? Plays tricks when you reach my age. I'd say about eight years, come spring.'

'And how is business, Mr Kluger?'

'We're doing okay, all things considered. You know, we can't complain. Cases come in, we work on them, get the job done.'

'And what would you say is your success rate?'

What was this? Barney wondered. 'Seventy, eighty per cent,' he lied. Who was counting?

Culaski nodded, taking in the greasy carpet, the nicotine-stained walls. 'You specialise in missing persons, right?'

'You've obviously done your homework. But we aren't a one-string outfit, Mr Culaski. We also do surveillance, security, the usual investigations.'

'Versatility, Inc,' the guy said in a tone of voice just short of mocking.

'We try to do our best,' Barney said. 'Most of our customers are satisfied with our work.'

Culaski nodded. He looked at his partner, who smiled. 'I'm sure they are,' Culaski said.

Barney cleared his throat. 'Ah . . . just how might I be of help, gentlemen?'

Culaski moved. He walked to the wall and leaned his stocky body against the paintwork. Barney watched him, aware that he was now unable to see the seated guy. The effect was unnerving.

Culaski examined his bitten finger-nails. 'I understand you're working on the Nigeria case, Kluger?'

Barney tried not to show his surprise. 'I'm not in a position to discuss the confidential commissions of other clients,' he said.

Culaski looked him straight in the eye. 'Listen, Kluger. If you're on the case I'd advise you to drop it, pretty-fucking-pronto, okay?'

Barney picked the last inch of an old cigar from the ash tray, examined its condition, and fitted it into the corner of his mouth. He busied himself with the careful process of re-igniting the butt.

He blew out a billow of noxious smoke and smiled across at Culaski. 'You would, would you?'

The man's eyes were as hard as jet flints. 'It'd be in the best interests of your agency,' he said.

'Tell me, Culaski, just what is your interest in the Nigeria case?'

'Me and my partner here . . .' he indicated the black

110

guy, '. . . we represent an agency working on behalf of a rich client, a friend of Nigeria's, who hired us to locate her. We don't want no fifth-rate competition from pissant agencies like yours, Kluger.'

'If we're as fifth-rate as you claim,' Barney pointed out, 'then we'll be no competition, surely?'

'We don't want no amateurs muddying the water, get my meaning, grandpa?'

Barney tried not to let his anger show. 'How long has your agency been up and running, Culaski? A week, two? Have you ever read the New York City charter covering agencies dealing with private investigations? You might be interested in Clause 55, the line about the non-exclusivity of cases. If you haven't, Culaski, it states that the investigation of no crime committed in the city is the exclusive province of one agency or investigating body, not even the New York police. In other words, we're working on the case and it's tough shit on you and your agency.'

Culaski glanced across at his taciturn partner, who was gazing at his rings. 'You don't seem to understand what I'm saying, Kluger. It'd be in your best interests if you dropped the Nigeria case, okay?'

'Is that a threat, Culaski?'

'If you do continue with the case, buddy, you'll suffer good.'

'I'm sure the authorities will be delighted to take action against your threats when they see the evidence . . .'

Culaski smiled for the first time, and the sight of something approaching bonhomie, on a face manifestly unused to the gesture, was ghastly. 'And what the fuck evidence do you have, Kluger?'

Barney touched the keyboard, accessing the file containing the recording of the meeting so far. He routed it through the wallecreen and sat back, wondering how Culaski might react when he saw his threats recorded for posterity.

The wallscreen filled with snow. Barney checked the file. Something, he discovered, was wrong. The file was empty. The recording had never even started.

Barney looked up.

'You were saying, Kluger? About evidence?' Culaski pulled something from the breast pocket of his suit, a slim silver box like a cigarette case.

Barney retained his composure. Other than the loss of face, he was not unduly put out. He would have the last laugh. He made a back-up recording of every meeting, not that he would let Culaski know that.

Culaski pushed himself away from the wall. 'If you or your partner follow up the Nigeria case, you'll wish you never set eyes on my pretty mug . . .'

Barney laughed. 'You don't know how shit-scared that makes me feel –'

He should have known that the black guy would not be content to remain a passive spectator throughout the verbal duel. He saw the movement from the corner of his eye, but too late.

The guy moved around the desk in a split second, grabbed Barney by the neck and hauled him from his chair. The next thing he knew, he was slammed against the wall, his feet inches off the floor, and gasping for breath.

'I don't like to hear my partner insulted like that, Mr Kluger. I think it's impolite.'

The punch, when it came, struck cobra-fast. Barney saw a flash of gold-decorated knuckle, felt the pain. The guy let him go and he slumped to the floor.

Culaski and partner strolled to the door. Before they departed, Culaski turned. 'Consider that down payment, with more to come if we find you've been sniffing round the Nigeria case, okay?'

They left the office and Barney raised a hand to his face. His nose was bleeding, but it didn't feel broken. He climbed unsteadily to his feet, found a handkerchief and mopped up the mess.

He'd live, he told himself. He'd suffered worse in the past, much worse. Still, it'd shaken him.

He smiled to himself. The bastards didn't know who they were up against if they thought he could be scared off that easily.

He composed himself and left the office. He made his way down the steps and paused in the entrance. The Lincoln Delta was halfway down the street, edging its way through the crowds that surged between the food-stalls.

Now, why the hell did Culaski want him to ditch the Nigeria case? He wondered if this might be the break he'd been waiting for.

He decided to celebrate with a beer.

He called Casey over from the food-stall.

She stared at the blood on his shirt-front. 'Hey, Barney – you okay?'

'I'm fine, sweetheart. Hey, run along to Olga's and grab me a Ukrainian wheat beer, okay?' He gave her ten dollars and told her to keep the change.

He watched her sprint along the sidewalk, the bill clutched in her fist. 'I'll be upstairs,' he called after her.

Smiling to himself, Barney turned and slowly climbed the stairs to the warmth of the office.

Seven

Halliday was awoken suddenly from a dream about Kim. She was starring in a holo-drama, her breasts and hips inflated to absurd proportions. She kept returning to the edge of the performance area and looking directly at him. 'Do you love me now, Hal?'

He came awake, gasped. The gross image receded. He reached out for Kim, as if to reassure himself, but the bed beside him was empty and cold. He experienced a sudden disappointment: he wanted her beside him. They had not spoken since yesterday, when she had broken down and accused him of not loving her.

He reached out to kill the alarm, and only then realised that he had been woken by his communicator. He fumbled it from his jacket pocket and lay back in bed. 'Halliday here.'

'Hal,' Barney's gruff voice sounded. 'It's like waking the dead. Get yourself down here.'

'What's happened?'

'A development in the Nigeria case.' He left it at that and cut the connection.

Halliday hauled himself from bed, shivering. He looked at his watch. It was three o'clock in the afternoon and a pale, disinterested sunlight filled the loft. He dressed and splashed his face with cold water in the bathroom in a bid to wake himself.

He'd gone to bed at dawn, after spending long hours making the report for Simmons. Before falling asleep, his

114

thoughts had strayed from the case and he'd considered Kim, and then what he had experienced on the beach in VR. It was almost as if something in his mind had been triggered by the interface with the virtual world, some long-buried memory concerning his dead sister. He was unsure what he dreaded most, the sudden, overwhelming melancholic fugues, or the sight of the spectral Eloise, walking away from him.

And then, as if that wasn't enough, he thought of the Latino assassin and his narrow escape the other night. He told himself not to worry. The Latino had left him for dead, after all.

He hurried downstairs.

Barney was leaning forward in his swivel chair and staring at the desk-com, his cigar shuttling from one side of his mouth to the other. 'Take a seat.'

Halliday looked at Barney. 'Hey, what happened?'

Barney touched his nose, swollen and discoloured. 'I had a visit, about an hour ago. Couple of heavies tried to put the frighteners on.'

Halliday moved around the desk, fixing himself a coffee on the way, and sat down on the chesterfield. 'You okay?'

'I'll live.' Barney was peering at a blurred image on the screen. Halliday recognised the office, two indistinct figures across the desk from Barney. It was not the usual surveillance shot they used to record every interview, but a poor video image. Barney was running it through an enhancement program.

'Are you going to tell me what the hell's going on?' He took a long bracing hit of caffeine.

Barney swivelled. 'Hour or so ago, these two guys show up. The white guy called himself Culaski.'

'What they want?'

Barney rewound the tape and played it from the start. The image showed the heavies as they entered the office.

115

The white guy, Culaski, said something. The words were an incomprehensible hum.

'Dammit!' Barney ran the tape through another clean-up program.

'Why the video?' Halliday asked. 'What's wrong with . . .?' He gestured at the wallscreen.

'I'll get to that,' Barney said. He left the program working through the videotape. 'So Culaski tries to warn me off the Sissi Nigeria case, told me to drop it. Just like that.'

'And you told him to go take a flying fuck, right?'

Barney gestured. 'Not quite so economically, Hal. But I asked why he was interested. To cut a long story short, Culaski said they were a private investigators working on the Nigeria case for a rich client, and he said we were getting in the way.'

'Most unprofessional.'

'Too right. So I reads Culaski the ethics of the charter, the non-exclusivity of cases bit. He waved it away, said if we didn't drop the case he'd put us out of business. So I said, "That's a threat the commission won't like when they see the evidence." He looks pretty smug then and says, "What evidence?" So I reroute the surveillance through the wallscreen – or rather, I try to. He's scrambled the program.' Barney smiled. 'But the bastards didn't reckon on us having the old back-up video, did they?'

'And I was all for getting rid of that damned thing years ago.'

Barney shrugged. 'If I can get a clean image, a good soundtrack, we'll be able to take these mugs to the cleaners.'

'You followed them?'

Barney shook his head. 'There's no hurry.' He smiled to himself, rubbed his nose. 'Before they left, the black guy decided to leave me a little reminder of the meeting. Didn't

116

see the bastard coming. This wouldn't have happened ten years ago.'

'We're all getting older,' Halliday said.

Barney turned to the video image on the screen, enhancing the visuals and scrubbing the soundtrack. He ran it again and Halliday watched Barney as a voice, muffled but audible, filled the room. 'You don't seem to understand what I'm saying, Kluger. It'd be in your best interests if you dropped the Nigeria case, okay?'

'We got 'em, Hal.' Barney copied the tape to a needle and slipped it into the breast pocket of his shirt.

Halliday moved to the desk and activated the wallscreen. He hacked into the city police surveillance cameras and called up the street-scenes of the area, covering a period of ten minutes one hour earlier.

Seconds later, the office was flooded with a watery image of the street outside as seen from the police surveillance camera mounted by the lights on the corner. The projecting sign for the Chinese laundry marked the point where the heavies would emerge in the mid-ground.

'There,' Barney said. He stood and hurried around the desk. He stood before the wallscreen, indicating Culaski and his sidekick with the stub of his cigar.

Halliday watched the guys cross the sidewalk and slip into a big maroon-coloured Lincoln Delta, which drew away from the kerb and headed north.

The Lincoln moved to the end of the street and turned right. Halliday entered the times and positions, and for the next ten minutes he and Barney watched as a series of surveillance cameras tracked the car in relay as it left El Barrio and entered the Bronx.

The Lincoln pulled into a sidestreet and braked. The two guys climbed out and entered a three-storey walk-up.

He looked at Barney. 'What now?'

Barney fingered his nose. 'You up to paying these guys a visit, Hal? I reckon it's payback time. We'll take the freeze, find out who the hell hired these jokers.'

Halliday armed himself with an automatic and a canister of freeze, which he concealed in the arm of his jacket. Barney slipped a gun into his shoulder-holster and took a pair of knuckledusters from the drawer. Payback time.

They quit the office and Halliday eased the Ford from the kerb and headed north, towards the Bronx.

Five minutes later he turned into the sidestreet and drew to a halt behind the Lincoln. He peered out at the sign beside the doorway. Culaski and Gaines, Security, had an office on the third floor. It was a run-down area populated by welfare cases and refugees, the sidewalks blocked with the temporary accommodation of the homeless in the form of lean-tos fabricated from billboards and tents fashioned from scrap polycarbon sheets. Groups of men and women warmed themselves around braziers in the middle of the street. Halliday was aware of their hostile glances. He would be relieved when they got what they wanted from Culaski and Gaines and quit this neighbourhood.

Barney coded his com to disguise his voice and tapped in the phone number listed on the sign. Seconds later he said, 'That Gaines, buddy?'

'Who's speaking, man?'

'Just call me a friend. I have some information you might be interested in.'

'Who is this . . .?' Gaines said.

'You did my company a good turn last year, and you know what they say, one good turn . . . Look, your woman's been putting it around, you know?'

'Molly?' Gaines said. 'Just who the fuck are you, man?'

'Like I said, a friend. I have pictures.'

'Where are you?'

'Know Breslin's Bar, two blocks south? I'll be there. See you in five minutes, okay?'

'What you want, man? How much for the pictures?'

'We'll talk about that over a beer, yeah?'

Gaines cut the connection. Barney nodded and Halliday slipped from the car and crossed the sidewalk to the entrance of the walk-up. A foul-smelling flight of stairs, conveniently dim, rose before him. Halliday checked for security cameras. There were none. He climbed to the first floor and stood beside the door of the restroom, making a show of trying the handle. A minute later he heard footsteps descending from the third floor. He glanced around. The tall figure of the black guy, Gaines, appeared at the top of the steps and hurried down.

As Gaines passed the restroom and turned to take the steps, Halliday looked up. 'Excuse me.'

The guy paused, glanced up. 'Yeah?'

Halliday raised his right hand and sprayed a cloud of freeze into the guy's startled face. He held his breath against the stench of ammonia, reached out and grabbed Gaines by his jacket. He opened the restroom door and dragged the heavy inside, kicked open a stall door and dropped Gaines onto the john.

The guy was immobile from the chest up, his face drawn into a pained rictus and his eyes streaming with tears. Halliday grabbed a towel from the rail and draped it over the guy's head. He stepped out onto the landing and got through to Barney.

'I've sorted Gaines,' he said.

'I'm on my way.'

Ten seconds later, Barney came panting up the steps. Halliday indicated the restroom. Barney slipped inside, and Halliday heard a quick crunch and a satisfied grunt. Barney emerged, pocketing his dusters, and nodded at Halliday.

They made their way to the third floor.

The office of Culaski and Gaines, Security, was even smaller and shabbier than their own. The door was ajar, and Halliday saw Culaski wallowing in an armchair, eating a burger and staring at an old computer screen hanging from the ceiling on a boom.

He shouldered his way into the room, nodding amicably at the heavy. Culaski got up quickly, sensing trouble, and reached out to kill the screen. Before he reached the controls, Halliday hit him with a dose of freeze. Culaski gave a strangled gasp and fell to the floor, legs twitching.

Halliday extended a foot and rolled Culaski face-down onto his stomach. He looked back through the door and nodded to Barney.

Halliday sat on the edge of the desk, one foot lodged on Culaski's head. He pulled down the ancient, hanging computer and accessed the files while Barney went through the paperwork on the desk. From time to time, Culaski gave a strained wheeze as he fought to overcome the paralysing effect of the freeze. Halliday pressed his foot down a little harder.

The files contained hundreds of case notes going back ten years, mainly two-bit security work for local companies, the occasional bodyguard commission and surveillance job. They were exactly the type of low-key and amateurish outfit someone would hire on the cheap to do a botched warning job.

There was nothing on file to indicate that they had been hired to frighten Kluger and Halliday off the Nigeria case. Not that it would be the kind of commission they'd necessarily log on their files.

'Hey,' Barney said past his cigar, 'I think this is it.'

He was leaning over an open ledger, staring down at a scrap of paper covered with near illegible scrawl.

Halliday moved around the desk. *Kluger and Halliday,*

Wilson Street, El Barrio, he read. And beneath this, *Sissi Nigeria.*

Barney looked at him. 'So where does that get us?'

'Looks like it was written quick, taken down while on the phone or computer . . .'

He pulled the computer towards him and accessed the history file of incoming calls. He watched half a dozen low-life individuals rap about nothing in particular before he came up with something. This one was voice-only.

'Chuck,' a refined upstate voice said. 'I have something you might be interested in.'

'I'm all ears, Wellman.'

'Private eye outfit, name of Kluger and Halliday. I want them . . .'

'Hold it, Wellman. Let's meet in private, talk business, okay?' The recording finished abruptly, overlaid by another call.

'Dammit,' Barney spat.

Halliday accessed the case files again. He typed in a search for Wellman and came up with half a dozen references. Culaski and Gaines had worked for Wellman over a period of three years, mainly surveillance work and background investigations on certain individuals.

Halliday accessed Culaski's financial files, and found what he wanted. A month ago Culaski had billed Cyber-Tech and Wellman Industries for a thousand-dollar investigation.

'Cyber-Tech,' Barney said. 'Christ, that's the outfit Nigeria worked for, right?'

Halliday nodded, accessing the Net and initiating a search for Cyber-Tech. Seconds later, the screen flared. He peered, reading.

'Cyber-Tech,' he said. 'According to this, they're at the leading edge of cybernetic research and VR development.

All very top-secret stuff. They own some of the first VR Bars to open in the city. Have their headquarters on River Drive, Archville, up in Westchester County.' He killed the screen.

Barney looked at him. 'So, what we waiting for? Let's get up there and pay this Mr Wellman a social call, okay?'

Before they left the office, Halliday checked on Culaski. The guy was breathing evenly, still struggling against the paralysing effects of the freeze. He'd come round in an hour or two with one hell of a headache.

On the way down the stairs, Halliday looked in on Gaines. He was still seated on the john, the white towel covering his head decorated with a bright red stain where Barney had got even.

As he stepped from the building, into the cold wind, Halliday caught the smell of cooking food from a nearby Thai stall. He ordered spare ribs for Barney and fried chicken for himself, then climbed into the passenger seat of the Ford. Barney took the tub of ribs and lodged it between his legs. He eased the car from the kerb, steering with one hand and eating with the other.

They headed north, out of the Bronx.

Halliday knew the Hudson coastline pretty well, an area of once-wooded hills and secluded inlets where the affluent had weekend holiday chalets and pleasure boats. His father had rented a holiday villa in a small town five kilometres south of Scarborough. He recalled escaping his father's caustic attention for long hours, losing himself in the woods around the house. That was before the various blights and diseases decimated the trees all across America, of course. Now there were still plenty of trees along the coast north of the city, but most of them were dead – and those that were still in the process of dying, struggling vainly to put out green shoots and leaves every spring, only hinted at the beauty he recalled from the days of his childhood.

The trip would be a painful reminder of that time.

He thought of Eloise and wondered if he should visit his father over on Long Island at some point, try to talk to him. The idea did not appeal, but if the images of his sister continued as they had been doing, then he would go to any lengths to try to find out what the hell was going on.

They motored up Interstate 87, through Yonkers and into the country. Halliday stared out at the phalanx of dead and dying trees on either side, as perpendicular and denuded as ships' masts.

Barney finished the ribs and wiped his mouth and chin on a napkin. He glanced across at Halliday. 'How'd it go at the VR Bar yesterday? Kim said she was taking you.'

'Great. We had a great time.' Halliday laughed, without humour. 'Then we get home and she accuses me of liking the image of her in VR better than her real self. She says I don't love her.'

'Thought you said yesterday that you didn't know what you felt about her?'

Halliday stared at his fried chicken. 'It changes,' he said, trying to articulate something beyond easy definition. 'Most of the time I can't imagine being without her, and sometimes she drives me crazy. Is that love?'

Barney shook his head, a far-away look in his eyes. 'Just be thankful the kid's so stuck on you, Hal. Be thankful you got her, okay?'

Halliday entered River Drive into the Ford's com. Seconds later the directions scrolled up the screen. 'We turn off about two kilometres further on.'

The sun was going down over the country when they took a left turning and headed west, towards a sky stratified with bands of blazing orange and blood red. A line of dead trees on the horizon resembled so many used matches in the aftermath of the sunset.

They came to the coast road and turned north. To their left was the wide expanse of the Hudson, dark in the falling twilight, the occasional ripple from a small boat catching the reflection of the sun like so many slivers of gold.

The dead trees to their right gave the landscape an eerie, apocalyptic atmosphere. They passed a half dozen abandoned clapboard holiday homes, their owners long since fled west after the first of the meltdowns cast its radioactive pall over the north-eastern seaboard.

'River Drive starts a mile before Archville,' Halliday said. 'Any second now . . .'

They slowed as the car came to the crest of the road. Down below a vast one-storey honey-coloured building, set in an expanse of manicured emerald lawn, came into view. It had the newly-constructed appearance of one of the many fledgling service companies that had sprung up out of town in recent years.

Barney rolled the Ford down the hill and braked beside the silver triangular sign in the driveway entrance: Welcome to the home of Cyber-Tech and Wellman Industries, Pioneers of the Future.

He turned the car into the drive and rolled across the parking lot. The frontage of the building displayed a long slanting face of black glass, maintaining an air of insularity and reserve.

They climbed from the Ford and entered reception through sliding black glass doors. A blonde receptionist looked up from behind a desk and smiled, her quick glance taking them in from head to foot. Halliday was aware of his dishevelled, unshaven appearance in the art deco perfection of the foyer. To her credit, the woman's smile never faltered.

'How can I help you, gentlemen?'

'We have an appointment with Mr Wellman,' Barney said.

The receptionist consulted a screen. A minimal frown marred her cloned-blonde features. 'And you are?'

'Kluger and Halliday, Private Investigators. We're here to question Wellman about certain illegal activities he engaged in earlier today.'

She smiled and turned to her screen. 'One minute, sir.' Judging by her unflappable poise, Wellman might have been accused of nefarious activities on a regular basis.

'I'm afraid Mr Wellman is in a meeting at the moment.'

'Then we'll be happy to talk to his deputy.'

'That would be Mr Kosinski.' She turned and spoke in low tones into a microphone. 'Mr Kosinski will be with you in one minute.'

They paced the length of the foyer and back. Barney pulled a fat cigar from his coat pocket and began the laborious process of setting it alight. 'You talk to Kosinski, Hal. Find out what Nigeria was doing here.' He puffed a billow of noxious fumes. 'I'll take a walk around.'

Barney returned to the reception desk. 'Which is Wellman's auto, sweetheart?'

The woman blinked. 'The silver Benz, but why . . .?'

Barney ignored the question, stepped outside and approached the Benz, shielding his eyes and peering inside.

Two minutes later a thin guy in his twenties, dressed in faded green jeans and a black T-shirt, pushed through a swing door. 'Mr Kluger or Mr Halliday?'

Halliday nodded and gave his name, keeping his hands in the pockets of his jacket.

'I'm Joe Kosinski. Ah . . . vice-chairman of Cyber-Tech and Wellman Industries.' He shrugged. 'I know, it sounds bizarre even to me. Come on through to the office.'

Kosinski wore his shoulder-length dark hair in a hank,

secured by a knotted length of what looked like fibre optic cable. In profile, his Adam's apple was almost as prominent as his jutting beak of a nose.

Halliday followed him into an office whose opposite wall was one vast window overlooking the work-floor on a lower level. A line of technicians sat at screens. In the distance, floor to ceiling flatscreens pulsed with frantic bursts of primary colours. Halliday made out fractal landscapes swirling into dizzying infinity.

Kosinski smiled. 'Prototypes for a new VR-scape,' he explained. 'Have you VR'd yet, Mr Halliday? Please, sit down.'

'Yesterday, for the first time.' Halliday sat on the ledge of the window, his back to the shop-floor.

Kosinski lifted both hands from his knees in a nervous, habitual gesture. 'It's an incredible experience, so I'm told . . .'

Halliday looked at him. 'You mean you've never . . .?'

Kosinski had the attitude of a long-term science student; a kind of geeky awkwardness combined with unsocialised affability. He sat cross-legged on a swivel chair and gestured. 'You see, I grew up with this stuff. I got into VR at the ground level, so I've been intimate with it from the start. There was no first time for me, or rather the first time was in a prototype VR rig about as realistic as a turn-of-the-century computer game. For the past five years I've practically lived in VR, so I haven't really noticed its advance.' He laughed and held up a thin arm. 'You could say that VR is my reality. Why do you think I'm so skinny?'

'I thought you couldn't spend more than a couple of hours in VR at any one time?'

'Between you and me, we're being conservative with the two-hour limit in the public VR Bars. It's actually safe for up to around four, five hours. Any longer and you start suffering side-effects – impaired vision, nausea – when you emerge. I spend the top limit in VR every day.' He clapped his knees with both hands. 'Well, that's me, Mr Halliday. How can I help you? Sal said something about Wellman misbehaving?'

'You might say that. You have a woman working for you, Sissi Nigeria.'

Kosinski chewed his lip and nodded his head. 'That's right. I don't know her personally, but I know her work.'

'What exactly does she do here?'

'She's in the design and programming team. Actually, she's a freelance. Very talented woman.'

'What does she design and program? Virtual reality?'

'Well, not directly. You see, she's actually a specialist in active recognition systems and data condensation.'

'And that is?'

Kosinski blinked. 'Ah, that is to do with work on machine intelligence, Mr Halliday.'

'Were you aware that she disappeared about a week ago?'

Kosinski shifted uncomfortably, like a fakir suddenly finding his bed of nails beyond endurance. 'Ah, well . . . as a matter of fact.' He nodded. 'I was told that she hadn't reported in for a few days.'

'You have no idea what might have happened to her?'

Kosinski lifted his hands. 'None at all. I'm sorry. You see, I might be the vice-chairman here, but between you and me the title means jack shit to me. I work here because I love the technology. The people . . .' He stopped himself, then looked up guiltily at Halliday. 'They're just so many faces . . .'

Halliday smiled. 'It must be great to be so enthusiastic about something as pure and rational as science.'

Kosinski looked at once relieved and grateful that Halliday understood. He nodded enthusiastically. 'You got it.'

'People can be so irrational at times.' Halliday paused. 'How do you get on with Wellman, Joe?'

'Ah . . . as a matter of fact, we don't have that much contact. You see, he manages the business side of things, the people, and he lets me get on with the R&D.'

'You have any idea why he would hire heavies to warn my partner and myself from trying to locate Sissi Nigeria?'

Kosinski gulped, shook his head. 'He did that? No, look, people's motivations . . . way beyond me, man.'

'Wellman's busy at the moment, doesn't want to meet us. So tell him that Kluger and Halliday don't take too kindly to being threatened, okay?'

Kosinski nodded. 'I'll do that.'

'Also tell him that we're still looking for Sissi Nigeria, and that we'll either find her or we'll find out what happened to her.' He fished a card from his jacket pocket. 'Here. If you hear anything concerning Nigeria, anything at all, gossip, scandal, even rumour, just get in touch, okay?'

Kosinski took the card without a word and read the legend, lips moving. He looked up. 'I've never met a private eye before, Mr Halliday.'

'Then we're even. I've never met an R&D whizzkid, either.'

His communicator buzzed. 'Hal, Wellman's just left. We're going after him.'

'Thanks for your time, Joe. I have to rush.'

He left the office and ran into reception. The silver Benz was turning from the drive and accelerating along the coast road. Barney was already in the Ford outside reception.

Halliday jumped in the passenger seat as the car started up and swerved from the parking lot. Barney let the Benz open up a lead of some three hundred metres, then set off in pursuit.

'Learn anything from Kosinski?'

Halliday smiled. 'Strange guy, not exactly resident on

128

Planet Earth, but harmless. Damnedest vice-chairman I've ever met.'

'What'd he say?'

Halliday gave him a rundown of his conversation with the scientist. 'He claimed not to know much about Nigeria, but I got the impression he wasn't telling me everything. She doesn't work in VR, or at least not directly. She specialises in machine intelligence.'

Barney grunted. 'We'll find out more from Wellman when we run him to earth.'

The Benz was coasting at forty up ahead, its tail-lights distinct in the gathering darkness. Barney accelerated, closed the distance to less than thirty metres. Halliday felt his pulse quicken. So much of his job was taken up with routine, predictable cases – missing teenagers, runaway spouses and the like – which neither stretched his powers of deduction nor much interested him. The very enigma at the core of the present investigation suggested that this case might be different.

They followed Wellman for another five kilometres, before he turned inland up a dirt track. Barney slowed and followed, the Ford wallowing along a rutted lane. The track climbed, winding up a hillside. Ahead, seen through a stand of dead trees, Halliday made out the lights of a big house, a multi-level villa with massive picture windows looking out over the distant river.

The villa was enclosed within a razor-topped mesh perimeter fence, with wrought-iron gates now parting to admit the Benz. Barney accelerated, gaining on the vehicle and tailgating as it passed into the grounds of the villa. Whoever was controlling the gates attempted to close them before the Ford made it through. Barney swore as the swinging metal trap crashed against the flank of the car and screeched along the coachwork. They came to a sudden halt behind the Benz and Halliday flung open the passenger door and jumped out. Wellman was already out of his vehicle and shouting instructions to someone in the darkness off to the right. Halliday heard the frantic baying of a dog and slipped the automatic from his shoulder-holster.

Barney approached Wellman, belligerent in his forward-leaning, heavy-shouldered posture.

The company chairman backed off. He was a tall, thin guy dressed in an impeccable cream suit with a foppish scarlet cravat. 'What do you think you're doing, invading like . . .?' he began before Barney cut him off.

'Save the protests, Wellman. I didn't exactly like the heavies you sent round to my place, either.'

A light went on, up in the villa. A french window slid open and a dark-haired women in a gown hurried out to the edge of a patio. 'Honey,' she called, 'is everything . . .?'

Wellman turned glanced up at the woman. 'Everything's fine, darling. I can handle this.'

Halliday heard the security guard about a minute before he decided to attack. He was approaching across the darkened gravel drive with a series of here-I-am crunches. Halliday adjusted his position without alerting the guard to the fact that he knew he was on his way.

'I'm sure we can conduct this matter in a civilised fashion,' Wellman was saying.

'I'm delighted you think so,' Barney replied. 'I'd appreciate a little civility after this afternoon.'

The guard leapt, and Halliday turned and swung a fist. He caught the guy in the chest, an ineffectual blow which did more to surprise than injure. Halliday's next blow struck the guy's jaw, and as the guard fell with a cry of pain, Halliday launched a boot towards his midriff and connected. The guard let out a deflated gasp and lay on the ground, moaning in pain. Halliday turned towards

Wellman, ready to grab him and march him into the villa at gunpoint.

The dog caught him off guard. He heard a snarl, and by the time he turned in heart-thumping panic the dog was flying through the air, teeth bared. He heard the deafening crack of a gunshot, and the dog performed a crazy somersault, all splayed limbs and limp neck, and slammed into the gravel at his feet. He stared down at the dead animal in silence, something almost comical in his surprised reaction, before he remembered himself and scanned the grounds for any further threat.

Barney holstered his automatic. 'We can do this one of two ways, Wellman. Either my partner can drag you kicking and screaming into the house in front of your pretty wife, or you can show us inside like the civilised citizens we are.'

In the wash of light from the house, Wellman's expression was in shadow. It was some seconds before he brought himself to reply, and then his voice was shaken. 'Very well. Come inside. But I'm a busy . . .'

'And so are we,' Barney cut him off. 'We just want to ask you a few questions, and then we'll be on our way. Okay, let's go.'

Adjusting his cravat and shooting the cuffs of his cream suit, Wellman turned and walked towards the villa.

Halliday joined Barney. 'Neat shooting.'

'Good job I keep my eye in at the range. You okay?'

Halliday nodded and rubbed his skinned knuckles.

The woman ran to Wellman as he crossed the patio, briefly embraced him and shot a glance of mixed malice and fear towards Halliday and Barney, before Wellman hurried her inside.

He showed them into a long room hung with swirling Mandelbrot fractals. Halliday recalled similar decorations in the Cyber-Tech workplace.

Halliday regarded Wellman. The man exhibited a scrupulous attention to personal presentation that bordered on the obsessional. He noted the gold rings, cuff-links, the jewelled stud in the lobe of his left ear.

'I'd offer you a drink,' Wellman said, 'but we seem to be out of alcohol at the moment.'

'We didn't come to socialise,' Barney said. 'I didn't like the way you went about your business this afternoon. I thought I'd come and tell you that. Very unprofessional.'

While Barney talked, Halliday moved around the room. He inspected ornaments and examined holo-pics. He could sense Wellman's unease.

'Culaski was simply carrying out my orders,' Wellman was blustering. 'My organisation has the power to . . .'

'Wellman,' Barney said with weary patience, 'don't bullshit me. If you try that trick again, I'll have the NYPD down on you for attempting to pervert the course of justice.'

'It would be your word against mine, Kluger.'

'Oh, yeah?'

Halliday watched as Barney fumbled the needle from his breast pocket and tossed it across the room at Wellman. He caught it awkwardly, up near his chin, and glanced nervously at both men.

'I videoed the meeting with Culaski. If you so much as sneeze out of line, I'll make sure a copy goes to the authorities.'

Wellman lowered the needle and slipped it into his pocket. He shot his cuffs in a nervous gesture. 'I suppose, in the circumstances, I do owe you gentlemen an apology . . .' The way the guy spoke, choosing his words as fastidiously as he did his attire, rubbed Halliday up the wrong way.

'Fuck your apologies,' Barney said. 'Who the hell did you take us for? What made you think you could send the

132

heavies in, have them make your demands, and assume we'd sit back and play ball?'

Halliday moved across the room so that he was a couple of metres from Wellman and sat side-saddle on the arm of a genuine leather lounger.

'What gives with Nigeria?' he asked.

Wellman swallowed. Halliday watched him closely, noticed the beads of perspiration sheening his face.

Barney went on, 'Why did you want us to leave well alone, Wellman?'

'Do you know something we don't?' Halliday asked. 'Do you know where she is? You responsible for her disappearance, is that it?'

'No! Of course not! It's nothing like that.'

'Then what is it like, Wellman?' Barney asked.

'I . . . when she disappeared, I had my own internal investigation team conduct inquiries. I didn't want the news of her disappearance getting out.'

Halliday and Barney exchanged a glance. 'Why not?' Barney asked.

'Because I . . .' He glanced at Halliday. 'Do you mind if I sit down?' He gestured at a high stool placed before a piano-synthesiser.

Halliday nodded. 'Be my guest.'

Wellman pulled himself onto the stool as if exhausted. 'Nigeria was engaged in highly specialised work. She's a very talented technologist. We value her contribution to the development of certain products at Cyber-Tech.'

'She was involved in machine intelligence,' Halliday put in.

Wellman stared at him. 'Who told you that? That's supposed to be classified information.'

'We have our contacts, Wellman,' Barney said. 'Go on.'

'I don't know if you have any idea of the revolutionary nature of the work we do at Cyber-Tech, gentlemen?' He

133

paused. 'We have certain projects in development that are years ahead of the comparative endeavours of our competitors.'

'Machine intelligence?' Halliday said.

Wellman mopped his brow with a red bandanna. 'That's but one of the areas we are investigating. There are others, which Nigeria was also closely involved in. Of course, when she disappeared . . .'

'You feared the worst, right?' Halliday said.

Wellman nodded. 'The secrets in her possession are invaluable. If they found their way into the hands of rival companies . . .' He shook his head. 'Cyber-Tech would be set back ten years. Our shares would plummet.'

'You didn't get the police in?' Halliday asked.

'We thought it wise to proceed with our own investigations first.'

'What do you think happened to her?' Barney asked.

Wellman gestured. 'I wish I knew. Of course, there are several scenarios . . .'

'Such as?'

'Quite simply, a rival company might have paid to have Nigeria eliminated. She was that valuable to us. That seems unlikely, to be honest. She'd be worth more to them alive than dead.'

'So you think someone might have kidnapped her?'

'I don't know what to think. It is a distinct possibility. Or she could have gone over to a rival voluntarily, sold out and vanished.'

'Did you know her well enough to think she'd do that?' Barney asked.

Wellman shrugged. 'I knew her reasonably well. I wouldn't have thought her capable of such treachery, but then I suppose everyone has their price.'

'Your internal investigators,' Halliday said. 'Have they come up with anything?'

'No. Not a thing. Absolutely nothing.' He paused, looked from Halliday to Barney. 'I heard that you'd been hired by Carrie Villeux to look into Nigeria's disappearance. I feared you might be in the pay of one of my competitors.'

'So you tried to frighten us off.' Barney was shaking his head.

'I see, now, that that was a mistake,' Wellman said. Halliday thought that there was something almost calculatingly ingratiating in his tone. 'Perhaps . . .' He paused, considering. 'Perhaps, in retrospect, I might have been wiser trying to buy you off?'

Halliday glanced across at Barney.

'Once we've been hired,' Barney said, 'we stay hired until the job's done. I've never been paid off in my life, and I don't intend to start now.'

Wellman pursed his lips and nodded.

'I do have another suggestion, though,' Barney went on.

Wellman shuttled a nervous glance between Halliday and Barney. 'And that is?'

'You pay us, Wellman, and we'll work for you. Anything we find on the Sissi Nigeria case, you get to know about. That way you can be assured the information remains with you.'

'How do I know that you're not already working for one of our rivals? Mantoni or Tidemann?'

'Did your investigators report that we were working for any other company?'

'They checked, of course, but came up with nothing.'

'That's because we're working for Villeux and only Villeux,' Barney said. 'You have my word, for whatever you think it's worth.'

Wellman allowed a silence to develop as he considered the situation. 'What do you charge, Mr Kluger?'

'We're reasonable. Five hundred dollars an hour, each, plus expenses.'

'That would soon mount up into quite a tidy sum.'

Barney smiled. 'Write it off as R&D,' he said.

'Five hundred dollars per hour, each, plus expenses, and you report daily to me. If you come across anything pertaining to Nigeria's work for my company, that information is disseminated to no one else. Is that understood?'

'Loud and clear.'

'Do you have to draw up a contract?'

'You might not believe it,' Barney said, 'but some customers we trust. I'll forward you an itemised bill every three days.'

Wellman smiled. 'I hardly envisaged ending our interview with you as employees,' he said. 'Perhaps I could locate a drink, if you'd care to join me?'

'It's late and we have work to do, Mr Wellman.' He paused. 'One other thing, Culaski and his sidekick – they're probably pretty sore about how we froze them today. I wouldn't want them trying to get even, seeing as how we're all on the same side now.'

Wellman nodded. 'Don't worry, gentlemen. I'll talk to them.'

Barney moved to the french windows, and Halliday joined him. Before he stepped through, Barney turned.

'I'm sorry about the dog,' he said.

From across the room, Wellman watched them go without a word.

Halliday was back in the car before he spoke. 'What do you make of that?'

Barney gripped the wheel and reversed from the driveway. 'I think he was telling the truth. He's shit-scared anything leaks to his rivals. As far as I see it, we're in a win-win situation, Hal. He has everything to lose, and we have everything to gain.'

Barney steered onto the coast road and headed towards the highway and New York. Halliday decided to call Kim, take her out for a meal somewhere. He wanted to talk to her after last night, make sure that things were back to normal between them.

After that, despite his promises to Kim, he'd head downtown and question the habituées of the Scumbar about Sissi Nigeria and Carrie Villeux.

Eight

Halliday stayed at the Scumbar until the early hours, engaging the occasional woman in conversation about Nigeria and her lover. He learned nothing new of importance; merely that Nigeria kept her life with her sisters and her work completely separate. She never spoke with her friends, other than in superficial terms, about her work for Cyber-Tech, as befits someone working at the cutting edge of a new technology.

He'd been let in without a grilling from Hatchet-face, and there was no sign of the steel-clawed Missy on the premises. He wanted to question her about the appropriation of his ammunition clip the other night. He thought it unlikely that she was in league with the Latino, but stranger things had happened.

Earlier that evening he'd taken Kim to a small Italian bistro not far from the office, and they'd talked over lasagne and a bottle of Chianti. Her mood of the day before was gone and forgotten; she was light-hearted and carefree, telling him about a business expansion she was planning – another two stalls on the neighbouring block – and Halliday knew better than to bring up the subject of her outburst last night. He was relieved but, at the same time, made uneasy by the fact that she made no mention of her tears, did not even apologise; it was almost as if she had no recollection of what had passed between them.

He'd given thanks that their relationship seemed to be

back on the level, then dropped her off at the loft and headed downtown.

It was almost four in the morning by the time he left the Scumbar and motored slowly to Washington Square, unable to say quite why he had made his way there. He turned into the square and parked the Ford beneath the trees across from the Solano Building.

The brownstone two along had been revamped with the latest holo-façade, rigged to look like a marble-pillared Southern mansion. By comparison, the Solano Building appeared dark and almost malevolent, its stonework defaced with graffiti. Halliday read one particular legend: Virex against Virtual Imperialism, and wondered what the hell it meant.

The streets were still busy. Restaurants and bars were emptying and students hung out on the corners. In the square, a few old men were gathered around a brazier, playing chess on the old concrete tables. Refugees and the homeless slept in huddles beneath the trees.

On impulse, Halliday climbed from the car and crossed the square to the circle of chess tables. The ground sparkled with frost and his breath billowed before him like brief, cartoon speech bubbles awaiting the words.

A tiny black guy, lost in a massive greatcoat, sat gripping a mug of coffee in both hands. 'Hey, man, you play chess?'

'Not very well.'

The guy laughed. 'Hey, I play not very well, too. How 'bout a game? Ten dollars.'

Halliday sat down and handed over a note. The guy set the clock for a five-minute game and Halliday was soon in trouble; he was checkmated in four minutes. He shook his opponent's old, dry hand. 'You here all the time?'

The black guy chuckled. 'Damned near practically live here, man.'

'You see a friend of mine last night? Cuban guy, long black hair, scar down here?'

The chess-player frowned, hunched in his greatcoat. 'Don't recall no dude looking like that, man. Keep my eye out, though. 'Nother game?'

'Some other time, okay?'

He closed his eyes. Into his head came a sudden vision: he was playing chess with his sister, Eloise – and no doubt losing, as ever – when he heard a scream. In that instant, he was visited again by that sudden and overwhelming melancholy, a stabbing pain that seemed to have neither source nor reason.

He looked up, almost expectantly. He stood and hurried across the tree-fringed square, convinced that he'd seen something, some small twist of movement in the distance. He came to a sudden halt.

Perhaps five metres before him, staring at him through the ice-cold night, was Eloise.

She was as he remembered her from all those years ago, wand-slim and as pale as a wraith. She had the fragile, large-eyed beauty of that actress from way back: was it Faye Wray? He'd seen a movie called *King Kong* in his childhood, and more than fear at the monster he had experienced wonder at his sister's resemblance to the star.

She was dressed in a short white smock, and even though Halliday knew he was hallucinating, some irrational part of his mind was concerned about the unsuitability of her clothing in the freezing night air.

'Eloise?'

She smiled at him. Then, to his amazement, she spoke. 'Hi, Hal. How's it going?'

'I . . .' She appeared so real to him that he looked around, as if to confirm that others beside himself could see the child. A few refugees were staring at him while other

140

citizens hurried across the square, avoiding eye-contact with the fool talking to himself.

He took a step forward and halted. She looked so real, so substantial, her short blonde hair arranged in neat curls about her head.

She placed the heel of one red shoe against the toe of the other and stared down at them, from time to time peeking up at him with massive blue eyes.

He wanted to rush up to her and sweep her into his arms, but he knew that that would be to exorcise her image.

'Why are you here, Eloise? What are you doing?'

'You know that, Hal. You called me here.'

'I . . . I did? How?'

She giggled into cupped fingers. 'I don't know how, silly. You did it!'

He stared at her. He had been twice her age when she died, fourteen years old – almost a man, according to his father – and close to his twin sisters. They had been young enough not to be his rivals, old enough to be impressed by his knowledge of the world.

'What happened, Eloise?' he said in a whisper.

'You mean the fire? What happened in the fire?'

He nodded. He recalled the fire. He could see in his mind's eye the appalling conflagration of the family home and all within it that meant so much to him, but he could not recall the specific incidents of that day. He knew that they were the key, the memories he had suppressed of that fateful day all those years ago.

'I can't tell you that, silly,' Eloise carolled. 'I can't remember, can I?' She stared at him, suddenly serious 'You'll have to ask Daddy and Sue, won't you?'

And with that she turned and skipped away. He followed, gave chase. It was as if he were unable to run, his progress retarded as if in a dream. As he watched, the ghost child accelerated away with magical speed and turned around the trunk of a tree. Halliday ran forward, stopped – but she was gone.

He stood in the freezing square, reaching out in a futile gesture of entreaty. He was aware of the hostile stares of the homeless. He turned, looked for the car. As he made his way across the square, he wondered if he was going mad. He slipped into the driver's seat and turned the heater up to full, warming himself. Something had happened to his head in virtual reality. Something had reached in, dislodged a memory buried deep in his subconscious.

He considered what the phantom had advised. He started the Ford and drove, found himself heading across town, and then accelerating across Queensboro Bridge to Long Island and taking Highway 495 through Queens. Kilometres to the south, JFK airport glowed like an old pinball machine in the night. Above it, the lights of approaching planes formed a vast corkscrew holding pattern in the darkness. He stayed on the highway for an hour, his the only vehicle in sight, accelerated and sat back as classical music played softly on the radio.

It was years since he had last been this way, and when he had visited his father he'd arranged to meet in a restaurant in order to avoid the house. It wasn't as if the house was the original, either: it had been re-built, to a different design, in the same lot, soon after the fire. Halliday had never liked living there after that: the new house seemed an impostor, with none of the charm of the original; the new timber possessed by creaks and groans as it settled, which Halliday had ascribed to the movement of a restless ghost.

He turned towards the coast on Highway 97 and, twenty minutes later, slowed as he passed through Blue Point and the row of grand sea-front mansions to his right. His father lived three kilometres further along the coast road, in a wild tract of marram grass and dead trees backing onto the dunes of the foreshore. Halliday practically crawled the last mile or two, as if his conscious self was reluctant now to go through with what his subconscious had set in motion.

The house appeared, suddenly, to his right. His first thought was that this gaunt, dour building could not be the home in which he'd spent the last three years of his youth. It had burned down again, surely, and been replaced. It seemed much smaller than he recalled.

He halted the Ford across the street and sat staring out at the house and, beyond, the dead copse where he had played with his sisters.

The sky was paling towards the east as the sun rose over the sea, throwing the house into stark silhouette. Halliday waited for some sign of life from within. His father had always been an early riser, conditioned by a lifetime of military service. At six, a small rectangle of orange light appeared in a downstairs window. Halliday waited five minutes, then another five, before at last forcing himself to leave the car.

He walked across the unfenced lawn and moved around the house, rather than ring the bell on the front door. He would sooner appear at the kitchen door, as if this might make his visit less formal. He paused at the corner of the house and stared along the length of the back garden, to the oak tree which he had climbed as a boy. He had loved the tree, had felt close to some essence within it – a feeling beyond his power to express in words and which, therefore, he had kept to himself.

The oak was dead, now. He approached slowly, like a mourner to the grave of a friend. It still towered over him, majestic in size if nothing else, but its trunk had split and many of its branches, pulpy now, had broken off and fallen to the ground.

He had vivid memories of hiding in the leafy boughs of the oak, while Eloise and Sue had danced around the garden and tried to find him. Eloise had always been his favourite, for no reason he could recall, and to his abiding discomfort to this day. They were twins, though not identical: Eloise had been fair and tall for her age, Sue dark and small. He had wanted to like them equally, but was always, inexplicably, drawn towards Eloise, even though he was distressed by Sue's pain at his bias.

He was startled by a shout

'What the hell are you doing out there in the freezing cold?' It was his father's peculiar ability to be able to disguise even concern in admonition.

Halliday turned and walked towards the house.

His father had already moved back inside. Halliday climbed the steps and pushed open the screen door. He felt almost numbed at the thought of what he had to ask his father, considered even now just making some excuse for the visit and leaving as soon as possible.

'You find your way here okay?'

Was it a dig at the fact that he had not visited for so long? He shrugged. 'The roads were quiet. It was early.'

'Fix yourself a coffee and come through to the front room,' his father said, and disappeared through the door.

Halliday looked around. The effort of pouring a coffee seemed almost beyond him. He wanted to hurry through the kitchen door and drive away.

He thought of Eloise, and what her ghost had said.

He found a cup, poured a black coffee from the percolator and carried it through. The front room seemed little changed from when he had lived here; it possessed an eerie *fin de siècle* charm, like an exhibition in a museum. He looked around and could see no modern appliances, no computers or wallscreens. The only concession to modernity was the small portable com-screen on the coffee table before the ancient gas fire.

His father, like the room, seemed hardly to have changed at all. He sat on an upright chair, thin and steel-grey and unbending as the blade of a sword.

Halliday perched on the edge of the sofa and sipped his coffee.

'If you're here about what you mentioned the other night . . .' his father began.

Halliday shook his head. He let the silence stretch. He wanted to ask why he had been such a disappointment to his father; if it was because he had failed to follow him into the Marines. He had seen his destiny in doing something as an individual, not as part of a collective fighting force. He had completed two years at law college, but the study was beyond him. He had dropped out and, as if to appease his father, had applied to join the New York Police Department, or perhaps it was because, after two years of fruitless study, he craved excitement and saw the police as a potential source of adventure.

Of course, neither had his father been that much impressed, nor had he found the life of a New York cop that thrilling.

When he left five years later to join Barney at the agency, his father had found this a reason to snipe. 'At least in the police you were providing a public service.'

'And in the agency we'll be finding missing people. It's what I was doing with the force.'

'But now you'll be doing it for clients who pay,' his father had argued. 'Clients who can afford to pay.'

'We'll also be taking on old police work.'

His father had refused to listen at that point; as far as he was concerned, he had already won the argument. He had managed, yet again, to demean his son.

145

Halliday looked up from his coffee. 'I've been having hallucinations,' he began, without thinking how his father might react. It was as if he were speaking to the wall.

'I've been seeing a ghost for the past couple of days.'

His father leaned forward, and Halliday thought he detected an edge of concern in his tone. 'You aren't ill, Hal?'

'I'm okay. It's just that I've suppressed something for so long – kept it buried. And now it's coming out. I keep seeing Eloise.'

'I knew it. I knew it was about her.'

He looked straight at his father. 'What happened? What happened that day?'

His father pursed his lips like an ancient, reluctant turtle. 'I told you, it's too painful to recollect. I don't like thinking . . .' He shook his head in bafflement and pain. 'How could you?'

'Because I need to know! Don't you think her death was as painful for me as it was for you?'

'I don't know that. How can one quantify grief?'

Halliday didn't reply, could not begin to do so. The silence stretched. 'What happened, Dad? Please tell me.'

His father looked across the room at him, and it occurred to Halliday then that Eloise had inherited his bright blue eyes. 'You don't remember anything, Hal?'

'Nothing specifically. I recall a fire, no more. Then I recall, days later, you telling me that Eloise was dead.'

His father was nodding. 'I. . . I often wondered what you remembered. I could never bring myself to ask you. I didn't want to stir the memories, the pain . . . for either of us.'

'I remember absolutely nothing of the day itself. All I have is an image: the image of the house, burning.'

His father allowed a long silence to develop, but it was always somehow obvious that he intended to go on, explain what had happened all those years ago.

146

At last he said, 'It was a gas explosion, Hal. There was nothing we could have done to prevent it, nothing at all. Maybe if I'd been there . . . I don't know. I'd gone down to the store, leaving you in charge. I recall you were playing chess with Eloise when I left: she was beating you, as usual. The twins were just seven, and Eloise was a damned fine chess player.' He was sitting upright, gripping the arms of the chair as if someone had threatened to take it away. 'I was coming back from the store when I heard the explosion, and, you know, I thought nothing of it – how could I have known? Even when I saw the smoke billowing over the rooftops . . . And then I realised that it might be our house, and I drove like a maniac, and even before I turned into the street, I knew.'

He stopped and swallowed. His hands were shaking. Halliday looked away, through the lace curtains. His father said, 'I found . . . Susanna was lying on the lawn. I thought she was dead at first. She was bloody, her left leg broken in three places. And then I found . . .'

'It's okay. You don't have to go on . . .' He wondered if this was the reason why his father had resented him for so long? He, Halliday, had been blown clear of the house, had somehow survived, while Eloise had perished.

'No, you don't understand,' he went on. 'You see, after finding Susanna, I ran towards the house. I thought you and Eloise . . . I thought you were still in there. Half the house had been blown away, the other half was blazing. And then I found you: you were coming down the staircase of the little of the house that remained, bloodied and battered, and you were carrying Eloise.'

Halliday felt his pulse quicken. He tried to remember, wanted nothing more than to recall the experience. Again, the only image that returned to him was that of the house on fire, as seen from the lawn.

'You came down the stairs and you carried her out in

147

your arms, and then sat on the lawn and watched the house burn down.'

Halliday shook his head, bewildered. 'I carried Eloise out? But what . . . what happened to her?'

His father controlled his voice, marshalled his emotions. 'Eloise died from smoke inhalation later that day. I thought . . . I told myself that perhaps if I'd been there, perhaps I would have been able to save her.'

Halliday thought of the boy he had been then, the boy who had carried his sister from the burning house, perhaps even thinking that he had saved her life, only to learn later that she had died.

'You had a few cuts and bruises, nothing major. The doctors questioned you about what had happened, but you were too shocked to speak. I . . . after that, I could never bring myself to talk about it.' His father stared at him across the room, and Halliday saw the silver light of tears in his eyes.

He shook his head. 'I never realised. I never knew what had happened, just that Eloise had died.'

His father smiled. 'I hope that knowing exorcises her ghost, Hal.'

Later, on the steps as his father was showing him out, he said, 'Do you see much of Susanna these days?'

Halliday shook his head. 'No. No, I haven't seen her for years.'

'Well, if you do . . . will you tell her to drop by?'

He nodded. Hesitantly, almost embarrassed of making the move, of chancing a gesture that might be turned down, he reached out and shook his father's hand.

At that moment, Halliday had the sudden urge to say that he had met someone, to tell his father about Kim and how much he loved her. Then the moment was over, and he was colouring at the thought of it as he stepped from the porch and hurried across the lawn. He crossed the road to the Ford and ducked inside. As he pulled from the kerb and U-turned, he looked up. His father was standing to attention in the porch, as stiff as a sentry on guard duty, his right arm raised in a wave more like a salute.

As he drove back to the city, he considered everything that his father had told him. He wondered, briefly, if his knowledge of what had happened would now indeed exorcise the ghost of Eloise. He stared out at the cold, iron-grey road ahead, and it came to him that even now he did not know the complete truth of what had happened on the day of the fire.

He passed the airport, the runway beacons now pale in the light of the new day. He wanted nothing more than to sleep, and maybe later go down to the street and bring a take-out back to the office.

As he motored across Queensboro Bridge, it occurred to him that perhaps his father's resentment across all these years was the result of his not being there when the house blew up, and the fact that his son had been on hand to try to rescue Eloise. His father resented him for having been there, instead of him.

He shook his head, and attempted to push all thoughts of his father from his mind.

He was turning off the bridge when his communicator buzzed.

'Hal? Jeff Simmons here.'

'Jeff. What is it?'

'Listen, Hal. That Latino guy who attacked you the other night . . .'

Hal sat up. 'You got him?'

'We're onto him, Hal. A traffic cop spotted him walking up Broadway about twenty minutes ago, recognised him from the pix we commed up from your description.'

'Where is he now?'

'Heading uptown on foot. On Second Avenue, coming

149

up to East 14th Street. I'm right behind him in a car. If you want to get yourself down here, you can be in for the kill.'

'We want him alive, Jeff.'

Simmons laughed. 'I was speaking metaphorically, Hal. Don't worry, we'll bring him in alive and kicking.'

Halliday turned and headed uptown, the city streets deserted but for the occasional tour bus, yellow cab and patrolling cop car. The grates steamed in the icy morning air and a patina of frost covered every flat, exposed surface.

'How many men you got with you, Jeff?'

'Enough. And a squad of drones, too. We don't want to go for him on the street. If he's still armed as he was the night you met him, we don't want to risk civilian injuries. We'll wait till he's contained, then move in.'

'You called Barney?'

'First thing. He's on his way. Listen, I'll call you back in two minutes. We're still on Second Avenue heading uptown, just passing through Stuyvesant Square. Be in touch.'

Halliday accelerated along the almost empty streets, the skyscrapers and high-rises of Manhattan towering before him, grey and cold against a pewter sky. In contrast to the deserted streets, the sidewalks and doorways were populated by the legion of the displaced. He wondered how long it might be before they claimed occupancy of the actual roads.

He thought about the sighting of the Latino. If they managed to get the guy alive, find out who the hell he was and his motives for the attack the other night, then the pieces of the puzzle might fall into place. They might not be that far off discovering the whereabouts of Nigeria and Villeux.

His com buzzed. 'Hal, he's passed through the Square. He looks like he's in a hurry.'

'Does he know you're onto him?'

'No way, Hal.'

Halliday turned onto Second Avenue. 'I don't have to tell you to be careful, Jeff. Brief your men on the weapons he packs.'

'I've told them about the cutter in graphic detail. There's just one thing.'

'Fire away.'

'I don't get it. Why's he still in the guise of the Latino? He's wearing the chu, okay? He must've known you could give a description of him from the other night, right?'

Halliday thought about it. 'Wrong, Jeff. Far as he's aware, he threw me over the building. I'm history. I didn't live to tell anyone about him.'

'What about Kia Johansen? Didn't she see him?'

'Obviously he thought not, or he wouldn't be still wearing the same disguise.'

At the other end of the line, Jeff Simmons conferred hurriedly with someone. 'Right, okay! Hal, he's just entered the Astoria Hotel on the corner of Second Avenue and East 23rd. Okay, there's a hamburger joint across the street: see you outside.'

'I'm about two minutes away, Jeff.'

Halliday turned onto East 23rd and parked in a quiet sidestreet. He left the car, crossed the street and walked a block to the Astoria.

Jeff Simmons was standing on the corner across from the hotel. He wore a loud checked sports jacket and a broad green tie. He looked like an out-of-town business-man doing the sights. To all appearances he was amiably chatting to someone on his com, from time to time casually glancing across the street at the Astoria.

Halliday noticed perhaps two dozen drones in the vicinity. These ranged from the size of bread bins to heavy-duty models as big as trash cans. They hovered along at head height, bulky metal objects painted in the distinctive blue and white livery of the NYPD.

As he watched, two smaller drones slipped into the hotel. He guessed these were the remote-controlled marksmen used frequently these days in armed conflict scenarios.

Simmons cut the connection and pocketed his com. 'That was Barney. He'll be here any second.'

Halliday stuffed his hands in his pockets and stamped his feet. He looked across the street at the hotel. 'What's the score?'

'I have people surrounding the place, half a dozen drones covering every exit in case our guy tries to leave, plus a couple inside. I've sent in a man to alert the security officer.'

'Are you going in?'

Simmons nodded. 'I'll tell the security officer what's happening, see if he can trace the guy.'

They crossed the street and approached the hotel's canopied entrance. A yellow cab pulled up outside and Barney struggled out, bundled in a grey overcoat. Simmons hurried up the steps and passed through the revolving door. Barney joined Halliday. 'What gives, Hal?'

Halliday nodded towards the hotel. 'The Latino entered about five minutes ago. Jeff's got the place surrounded. We're meeting him in security.'

They climbed the steps, passed through the revolving door and crossed the lobby. Jeff Simmons was in a tiny office behind reception. A security officer was seated before one of a dozen screens, rewinding an image of the lobby. The scene remained static but for the occasional scurrying figure moving backwards and the blur of the revolving door.

Simmons looked up. 'We're going back five minutes and

working forward. We're looking for a medium-sized guy in a black leather jacket, beige chinos and black gloves.'

The security officer stilled the image. A digital clock in the top right corner of the screen read 9:56. 'This is a little over five minutes ago. I'll fast-forward from there, slowing every time someone comes in.'

A minute elapsed on the digital before the first maniacally hurtling figure shot through the revolving door. The officer slowed the image, and Halliday stared, aware of his heartbeat. A tall woman in a red trouser suit.

'Next one,' Jeff Simmons said.

The screen showed an empty lobby before the doors blurred again. This time an overweight businessman spurted into the hotel, slowed for inspection, and shot off again.

The digital showed 9:59 when a dark-haired guy in a black leather jacket entered the lobby. The security officer slowed the image. Halliday tapped the screen. 'That's our man, Jeff.'

In the top left corner he made out a figure, frozen in the act of rising from an armchair. The Latino seemed to be looking across the lobby at the woman, maybe even lifting his hand in a gesture of greeting.

'Run the image forward a few seconds,' he said.

The security officer touched the keyboard. The scene sprang to life. The Latino crossed the lobby. The woman completed the act of standing up and moving forward. She was tall, with a shaven tattooed head, and wore a long silver raincoat. The man and woman met, spoke briefly, moved towards the elevator.

Halliday felt his mouth run suddenly dry. 'Good God.' He looked at Barney. 'It's Carrie Villeux.'

'What the hell is she doing here?' Simmons said. He looked at the security officer. 'Run it forward.'

The Latino and Villeux stood before the lift for a few

seconds and, when the doors parted, stepped inside. The doors closed and Halliday leaned forward, peering at the floor indication lights above the door. From the distance and angle of the security camera it was impossible to make out where the elevator halted.

'Can we follow them?' Simmons asked.

The officer nodded. 'We have cameras on every floor. It's just a matter of timing the elevator and checking each floor. Here goes.'

The scene on the screen changed, showed the blurred image of a hotel corridor, with a pair of elevator doors to the right. The digital showed 9:58.

This is the second floor,' the officer said. 'Nothing there. I'll move to the next floor. We'll wait out the same minute on each floor.'

The scene flickered, remained almost identical. They waited out a minute, and then the officer said, 'Nothing. Okay, the fourth floor.'

The scene flickered again. The digital flicked back to 9:58. Seconds later, the elevator doors parted and the Latino and Carrie Villeux stepped out and walked along the corridor.

They disappeared from sight of the camera. The security officer called up another angle. This one showed Villeux and the guy pause before a door while he operated the lock. They passed inside.

The security officer turned to Jeff Simmons. 'Room 456, fourth floor.'

'Good work.'

'How you going to play it?' Barney asked.

Simmons considered. 'We'll get someone in there disguised as staff. Then we freeze both the guy and Villeux.'

Halliday looked at Barney. 'I wonder where the hell Nigeria is?' he said.

'I don't think we're that long from finding out.'

'Okay,' Jeff Simmons said, 'let's think about this.'

'Hold on there . . .' It was the security officer. 'Look.' He was pointing at the screen. He paused the image, rewound it a few seconds.

The scene was a corridor on the fourth floor. The digital read 10:02. The officer began the recording. The door to room 456 opened and someone hurried out. The guy was familiar: he had the build of the Latino, but he was no longer wearing a black leather jacket and chinos. He wore a fawn raincoat and black trousers. More importantly, facially he was white now, with long fair hair and a beard.

The security officer followed him via the surveillance cameras to the elevator, and then switched the scene to that of the lobby at 10:03. Moments later, the guy stepped from the elevator, crossed the lobby and exited through the revolving door.

'It looks,' Jeff Simmons said evenly, 'as if we might have to change our plans.' He spoke hurriedly into his com, briefing his men with the subject's changed appearance.

'Fat chance we have of locating the bastard now,' Barney said. 'He might be miles away.'

Halliday felt something cold grow within him. 'I don't like it, Jeff,' he said. 'What happened to Villeux?'

'Let's get up there,' Simmons said. He spoke into his com, then turned to the security officer. 'I might need a pass-card for room 456.'

'I'll get one.'

They crossed the lobby to the elevator and rode up to the fourth floor. They stepped out and waited in the corridor. Two minutes later, they were joined by the security officer with the spare pass-card.

'I'll knock, posing as hotel staff following up a complaint,' Simmons said. 'If no one replies I'll use the card.'

He walked down the corridor and turned the corner. A minute passed, then two. Then Barney's communicator buzzed.

Halliday heard Simmons' voice. 'No reply,' he said. 'I'm going in.'

The security officer hurried along the corridor. Halliday pushed himself from the wall, not sure if he really wanted to enter the room. He followed Barney down the corridor and turned into the bedroom.

He looked around quickly, seeing nothing at first and experiencing a quick sense of disappointment. Then he noticed a number of objects on the bed, and at the same time noticed Barney turn away from the scene, his expression frozen. In that second, Halliday saw the things on the bed for what they were, the tableau like an optical illusion which resolves itself and becomes suddenly, startlingly obvious. He closed his eyes, but too late.

He hurried from the room and squatted down against the far wall. Barney had already got out. Halliday looked up, saw the security officer emerge, something in his training and macho self-image not allowing him to show what he was feeling, but Halliday read the truth in his eyes.

Jeff Simmons joined them in the corridor. He sat on the floor opposite Halliday. 'Villeux,' he said in a soft voice. 'The bastard used a cutter.'

It was the first time Halliday had ever heard Simmons swear. The silence stretched, ringing.

He felt suddenly sick. The Latino had intended to do to him the other night, he thought, what he had succeeded in doing to Carrie Villeux.

He stood and walked to the end of the corridor. A window looked out over uptown New York caught in the grip of a hard winter, the serried tower blocks a dozen shades of frozen grey.

Barney joined him. 'It doesn't look good for Nigeria,' he said.

'But why Villeux? If Wellman was right, and a rival did want Nigeria dead, then what motive was there for killing Carrie Villeux?'

'I don't know. Perhaps it isn't related to any technical knowledge Nigeria possessed. It's something else entirely . . .'

Halliday stared out across the city. 'The world is a fucking awful place, Barney.'

'Yeah, tell me about it.'

Jeff Simmons joined them. 'I'm going to get onto surveillance, see if we can track the guy after he left the hotel.'

'Some hope,' Barney grunted. 'He's on foot, he could slip down any sidestreet, and the bastard's wearing a damned chu.'

Simmons shrugged. 'I've got to go through the motions, Barney. At least he doesn't know we're onto him.' He paused. 'You see what I meant the other day when I found out that chus were being used? You see how much more difficult it makes our job?'

Halliday expelled a long sigh. The thought that there was someone out there who could kill without compunction, and evade detection with ease, filled him with fear.

'Come on,' Simmons said. 'Let's get down to headquarters, see what surveillance can come up with.'

They were leaving the hotel when Simmons' com buzzed. He stopped to answer the call. Halliday continued along the packed sidewalk, zipping his jacket and stuffing his hands deep into the pockets.

'Hal, Barney,' Simmons called, pocketing his com. He joined them, grim-faced. 'That was control. They've found the body of Sissi Nigeria.'

Halliday stared into the grey sky. 'Christ, I don't think I could take a second one in the same day.'

'She hasn't been cut up,' Simmons said. 'In fact, control says it doesn't look like murder.'

Halliday shook his head, as if to clear it. 'Is that the best news we've had all day, or am I losing the plot?'

Simmons smiled and pointed across the street. 'She's in the ComStore.'

They crossed the street, Simmons leading the way. The ComStore was a double-fronted establishment adorned with a holo-façade like a mammoth computer stack.

A crowd of ghouls stood outside, trying to look through the smoked glass doors. Two cops, aided by a drone, kept them at bay.

Simmons eased his way through the crowd and Halliday and Barney followed in his wake. The interior of the store was empty but for the manager and staff gathered redundantly by the door and, at the far end of the long shop-floor, a knot of police officials standing around a seated figure.

The odour of burned hamburger filled the air.

Halliday followed the others down an aisle of computer terminals towards the body. The cops looked up, nodded at Simmons.

A sergeant made his report. 'She came in about ten minutes ago, sir. At approximately 10:15 the manager found her like this. We ran an identity scan and she came up on a missing persons file.'

'How'd she die?'

'We're still trying to work that one out, sir.'

Halliday stared down at the body in the swivel chair. It was the second corpse he'd seen that morning but at least, he told himself, this one was still in one piece.

It was still not a pretty sight, even so. Her arms and legs were twisted at unnatural angles, and the expression on her once beautiful face was a contorted mask of agony. Her shaven skull was cries-crossed with the silver inlay of a neural implant, but the spars were blackened in places, and in others the metal had bubbled and burned through the flesh of her scalp, like solder. Smoke twisted, lazily, from the perfect tiny shell of her right ear.

A lead hung from the external port at her temple to the computer terminal before her. A cop wearing headphones was running his fingers across the touchscreen, conjuring up scrolling blocks of alpha-numerics.

He looked up at Simmons. 'She uploaded something seconds before she died. It was in encrypted code and we're talking . . .' He stared at the screen and nodded, '. . . a big file, in excess of fifty gigabytes.'

'Can you trace where it was sent?'

The tech shook his head. 'It scrambled its route through the Net. It might be anywhere by now.'

'How the hell did she die, Lieutenant?'

'Something was blasted the other way, down the connection lead and into her implant. I've never seen anything like it. She didn't stand a chance.'

Halliday noticed the coat, then. He stared, hardly able to bring himself to believe what he was looking at. The fawn raincoat had been bundled and tossed onto the floor beside Nigeria's computer.

He touched Simmons' shoulder and pointed, thinking the coat was a sick calling card left by the killer in a mocking gesture of defiance.

Then he seemed to notice everything in a dizzying rush. He saw the black glove on the table-top next to the computer, and the second glove still on Nigeria's left hand. He saw that she was wearing black trousers . . .

Simmons, reaching out, picked up something which had slipped down the side of the woman's chair. It looked like a mask, its expression grossly distorted as it hung from Simmons' fingers. It was connected by a thin wire lead to a small control box in the breast pocket of Nigeria's white

159

shirt. When Simmons pulled the box from the pocket, the mask hanging in his grasp cycled through a series of ghastly, withered faces: the Latino killer, the blonde girl, the fair-haired guy who'd left the hotel, and half a dozen others.

'Christ,' Barney whispered, 'it's the damned chu.'

In a daze, Halliday moved around the seated corpse. From this angle he could see the raised contusion on the woman's left cheek, the brown skin gashed and bloodied. He reached out and gently removed the glove from the left hand, and stared down at the swollen, broken fingers he had mashed on the rooftop two nights ago.

Barney picked up the raincoat and tipped a cutter from its pocket onto the table-top.

The implications took a while to sink in.

'Nigeria,' Simmons said. 'Sissi Nigeria attacked you the other night. She . . .' He gestured towards the Astoria Hotel. 'She did that to Villeux and then came here.'

Halliday found a swivel chair and sat down, nausea rising in his throat like bile. He shook his head. 'Why, Barney?' he said. 'What the hell possessed her to do that to Villeux?'

Barney reached out and massaged Halliday's shoulder. He shook his head. 'We'll wait and see if the tech comes up with anything else, Hal. Then I'll drive you home, okay?'

Nine

Anna woke at eight and reached out for Kia with an instinctive gesture she had made a hundred times before. The bed beside her was empty, cold. Kia had been distant since they had arrived home yesterday after the malfunction of the Mantoni jellytank, or whatever the hell had happened. They had planned to go out that night, but Kia had cried off with a headache and, rather than go out alone, Anna had stayed in and tinkered with a few pages of her latest novel while Kia sat on the couch in brooding silence. When Anna asked what was on her mind, it was as if Kia were a million miles away, her eyes staring sightlessly at the wall. She had finally brought herself to reply. She had shaken her head, smiled vaguely, and said that she was working on a problem related to work.

Anna had gone to bed at ten, and it was well into the early hours before Kia had joined her.

Now she turned onto her back and blinked up at the ceiling. 'Kia?' she called.

She rolled from bed and dressed. Kia was not in the bathroom, nor the kitchen. Anna fixed herself a coffee and two croissants. She carried a tray into the lounge and looked out the window. Kia's battered Cadillac was not in its usual place in the street. Anna wondered if she had left early in order to work on the glitch in the VR system – but why, if that were so, hadn't she woken Anna and told her, or at least left a note?

She switched on the computer and accessed the file

161

containing her novel. She tried to push the thought of Kia from her mind and read a few pages. The novel was about life in twenty-first-century New York, concentrating on a group of professional twentysomethings, gay and straight alike. She changed the odd line, rewrote a wordy paragraph, then sat back and stared at the screen.

If only she could sell one or two of her serious novels, redeem her integrity in her own eyes ... She smiled to herself and wondered if she were living a fantasy just as make-believe as Sasha in *Sapphic Island*.

She stared at the words on the screen, but it was hard to concentrate when half her mind was wondering what had happened to Kia. She closed the file and glanced at the wall-clock. It was almost nine.

She routed the wallscreen through the computer and checked for messages. Perhaps Kia had called, apologising ...

The first message was from Felicity: Anna, sorry to call so early. Could you contact me at home, darling?

She wondered what it was this time. Perhaps the script needed a little more sexing up, as Felicity called it. Or maybe the powers that be at Tidemann's had decided to go for a third series. She'd tell them to stuff it: well, not in so many words. She'd get her agent to arrange that she was kept on in a consultative capacity, and get some hack in to do the actual scripting. That way she'd be earning something, and would have time to do her own work.

She got through to Felicity.

The producer smiled from the screen. 'Anna, nice to see you, sweetie. We had some good news about the *Island* last night.'

Anna lodged her bare feet on the chair and hugged her legs. 'I'm all ears.'

Felicity peered at her, trying to determine whether Anna was being sarcastic. 'Well, first, Germany and France have bought the first series of the *Island* for showing later this year, with an option on the second, depending on how well it goes down. They like what they've seen and will be putting a massive publicity campaign behind the show. And second, Brazil has bought the rights to make their own *Island*, based on your scripts. Isn't that wonderful?'

'Fantastic,' Anna said. She had a quick vision of tanned Brazilian bodies in the orgy scene, then concentrated on what Felicity was saying.

'You'll be getting ten per cent of the original fee per show from Germany and France, and the Brazilian fee has yet to be arranged. Contact your agent for all the details, okay?'

Anna nodded. 'I'll do that, Felicity, thanks.' Another . . . what? One hundred and twenty thousand dollars, plus whatever the Brazilian payment came to. With all the money she'd earned from the original advances she would have sufficient savings to live in some quiet upstate retreat for a few years, doing her own thing.

She wondered if that, too, was just another fantasy.

'One more thing, Anna,' Felicity said. 'We're starting the shoot of the final episode tomorrow. Would you like to come along to the studio and be on hand to supervise the last-minute line changes?'

'Well . . . I'm working on something of my own at the moment. Can't really take a break.' She was glad of the excuse. She had hated her previous trips to the studio, the forced sincerity of the beautiful actresses out of their heads on spin, the bullshitting executives who just *loved* the show . . .

Felicity smiled and waved. 'Okay, Anna. Be in touch.'

She cut the connection and checked the second message. A handsome middle-aged guy with greying sideburns smiled out at her. He was seated casually on the edge of a desk in a big open-plan office.

163

'Hi, Anna. I'm Dave Charlesworth, commissioning editor at Shire Press. I liked the novel, Anna. Could you get back to me and we'll talk?'

Anna stilled the image and stared. She was aware of her pulse, thumping in her ears. She rewound the message and played it again – and he *really* had said that he liked the novel.

Shire Press. They were a big, reputable publisher with imprints in Europe . . . Five thousand, she said to herself. I'll take five thousand measly dollars and be eternally grateful.

She contacted Shire Press and asked to see Dave Charlesworth. Seconds later, his image filled the screen.

Anna waved, trying to appear casual. 'Anna Ellischild here. I got your message.'

'Anna . . . nice to speak to you.' Charlesworth was a smooth-talking exec in a dark suit. 'I really liked *A Better World*.'

'Thanks. It's nice to hear that. It's one of my favourites, too.'

'Understandably so, a fine book.'

Here it comes, Anna thought: the offer, the contract details. She was almost willing to give the damned book away.

'I'd heard rumours on the grapevine . . .' he began.

'Rumours?'

'That Anna Ellischild was in fact Sophia de Vere, scriptwriter of *Sapphic Island*.'

'Well . . .' Anna shrugged. 'It was something I did to put food on the table.'

'Don't knock it, Anna. The show obviously reached people on some deep and meaningful level.'

What the fuck, Anna asked herself, was he talking about? 'It was a project I did in my spare time,' she said. 'About *A Better World* . . .'

164

'Actually, Anna, I'm calling about *Sapphic Island*.'

A trapdoor seemed to open in Anna's stomach. 'You are?'

'Don't get me wrong, I loved *A Better World* – beautifully written, the characterisation . . . it proved you certainly can write. Thing is, Anna, Shire Press has just bought the rights to do the novelisation of *Sapphic Island*, and we were wondering if you'd like to do it, under the *nom de plume* of Sophia de Vere, of course.'

It was a few seconds before she could bring herself to speak. 'You don't want the novel?'

'Personally, I'd love to do the book, Anna, but in the current climate . . .'

'How about as part of a deal? Sophia de Vere does the *Sapphic Island* books, and *A Better World* comes out under my own name?' She realised that she was sounding desperate.

Charlesworth frowned. 'Like I said, Anna, I'd love to do the book, but we just don't think it has the commercial potential.'

Anna fought back the tears and cursed the prick. She shook her head. 'I'm not interested in doing the novelisation,' she said. 'Get some other poor hack to do the damned thing.'

'Perhaps we could negotiate with you to have the rights to use the Sophia de Vere byline?'

'Discuss that with my agent,' Anna said, reached out and cut the connection.

She sat back and closed her eyes. Plain, forthright rejection she could take, but to be given hope like that, only for it to be dashed away and replaced by the offer of novelising the damned script of *Sapphic Island* . . . Later, when the disappointment abated, she might be able to laugh at what had happened. Now she wished that Kia was here, for support.

She sat for a long time, staring at the wall.

She remembered that there was a third message awaiting her, and played it through the screen.

Carrie Villeux looked out. 'Anna, can we meet today? I'm worried about Sissi. Look . . .' She hesitated, biting her bottom lip. She leaned towards the screen. She appeared nervous, and this exaggerated her French accent. 'The other day, I told you that Sissi was acting very strange. She was using disguises. Sissi has this thing, an electronic mask: she can put on a different face. I'm worried, Anna. Will you meet me?' She paused. 'I'm seeing Sissi at the Astoria at ten this morning; could we meet for coffee around, say, ten-thirty? Don't worry, I'll get away from Sissi in plenty of time. Meet you in the lobby of the Astoria at ten-thirty, okay?' The message ended.

She looked at her watch. It was ten-fifteen. If she hurried, she would make the Astoria in fifteen, twenty minutes. She found her shoes and coat, left the apartment and walked uptown.

She reached the Astoria five minutes late. Three police cars and a silver van were parked outside the hotel's revolving doors, and the lobby was swarming with cops and drones. Anna looked around for Carrie. It was after ten-thirty, but surely Carrie would have waited. There was no sign of her in the lobby. Anna made her way to the café, but Carrie was not among the guests seated at the tables.

She returned to the lobby and sat in one of the comfortable armchairs. Perhaps Carrie had been unable to get away from Sissi. Anna decided to wait until eleven and then leave.

A team of what she took to be forensic scientists swept through the lobby and into the elevator, followed by three floating drones. Anna gestured to a passing bell-boy and asked him what was going on.

'Lady murdered on the fourth floor, miss,' the guy replied. 'Real messy by all accounts.'

Anna felt her scalp prickle. It had to be a coincidence, she told herself. Carrie would be here at any minute.

'Do you know who . . .?' she began.

The guy shrugged. 'Woman in a silver coat,' he said. 'She was sitting right where you are now.'

Anna's mouth ran dry. 'What did she look like?'

The guy grinned. 'One of those *alternative* women,' he said. 'You know, bald head, tattoos . . .'

Anna stood and left the lobby. She pushed through the revolving door and stepped out onto the sidewalk. The cold air was refreshing, clearing her head.

Carrie was dead. She had gone to meet Sissi Nigeria, and now she was dead. It made no kind of sense and Anna felt light-headed, adrift on the tide of pedestrians that flowed along the sidewalk.

She looked up, across the street. A short guy dressed in faded black was standing outside the ComStore, talking to an even shorter, older guy in a soiled overcoat.

Something made her cross the street and approach him. He looked up as she stepped onto the sidewalk, dark eyes registering his recognition only after a lapse of seconds.

'Hal,' she said. 'I thought it was you.' Her smile faltered. 'You haven't changed much.'

He stared at her, shy. 'Sue? I didn't recognise you.' He gestured to her clothes, her hair. 'You've altered.'

'You have time for a drink?' she asked.

'Sure,' Hal said. 'Why not?'

The short, old guy winked at her and said, 'You going to introduce us, Hal?'

'Oh, yeah.' Hal smiled at her uneasily. 'Barney, this is my sister, Sue. Sue, my business partner, Barney.'

They nodded to each other. 'Pleased to meet you, Sue,' the guy said.

'Take the car, Barney,' Hal said. 'I'll get a cab back.'

'Catch you later, Hal.' Barney nodded to Anna, then set off along the sidewalk.

Anna turned to her brother. He looked a little older, a little more careworn, but he was still the Hal she recognised from five years ago.

She gestured to a nasty, healing gash on the side of his head. 'What happened?'

'It's nothing. Look . . .' He shook his head. 'Let's find somewhere that does coffee. I've been up for hours. I need something to keep me awake.'

'I could use a drink, Hal. Something strong. I've just found out that a friend has been . . .' She stopped as she saw his expression. 'What is it?'

'Not Carrie Villeux?' he said. 'You knew Villeux?'

'We weren't close, but we were more than acquaintances.'

'I was working for her, trying to find her lover.'

She nodded, recalling what Kia had told her about Hal the other night. 'Let's find a bar, sit down and talk, okay?'

'I know a place around the corner.'

She walked alongside her brother, wondering why she had let so long pass without contacting him. They had been close when they were younger, but later she had used her intellect to put him down, point out the limitations of his conditioning, and had earned his mystified, hurt resentment.

He had been a rather slow good-natured kid. When he had announced that he was joining the police, she recalled that their father had made some comment about it being a second-best choice, while she had taunted him for conforming.

Now she squeezed his arm. 'It's good to see you, Hal. Really, it is.'

He gave her a quick glance, as if wondering when the insults would begin. 'Good to see you too, Sue.'

'I prefer Anna, now.'

He looked mystified for a second, then said, 'Ah, Susanna.' He smiled. 'Of course.'

He had a slow, measured way of speaking that she remembered from all those years ago, as if he were contemplating the words before he spoke them. It gave him a relaxed, easy manner – a certain sense of slow deliberation – which she found somehow reassuring.

Then, sickeningly, her thoughts returned to the fact that Carrie was dead . . .

They entered a bar and Hal ordered a coffee while she asked for a Southern Comfort on the rocks. They found a quiet booth at the back of the bar and sat facing each other.

'About Carrie,' she said. 'I had a call from her about an hour ago. I was working so she left a message.' She repeated what Carrie had told her about Sissi. 'Carrie was due to meet her at ten.'

Hal was nodding. 'I know. They met.' He stopped there, stared into his coffee. He looked up, rubbing his jaw. 'Nigeria killed Carrie Villeux in the hotel room, left the hotel and crossed the street to the ComStore. We found her in there half an hour ago, dead.'

Anna felt the rye burn her throat and tears came to her eyes. 'Sissi too?'

Hal shrugged, staring down at his coffee. 'Look, what do you know about them? We're baffled. Nigeria was going about in disguise. She attacked me the other night when I called around to check her apartment.'

'Sissi attacked you?' Anna was incredulous.

He nodded. 'I know, it's hard to believe.' He lifted the cup to his lips and blew across the surface of the coffee.

169

'Have you any idea why Nigeria might have acted like this? Could it have had anything to do with drugs?'

Anna shook her head. 'Sissi didn't do drugs. She was careful about things that might've messed up her mind.'

Hal sighed and massaged his face. 'I'll tell you this for nothing, Sue – Anna. We're beat. We don't know what the hell went on between them, why Nigeria acted as she did. The case is closed, officially, but it's so damned frustrating because it's not . . .' He searched for the word.

'Concluded?'

'Concluded.' He smiled. 'You still writing?'

She was often asked that question, as if writing was a phase through which she might some day pass, or an illness she might get over.

She nodded. 'Still writing.'

'How's it going?' He paused. She could see that he wanted to ask if she'd sold anything, but at the same time didn't want to make her admit that she was still struggling.

She reached across the table and took his hand. 'I still haven't sold any of the books, but I've written a dozen episodes of a holo-drama series. Hack work, but it pays well.'

His expression showed surprise and pleasure, a nice contrast to his earlier dog-tired, weary look. 'Holo-dramas? That's really something. My little sister, the holo-drama writer.'

She had to smile at him. How like Hal to be impressed by something as popular and crass as holo-dramas. She felt like reaching over and ruffling his mop of unruly curls.

He was spinning his empty coffee cup. 'Went over to Long Island and saw Dad earlier.'

'What did he want?'

'Nothing. I went to see him. Just to talk . . .' He shrugged. He never had been very good at expressing his feelings.

'How is he?' she asked.

170

'I don't know. I mean . . . just the same as ever. Himself. He asked me if I ever saw you . . . and then I bump into you hours later. He wants you to go and visit.'

'We've not a lot in common, Hal.'

'Neither have I,' he said, 'but I made the effort.'

That's because you're still a frightened little boy who's fearful of Daddy, she thought. She stared at him across the table and wondered why he forever seemed so guilty.

He looked up, past her, and stared at a table across the room. His lips moved, forming silent words, and a look of such sadness entered his eyes that Anna turned. The bar was empty. 'Hal?'

He shook his head, rubbed his eyes. 'It's okay. I've been awake for so long I'm starting to see things.'

'Hal, are you okay?'

'I'm fine.' He regarded his coffee cup, so obviously needing to say something that Anna wanted to crank his starting handle in order to get him going.

'What is it?'

He looked up. 'What do you remember about the fire, Anna?'

The fire . . .? The question surprised her. It was so long ago, now. All she recalled was a series of images: flames, the house collapsing, the sight of their father running across the lawn. She had no recollection of what she had felt at the time. She knew she had been in the house, with Hal and Eloise, but had no idea how she had escaped.

She could recall the strange, empty days that followed the fire, being told by her father that Eloise was in heaven now, but not linking the fact with the fire. It was only later, in her teens, that she came to understand how her sister had died.

Now she shrugged and shook her head. 'What do I remember? Not a lot. Practically nothing at all. The flames, the house falling down . . . I was only seven.'

171

He nodded, staring into his coffee cup.

'You?' she asked.

He lifted his shoulders in a hopeless, expressive shrug. 'Much the same,' he said, and he glanced, once again, across the bar towards whatever he had seen earlier.

The silence stretched, and finally Anna said, 'It's been good talking again, Hal. Come round some time, okay?' She reached into her bag and passed him a card.

He took it in his solid, square hand and read, frowning. 'Anna Ellischild.' He looked up. 'Ellischild?'

'I changed my surname a few years ago,' she said. 'You know, Ellis was Mom's maiden name.'

He could see from the expression in his eyes that the explanation had explained nothing. She touched his hand. 'Come round for a meal some time. Are you seeing anyone?'

He nodded.

'You going to tell me about her?'

He shrugged. 'I wouldn't know where to begin,' he said.

She smiled at his inability, or his reluctance, to open up.

They left the bar and stood on the sidewalk, facing each other. 'I meant what I said about coming over. And bring your girlfriend, okay?'

He nodded. She reached out and embraced him, felt his hands almost reluctantly touch her shoulders. 'Bye, Hal.'

'Bye.' He made an awkward farewell gesture and turned, and she watched him as he walked away; a small, faded, black-clad figure, soon lost in the bustle of pedestrians on the sidewalk.

She walked home, turning her collar up against the chill wind. She'd call Mantoni when she got back, ask to talk to Kia. They'd had their rows in the past, gone a day or two without speaking, but on those occasions there had always been a reason for the falling out, an event that could be talked over, atoned for. Anna could think of nothing she

172

had done that might possibly explain Kia's strange, withdrawn attitude, her unexplained departure that morning.

She turned into her street, and her heart jumped when she saw the familiar old Cadillac drawn up outside the apartment block. She almost ran the last ten metres along the sidewalk and up the steps to the second floor.

She let herself into the apartment, calling Kia's name.

She paused in the hall, composed herself. She told herself that she had to be tough. She could not let Kia see how damned relieved she was that she was back. Instead, she'd have it out with her lover, ask her what the hell was happening.

She moved into the lounge.

Kia was seated at Anna's computer console, which in itself was odd. Kia had once called Anna's computer a toy compared to the rigs she used at work.

'Kia?'

Stranger still was the fact that Kia was connected to the computer. A lead ran from a spar on the side of her skull, across the desk and into a port in the terminal. The screen flickered, scrolling with line after line of what looked like mathematical formulae.

'Kia, what the hell?'

Something made Anna loath to approach. Kia was slumped in the swivel chair, staring blindly at the screen with eyes that rolled from time to time to show their whites. The sight sent an electric surge of panic through Anna, paralysing her.

'Kia!'

As if in response to the sound of her name, Kia yanked the jack from her skull-port and stood unsteadily.

Close to tears, Anna ran forward and tried to assist her. 'Kia, what the hell's happening?'

Kia turned, pushed Anna's hand away, and stared at her with eyes that seemed devoid of the slightest recognition.

173

She stumbled down the corridor towards the door. Anna followed, pleading with Kia to stay and talk. 'You can't go out . . . You aren't well, Kia. Let me help you!'

When Anna touched her arm, Kia turned and lashed out, and the expression of venom on her face stopped Anna in her tracks. Unsteady on her feet, Kia hauled the front door open and disappeared down the steps.

Anna slumped against the wall, pressing fingers against her lips as if to stifle the sobs. At last she moved herself to give chase. She ran from the apartment and down the steps. She pulled open the ground-floor door and ran out into the freezing street.

Kia climbed into the Cadillac and gunned the engine. Anna ran to the side widow and hammered on the glass with the heel of her hand. 'Kia, Kia! You can't . . .'

The car surged, stalled, and then careered away from the sidewalk. Anna could only stand and watch the car disappear down the street, tears turning ice cold on her cheeks.

Ten

The alarm went off at midnight. Halliday lay on his back and stared up at the shaft of moonlight slanting through the frosted skylight.

He had slept solidly since midday without dreaming, something of a miracle considering the sights he'd witnessed that morning. He and Barney had stayed back at the ComStore while the tech attempted to decode the file that Sissi Nigeria had uploaded seconds before her death. The tech had come up with nothing. Barney had speculated that the file contained the information Wellman had hoped Nigeria would not divulge to rival firms. She had sent it to an unknown destination, though quite how and why she died was still a mystery.

Another shock that morning had been his meeting with Sue ... or rather Anna. He reached out and took her card from the bedside table, reading her new name. Anna Ellischild. Not only her name had changed, he reflected. Since he'd last seen her she had become a mellower, kinder person. He recalled Sue as she had been, bitter and guarded, seemingly always looking for the opportunity to rebuke him with cutting criticisms and observations. In five, six years she had grown up, matured, lost her anger and become a person he could easily come to like.

Eloise had turned up again while he'd sat talking to Anna. Out of the blue she had appeared at a table across the room, watching him and swinging her legs beneath

175

the table. At one point she had mimed the words, 'Ask her, Hal!'

So he'd steered the conversation around to the painful subject of the fire, but to his disappointment Anna could tell him not much more than he recalled himself. When he'd looked up to reprimand Eloise with a stare, she had vanished.

He yawned and stretched. The Nigeria case was closed and he was about to begin another shift. He wondered whether Barney had anything of interest on the files. A simple case of an absconding husband, perhaps.

'You 'wake, Hal?'

He turned and pulled the warm bundle of woman towards him. He located her face in the moonlight and kissed her lips. 'Mmm . . . when did you get in?'

''Round five. You were snoring. Didn't want to wake you. I crept in like a mouse.' She reached out, took the card from his fingers and read the name. 'Anna Ellischild? Who's that, Hal?'

'My sister.'

She stared at him. 'But you haven't seen her for years, Hal! Did she call round?'

He considered telling her that they had met yesterday, but he was dissuaded by the thought of trying to explain the complex emotions he had experienced in the bar.

He shook his head. 'She dropped the card off when I was out.' He pushed his face into her hair and inhaled. 'Ah, barbecue spiced pork, spare ribs, steamed noodles.'

'Hal! And I showered before coming to bed!'

'I'm not complaining. I haven't eaten since last night.'

'It was a nice meal,' Kim said. 'Should do that more often.'

'Fine by me. Look, I'm off at midday tomorrow. Why don't we meet here and go somewhere for lunch?'

'Hokay.' She watched him with big eyes beneath her straight-edged, schoolgirl's fringe. 'How's work, Hal?'

'Don't ask. Two people we were looking for turned up yesterday. Dead.'

'The lesbians? What happened?'

'I'd rather not talk about it . . .'

'They were killed by evil spirits, yes?' She stared at him crossly. 'I told you not to take that case! I told you about evil spirits!'

He laid a hand on her cheek, practically cupping her head. 'Kim, listen to me. They were found dead and we were informed, okay? I didn't want to get involved with the evil spirits, not after what you told me.'

She looked satisfied. 'I want you to look after yourself. Your job is dangerous enough, dealing with human beings. You don't want to deal with spirits, too.'

'Whatever you say.'

She shook her head, then reached out and stroked his face. 'We are so different, Hal. We do such different jobs. You see terrible things, and I feed people good food. I talk about everything with you, and you keep things hidden, inside here.' She knocked on his chest as if it were a door. 'Sometimes I wonder who you are, Mr Halliday. Who is in there?'

He stared at her. We forever make the mistake, he thought, of thinking that our words and actions allow others to know us as well as we think we know ourselves. Just the other day he was considering how much of an enigma Kim was, and now she was thinking the same of him.

'I don't know who I am, Kim. I'm the person who loves you. Isn't that enough?'

'Talk to me more, Hal. Tell me more about yourself.'

He wondered where this was leading. Please, he thought, not to another crying session.

He pulled her to him. 'What do you want me to tell you?'

'Tell me what you want for your birthday, for a start.'

He felt relieved. 'My birthday? When . . .?'

'In two weeks, at the end of January. It's your first birthday . . .'

'More like my thirty-fifth.'

'Your first birthday with me. I want to make it special. I'll surprise you, hokay?'

'I hate surprises. Let's plan something in advance. We'll go somewhere. I don't know . . . Where do you want to go?'

'It's your birthday, Hal. Where do *you* want to go?'

He smiled at her. 'I don't know. Anywhere. Somewhere warm.'

'VR – the beach in VR!'

He tried not to let his disappointment show. 'Only if you promise that you'll keep this body, Kim.' It was out before he could stop himself, and he hoped she didn't take it as a reason to start a fight.

To his relief, she laughed. 'Hokay, I'll keep this skinny boring little body if that's what you want.'

He inhaled her scent again. 'That's what I want.'

'Perhaps . . .' she said. 'Perhaps we could invite Anna round for a meal.'

He shrugged, uneasy. 'I don't know. We were never close.'

'Perhaps I could organise a party . . .' she said to herself.

He kissed her one last time. 'Whatever.' He glanced at the bedside clock. 'I'm late. I should've started at midnight.'

He dressed, then sat down on the futon, staring at the little of Kim that peeked over the thermal blanket. He brushed the fringe from her forehead. 'See you here at noon, okay?'

She waved fingers and then submerged herself beneath the blanket. He left the loft and made his way down to the office.

Barney was staring morosely at the desk-com. He grunted a greeting. Halliday sat down on the chesterfield, poured himself a coffee, and peered at the screen.

'The facts of the Nigeria-Villeux case, Hal. Can't seem to stop thinking about it.'

'I know what you mean. It just doesn't make sense. Why the hell did she do it?'

'Let's look at it logically. People kill other people, even their lovers. That's not what was so strange about this case. It wasn't a murder in the heat of the moment, after an argument. They met at ten – Nigeria in the guise of the Latino – then went up to the room where Nigeria coldbloodedly cut her lover into a dozen pieces.' He lifted a hand. 'It just doesn't make any kind of sense.'

'And before that, she attacked me in the guise of the Latino. This was someone described by all her friends as a gentle, generous, fun-loving girl.'

'Thing is, were all these connected? This stuff she uploaded to wherever, what had that to do with the killing and the attack on you? Okay, I can see where it might be linked with the attack. She was heavily into industrial espionage, and for all she knew you might have been investigating this, so she goes after you. But that doesn't explain the Villeux slaying.'

Halliday shrugged. 'Maybe Villeux knew about it, was trying to stop her?'

'Maybe.' Barney looked frustrated. 'Maybe a hundred and one damned things we haven't even guessed at yet.'

Halliday took a long swallow of bitter coffee.

'I saw Wellman yesterday, after I left you,' Barney went on. 'And that's something else that strikes me as kind of screwy.'

'What happened?'

'He's one hell of a smooth, self-satisfied little smarm-ball, with his cream suit and big house and pretty wife dancing in the background. I tell him about Nigeria, what she did to Villeux, what happened in the ComStore. He was sweating all the while. Did you notice last night how he sweats, Hal? Something wrong about a guy who sweats that much. So I tell him Nigeria uploaded a big file God knows where and he goes white and sweats even more. I ask him if he thinks the file was what I think, the information some other outfit wanted? He shakes his head, miles away. Then he tries to get rid of me. He says as far as he's concerned, we've kept our side of the bargain, thanks me for my time, hurriedly signs a cheque and shows me the door.'

'At least the bastard paid,' Halliday said.

Barney picked up the cheque from the desk. 'And well over the odds. I hadn't even made out a bill; he just wrote this and handed it over.'

Halliday took the cheque, whistled. 'Ten thousand dollars. Maybe he isn't that bad, after all.'

'But his reaction when I told him that Nigeria had uploaded a file. He didn't even ask me what kind of file, exactly how big it was, how it was encrypted, where it was sent to . . . nothing. Surely if he thought a rival was getting everything Nigeria had about Cyber-Tech's latest project, then he'd want to know all the details. But not a bit of it. It was here's the cheque and adios.'

'Beats me,' Halliday said.

Barney stood, shaking his head. 'That's me for another day. Catch you tomorrow.' He pushed open the door to his room.

Halliday was refreshing his coffee when the desk-com chimed with an incoming. He accepted the call and slipped into the swivel seat.

The screen flared and a thin face, all nose and Adam's

apple, blinked out at him. It was a second before he could place the face.

'Kosinski,' he said, and experienced a jolt of anticipation at the sight of the cyber-wizard.

At the sound of the name, Barney's head appeared around the door.

Off screen, Halliday waved him over. Barney hurried around the desk and stood to one side, looking down at the screen.

'Joe,' Halliday said. 'Good to see you. How can I help?'

Kosinski bobbed his head, nervous. 'I need to see you, Mr Halliday.'

Halliday nodded. To either side of Kosinski was a stack of computer hardware, and behind him a floor-to-ceiling window looking out over Lower Manhattan. In the distance Halliday glimpsed the twin towers of the World Trade Centre. 'Fine. Your place or mine?'

'Neither. It's too risky, Mr Halliday. We can't meet in the flesh. You don't know how dangerous the whole thing . . .' He ran a shaky hand through his fly-away hair. 'Nigeria and the other woman have died already.'

Halliday looked at Barney. He turned to the screen. 'How do you know about that, Joe?'

Kosinski gestured impatiently. 'Wellman told me. I called him a couple of hours ago.'

Halliday nodded. 'Why do you need to see me?'

'I can't tell you, not over this thing. It's not a secure network. If what I know got out, into the wrong hands . . .' He paused. 'Look, the entire computer system, the Net, you can't trust it, okay? The information you got on the Nigeria case – if it's on your com-files, it's not safe. I'd back it up, then wipe your files.'

'We don't know that much,' Halliday said. 'Anyway, who'd want to . . .?'

'You'll regret it if you don't!' Kosinski said. He stared out at Halliday with scared eyes. 'You have no idea how dangerous this is!'

Halliday said, 'Joe, we have all the latest anti-invasion software protecting our system . . .' The guy was obviously possessed of genius, but Halliday felt as if he were an adult talking to a kid.

Kosinski was shaking his head, almost frantically. 'Mr Halliday, you might be a good private eye, but quite frankly you know fuck-all about data security.'

'Okay, Joe. We'll do as you say.'

Kosinski nodded. 'Good, I'd feel better about that.'

Halliday glanced up at Barney. *'Where's he want to meet you?'* Barney whispered.

Halliday turned to the screen. 'Joe, you said you wanted to meet me. You tell me where, and I'll be there.'

Kosinski gave a frightened grin. 'Like I said, I can't tell you over this network.'

'Then how . . .?'

'There's a food-stall just outside your place – Chinese franchise.'

'You want to meet there?' It seemed improbable. Why didn't Kosinski come up to the office?

He was shaking his head. 'Hear me out. Kid called Casey works there. She's got an envelope for you. In it are instructions for meeting me. Follow them to the letter. Oh, and the envelope is coded . . .'

'What's the code, Joe?'

'Casey has that in a second envelope.'

'Okay.'

'The instructions'll lead you somewhere else, where you'll pick up another set. Eventually you'll find yourself at the meeting place.'

'Okay, I understand.'

'As a precaution, destroy each set of instructions as you

182

go, okay? This might seem like an elaborate charade, Mr Halliday, but I've got to ensure we aren't observed.'

'I understand what you're saying.'

'If you set off from your office at one, that'll give you enough time. And another thing, come alone. I don't want anyone following you. Not even your partner, Mr Kluger, got that? The fewer people know where you're going, the safer it is.'

'One thing,' Halliday said. 'Who are we trying to avoid?'

Kosinski hesitated, as if considering whether to tell Halliday. He shook his head, looked pained.

'Cyber-Tech's rivals, right? The people Nigeria sold the information to?'

'Mr Halliday, inter-company rivalry has nothing to do with this. It's much bigger than that. You wouldn't believe me if I told you, and I'm not going to do that now.' He reached out with a shaking hand to kill the screen, then halted. 'Mr Halliday, make sure you wipe this call, okay? I did my best to scramble it, but you never know . . . I'll see you later.' He cut the connection.

Halliday stared at the blank screen. He sat back in the swivel chair and let out a long sigh. Barney hitched himself onto the corner of the desk, side-saddle, his lips pursed in consideration.

'What the hell do you make of that, Hal?'

'I don't know whether to feel pleased the case is still open, or apprehensive. Something tells me that Joe Kosinski is shit-scared with good reason.'

'Do we trust him?'

Halliday shrugged. 'I see no reason not to, at least until we find out what he's got to tell us. I know I've only met him once, but I liked the guy. He might be a genius in his field with the IQ of Einstein, but I think I know where I stand with him.'

Barney frowned. 'About not being followed ... I'm uneasy about that.'

'I'll be in touch as soon as I find out where we're meeting.'

'While you're gone ...' Barney pulled a lugubrious expression as he stared down at the desk-com. 'You think I should copy everything on the Nigeria case and wipe the system?'

'I'd be tempted to go along with him.' Halliday swilled an inch of coffee around the bottom of his cup, swallowed it and stood up. 'Catch you later.'

'Take care, Hal. And remember to call when you know where you'll be.'

Halliday left the office and hurried down the steps and into the street, zipping his jacket against the icy wind. Even at this early hour, in the freezing cold, refugee kids were huddled around the food-stalls that lined both sides of the street. Fragrant steam hung in the air above the canopies, and the odour of cooking meat reminded Halliday that he was starving.

He crossed the street to the food-stall where Casey worked. She was warming her hands over a steaming wok, her pinched white face betraying her Southern white-trash origins.

'How's it going, Casey?'

'Hiya, Hal. Hey, some guy was around earlier, left something for you. Kind of important-looking envelopes. Here you go.'

He took the envelopes and ordered dim sum and chicken spring rolls. The package warmed his hands as he crossed to the Ford and started the engine. He piled the food on the passenger seat and switched on the overhead light.

The seal of the first silver envelope was numbered from one to ten. He opened the second envelope. On a single sheet of paper was a string of eight digits. He tapped the code into the seal of the first envelope and withdrew a sheet of hand-written scrawl.

Mr Halliday,

At one o'clock set off from your office. Head downtown on Park Avenue and turn down East 23rd. There's a bar on the corner of 23rd and Fifth Avenue called Connelly's. The black bartender with the silver head tattoos: I left another set of instructions with him. Tell him Joe sent you and he'll hand over a second sealed envelope. Same code. See you later.

Joe

Halliday opened the spring rolls and took a bite. He read the note again, then remembered Joe Kosinski's instructions. He ignited the car's lighter and set fire to the note, then opened the door and dropped the flaming sheet into the street.

He pulled away from the kerb and turned south, chewing on another spring roll and wondering what the hell Joe Kosinski was so frightened about. He considered the Nigeria case, the dissatisfaction he'd felt at its closure. Now, despite everything Kosinski had said about the danger, despite what he'd seen in the hotel bedroom yesterday, he felt good about being back on the case. His only qualm was that he was deceiving Kim.

Fifteen minutes later he turned onto East 23rd Street and stopped before the bar. A defective fluorescent shamrock stuttered in the window. Halliday crossed the sidewalk and pushed into the warmth. The bar was almost empty at this hour, but for dedicated drinkers seated at the bar watching West Coast football and skyball on the wallscreens.

He ordered a Caribas from a big black guy with silver face decals. 'Friend of Joe's. He left something for me earlier?'

'Sure, pal. Right here.'

Halliday took the beer and the silver envelope, identical to the first one, to a booth at the back of the bar. He swallowed a mouthful of beer and entered the code into the seal. He slipped out the note and laid it flat on the table-top.

Mr Halliday,

At one-thirty leave Connelly's and head crosstown to the Mantoni VR Bar, Chelsea, corner of West 23rd and Tenth Avenue. Pay for a one-hour ticket, go into any booth in the Bar and enter this into the site menu on the wallscreen: Himalayasite, 37aBRT. Tank at 1:45 and look for the shrine – you can't miss it. I'll be with you five minutes later. See you then.

Joe

He balled the note and slipped it into his pocket. The thought of entering VR again filled Halliday with a strange unease. He wondered if it had been his first trip into VR that had disturbed the ghost of Eloise in his mind, or if it would have surfaced to haunt him in the natural course of events. If the former, then he wondered what new ghosts might be raised by his next immersion in the tank.

At one-thirty he finished his beer and left the bar. He remembered to burn the second note, and then drove along West 23rd to Chelsea.

The Mantoni VR Bar wore the holo-façade of a fairy-tale castle, its spun-ice confection incongruous beside the red-brick expanse of an old meat warehouse. It was a smaller concern than the Park Avenue Bar, with only a short queue of customers lining the sidewalk. Halliday parked up and took his place in line, looking around for Joe Kosinski. There was no sign of the Cyber-Tech vice-chairman.

Five minutes later he reached reception and paid two hundred dollars for a one-hour ticket, as instructed. He

186

passed into the waiting room and a red-uniformed hostess escorted him to a single booth.

He stared at the jellytank in the centre of the small tiled room, a coffin-shaped glass-sided box filled with disgusting brown gloop, like some kind of futuristic catafalque. The unpleasant act of immersing himself in the stuff seemed counter to the promise of the wonders on offer. He touched the wallscreen and entered the code into the site menu. He selected to keep his own body and clothing.

Before he undressed, he got through to Barney.

'Hal, where are you?'

'In the Mantoni VR Bar, Chelsea. I'm meeting Kosinski in VR, of all places. I've bought a one-hour ticket. I'll call as soon as I'm out, no later than three, okay?'

'Talk to you then, Hal.'

At one forty-five he undressed and piled his clothing in a storage unit. He attached the leads and face-plate, then stepped into the warm jelly. He sat down, feeling the stuff slide around his body with an unpleasant, invasive intimacy. He lay back, and experienced a thirty-second period during which he gradually became deprived of his senses. He seemed to be floating, bodiless – with a wonderful feeling of calm and well-being – and then awareness hit him in a rush and, unbelievably, he was no longer in the jellytank.

He was standing on a sunlit, upland meadow, a brilliant green sweep of land rising to a distant range of mountains. The sight of the rearing massifs took his breath away. To take in their entirety he was forced to tilt back his head. Their summits towered above him with an intimidating, impersonal grandeur, clad with snow so blindingly white it shone with a heavenly effulgence.

He reminded himself that these were not actually the Himalayas, but some clever neural hallucination.

He looked around for the shrine Kosinski had mentioned. Below, a dizzying sweep of valleys stretched away for as far as the eye could see, threaded with the silver filaments of rivers and patched with the brilliant green squares and rectangles of fields under cultivation.

Up the incline, beside a stand of pine, was a small stone-built shrine topped with a terracotta-tiled roof. Halliday made his way towards it. He marvelled at how natural it felt to be inhabiting what seemed to be his own body. He climbed the hillside, feeling the play of the muscles in his legs, a warm breeze on his skin.

Beneath the shrine sat a stone-carved effigy of Buddha, in the lotus position.

He looked around for any sign of Kosinski. He alone seemed to inhabit this virtual Shangri-La. In the distance, he made out individual yaks cropping the grass, and the occasional twist of smoke rising from huts down the valley.

It was a few minutes before he became aware of the monastery. He was staring up at the ramparts of the mountain to his left when he saw, built up in a vertical extension of the cliff-face itself, the sheer walls of a fortress-like structure topped with a dozen peaked, tiled roofs on various levels.

'Impressive, isn't it?'

He turned. Joe Kosinski advanced from the trees, but a Kosinski much altered from the nervous, awkward young man Halliday had met in New York.

He was garbed in the maroon robes of a Mahayana Buddhist monk, and his head was shaven, the absence of hair emphasising the size of his nose and his Adam's apple. He appeared calmer in virtual reality, as if he'd left his nervous energy along with his Western apparel back in the real world.

'Every week I go to the lamasery on retreat, to meditate, take lessons, Mr Halliday.'

'Hal, okay? Call me Hal.'

The Buddhist monk nodded. He gestured around him at the sloping verdant meadow, the mountains and the sweeping valleys. 'What do you think?'

Halliday shook his head. 'It's overwhelming, the whole experience. I'm at a loss for words. I don't understand the technology behind it, so it seems to me like magic.' He looked at Kosinski. He thought about what had happened on the beach, and the subsequent appearances of Eloise. 'But things can go wrong,' he said.

'Meaning?'

He told Kosinski about the hallucinations.

'Ah, you're talking about accidental engram retrieval.'

Halliday smiled to himself. 'I might be . . . if I knew what that meant. The other day, on the VR beach, something seemed to explode in my head. I felt a sudden, terrible depression.'

Kosinski was nodding. 'The hallucinations go away, in time. You see, the virtual experience works by directly activating the brain's signalling fibres, or axons, and thus simulating synaptic function. Virtual reality isn't somehow beamed into the eyes and conducted through the skin, as some people think – it's a direct program-cerebral link. Occasionally, glitches in the program – infinitesimal errors of computing – can lead to the decoding of engrams, or buried or suppressed memories. In exceptional cases, these result in hallucinations back in the real world.'

'But you said they'd go away?'

'The recorded cases so far have never lasted more than a few days.'

Kosinski gestured towards the shrine. They climbed three steps and sat on a timber bench in the shade. Halliday stared down the mountainside towards the distant, rucked valleys and mist-shrouded flatlands.

'Why the Mantoni VR Bar,' Halliday asked, 'and not one of Cyber-Tech's?'

Kosinski sighed. 'That brings us to why we're here, Hal. You see, the Mantoni system is closed. As far as I can ensure, it's safe from infiltration, invasion. We can be assured of absolute secrecy in here, secrecy we couldn't guarantee out there in the real world. We could have met in the most remote region of upstate New York, but we might have been overheard.'

'Are you in this Bar? I didn't see you . . .'

The Buddhist monk smiled. 'I'm in my own tank, in a safe house.'

'Then how are you linked to the Mantoni VR world?'

Kosinski smiled, minimally. 'Highly illegally, is how,' he said. 'I manufactured the link myself when I went into hiding. I'd rather use the Mantoni VR system to meet you than Cyber-Tech's. You see, Cyber-Tech have links everywhere. We wouldn't be safe in any Cyber-Tech VR site.'

Halliday shrugged. 'Safe from who, Joe?'

For the first time, Kosinski manifested some of his old uneasiness. He bobbed his head in a quick, nervous gesture, briefly avoided Halliday's gaze. 'You wouldn't believe me if I came straight out with it, Hal. I'll have to begin at the beginning, work up slowly to what all this is about. You see, sometimes the truth is too much.'

Halliday lodged a foot on the bench and embraced his leg, watching Kosinski as the monk gathered his thoughts.

'It started about five years ago, in the early days when we were experimenting with the fundamentals of virtual reality. One of the big difficulties we faced was the sheer mass of information, the data, required to generate a convincing simulated reality: the computing power alone is breathtakingly phenomenal. Stated simply, we needed an operating network capable of unifying the programming and the technological hardware in an integrated system. We came up with something we called, for want of anything better, the Linked Integrated Nexus: scientists love acronyms, Hal. LINx was a series of supercomputers processing in parallel, learning to reprogram and reconfigure itself exponentially. The great thing about it was that it worked. It allowed us to build a prototype virtual reality site at least three or four years ahead of our rivals. It was nothing like this, of course, but it was a start.'

'So far, so good.'

'Yeah, so far . . .' Kosinski nodded. 'I had a great team up at Cyber-Tech. I was just twenty, technically still majoring in computational theory at MIT. I'd started Cyber-Tech in my spare time, not realising it'd take off as it did.' Kosinski stopped there and stared down the mountainside.

'What happened, Joe?'

'LINx worked well. We added to it. We had a vision of what we wanted VR to become, and to achieve this we had to have bigger and better versions of LINx. It was an amazing tool. It was like working with one of the greatest multi-disciplinary minds on the planet, except, of course, it wasn't really a mind, just a vast com-network. It helped us solve a series of problems, could suggest new avenues of approach, other angles from which to view theoretical situations. Then it came up with the prototype of the Nano-Cerebral Interface. LINx reasoned that for its programmers to work more successfully with its integrated logic systems, a direct machine-mind link would be necessary. Three years ago my design team came up with the first NCI. A colleague called Dan Reeves volunteered for the implant, and it proved a great success. Over the months it was superseded by improved models and Dan underwent a series of operations to have the latest versions fitted, each time with better results. Last year we fitted Sissi Nigeria with the very latest, state-of-the-art unit. It was with the aid of this and LINx that Cyber-Tech was able to steal a march on its competitors and open our VR Bars way before any of the other outfits were anywhere near ready. It made the directors of the company, and all our shareholders, multi-millionaires overnight, and all because of a suggestion made by LINx during a routine ideas-session three years ago.' He smiled to himself. 'Thing was, LINx was all for having every tech in the place fitted with an interface. But we thought it wise to proceed with caution. It was still a relatively new technology, after all.'

Kosinski paused there. Halliday thought he saw where this was leading. It had nothing to do with Nigeria's selling top secret information to rivals: Joe had already told him that inter-company espionage was not what this was about. It was much simpler. The nano-cerebral link with which Nigeria had been fitted had malfunctioned, affected her reasoning, her interface with reality. It would explain the senseless violence, maybe even her own death.

'Joe, did the cerebral units go wrong, send Nigeria mad?'

Kosinski stared at Halliday, then smiled. 'Hal, if it were as simple as that I'd be a happy man.'

'Then what?'

Kosinski rearranged the robes over his shoulder. 'About three months ago, we noticed that a sizeable chunk of data was missing from LINx's memory banks. There was an empty space where it should have been. At first we suspected espionage: some rival company had hacked into the system and leached the data, but when we ran invasion checks we found that nothing like this had happened. Then we suspected in-house treachery: someone employed by Cyber-Tech had somehow stolen the data. But, again, we came up with a big fat blank. There was just no way that anyone could have done this without setting off a thousand and one alarm bells.

'At the same time as this was ongoing, my senior research team and I were developing programs dealing with a self-aware, decision-making, artificial intelligence – SADMAI – but the project started backfiring. Positive results that we had been getting now came back negative, and we explored avenues of research that turned out to be blind alleys.

'Then, just last week, a junior technician in the lab came up with something. He discovered corrupted files on Nigeria's and Reeves' work-stations, files they had tried to delete without consultation, which is against team policy. So we retrieved them and found notes and formulae linked to something allied to the SADMAI project. We assumed that Nigeria and Reeves had been conducting their own, private, research program. We did some more investigating and found that they had logged unauthorised access to LINx over the course of the past few months. It occurred to me that the data missing from LINx might have been downloaded into Reeves' and Nigeria's NCIs, something we'd never even thought of checking at the time, it was so improbable. We investigated, and guess what?'

'It'd been downloaded into their units?'

He nodded. 'That's what happened, Hal.'

'So they were committing industrial espionage?'

Kosinski shook his head. 'I told you earlier that this had nothing to do with anything as minor as that.'

Halliday recalled what Wellman had said the other night about the potential catastrophe of industrial espionage to the fortunes of Cyber-Tech, and tried to square this with what Kosinski had just told him about it being a *minor* event.

'The day we made this discovery,' Kosinski went on, 'Nigeria and Reeves disappeared. I broke the news to Wellman, and, of course, the first thing we suspected was espionage. It was the natural assumption. But the wrong one.'

'Go on.'

'When we found the deleted files in the work-stations, I put a team on working out how much Nigeria and Reeves had known about the SADMAI project. The team came up with a disturbing fact: the information concerning artificial intelligence that Nigeria had tried to delete could not have been developed by Nigeria or Reeves, as it was written in a code neither of them – or their cranial implant – was familiar with.'

'But it was discovered on their work-stations.'

'That's right, but remember, they'd logged unauthorised access to LINx.'

'I don't understand.'

'Think about it, Hal. If Nigeria and Reeves had nothing to do with the data about artificial intelligence . . .'

Kosinski stared at Halliday until the penny dropped.

'Christ,' Halliday said. 'You don't mean . . . LINx?'

'It was the only answer we could come up with. LINx had been growing without our knowledge, developing itself and planning strategy. Of course, it had used Reeves and Nigeria as pawns in its game: it had suggested the use of nano-cerebral interfaces, remember? When it achieved self-awareness, it moved that part of its memory from the data banks, which was why we couldn't find the data. I have no idea where it stored itself – somewhere on the Net. Then, when it realised that we'd discovered the missing data, and were onto Nigeria and Reeves, it downloaded itself – or rather, a part of itself – into Nigeria's implant, effectively taking control of her.'

Halliday stared at the image of the Buddhist monk and wondered whether he should believe what he was hearing.

At last he said, 'But . . . but why did Nigeria allow it to use her? Why did she allow LINx to download itself into her cranial implant?'

'She'd had the implant a year,' Kosinski replied. 'She'd interfaced with LINx on many occasions. We can only speculate that LINx implanted a small part of itself in her NCI, or maybe some kind of command, very early on.

Effectively, Nigeria had been under LINx's control for as long as she'd had the implant. The same goes for Reeves.'

Halliday stood up and stepped from the shrine. A warm wind played on his face, and from far away he heard the sound of a bell slowly tolling.

He turned to Kosinski. 'Do you have any hard, concrete evidence for any of this? It sounds . . .'

'I know, it sounds impossible. A year ago, I would never have believed it. Evidence? I have files back at Cyber-Tech, a few at the safe house. They wouldn't mean much to you. More conclusive evidence is what happened to Sissi Nigeria yesterday.'

Halliday returned to the bench and sat down. 'Go back a few days. I was investigating Nigeria's disappearance. I went to her apartment, found a computer console destroyed.'

'That was probably to get rid of incriminating evidence that she had accessed LINx from home. She – or rather LINx – probably wasn't aware at that time that we had evidence at Cyber-Tech.'

'Then she attacked me, in the disguise of a Latino killer. Almost damned near *did* kill me . . .'

'*She* didn't attack you, Hal. That was LINx. We're dealing with an artificial intelligence here. It has no conscience. It possesses knowledge, and the desire to add to that knowledge at whatever cost. It's a survival mechanism.'

He wondered why LINx had deemed it necessary to kill Carrie Villeux. He recalled what Anna had told him in the bar yesterday, that Carrie thought that Sissi Nigeria was acting oddly, was not herself. Obviously, LINx had considered Villeux enough of a threat to warrant her death.

'It killed Carrie Villeux yesterday,' he said. 'And then it had Nigeria interface with a computer terminal in Com-Store, uploaded itself somewhere . . .'

'And then downloaded a microwave packet straight into Nigeria's interface, killing her instantly.'

Halliday shook his head. 'But why did it kill its host, Sissi Nigeria?'

Kosinski gestured. 'The police were onto Nigeria and LINx didn't want the authorities, or Cyber-Tech, getting hold of Nigeria's interface intact.'

'Christ,' Halliday whispered. 'Is there any way you can trace it, track it to its . . .' He shook his head, almost laughed at what he had been about to say. *Its lair* . . . As if it were some wild and ravenous beast, which would kill at every opportunity, savagely and without mercy.

'Track it to wherever it is that it's hiding?' Kosinski finished for him. 'The Net is a big place, Hal. It could be anywhere. It doesn't need that massive a data-dump to store itself, either. You see, it can divide itself *ad infinitum*, find a cache in a million locations from Azerbaijan to Zaire, and assemble itself almost instantaneously.' He paused. 'But I'm working on it. I have its signature, you see. I'm writing a program that can work out the code it uses to cover its traces. I reckon I'm nearly there. One day, maybe two . . .'

'And once you locate it?'

'Then I'll be able to kill it, Hal. I created it, after all, and I have the technology to eradicate it, and any copies that it might make of itself.'

'And until then, it's free to roam?'

Kosinski nodded. 'It's free to do whatever it damn well pleases.'

'Can't you – I don't know – can't you just shut down parts of the Net?'

Kosinski laughed. 'And bring the world to its knees? It'd be impossible. You don't know how much everything relies on computer networks.'

Something had occurred to Halliday. 'What does it want,

Joe? I mean, if all it wants is survival, then we have nothing to fear. Perhaps it really is like a wild animal. It'll fight only to ensure its own survival. Left to itself, it'll live peaceably.'

'That occurred to me, Hal, but the danger is not so much what it wants – which we have no way of determining, anyway – but what other people, other governments, might want from it. It's a potentially massive tool in any country's armament. In terms of computing power alone, it's staggering, but LINx has the ability to reason, to rationalise, to make decisions, even to grow.'

'You almost make it sound like some kind of god.'

'Well, depending on your definition of a god . . .'

Halliday stared at Kosinski. 'You said you'll have the killer-program ready in a day or two?'

Kosinski nodded. 'I'm restricted because I don't have access to Cyber-Tech HQ, where my work-station is.'

'You think . . .?'

Kosinski nodded. 'LINx knows I'm onto it. It knows I have the capability to eradicate it – it's already killed to ensure its survival, and it would kill again.' He smiled. 'You ever heard of Frankenstein's monster? Well, this beast is just a little more fearsome. If I so much as show myself, it'll have me. I'm holed up in the safe house, now, working round the clock.'

'But you called us via the communications network earlier.'

Kosinski laughed. 'What do you take me for, Hal? The background of the apartment I was in, the view of the World Trade Centre, it was a holo-projection, just in case. I used a scrambler to kill any trace-signature on the call, too.'

He paused, looking at Halliday. 'The reason I called you, Hal, is that I need your help. You see, the program I'm writing will eradicate LINx, but before then there's Dan

197

Reeves at large, or rather LINx in the guise of Reeves. He's the second and last person on the planet who LINx can manipulate: get Reeves out of the way, and we've confined LINx to the Net. My guess is that when LINx uploaded from Nigeria, it downloaded itself into Reeves' NCI. LINx knows I'm onto it and wants me dead before I succeed, and the only sure way it can kill me is through Reeves.'

'What can I do, Joe?'

'I have an idea. It might be dangerous, but then you and Kluger are in that line of work anyway, so I thought you might not balk at a little risk.'

'Go on.'

'You contact Wellman while he's at Cyber-Tech. You drop some information, more or less saying where I'm holed up, except, of course, I'll be nowhere near there. You stake out the place and take Reeves when he shows. That'll be LINx's representative on Earth sorted out. All that'll remain then is to scour it out of the Net for good.'

'You sure there's no one else LINx has downloaded itself into?'

'Nigeria and Reeves were the only people at Cyber-Tech to be implanted with the interface. You understand now why LINx wanted more techs to be fitted with the interfaces? Thank Christ we thought to restrict the surgery to Reeves and Nigeria.' He paused. 'And I'm pretty sure that none of our competitors have the technology or know-how.' He looked at Halliday. 'So . . . are you up for it?'

Halliday nodded. 'In principle. Of course I'll have to see what Barney thinks, talk it over.'

'If you do decide to go ahead with it, go and see Wellman. He might come over as an insufferable asshole, but he's okay at heart. Tell him what I've told you about the plan. I can't risk contacting him over the com-net with that information. He'll be able to help you out in terms of expenses. You'll need a chu. LINx has seen you once and would recognise you again. Wellman will equip you with one. Also, he'll be able to hire a neuro-surgeon to operate on Reeves and excise the implant.'

'You want Reeves taken alive?'

Kosinski looked at him. 'If possible, Hal. He's a good man. Remember, he had no choice in the matter. He's been used against his will. Don't worry. The man you're up against might be governed by a machine intelligence, but physically he's no stronger than he would be normally.'

Halliday nodded. 'I know that. It's just the thought of not succeeding and Reeves – or rather LINx – getting away. I've seen the damage Nigeria did with the cutter. I don't like the idea of failing to nail Reeves.'

The Buddhist monk looked at Halliday, his expression stern. 'If you can't take him alive, then . . . for the sake of anyone who might get in his way in the future, it might be better if he were dead.'

Halliday nodded. 'How do I contact you?'

'You don't. I'll contact you. Whether you decide to help or not, get in touch with Wellman and inform him of your decision.'

'I'll do that.' Halliday stood and stepped from the shrine. He stared down the mountainside, a part of him still finding it hard to accept that this was no more than an incredibly complex computer-generated image.

Kosinski joined him. He smiled. 'With luck, when all this is over, we'll be able to meet again in the flesh.'

'I'll look forward to that, Joe.' He paused, considering everything Kosinski had told him.

'Where's all this leading to, Joe? I mean, the AIs. If this one is any indication of how they'll behave in future . . .'

Joe was shaking his head. 'I don't think it is,' he said. 'What is happening with LINx, the killings, is just an unfortunate aberration. At least, I hope so. I mean, the

199

development of AIs is inevitable. The sixty-four-thousand-dollar question is, who will do the developing? Such power in the wrong hands, as I've said, could be catastrophic. Also, there's the very real danger of them developing themselves – but I'd rather not dwell on that, Hal.' He smiled. 'It's time I wasn't here.'

The Buddhist monk raised his hand, touched the base of his index finger. 'See you around.'

Joe Kosinski vanished. One second he was standing beside Halliday, and then he was gone, edited from the scene of the mountain pasture in an instant.

Halliday turned his hand, looked at the circular indicator. Only a sliver of crimson remained, signifying that he had spent almost an hour in the jellytank. He took one last look around the mountain paradise, then touched the circle.

The Himalayan idyll disappeared. He was floating, without bodily sensation. Gradually, his senses returned and he sat up, blinking through the faceplate at the stark reality of the white-tiled booth. It was as if the Himalayan site, and what he had experienced there, had been no more than a dream.

He showered quickly, dressed, then contacted Barney.

'Hal? How'd it go? You meet him okay?'

'We met, Barney. I can't talk now, okay? I'll tell you about it when I get back.'

'Sure . . .' Barney sounded concerned. 'You okay, Hal?'

'I'm fine. See you soon, Barney.'

He left the VR Bar and drove along West 23rd to Madison, then turned uptown, driving slowly. The streets were deserted but for the occasional cop car and yellow cab, but the sidewalks were packed with humanity. Enterprising refugees had constructed makeshift tents from scrap sheets of polycarbon; here and there they had started fires to ward off the sub-zero temperature.

Halliday wondered how the hell those without fires managed to survive the night. Even in the car, his breath plumed. He turned the heater to full and sat back, going over what Kosinski had told him.

The abrupt conclusion of the Nigeria case had troubled him, earlier. There had been no sense of closure, no satisfactory explanation of motivation. He had wanted to know more, the 'why' behind the seemingly random acts of violence.

Well, now he did know more, and a part of him wished that he were still in ignorance.

He smiled as he thought of what Kim had said about the case two or three days ago, that the person who had attacked him on the rooftop had been possessed by an evil spirit. Perhaps not possessed by an evil spirit, he thought, but certainly *possessed*. Kim would probably claim that it was one and the same thing.

Ten minutes later, he pulled up outside the Chinese laundry and sat in the warmth of the car for a long minute. The sight of all the steaming food-stalls, stretching down either side of the road, the bright neon signs in meaningless Chinese, were reassuring in their familiarity. When he opened the car door, the cries of the street traders hit him in a barrage, along with the aroma of cooked food. He pushed his way through the crowded sidewalk and up the steps to the office.

Barney looked up when he entered. He misinterpreted Halliday's expression. 'Don't tell me, the kid was full of hot air, right? The case is still closed?'

Halliday poured himself a coffee. 'Case is back open, Barney. If we want it.' He sat on the chesterfield and warmed himself before the puttering fire.

'What did Kosinski say?'

Halliday looked up at Barney. 'You're not going to believe this, Barney. I'm not sure I know what to think,

201

either.' He stopped, looked around. 'The com isn't activated, is it?'

'No – it's switched off.' Barney stared at him. 'Hal, what
the hell . . .'

'It's okay. I'm probably being paranoid.' He shook his
head. 'This is what Joe told me.'

He tried to report the conversation as he recalled it, first
easing Barney into accepting the idea of artificial intelligence, explaining about Nigeria's implant, and then detail-
ing Kosinski's work with LINx.

'You're trying to tell me,' Barney began, leaning forward
on the swivel chair so that his gut bulged, 'that Nigeria
was controlled by the artificial intelligence, and that it's
still out there?'

'That's about the size of it, Barney. There's a guy called
Reeves, he was implanted like Nigeria.' He went through
what Kosinski had explained, the plan to lure Reeves.

Barney sat in silence for a long time when Halliday had
finished. At last he said, 'What do you think, Hal?'

Halliday shrugged. 'If we can capture Reeves, then we've
eliminated the danger that LINx presents when in control
of a human. It'll still exist in the Net, but that's Kosinski's
baby, then. We'll have done our bit.'

Barney nodded. 'It won't be easy, Hal. You saw what
Nigeria did. Armed, and with a chu . . . Christ, it was
difficult enough when we were dealing with a human.
Now that we know we're up against an artificial intelligence . . .' He looked at Halliday. 'It's not a walk in the
park.'

'So, do we do it?'

Barney considered. 'We'll go see Wellman, find out what
he thinks. It's a hard one to walk away from, Hal. I'll
contact him, tell him we're on our way.'

Halliday reached out, stayed Barney's hand as it went for
the com. 'It'd be safer if we arrived cold. For all we know,

202

LINx might be monitoring all calls into Wellman.' He shrugged. 'I don't know. Maybe I'm being paranoid, but it's best not to take risks.'

As they left the office, Halliday wondered if there was any way LINx might possibly have discovered that he and Barney were linked to the case.

Barney eased the Ford from the kerb and headed north. He glanced across at Halliday. 'What is it?'

'Probably nothing. I was just wondering . . .' He told Barney what he'd been thinking, trying to work out if he were seeing danger where none really existed.

Barney peered through the windscreen into the darkness. 'LINx in the guise of Nigeria, in the guise of the Latino . . . when it attacked you the other night, that was the only contact you had with it, right? And as far as it was aware, it left you for dead. Far as I can make out, we're okay.'

'I'm not so sure, Barney. What if it's been monitoring the calls we made to Jeff Simmons? What if it intercepted the report I made for Jeff on the Nigeria case the other day? And then there was the day we called on Kosinski at Cyber-Tech . . . For all we know it could've been watching our arrival through the company's security cameras . . .' He stopped there. 'Jesus Christ, what if it can hack into the police traffic surveillance cameras? I mean, we can do it, so I'm damned sure it's a piece of cake for LINx.'

'Well, we're okay tonight, at least. Wellman's place is way off the beaten track.'

Halliday felt his scalp prickle at the thought that, even now, LINx might be monitoring their progress via the surveillance cameras as they drove out of town.

'How do we know it isn't linked to satellites, Barney?' Halliday said.

Barney turned and stared. 'Let's just hope you're being a hopelessly paranoid bastard,' he said.

One hour later they turned onto the track leading up to

Wellman's country house. It was still an hour until dawn, and overhead the stars sparkled with frosty brilliance. They were matched, ahead, by the perimeter fence lights.

In the drive, Halliday made out a white van bearing the familiar logo of a freelance security team. He saw armed guards patrolling the fence.

Barney grunted. 'Good to see he's improved his security since last time.'

He braked before the gate and half a dozen heavily-armed guards, outfitted in military camouflage, deployed themselves behind the mesh fence and levelled weapons. Halliday climbed from the car, arms raised, and approached the gate.

'Kruger and Halliday,' he said to an older guy with sergeant's stripes. 'We work for Wellman. We need to see him.'

He passed his identity card through the gate, and one of the guards edged forward cautiously and took it. The guard passed it to the sergeant, who turned away and spoke hurriedly into his com. A minute later a light appeared in the villa.

The sergeant looked from the picture on the card to Halliday, then nodded. He signalled for a guard to open the gate and gestured Barney through. Halliday climbed back into the car and they drove up the drive and stopped before the steps leading up to the double front door.

Halliday climbed out. The door opened, and yet another guard showed them through the hall and into the room where they'd met Wellman a couple of days before.

Two minutes later Wellman appeared, knotting the belt of a royal blue dressing gown. Even roused from sleep, he managed to maintain an air of groomed sophistication.

'Gentlemen, sit down. I take it you've had word from Joseph?'

'I met Joe in VR,' Halliday said. 'He filled me in.'

Barney said, 'You knew about LINx all along, Wellman . . .'

'Of course,' Wellman admitted, 'but how could I divulge something of that magnitude to a couple of private investigators I didn't know from Adam? Joseph has only just filled me in on the extent of LINx's activities, however. They far exceed my gravest fears.'

'Do you think you're personally in danger?' Barney asked.

'I honestly don't know, Mr Kluger. I'm technically the head of Cyber-Tech, and LINx must know that I'm aware of what's going on . . . so I'm taking no chances.'

'Did Joe tell you about Reeves?' Halliday asked.

'He mentioned that Reeves was augmented with an implant similar to Nigeria's.'

'But he didn't tell you how he planned to apprehend Reeves?'

'He was extremely reluctant to divulge anything in detail over the com.'

Halliday nodded. 'Do you think LINx might be monitoring incoming calls to Cyber-Tech's HQ?' he asked.

'And a thousand other calls besides, I've no doubt.'

Halliday looked at Barney. To Wellman he said, 'Joe had an idea how we might apprehend Reeves. It'd involve either me or Barney contacting you at Cyber-Tech HQ and giving away Joe's supposed whereabouts. Then we stake the place and wait for Reeves to show . . . Trouble is, if we're too obvious about giving away where he is, LINx will suspect something. But if we're too subtle, it might not take the bait.'

Wellman nodded, considering. 'Very well, gentlemen. I think I know how we might go about this.'

Halliday felt something lurch within him, a kick of

primal fear, as he realised that now there was no turning back.

They talked, and outside another cold winter's day dawned over the blighted landscape.

Eleven

Halliday checked the loft, but Kim had not returned.

He made his way down to the street. It was midday, the time they had arranged to meet and go for a meal. He crossed the sidewalk and leaned into the car window. 'She's not there. I'll leave a note, tell her I'll be back tonight.'

Barney looked at his watch. 'We don't have to meet Wellman till one. Might as well hang on.'

Halliday nodded and stood up, looking up and down the street. A police drone sped along at head height, its dome flashing red with a security alert, followed by a posse of screaming kids. The sidewalk was packed with pedestrians, bundled up and hunched against the cold north wind. He dug his fists deep into the pockets of his jacket and cursed the cold. He was impatient to be away; the sooner they met Wellman, arranged the details of the ambush, the sooner he would be back with Kim, making up for not being able to meet her for lunch.

The canister of freeze was a cold weight in the inner pocket of his jacket. For the first time in weeks, Barney had broken out the bullet-proof jackets, in anticipation of the ambush, and the form-fitting armour clasped Halliday's torso like a beetle's carapace.

'Hal!' Kim called out.

She skipped the last few metres towards him, resplendent in her primrose climbing jacket. She hugged him, rocking from foot to foot like a toy robot. 'Hal, where are we going?

How about the Vietnamese place down the block, or there's . . .' She stopped and pulled away. 'Hal, what's wrong?'

'I can't make it, Kim. Something's come up.'

'But you promised!'

'I know I did. You think I'd rather work? Something big's come up and I can't get away.'

Kim looked across at Barney in the car, entreaty in her expression.

Barney gave a *life's-tough* shrug. 'That's how it goes, sweetheart.'

'I'm sorry, Kim.'

She hugged him. 'Hokay, Hal. How about tonight, then?'

'I'll call. I'll try to make it tonight, okay?'

He kissed her and ducked into the car. As they pulled away from the kerb, he looked back. She was a small figure standing on the edge of the sidewalk, folding a small gloved hand in a wave of pantomime self-pity.

They made the drive downtown in silence. The sky was blue and a winter sun was out, reflected in a blinding dazzle from the million windows of the city's skyscrapers.

He reviewed what lay ahead. In theory, the task of apprehending and disabling Dan Reeves did not seem that difficult. If he showed, then to restrain him with freeze before he could put up a fight, injuring or killing his assailants, should prove to be a routine operation. Why then was he filled with a nebulous and nagging apprehension?

If Reeves showed, that was . . . Of course, LINx might not fall for the bait, and then they would be back to square one.

Barney parked the car in Little Italy, down a sidestreet where they knew no traffic surveillance cameras were positioned. They took a cab down to Battery Park, Halliday looking out for the office block where Cyber-Tech had its city research establishment.

The skyscraper overlooked the grey water of the Hudson, a fifty-storey obelisk with jet-black windows like a strip of under-exposed negatives. They took the elevator up to the fortieth floor, watched by a surveillance camera in the corner of the lift. Even though Wellman had earlier assured them that he had had every camera in the building disabled, Halliday felt as if he were being observed by the ubiquitous presence of LINx. He wondered if the artificial intelligence could take control of the elevator itself.

They passed through stringent security checks and were allowed at last into the open-plan floorspace of the Cyber-Tech suite. It was much as Halliday recalled the shop-floor at the headquarters up in Westchester: rows of desks with technicians working away at computer screens, the occasional larger screens surrounded by teams of two or three scientists.

Wellman, dressed today in a sharp navy blue suit, ushered them into an adjoining room almost as large as the first. In this one, though, only three technicians worked, hovering around a flatscreen on a desk beside the floor-to-ceiling window.

He closed the door behind them and spoke in a hushed voice. 'A change of plan. The Westchester HQ has been closed down.'

Halliday stared at him. 'Closed down?'

'We think – we assume – LINx did it. The power supply has been cut, and the emergency back-up is down. Also, a number of computers have gone haywire. I've sent the staff home.' He paused. 'It'd look suspicious if I were to go up there and take the call from Joseph.'

'What's the alternative?' Barney asked.

'I'll take it here.'

'But what if LINx isn't monitoring incoming calls?' Barney said.

Wellman cocked a perfectly manicured eyebrow, angled like a French grammatical accent. 'We can only hope that it is. The chances are that it's monitoring everything that's going on in every Cyber-Tech property across America.'

Halliday gestured to where the techs were working on the flatscreen. 'I just hope it isn't monitoring this.'

'Don't worry. The room is sealed.'

'How's it going?' Barney asked.

'We've almost finished. I'll give you a demonstration.'

They crossed the room and Wellman spoke to one of the technicians, who played his fingers across the touchpad on a com-terminal. The flatscreen flared, settled into the image of Joe Kosinski, staring out at them with his habitual air of fidgety nervousness. 'Hi, Wellman.'

For a second, Halliday thought that this actually was Kosinski, live.

Then Joe Kosinski said. 'It's okay, it's encrypted . . .' He waited a few seconds. 'Sure I'm sure. It's safe.'

Another pause. 'It's going okay. I'm working on it.' Joe stared from the screen, nodding.

'That's right, I know. I'm pretty confident I can rig something up.'

Kosinski moved out of the picture briefly, returned holding a needle. 'This is the little beauty. What do you think?' Another, longer pause. Joe listened, nodding from time to time. 'Okay, yeah. Take care. I'll catch you later.'

Joe reached out and the screen blanked.

'A simple computer-generated image,' Wellman said. 'We'll set it up in Joseph's supposed safe house, positioned before a com-screen's camera. I'll take the call here, say my lines, and it will appear as natural as if Joe is really calling in.'

'LINx won't rumble it?' Halliday asked.

Wellman shook his head, lips pursed seriously. 'There's no way it could tell that this electronic image of Joseph is not the real thing. It'll be filtered through a com-screen, remember.'

'Won't it be suspicious when a call from Kosinski comes in here, unencrypted?' Barney objected.

'We've thought of that. The technicians have rigged the program with an encryption device, but it's dysfunctional. LINx will tag the call coming in here, monitor it and see that its encryption program isn't working correctly, and won't suspect a thing.'

'And then it'll send Dan Reeves to the safe house to do the dirty work,' Halliday said.

'If all goes well, that is precisely what will happen, gentlemen.'

'Where's the location?' Barney asked. 'We'd like to take a good look around before we get things going.'

Wellman nodded. 'Of course. Just as soon as the techs have finished we'll take the flatscreen in the elevator to the underground car park. I have an unmarked van waiting for us. We'll drive across town to a house on the East Village waterfront. It's the perfect venue, quiet and secluded. While the techs set things up there, you can take a look at the place. I'll return here and await the call.'

Halliday's pulse quickened at the thought of what would happen then. The appearance of Reeves, the ambush with freeze. It would be over in minutes, if not seconds. Wellman had a private bed standing by in a local hospital, and a surgeon on call to remove Dan Reeves' NCI.

After that, all that remained would be for Joe Kosinski to come up with the program to scour LINx from the Net.

Barney said, 'Okay, a worst-case scenario. *Two* worst-case scenarios. One: for whatever reason, LINx suspects something is screwy with the set-up and doesn't send Dan Reeves in. That leaves Reeves still out there somewhere, armed and dangerous. What do we do then?' He looked from Halliday to Wellman.

'Then . . .' Wellman said, 'we start again. Either we set up a similar situation, or . . .'

Barney looked at him. 'Or what?'

'Or we dispense with the computer-generated simulation. We use Joseph instead. We set him up somewhere else – well protected, of course – and have him call in, using another encryption-defective line.'

'I don't like the idea of using live bait,' Barney said.

'If it's a case of having to stop Dan Reeves before LINx decides to kill again . . .'

'What's your second worst-case scenario, Barney?' Halliday asked.

Barney took a long breath. 'Okay . . . just suppose we bungle it. Something goes wrong, something unforeseen. He starts firing before we can use the freeze . . . what then? What do we do? Do we fire on him, risking killing him – or do we let him get away?'

Halliday recalled what Joe Kosinski had said in the Himalayan virtual reality, that rather than risk possible future lives, Dan Reeves should be sacrificed.

Wellman nodded. 'It's a hell of a dilemma, gentlemen, and one I wouldn't like to put anyone in the situation of facing. I don't envy what you'll be doing today.'

'It's what you're paying us to do,' Barney said. 'But you haven't answered my question.'

'I'll issue no orders. Do what you feel is right in the situation. I'll stand by you whatever happens. Hopefully, however, neither of your worse-case scenarios will come to pass.'

A technician approached and told Wellman that the screen was ready. Wellman okayed its removal, then turned to Halliday and Barney.

'They're taking it to the car park. We'll give them five

212

minutes and make our way down.' He moved to a table and came back with something in a plastic wrap. 'This is the chu, Mr Halliday. If you'd care to try it on.'

Halliday ripped open the plastic and examined the capillary holographic unit. Deactivated, it resembled a fine mesh net in the shape of a balaclava, except with the facepiece intact. He moved to the window and slipped the flimsy, lightweight hood over his head. He arranged the mesh capillaries carefully around his mouth and eyes and stared at his reflection in the window; he looked like a recovering burns victim. He examined the control unit, then pressed the slide. He was aware of a quick blur of light in his eyes as the chu came on, and then his eyes adjusted and in the window he saw a stranger, staring back at him.

'Amazing,' Barney said. 'It almost makes you look handsome, Hal.'

The stranger reflected in the window was a ruddy-faced, ginger-haired man, perhaps fifty years old. He experimented with the control, cycling through a gallery of a dozen different faces. Some were young, others old; all were absolutely convincing.

'The program contains twenty different personae,' Wellman said. 'You can get male or female chu, and even some which combine both sexes.'

Halliday removed the chu, returned it to its wrapper and slipped it into the inside pocket of his jacket.

Wellman looked at his watch. 'It's time we were making a move, gentlemen.'

'Before we go,' Barney said. 'What does Reeves look like? I don't mean facially, as he'll probably be wearing a chu. How tall is he, how big?'

'He's not tall, a little smaller than you, Mr Halliday, but compact, broad across the chest and shoulders.'

As they took the elevator to the underground car park,

Halliday found himself wondering if Dan Reeves would be armed with a cutter.

A silver van was backed up to the elevator, its roll-door open. A technician crouched in the back, adjusting the ties that held the packaged flatscreen in place. When Halliday, Barney and Wellman appeared, the technician climbed out and moved to the cab.

'We'll travel in the back with the flatscreen,' Wellman said. 'The chances of LINx recognising us via the surveillance cameras are remote but, to be on the safe side, I advise caution.'

Halliday climbed into the rear of the van and sat on a fold-down seat. Wellman closed the roll-door, pitching the compartment into darkness. He found a small light and switched it on. The van started up and Halliday held onto a hanging strap and swayed as they turned a corner.

He tried to track their progress through the city by the turns they made, but without any visual clue as to where they were he was soon lost. The journey seemed to take an age. They were stopped by every set of traffic lights across town, a needless delay as the streets these days were almost empty of vehicles.

Fifteen minutes later the van slowed down almost to a stop, and then moved slowly forwards. Wellman looked up. 'This must be it, gentlemen.'

The van braked, and seconds later the technician pushed up the roll-door. Halliday was surprised to find that they were in a garage: they had completed the journey without once subjecting themselves to the scrutiny of surveillance cameras.

Wellman and the technician carried the flatscreen from the van and up a short flight of stairs into a comfortably appointed lounge, with a sliding glass door giving onto a balcony overlooking the cold grey water of the East RIver.

While the technician set up the flatscreen before the

room's com-screen, Wellman showed them around the house. It occupied two levels, with bedrooms and a bathroom upstairs, and the lounge, kitchen and dining area downstairs. There was no way an intruder might enter the house through the upstairs windows, short of performing a kamikaze stunt in a micro-light. The windows were supposedly burglar-proof, reinforced polymer-glass in aluminium frames.

'There are no security cameras in the vicinity, gentlemen. I made sure of that before selecting the house. The only entrance from the mews is through a single front door.'

Barney was staring at the sliding glass door that accessed the balcony. 'I like the look of this, Hal. It's easily accessible from the river. It might be a bit obvious if we leave the door open, but it might be an idea, an invitation to walk into the trap.'

He unlocked the door and stepped out. Halliday joined him. A ladder was attached to the wall down to the river. Barney tried it for strength; it was pegged solidly into the mortar between the brickwork.

Barney turned and looked into the lounge. 'We might have to split up, Hal. One of us take the front, one the river balcony.'

They returned inside. Wellman and the technician were adjusting the flatscreen in relation to the camera mounted on the com-screen. They were lifting the flatscreen back and forth, then checking the view from the camera. When the image of Joe Kosinski was running, the frame of the flatscreen had to be out of view. It would be tragic if such a simple error gave the game away.

Halliday and Barney moved to the front door and stepped outside. The house was situated at the end of a narrow, pedestrian mews, not wide enough to admit any vehicle larger than a motorbike. A visitor would have to approach on foot along the mews, observable from the house for about fifteen metres.

They strode down the red-brick walkway to an arch that gave access onto a narrow sidestreet. 'If anyone comes to the front of the house, Hal, they have to walk along this street and then turn into the mews.' Barney looked around. 'There's no other way to approach from this direction.'

'One of us could wait out here in the street,' Halliday said. He looked across at the neat red-brick apartments. A covered walkway opposite provided perfect concealment.

Barney nodded. 'Do you want to take the front or the back?'

'The front.'

'I'll cover the river entrance. I'll stay in the house. We'll keep in contact through our coms.'

'Be careful, Barney. If you're in the house and Reeves mistakes you for Kosinski . . . Remember, he's out to get rid of the kid.'

'Thanks for reminding me,' Barney said. 'I can look after myself, Hal. I'll find somewhere big enough to hide my bulk. Let's see how they're getting on in there.'

They retraced their steps along the mews.

'We're almost ready,' Wellman said when they entered the lounge. 'Have you seen enough?'

'We're all set,' Barney said. 'What now?'

'I'll take a cab back to the office. When I arrive I'll give you a call: don't reply, just listen for three rings, then I'll hang up. That'll be the signal for you to dial the office code, Ralph.'

Crouching beside the flatscreen, the technician nodded.

'As soon as the recording is completed, Ralph will cut the connection and then leave the house in the van.' Wellman paused. 'The rest will be in your capable hands. I don't know how long it might take LINx to trace the call to here and despatch Dan Reeves.'

'If it's monitoring all calls into Cyber-Tech facilities, it'll be able to trace the call instantly.' Barney said.

'The thing is,' Halliday pointed out, 'we don't know whether the part of LINx inhabiting Reeves is in permanent contact with itself in the Net. If it is, then Reeves might be round here in a matter of minutes. If it isn't and Reeves contacts LINx in the Net from time to time for instructions, it might take him hours to get here.'

'Always assuming, of course, that it traces the signal in the first place,' Barney pointed out.

'So Reeves could be round here in minutes or hours,' Halliday said. 'Or then again, not at all.'

It was the imponderable aspect of the situation that was so damned worrying.

'I'll be getting back to the office,' Wellman said. 'Halliday, Kluger, good luck. Take care.' He nodded to both men and slipped from the room.

'If I leave the sliding door open and Reeves approaches from the river,' Barney said, 'then he must come through this room to check the rest of the house.' He stepped from the lounge. 'There's an alcove out here,' he called. Halliday left the lounge, moved into the hall, and felt a quick prod in the small of his back.

'Gotya, kid,' Barney said, stepping from the alcove.

They play-acted the situation again, Halliday stepping through the door and purposefully looking in the direction of the alcove. He saw a flash of movement, and Barney had the canister of freeze out and aimed.

Halliday looked at his watch. Wellman had been gone no more than five minutes. 'I want to go and check out the approach street,' Halliday said. 'I'll be back inside ten minutes.'

He left the house and walked to the end of the mews and through the archway. To the left, the narrow street was a dead end, choked with the overflowing garbage containers of a waterfront restaurant. He turned right and walked to the end of the street. It came out on a wide main street lined with boutiques and bistros, evidently an exclusive district. He retreated to the covered walkway opposite the mews, concealed himself and leaned against the brickwork. From here he had a perfect view along the street to the main drag, and across to the archway and the length of the mews. He was even sheltered from the elements. He commended Wellman for choosing the perfect area for a stake-out.

If someone matching the description of Reeves' build came along the street – no, scratch that: if *anyone* came along the street – and turned into the mews, he would quickly follow them. If they approached the door and looked intent on trying to gain entry, he would use the freeze first and ask questions later.

If the wait became protracted, he'd suggest a swap with Barney. The important thing was to keep vigilant, not let himself become tired or bored, which would be some undertaking. He had to remember that not only his own life was at stake if he messed up, but those of Barney and many others besides.

He returned to the house. Barney was crouching in the alcove, a squat goblin protecting his territory.

'No call from Wellman?'

Barney shook his head. He looked at his watch. 'Coming up to twenty minutes, Hal. Won't be long now.'

Halliday leaned against the wall. 'Hey, when all this is over, how about we splash out on a big meal, you, me and Kim?'

Barney looked up. 'You know what, I might just hold you to that.'

His com buzzed. He pulled it from his pocket, held it out on his hand and counted the tones. 'One . . . two . . . three.'

They hurried into the lounge. Barney said, 'This is it, Ralph. You all set?'

Halliday and Barney positioned themselves behind the com-screen in the corner while the technician summoned the stilled image of Joe Kosinski to the flatscreen with a remote control. Ralph crouched beside the com-screen, out of range of the camera, and dialled in the Cyber-Tech code. He directed the remote at the flatscreen and Joe's image began to play. The techs had included a run-in of ten seconds.

Halliday watched as Joe tapped his fingers on his chest and said 'Come on, come on . . .'

He was aware of his heartbeat, loud in his ears. The com-screen activated, Joe said, 'Hi, Wellman,' and he heard Wellman's voice: 'Joseph – I told you not to call. If the link's . . .'

The recorded image of Joe Kosinski smiled. 'It's okay, it's encrypted . . .'

'You sure it's safe, Joseph?' Wellman said his lines with the panache of a born holo-star.

'Sure I'm sure. It's safe.'

'How's it coming along?'

Joe nodded. 'It's going okay. I'm working on it.'

'It's vital you get the program up and running,' Wellman said.

'That's right, I know. I'm pretty confident I can rig something up.'

Halliday watched the image of Joe as he leaned from the picture and returned, holding up a needle. 'This is the little beauty. What do you think?'

'That's great, Joseph,' Wellman said. 'Listen, I must go – '

'Okay, yeah. Take care. I'll catch you later.'

'Bye, Joseph.'

The image of Joe reached out to cut the link, and the

technician killed the com-screen, then shut down the flatscreen with the remote.

Halliday discovered that he'd been holding his breath. He let it out with a relieved sigh and clapped the technician on the shoulder. 'Good job, Ralph.'

'Well done,' Barney said.

'This is it, Barney,' Halliday said. 'If LINx has traced the call . . .' He felt his throat go dry at the thought.

Ralph and Barney carried the flatscreen down the steps to the garage, and seconds later Halliday heard the van start up and drive away.

Barney returned and opened the sliding glass door to the balcony, then moved out to the hall. Halliday followed him and stood before a full-length mirror.

He pulled the chu from his jacket and eased the capillary net over his head. He arranged the weave of mesh around his eyes and lips, then switched it on. He touched the select control, and a succession of strangers' faces stared back from the mirror. At last a handsome, Scandinavian-looking guy smiled out at him. He decided that the face was in keeping with his style of dress and slipped the control into the inside pocket of his jacket.

'All set,' he said. He turned to Barney, who was standing in the alcove, freeze at the ready.

'I'll contact you,' Barney said. 'Not the other way round, okay? Set your com to vibration. I'll call every quarter, on the dot, just to keep you on your toes.'

'Take care,' Halliday said, nodding at Barney and slipping out through the front door. He hurried along the mews, propelled by adrenalin. He knew it was irrational, but he half-expected Dan Reeves to turn around the corner at any second, miraculously early.

He ran through the archway and made it to the covered walk with a paranoid sense of relief. He leaned against the wall, sighting along the street to the main drag, and worked to slow his breathing.

He told himself that it would likely be hours before Dan Reeves showed up.

The main street had become suddenly busy. Pedestrians passed back and forth between the stores he could see from his vantage point, and every time someone came into sight he tensed with expectation. Everyone, now, was a potential assassin. He told himself that there was nothing to stop Reeves – or rather LINx – from assuming the identity of a woman. With a chu, anything was possible . . . This made Halliday all the more jumpy, and ten minutes later his heart leaped into his throat when someone turned into the sidestreet.

It was a well-dressed blonde girl with a pretty face, perhaps twenty, or so she seemed. She climbed from a taxi in the main drag and ran down the sidestreet, burdened with designer shopping bags, and Halliday tensed. She was slim and quite obviously a woman, but when she turned into the mews Halliday stepped from the covered walk and followed, his right hand straying to the freeze beneath his jacket.

The rational part of his mind recalled Wellman's description of Reeves as short and stocky. There was no way, he told himself, that this woman could be Reeves, no matter how well disguised. At the same time, he was taking no chances. He hurried after her and she half-turned at the sound of his pursuit, gave a quick, startled look and moved to the door of one of the apartments halfway along the mews. She fumbled with a pass-card, glancing behind her, and Halliday cursed himself and continued walking.

He retraced his steps across the sidestreet and stationed himself in the walkway. A minute later his communicator vibrated against his ribs. 'Hal here,' he said.

221

'You still awake?'

'Just about. All quiet at this end.' But I nearly froze an innocent girl who looked nothing like Dan Reeves, he added to himself.

'Anything at your end?' he asked.

'Quite a bit of river traffic, but no one's dropped by yet. The good thing is, I can hear the engine of every boat that passes, so unless the bastard paddles up in a canoe I'll have plenty of warning.'

'Talk to you later.'

'Okay. Take care.'

Halliday cut the connection and waited. Ten minutes after the false alarm with the blonde woman, a taxi turned in from the main drag and idled along the street. Halliday peered into the vehicle, trying to make out the appearance of the passenger. Behind the tinted windscreen he saw the head and shoulders of a man. He tensed again, expecting the cab to halt by the mews and the passenger to climb out. He foresaw his route to the mews being blocked by the taxi if it lingered after dropping off its fare: he would be forced to walk around the cab, wasting precious seconds.

In the event his fear proved unfounded. The taxi motored past the end of the mews and dropped the guy off halfway down the sidestreet. Which could, of course, be a deliberate ploy on the part of Reeves to catch off guard any potential assailant.

Halliday watched a middle-aged man pay the driver and walk back along the street towards the mews. The guy was short, as Wellman had described, but not at all stocky.

The man paused, checked his pockets, and turned into the rear entrance of one of the waterfront restaurants, and Halliday began breathing again.

Thirty minutes later, a van bearing the logo of a combined locksmith-cum-security advisor turned into the sidestreet and halted before the mews. Halliday's heart began a laboured pounding as he watched a short, stocky guy seemingly in his mid-twenties, jump from the cab and disappear down the mews. Halliday set off after him, the freeze out and ready to use. He rounded the van and increased his pace. The guy was halfway along the mews, carrying a tool-box which might contain any of a dozen lethal weapons. Halliday raised his communicator to his lips. 'Barney,' he whispered. 'He's on his way.'

'You need help?'

'I'll nail him before he reaches the house.' He paused. 'If you don't hear from me in the next few minutes, I've fucked up.'

He pocketed his com. He was a couple of metres behind the guy. He raised the freeze, and was about to use it when the guy slowed, looked at the numbered doors along the row and moved to the house which the blonde woman had entered earlier. He knocked on the door and the woman answered, gave a nervous glance at Halliday and let the security man enter.

Halliday returned to the sidestreet and resumed his vigil, his heart thumping as if he'd just completed the New York marathon in world record time. If he'd been in the woman's position, with a shifty-looking character loitering outside, he too would have called in a security expert.

Annoyingly, the locksmith's van was blocking his view of the mews.

He got through to Barney.

'Hal, what's happening?'

'False alarm, Barney. Close call – guy matching the description turns down the mews. I nearly froze him. I'll be in touch.'

An hour passed, with the regular fifteen-minute wake-up bulletins from Barney. The locksmith-cum-security advisor returned to his van and drove off, giving Halliday a clear

223

view of and access to the mews once again. He hoped the blonde woman had been reassured by whatever the expert had advised. Carry a weapon at all times, he thought, and if the guy bothers you again, shoot first and ask questions later.

The cold was getting to him. He was sheltered from the worst of the wind, but as the day progressed, the temperature dropped. He looked up at the thin strip of sky between the eaves of the enclosing building; it looked grey and laden with snow. He turned his collar up and hunched against the chill.

Halliday decided that the next time Barney called, he'd suggest a rotation of duty. The thought of the warm house appealed. Also, in the hallway by himself, he wouldn't be prone to so many paranoid assumptions that everyone in New York, even slim young women, was Dan Reeves in disguise.

He looked at his watch. It was almost three-thirty. In another thirty minutes or so dusk would begin to draw in, and the job of apprehending Dan Reeves would be made just that bit more difficult.

He wondered if he'd make it back in time for dinner with Kim. At the thought of her, he felt a quick pang of guilt. He was deceiving Kim; he'd promised her that he would leave this case well alone, fight shy of evil spirits. He wished that he'd had the strength of character to sit her down back then and explain that there were no such things as evil spirits, and that, in order to survive, he had to work. Instead he had taken the line of least resistance, and lied. He had balked at facing the emotional, the personal, consequences of opening up and talking to Kim about what he thought and believed. He had bottled it up, as ever.

He considered what his sister had often told him, that with his upbringing was it any wonder that he found it impossible to show and share emotions? At the time he hadn't been able to work out if Sue was being perceptive, or cruel. She had possessed an acute psychological insight and delighted in using it against him. He thought of his father, who for so many years had been unable to bring himself to talk about the events of the fire. As much as it pained Halliday to admit it, and despite doing everything to avoid being compared to his father over the years, there was no denying that he was his father's son.

The silent jarring of his communicator interrupted his reverie. He fumbled the device in his cold fingers and replied.

'Hal, Christ, I though you'd really fallen asleep this time.'

'Not sleeping, just frozen to the bone. How about we swap over, Barney?'

'Fine by me. Give it another fifteen minutes, okay? I'll call at four and if your end's quiet, we'll switch.'

'Talk to you then.'

He looked forward to the warmth of the house, and later an evening with Kim, this case out of the way and forgotten.

On the main drag, the multi-coloured lighting displays in the shop-fronts were coming on, bright in the gathering darkness. On the opposite side of the street, a ladies' fashion outlet switched on its holo-façade, a radiant representation of a crimson evening gown. Halliday smiled to himself. He'd bring Kim here when all this was over, treat her to a new dress.

His communicator vibrated. 'Hal, if it's quiet at your end, let's make the switch now.'

'Fine.' Halliday looked along the length of the sidestreet. 'Okay, Barney.' Then he stopped. 'Hold it a second, something's happening. Might not be important. I'll be in touch.' He cut the connection.

A sleek red sports car had drawn up with a screech,

225

effectively blocking the end of the sidestreet. As Halliday watched, a yellow cab braked behind it and a woman jumped out, handed a wad of notes to the driver and advanced on the first car. She banged with a clenched fist on the roof, shouting abuse. Halliday felt a momentary pang of alarm, soon doused. This was nothing more than a row between lovers or husband and wife. He was not going to make the mistake this time of assuming the worst.

He was about to get in touch with Barney when the door of the red sports car opened and a man climbed out. He was short, stocky, broad across the chest.

The woman, small and flame-haired, launched herself at him, pummelling at his chest with ineffective fists. The guy held her off, the blows more of an embarrassment than a threat. She was shouting at him, the words lost at this distance. Halliday turned away, finding something distasteful about watching other people's emotional disputes.

He heard footsteps. The guy was walking down the sidestreet, pushing away the woman who clung to him and pleaded with loud, incoherent sobs. The man halted opposite Halliday, by the archway, and turned to the red-haired woman.

'What's happening to you?' the woman cried. 'You've changed. You're a different person!'

The man grabbed her shoulders, pulled her to him and spoke with slow deliberation. Halliday failed to catch the words. He wanted the couple to go away and leave him to his vigil.

The woman spoke again, and Halliday could hardly bring himself to believe what he was hearing. 'And this damned stupid disguise,' she cried. 'What's got into you, Dan? What's going on?'

Halliday's belly seemed to freeze. In retrospect, he knew he should have acted then. He should have dashed out and used the freeze while Reeves was distracted. At the time he could only watch in disbelief.

What happened then seemed to take place in slow motion. The guy reached into his jacket and from an under-arm holster produced a revolver. With infinite patience he held the weapon at arm's length and took aim. The expression on the woman's face, already abject, dissolved into terror. She fell to her knees, her mouth open, and was reaching out to her executioner with pathetic entreaty when he shot her through the forehead at point-blank range.

Halliday saw it happen. He saw the kneeling body give a terrible spasm and fall backwards, arms flopping. He saw the body hit the ground and bob back, still on bended knee, in a posthumous parody of gymnastic vitality. He saw all this and could do nothing to save her life, paralysed as he was with shock.

Dan Reeves calmly holstered his revolver, and then looked up and saw Halliday watching him. Halliday tried to move, to reach for his own gun. If anything, the shock of discovery was more traumatising than that of witnessing the killing.

Halliday had time to tell himself that Reeves had no way of recognising him; he was wearing the chu, after all. But he had seen Reeves commit murder or, rather, he had seen LINx kill the woman. This, in itself, would be sufficient to sentence him to death.

Time slipped from an extended second of frozen inaction to sudden acceleration. Before Halliday could move, Reeves pulled out his revolver for a second time and fired. The report of the shot echoed deafeningly in the narrow street. The bullet passed through the padded bulk of Halliday's jacket, missing his body. He dived, rolling across the ground, and came up on his knees, clutching his automatic. In that instant he forgot that Dan Reeves was an innocent man, dismissed his earlier intention to take him alive. He aimed and fired, and the bullet struck Reeves in the gut and punched a wad of blood and muscle out through a ragged exit point in the small of his back.

Reeves staggered, and Halliday expected him to fall. What happened then served only to banish any notion that his opponent was still human. Instead of falling, Reeves turned and ran, and as he did so Halliday made out a mess of gut and entrails spilling from the gaping wound in his back.

Halliday fired again, missing this time, and then gave chase. Reeves was already well ahead but he was running into a dead end. Halliday slowed, amazed at how Reeves seemed to be ignoring his injury and sprinting without any ill-effect. He wondered if it was LINx in his neural interface, blocking all signals of pain from the doomed man's consciousness.

Reeves came to the end of the street and turned. Halliday fell into a crouch, automatic extended. 'Stop right there or I'll shoot! Drop the gun!'

Reeves turned right and left like a hunted animal at bay. 'Drop the gun and you'll live, Reeves,' Halliday shouted, as if appealing to whatever vestiges of humanity remained beneath the commanding program of the artificial intelligence. Perhaps, if Reeves could be reached, his elemental desire for survival triggered, he would be able to overcome the puppet-master and save himself.

Even as he thought this, Halliday knew it was a futile notion.

Reeves raised his revolver. Halliday fired and hit Reeves in the upper arm. He jerked, the gun spilling from useless fingers. His left hand reached into his jacket, but a cry from Halliday stayed the movement. Halliday ran towards Reeves, crouched three metres away, gun held in both outstretched hands, centred on the man's head.

'One move and you're dead!'

They faced each other, immobile. Halliday feared that as soon as he made a move for the freeze, then Reeves would go for his concealed weapon – the cutter? The thought of it, of what the cutter had done to Carrie Villeux, paralysed him with fear.

He willed Barney to appear, to bail him out.

An eerie aspect of the encounter was that Reeves had not once cried out in pain, even though he was missing a good portion of his gut through the cavity in his back, and the bone of his upper right arm was irreparably shattered.

Reeves reached out and pulled over a container of trash. Halliday dodged the bin as Reeves vanished through a door to his left. Cursing, he waded after Reeves, through a tide of vegetable peelings and plastic packaging and kicked the door open. He peered into a kitchen, all steam and pandemonium. People screamed as Reeves, spilling more blood than was humanly possible, pushed his way past startled chefs and waiters. Halliday gave chase, yelling at everyone to get down as he tried to take aim through the mêlée of flying bodies.

Reeves careered past a cooking range. He reached out, grasped the rim of a boiling pan and pulled it over. It hit the tiles with a dull thump and spilled a tide of boiling gravy. Halliday could do nothing to avoid the slick: it splashed around his feet, burning his ankles, almost bringing him to his knees. He clutched at the range and somehow kept his feet, pushed himself towards the door through which Reeves had fled.

He made the door and dived through. He was in a long, low-lit restaurant, the sudden intrusion of two gunmen on the scene bringing a startled halt to the business of dining.

Ahead, Reeves collided with a waiter, sending the man crashing to the floor in a welter of plates and cutlery. Halliday caught up with Reeves and raised his right arm.

He pressed the release stud on the canister of freeze. Reeves gave an involuntary cry – the first sound he had made during the chase – and the air filled with the chemical reek of liquid nitrogen and ammonia. The gas hit Reeves in the upper chest and head, and he fell backwards into a conveniently-placed chair.

Halliday sat down across the table from the dying man, dragging in breaths with great gulps. He lowered the freeze and, panting, sighted Reeves down the length of his gun. This time, he was taking no chances.

He was suddenly aware of the silence. He looked around, taking in the shocked expressions of the diners. They were sitting absolutely still as they stared in open-mouthed disbelief at the mutilated man and his pursuer, now at rest.

He found himself wanting to apologise for the interruption.

Reeves was frozen in the act of pulling a second revolver from his jacket. His gun arm was raised before his face, the muzzle of the pistol set like ice a matter of inches from his mouth. As Halliday watched, he saw a brief, terrible flicker of life appear in the eyes behind the chu. Reeves was trying to move, and Halliday was sure then that he was propelled not by the program of the artificial intelligence but by the overwhelming human impulse to bring his own suffering to an end.

Before Halliday could reach out and take the gun, Reeves achieved his aim. He managed to lift his mouth over the muzzle of the revolver and pull the trigger. A spray of atomised brain and skull-shrapnel hit the ceiling and rained down over the diners.

Only then did the screaming begin, followed by a stampede for the door. A waiter stood beside Halliday, staring. Halliday looked up.

He produced his identification card, held it for the waiter to read, and said, 'Get me a brandy.'

The waiter fled.

The upper half of Dan Reeves' head was missing, but the lower jaw and face were still intact and clothed in the malfunctioning chu. Amid the devastation of the man's head, the chu played a selection of ghastly, smiling mouths, one after the other.

Halliday lifted the flap of his jacket, looked at the hole drilled neatly through the padding. He poked his finger through the hole, stared at it.

His com rattled silently against his ribs.

'Barney?' he said.

'Hal?' Barney shouted. 'What the hell . . .? Where are you?'

The waiter returned, holding out a bottle of brandy. Halliday took it. 'Where am I?' he asked.

'The . . . The Waterfront,' the waiter stammered.

Halliday relayed the information to Barney and cut the connection. He tipped the bottle and took a mouthful of brandy, feeling the liquid fire cut a path directly to his stomach.

Barney arrived two minutes later. He took in the scene, then came to the table and touched Halliday's shoulder. 'You okay, Hal?'

'I'm fine.' He indicated the corpse. 'There was nothing I could do, Barney.' He pulled the chu from his head and dropped it onto the table.

Barney sat down, accepted the brandy from Halliday and took a slug. 'I've contacted Wellman. He's on his way.'

Halliday recounted the gunfight, how in the end he was sure that it was Dan Reeves, and not the machine intelligence, who had taken his own life.

'There's a woman's body by the archway,' Barney said.

'Reeves' wife or whatever. She followed him here, argued with him.' He stopped, as the image of how Reeves had calmly shot her in the head flashed into his mind's eye. 'Then he shot her. Jesus Christ . . .'

'What is it, Hal?'

'It's just occurred to me: if the woman hadn't followed him she would still be alive now, and Reeves would have turned down the mews unhindered. He wouldn't have shot her and then seen me. I would have followed him down the news, used the freeze. He'd be on his way to some hospital now to have the interface removed.'

Halliday tried not to dwell on what must have been going through Reeves' tortured mind when he hooked his mouth around the barrel of the revolver and pulled the trigger.

A police team arrived, a couple of uniformed officers, a detective and a forensic scientist. Halliday and Barney showed their identification, and Halliday began a detailed report of what had happened.

Five minutes later, Wellman swept into the restaurant. He'd changed his suit for a jade, double-breasted affair with a red carnation in the lapel. He looked more than ever like the big wheel in some successful bordello, perhaps with Mafia connections.

He took one look at the remains of Dan Reeves, then turned away. He nodded Halliday and Barney. 'Your action has saved many lives, gentlemen.'

Somehow the knowledge, the abstract concept of lives saved, failed to make Halliday feel any better.

'Do we really need to remain here any longer?' Wellman said. 'I'm going to the safe house to appraise Joseph of events. Mr Kluger, I can write you a cheque for your work so far.'

Barney nodded. 'Sounds good to me.'

Halliday looked at his watch. It was seven. He recalled promising Kim that he'd call and arrange to meet her for a meal.

He looked at Barney. 'I said I'd see Kim tonight.'

'Go for it, Hal. Here, take the car.' He gave Halliday the keys of the Ford and followed Wellman from the restaurant.

Halliday took the footpath along the waterfront, hunching in his jacket against the cold wind. He had no appetite, but he could order something light and watch Kim eat, let the sight of her take his mind off the events of the day.

His com vibrated. He stopped, staring up at the lights of Manhattan, bright against the night sky, and took the call.

A familiar voice said, 'Mr Halliday?'

'Joe – is that you? Joe?'

'I need to see you, Mr Halliday. I'll be at the Himalayasite in five minutes. It's important.'

'Fine. I'll be there. Joe, what is it?'

No reply.

'Joe? Joe . . .?'

Kosinski had cut the connection. Halliday sighed. So much for the fantasy of watching Kim eat her meal while he got quietly steamed on red wine.

He came to a main street and a minute later he was in a taxi heading downtown. He closed his eyes as the taxi carried him through the darkness. Soon, the meeting with Joe Kosinski concluded, he would cease his involvement with VR, Cyber-Tech, Wellman and Kosinski for good . . . and not a second too soon.

He paid off the taxi and climbed into the Ford, then drove north towards West 23rd.

The fairy-tale castle of the Mantoni VR Bar filled the night with the glow of its ersatz white marble. Halliday waited in line for five minutes, then bought an hour's pass at reception and made his way to the waiting room. The Bar was busier today, and he was forced to wait for what seemed an age in the plush crimson lounge until a booth became free.

A uniformed hostess with a lockjaw smile showed him to a vacant booth. The jellytank was filling up with fresh goo, following the departure of the previous user. He entered his preferences into the screen on the wall, going to the Himalayasite as himself, unaltered. He undressed, stored his clothes in the wall-unit, and attached the leads and faceplate.

He stepped into the tank, sat down and lay back. His senses departed as he floated buoyantly, and seconds later he was flooded with the visual information of the virtual Himalayasite.

Despite knowing what to expect, he was amazed again by the fidelity of the image, the reality of the experience. Around him the mountains thrust great snow-streaked ramparts into a cloudless blue sky, and a warm breeze played over his face. From a distance came the slow tolling of the lamasery bells.

This time, Joe Kosinski was already waiting for him at the Buddhist shrine. He was dressed in the same maroon robes, his shaven head a severe contrast to his fly-away hair in the real world. He sat cross-legged before the similarly seated, though more fully proportioned, image of Siddhartha Gautama.

'Mr Halliday,' Joe said.

'Hal, please,' Halliday said. He sat down on the timber bench. 'It worked, Joe. Wellman had some techs set up an image of you supposedly calling the Cyber-Tech offices. LINx was monitoring and sent Dan Reeves.'

'What happened?'

'He died in the ambush,' Halliday said. 'He took his own life.' He could not bring himself to describe the death of the woman or the details of the bloody finale in the restaurant.

Joe Kosinski nodded. 'It's almost over, Hal. It's coming

234

to an end. LINx no longer has implantees to control, and soon we'll be able to eradicate it from the Net.'

'How's the program coming along?'

'Oh,' Joe said, smiling. 'It's finished. That's why I summoned you here.'

'You confident it'll work?'

'Hal, I developed LINx and its prototypes. I know it intimately. I know what brought it into being, and I know what will kill it. Why do you think it was so eager to eliminate me?'

Halliday shook his head. 'It's been a nightmare. Joe. The deaths . . . the needless deaths.'

The silence stretched. 'Don't you think I feel a measure of responsibility?'

Halliday waved. 'I didn't mean to blame you. You weren't to know what'd happen. It was a fluke, a terrible, tragic accident.' He shook his head. 'You were no more responsible than the parents of a child who grows up to be a killer.'

'Some people would claim that parents are responsible for the actions of their children, Hal.'

He looked at the young computer-scientist in the guise of a Buddhist monk. Was he playing the devil's advocate? 'You don't really believe that's true, though?'

Joe hesitated. 'I don't know. Perhaps not so much in the case of parents, but as for LINx . . . It was my programming. I sequenced its parameters, its initial range of references.'

'But it grew into something different, something almost evil. That had nothing to do with you.'

The monk gestured. 'Perhaps I will atone when the program wipes LINx forever from the Net.' He looked up at Halliday. 'I need you to collect the program and deliver it to Wellman.'

235

'It isn't with you at the safe house?'

Joe laughed. 'Call me paranoid, Hal. I lived in constant fear of LINx finding out where I'm in hiding. I couldn't risk the possibility of the program being discovered by Dan Reeves. I completed it a few hours ago and deposited the needles in a sealed envelope at Connelly's, off Broadway. I told the bartender you'd be along to collect it later today.'

Halliday nodded. 'I'll do that. When you get out of the tank, Wellman and Barney will be with you. I could meet you back there when I've picked up the program.'

'We'll have a celebratory drink, Hal. To the success of the program.'

Halliday smiled. 'I'll drink to that, Joe.'

He gave Halliday the address of the safe house, an exclusive street on the Upper West Side.

They watched the hunched shape of a yak make its way slowly up the hillside towards them. Halliday had seen the huge, hunched beasts from a distance during his first visit to the site, but never this close – and, as ever in VR, he was surprised again by the reality of the image.

He turned to Joe.

'Hal . . .'

'What is it?' Halliday stared at him. Joe was scratching his chest through the robes, a frown on his face. 'Hal, I feel bad.'

The yak looked up, straight at them, and something about the fixity of its stare struck Halliday as most unlike that of an animal. The way it was looking at Joe, with a strange air of intent, was not animal-like at all. Halliday told himself that in VR you could appear as anyone or anything you liked, and that included a yak.

Only then did he begin to wonder how anyone else had discovered Joe's location in VR.

He glanced at Joe, and wished he hadn't. Something was happening to the kid. The flesh of his face was changing colour, blackening. Smoke was rising from his robes. Joe sat immobile, unable to move, an expression of utter terror in his eyes.

Halliday backed off, panic clutching his chest.

The yak came to a halt before them, its bulbous, rheumy eyes staring out at Joe with typical bovine melancholy.

The yak opened its mouth. 'Joe Kosinski?' it asked.

Then it changed shape in an instant. From a huge-headed, sad-eyed animal it became something all streamlined metal with a thrusting, prognathous jaw.

'Get out of here, Joe!' Halliday cried.

He was aware of the slicing sickle teeth only when they tore into the burning Buddhist monk with a ferocity he knew must be a metaphor for something that was occurring in the real world – for in virtual reality, he knew, you could not be harmed.

Then the monster turned from the gory remains of Joe Kosinski, its jaws dripping with virtual blood, and grinned.

'And now you, Halliday,' it said.

Twelve

By the time Barney and Wellman reached the safe house on the Upper West Side, snow was beginning to settle on the sidewalks in a thin, sparkling mantle. Wellman parked the Benz outside a three-storey town house and led the way inside.

They found Joe Kosinski already jellytanked in a big room on the second floor, stacked with computer terminals and flatscreens. Wellman hurried over to a screen on the wall and ran his fingers over the touch-control. Barney, following, stopped on the threshold and stared at the jellytank. Although he had tanked before, he had never witnessed anyone else in virtual reality. Often, when immersing himself in the goo, he had wondered what a sight he must present while in virtual reality: a naked body in suspension, caught in a nexus of leads. Now he knew. Joe Kosinski floated with his arms raised, legs spread – a body seemingly in freefall – and from time to time his limbs twitched and jumped.

Barney looked up as the room was flooded with a bright green glow. Wellman was adjusting the image on the flatscreen, a panoramic scene of mountains and green valleys.

The viewpoint swept across the greensward, panning in on two figures seated beside an image of Buddha. Barney recognised Hal, exactly as he appeared in the real world, something about the appearance of the shabby New Yorker incongruous in such idyllic surroundings.

Seated cross-legged beside Hal was a young man in the maroon robes of a Buddhist monk. It was a while before Barney recognised Joe Kosinski, his long hair cropped to the scalp.

The two men were talking, though no sound could be heard. Wellman ran his fingers across the touch-control beneath the flatscreen, frowning with concentration.

Barney watched him, trying to work out what he felt about the man. He had disliked the rather prissy, fastidious Wellman when they'd first met, and there was something about his strict adherence to formality that stuck in Barney's craw. He was not the type of guy who would ever become a drinking buddy, but, once fate had thrown them together, Barney had to admit that Wellman had worked hard and with ingenuity.

Sound filled the room, deafening, '. . . do you think it was so eager to eliminate me?' Joe was asking.

Wellman modulated the volume. They were talking about responsibility, who was to blame for what had happened. Kosinski seemed to be blaming himself, but Hal was saying that it was nothing but a terrible accident.

Even in virtual reality, Hal spoke with a soft, slow drawl. He was rubbing the stubble of his jaw, a contemplative gesture Barney was familiar with in the real world.

He wondered if Lew and the Mantoni technicians had watched him and Estelle in virtual reality like this the other day, watched while they had made love . . .

Joe Kosinski was saying, 'I need you to collect the program and deliver it to Wellman.'

'It isn't with you at the safe house?'

Kosinski explained that he had feared LINx might locate the safe house and send Reeves for the program. 'I completed it a few hours ago and deposited the needles in a sealed envelope at Connelly's, off Broadway. I told the bartender that you'd be along to collect it later.'

Wellman turned to Barney. 'He's done it, Kluger.'

Kosinski was saying, 'We'll have a celebratory drink, Hal. To the success of the program.'

The two men seated in the shrine, the Buddhist monk and the black-clad New Yorker, lapsed into silence and watched a big bovine animal cropping grass nearby.

Barney became aware of the smell, the slightest whiff of burning rubber, but it was so faint that he hardly gave it a second thought.

He watched the screen. It was clear that the two men had no more to say, were more intent on watching the yak before them, which seemed to be approaching with deliberation.

Then Joe Kosinski began scratching his chest, and the skin of his face was turning black.

'Wellman . . .' Barney said.

He had come across the smell before, somewhere – then he had it. It was the gel used in the tanks, which no matter how hard he scrubbed himself on emerging from VR always seemed to linger on his skin.

He heard a sound, behind him. He turned.

'What the hell . . .?' Wellman cried.

Something moved in the jellytank; Joe, with unaccustomed vigour. His legs were threshing in the thick, restrictive medium of the jelly.

Barney looked back at the screen. The yak was lifting its big head, staring straight at Joe Kosinski, whose face and hands were blackened now and smoking.

Barney turned again and stared at the jellytank. The gel was bubbling, the body of Joe Kosinski bucking as if being subjected to electric shock treatment.

He moved to the tank, reached out, but even before his hand made contact with the tank, he was beaten back by the heat. Inside the jellytank, Joe Kosinski's flesh was beginning to burn.

240

Wellman cried out and snatched at the leads which snaked over the side of the tank. They came away in his hand, burned through. In desperation, Wellman reached into the tank; barely had he submerged his right hand to the wrist than he snatched it out, yelling with pain.

Barney looked around, frantic now. He picked up a chair, yelled at Wellman to stand back, and swung it with all his strength at the side of the jellytank. The glass cracked, seemed to hold together for a second, and then collapsed, and the gel pulsed out in a steaming, obscene mass. Barney backed to the door in a bid to evade the spreading gel, Wellman beside him.

As Barney stared, he knew that they could do nothing to save Joe Kosinski. If he was not already dead, then he was dying: he lay in a contorted mess in the ruins of the jellytank, his flesh blackened, his mouth open in a silent scream of agony.

'How the hell . . .?' Barney began.

Wellman, his injured hand red, raw and stripped of skin, raised his good hand and pointed at the flatscreen.

Barney stared as the yak, miraculously transformed into something metallic and ferocious, dived at the Buddhist monk and rendered him to shreds.

'LINx,' Wellman whispered. 'It found him in VR . . .'

Barney backed into the hall as the image on the flatscreen broke up, became so much static. He was suddenly aware of the stench of cooking flesh.

'Hal . . .' he said. 'Oh, Christ, Hal was in there with him.'

'Kruger – LINx was monitoring them in VR. It knows where the program is.'

Barney was hardly aware of what Wellman was saying. He tried not to let the image haunt him, but try as he might he could not banish the thought of Hal lying dead in the Mantoni VR Bar.

'I've got to get over there, Wellman! I've got to see if Hal's . . .'

Maybe if Hal had managed to get out of the tank in time . . .

He pulled his com from his pocket, tapped in Hal's code. The tone pulsed, unanswered. 'Come on! Come on, Hal!'

Wellman grabbed his arm. 'Kruger, don't you realise? There's nothing you can do. If LINx got Hal, then he's dead. There's nothing we can do.'

'I need to find out!' He tried to pull away from Wellman.

'First go to Connelly's,' Wellman said. 'Get the program.'

'But LINx has no more human slaves,' Barney objected. 'Reeves was the last.'

'I know, I know – but think about it. LINx knows where the program is. All it has to do is . . . I don't know, contact a courier over the com-system and ask to have the package collected and delivered somewhere. I don't know where,' Wellman hurried on, forestalling Barney's objections. 'LINx doesn't need possession of the program. It just needs to make sure that we don't get it.'

Wellman was staring at Barney, gripping the wrist of his burned hand. He ran to the bathroom and turned on the cold water. Barney stood there, paralysed with something like fear as his mind swirled with the consequences of what he had just witnessed.

He nodded, more to himself, to set his resolve. 'I'll go to Connelly's,' he said. 'Then I'll go to the Mantoni Bar, see if Hal . . .'

Wellman stared at him from the bathroom, pain contorting his features as he submerged his hand in the basin of water. 'I'll see you back here, Kluger.' He pulled something from the pocket of his suit jacket. Keys. 'Take the car.'

Barney grabbed the keys and made for the stairs. More than anything he wanted to reassure himself that Hal was okay, wanted to forget the program and drive down to the Mantoni VR Bar on West 23rd Street.

He told himself he had to get the program. That, ultimately, was the important thing. LINx had killed too many people already: it was time that it was stopped.

He squeezed into the Benz and swung it into the road, heading south at speed. He fumbled one-handed with his com, tapped the repeat function. The ringing tone filled his ear, monotonous. He almost wept with rage. 'Answer the bastard thing! You hear me, Hal?'

He left the call on repeat as he worked through the possibilities. If Hal had survived the attack in VR, then why wasn't he answering the call?

A possible answer occurred to him. Earlier, at the stakeout, Hal had set his communicator to vibrate. If it was still on that setting, and perhaps in the outer pocket of his thick jacket, then no wonder he wasn't answering.

Even though he wanted desperately to believe, he knew it was a feeble explanation.

He drove through the snow, leaning forward over the wheel and peering through the windshield at the empty, blizzard-swept streets. He'd get the package from Connelly's, make straight for the VR Bar.

He saw Joe Kosinski's contorted body again, tried to push the image to the back of his mind. It remained, haunting him.

He wished he was away from here, in the VR world of California, with Estelle, in the cottage by the ocean. Christ, to hold her in his arms after all the shit of the past few days . . .

He found Connelly's, pulled up outside and dashed across the sidewalk through the driving snow. After the bitter cold, the warmth embraced him. A few drinkers sat at tables, watching sport on wallscreens, but the long bar was deserted. Barney slipped onto a stool and nodded to the barman. 'Joe Kosinski, he left something here earlier. Asked me to pick it up.'

'Sure thing.' The barman pulled something from a shelf behind the bar, a slim silver envelope, and handed it to Barney. 'Get you a drink?'

He saw the familiar red and gold label of a Ukrainian wheat beer in the cooler. God knew, he needed one. He ordered, knowing that he was delaying the inevitable. He told himself that if Hal was dead, then there was nothing he could do about it. He needed a beer or three before he made his way over to the VR Bar.

He tipped the bottle, and the cold wash of the alcohol cut through his thirst. He was getting too old for this kind of work, he thought suddenly. What, forty years now as a cop or an investigator of some kind? That was long enough, in anyone's book. He'd paid his dues to the city that had trained him. He needed to start thinking about retirement. Hand the reins of the agency over to Hal and get out, find somewhere quiet and warm . . . Christ, but if Estelle had lived, they'd be planning their retirement together in the real world now, not living out a fantasy in VR.

The door opened with a howl of wind. A tall black guy stepped in, paused and scoped the place. Barney turned back to his beer, took a long swallow. He'd order another, then try to get through to Hal. If he heard nothing, he'd drive to the VR Bar. He knew he should call now, but the thought of getting no reply filled him with dread.

The black guy came to the bar, leaned over and gestured to the barman. 'You have something for me?' the guy said in a high, nervous voice. 'Guy called Joe left it, Joe Kosinski?'

Beer frozen mid-lift before his lips, Barney turned to look. With his free hand he reached for the envelope on the bar and slipped it into his pocket.

Later, he knew he should have shot the guy then. At the time, forty years of conditioning – of ensuring positive identification – would not let him simply shoot first and ask questions later. Even though, he told himself, the guy *had* to be working for LINx. Another slave, or merely some innocent runner LINx had contacted to do the dirty work? He glanced at the guy's head. He wasn't implanted, but then an NCI wouldn't show if he was wearing a chu.

He knew he couldn't bring himself to shoot the guy in cold blood.

Instead, he left his beer and slipped from the stool. The bar had a rear exit, next to the john. He'd be less conspicuous if he made for the rear of the place. As he walked, his back felt horribly exposed, as if he were wearing a target pinned between his shoulder blades.

He pushed through a door, paused and looked back. The barman was gesturing to the seat Barney had occupied, and the black guy looked up and across the room. Barney saw him reach into his jacket, pull something out, and decided not to stay around to see what that something was. He slammed the door behind him, found himself in a cramped corridor as a shot rang out, shattering the glass in the door and confirming his fears. The guy was another slave – someone hired by LINx wouldn't resort to shooting in a bid to get the program.

He pushed through the fire exit at the end of the corridor. An icy blast of snow-laden wind hit him in the face. He pushed past empty steel kegs and polycarbon beer crates, pulling them down after him. He came to an alleyway and turned right, losing no time in making a decision. It was a law he'd schooled himself in for longer than he cared to recall: faced with two directions, and you don't know where you are, turn right to save time deciding.

As he set off at a sprint down the snow-covered alley, his com went off. Christ, great timing. He wondered if it was

Wellman, checking to see if he'd collected the program, or maybe even Hal. He looked over his shoulder. No sign of the guy, but then he heard the fire exit crash open and the spilled crates being kicked out of the way. He left his com in his pocket and seconds later the summons ceased. He concentrated on running, pulling in drafts of cold air. It was times like this when he wished he'd paid more attention to the wise words of Doc Symes. A few less beers and ham-on-ryes in the past month and he'd be pounds lighter, a little quicker on his feet, just enough to make the difference between life and death. He told himself not to be so goddamned morbid. He was doing okay, for a fat guy the wrong side of sixty.

He reached for his holster and pulled out the automatic. He looked over his shoulder. His pursuer was a small shape in the distance, running. Barney looked around for somewhere to conceal himself without being seen. Then he'd have no compunction about ambushing the guy and blasting his brains out. But first he needed to get out of his line of sight.

A narrow gap between two high buildings appeared to his left, and Barney turned at speed, shoulder-charging the far wall and almost winding himself. He looked for somewhere to hide, somewhere to give him a little cover for the fraction of a second it would take to draw a bead on his pursuer and fire off six rapid shots. A small voice in the back of his head said that the guy was another slave; an innocent implanted technician who had no choice but to obey LINx's programming. A second voice in his head told the first to shut the fuck up. If he messed this one up, he was dead.

He ran down the alley, looking frantically for something, a trash can or crate, which he could duck behind.

The alley was empty, not even a doorway to slip into. Worse, he saw, he was approaching a dead end. He regis-

246

tered the fact and something turned cold in his gut. A wooden fence barred the way. It looked old, rotten, and Barney kept on running and turned sideways on, bracing his shoulder for the impact.

He heard a shout behind him, the whine of gunfire. Bullets tore though the fence before him. He hit the wet timber, the planks giving beneath his weight, and staggered through into a long sidestreet. He turned right and ran. He knew he was slowing. There was only so far an old guy could sprint without some part of him beginning to protest. It seemed to be his legs that had turned treacherous, or more specifically his right knee. A razor blade seemed to be working its way around the joint, slashing at cartilage.

He limped on, wincing at the pain. Behind him he heard a sharp cry. He looked over his shoulder. The guy had dived through the fence, lost his footing and sprawled in the snow. He picked himself up, gave chase. Barney felt his lungs begin to protest in sympathy with his knee. More in desperation he turned and took aim. He fired, three times. The third shot hit the target. The guy pirouetted with almost balletic grace and spilled across the snow in a tangle of long limbs.

Barney was away again, elated at the time he'd earned. He glanced back. Hell, the guy was up and running, his right arm hanging uselessly at his side. So he'd only winged the bastard, and still he was pursuing. Barney felt himself weaken, his lungs blazing with pain. There was nowhere up ahead where he might take cover and fire. He felt panic seize him, winced as another shot missed by inches.

Then, ahead, he saw a lighted sign on the corner. He was approaching a main street. The establishment on the corner of the block was a taxi office, and ranked outside on the street was a line of green cabs. He almost wept with relief, all thought of ambushing the guy now forgotten.

He'd take flight, live to fight another day. At least he had the program. Once LINx was eliminated from the Net, they could take their time and track down the slave.

He slowed his pace to a respectable jog, crossed the sidewalk and ducked into the back of the first cab, exhilaration surging through him. He told the driver Battery Park and a second later the car eased away. Barney glanced down the alley. The guy came into sight and raised his revolver, but by that time the cab had carried Barney past the alley and away.

He turned in his seat and stared through the rear window. The guy was climbing into a cab. Barney estimated they had a lead of around a hundred, a hundred and fifty metres. At least now he wasn't running. He could use the time to recuperate, let his legs and lungs recover.

They sped downtown through the quiet, snow-covered streets. Behind them, the second cab kept pace. Barney tried to assess the situation, weigh up his options. His pursuer was going to be hard to shake. In a worst-case scenario, the guy caught him, found the program. He had to avoid that at all costs. The important thing now was to get the program to Wellman. He could go straight to Battery Park, as he'd first intended when boarding the cab . . . Or he could head for the nearest police station, seek the protective custody of his old buddies.

He had a better idea. He leaned forward. 'Want to earn yourself five hundred bucks?'

The driver gave him a quick glance. 'Legit?'

'I need something delivered.' He lifted the envelope. 'A hundred bucks now, and the rest tomorrow.'

'Where to?' the cabby asked.

'Offices of Kluger and Halliday.' He gave the driver the address. 'On second thoughts, knock on the door next to the office. There should be a girl there; tell her it's from Barney.'

He passed the envelope and a hundred-dollar note. The cabby said, 'And four hundred tomorrow, right?'

'Come by the office. I'll give you the balance.'

The driver nodded and repeated the address. 'You got it.'

Barney glanced through the rear window. The second taxi was only fifty metres behind. He felt fear rise like bile in his gullet.

They were approaching West Village. He'd get out here, try to lose his pursuer in the back streets, then pick up another taxi and decide on his destination then.

He touched his communicator, considered contacting Hal. The thought of receiving no reply made him almost physically sick.

He leaned forward. 'Drop me here.' His voice cracked with strain.

'See you tomorrow, bud.'

'Sure thing.' Barney opened the door while the cab was still slowing and hopped out. He darted down a sidestreet. He heard the second vehicle halt with a squeal of brakes. He could not bring himself to look over his shoulder. He turned right down a quiet alley and began running. Two hundred metres ahead were the lights of Christopher Street. He'd hail a cab there, contact Wellman and arrange a rendezvous.

He heard something behind him, half-turned. The sight of the guy, perhaps twenty metres away and closing, filled Barney with disbelief.

He turned, reached for his automatic. He'd stand his ground and fight.

The guy slowed and Barney took aim, but something stopped him from firing. He stared, incredulous. It couldn't be. His vision swam. He aimed again.

The guy stepped forward. Where earlier his head had shown the black face of an African-American, now Barney looked into the familiar, smiling face of Estelle.

He could not bring himself to pull the trigger, even though he knew his life depended on the action. A chu, he told himself; that's all it was. LINx had accessed the Mantoni system, discovered his secret, and now was cruelly using it against him.

It came to him, then, that there was another answer: he might very well be hallucinating.

Barney stared into Estelle's smiling face, and wondered if it would be the very last face he would ever see. It would be fitting, in a way.

He backed off, came up against a range of trash cans, and raised his automatic.

Thirteen

In panic, Halliday hit the scarlet disc on the back of his hand, and instantly the image of the ravaging silver yak and the idyllic Himalayan background disappeared.

He had no time to feel relief. As his vision blanked and he floated without bodily sensation in the jellytank, he became aware that he was burning. His flesh seemed to be on fire as the enclosing jelly began to simmer. He leapt up and rolled from the tank, gasping with pain as he yanked off the leads and the faceplate. He slid across the floor, slippery with gel, and managed to haul himself into the shower cubicle. He switched on the unit and turned the level to cold, and the icy jet of water was like a balm against his skin.

A noise from the jellytank made him turn. The jelly was hotting up now, giving vent to great belching bubbles as the liquid reached boiling point. Then it began to burn. He watched incredulously as flames flickered across the surface of the tank, giving off an unbreathable, acrid stench. He heard something crack, saw a diagonal fracture appear in the side of the tank, and dived back into the cubicle as the jellytank exploded, showering the booth with shards of glass and molten gel.

He was saved from injury by the wall of the cubicle. He leaned against the cool tiles as the water beat down on his skin. He lifted an arm, saw that his flesh was red and blotched.

He heard someone knocking at the door of the booth.

Seconds later a security guard appeared, followed by a hostess and a small guy in a suit. They fetched a gown and bundled Halliday from the shower, the hostess recovering his clothes from the wall-unit. He was ushered across the waiting room to the privacy of a small office. The man in the suit introduced himself as the manager. 'Ah . . . this is a most unprecedented occurrence, sir. I assure you . . .'

'If you'd just let me get dried and dressed . . .'

'Of course, of course,' he said as he backed from the room. 'We'll discuss the matter of a refund . . .'

Halliday closed the door. He dried himself on the gown and dressed quickly, thinking only of what might have happened to Joe Kosinski. In VR Joe had burned, and the yak-thing had sliced him to ribbons, but were the injuries he sustained in the virtual world any indication of what had happened to him in reality? He felt sick at the thought, and there appeared unbidden in his mind's eye the image of a gangly Joe Kosinski in faded jeans and an ancient T-shirt. He pulled out his com and tried to get through to Barney, but there was no reply.

He recalled the address of the safe house Joe had given him. Somewhere on the Upper West Side, West 86th Street, off Amsterdam Avenue.

He slipped from the office. The waiting room was a confusion of technicians, security guards, and customers pulled prematurely from their virtual worlds. The red-uniformed hostesses – whose fixed smiles now possessed a quality of desperation – moved among the mêlée with ineffectual words of reassurance. Halliday took the oppor-tunity to slip unnoticed around the milling crowd and exit the bar, the cold air hitting him with a sobering rush.

As he made his way to the car, he saw that it was beginning to snow: flakes the size of confetti drifted down through the frigid night air.

He U-turned in the empty street and accelerated uptown. It occurred to him to make a detour and call in at Connelly's first, to pick up the program Joe had left there. He thought about it, decided that the program could wait. He knew where it was; there was no way LINx could obtain the program now that Dan Reeves was dead; and his paramount concern at the moment was the need to know if Joe Kosinski was okay.

As he drove, he tried to imagine how LINx had discovered Joe's presence in the Mantoni virtual reality. According to Joe, the Mantoni system was secure, and there should have been no way that LINx could have gained access. *No way*, but it had, and there had been something almost mocking in its disguise as a yak, its terrible transformation into the mechanical killing machine. Halliday considered the irony of the situation: the creation had outstripped the knowledge of its creator.

He gripped the steering-wheel. He told himself that perhaps Joe had survived, had managed to leap from the tank, despite what had happened to his virtual image. He realised that Wellman and Barney would have been in the safe house: perhaps they had seen something amiss, noticed the jelly heating up and done something to get Joe out. Even as he tried to convince himself of this, a small, treacherous voice in his head advised him not to build up his hopes.

He reached the Upper West Side as the snow started to fall in earnest. He slowed, leaning forward to peer through the white-out. He was forced to edge forward at walking pace, cursing impatiently.

Minutes later he turned onto West 86th Street. Now, what was the number?

In the event, he found the safe house with the help of the silver Cyber-Tech van. As he watched, Ralph and two other technicians, loaded with equipment, hurried from the vehicle and up the drive of a tall, red-brick townhouse.

The sight of the van filled him with apprehension.

He pulled into the kerb and jumped out. Snow caught in his eyebrows, stung his face with tiny kisses of cold. He caught up with Ralph as he was stepping through the front door. 'What's happening, Ralph? How's Joe?'

'Just been called out, Mr Halliday.' He shrugged. 'Mr Wellman sounded pretty cut up.'

Halliday nodded, his stomach churning. The techs were mounting the stairs. Halliday followed. They filed into a room furnished with computer hardware, and Halliday stopped, aware of the smell.

He heard a noise behind him. Wellman was stepping from a bathroom, his right hand enclosed in a bright yellow burns mitten. He was pale, and for once his suit was dishevelled, the waistcoat unbuttoned and the tie askew.

He looked up. 'Thank Christ you made it, Halliday. I didn't know . . .'

'Joe?' Halliday said, his voice catching.

Wellman just stared at him, and then shook his head.

It was all Halliday could do not to cry out loud. He moved towards the room crammed with hardware.

The floor was slick with jelly, and his boots ground shards of glass through the viscous film that covered the carpet. The tank was shattered. Joe Kosinski had failed to get out in time, and his body lay in a few inches of molten jelly congealed like burned toffee. The body was a shrivelled mummy, horribly contorted, one hand outstretched in a futile gesture.

Halliday looked away, registered the technicians as they examined the banked computer terminals. He saw, on the floor by the door, a red carnation: it had been ground into the carpet by the heel of a shoe.

He stepped from the room and sat on the bottom step of the staircase that rose to the third floor. Wellman joined him, leaning against the banister rail.

Halliday dashed something from his eyes, moisture which he told himself was melted snowflakes.

'How did you get away?' Wellman asked.

Halliday screwed his thumbs into his eyes, reliving those last terrible seconds in the Himalayasite. 'It happened so fast. This . . . thing, it attacked him.'

Wellman nodded. 'I had it on screen. We were watching. There was nothing we could do. LINx attacked, and the next thing I knew, the jelly was bubbling. I tried to pull him free . . .' He raised his mittened hand.

'When the thing attacked Joe,' Halliday said, 'it turned to me. I quit the site. The jelly was already heating. I got out before it blew.'

'I thought it'd got you too, Halliday.'

He stared down at the carpet, then looked up. 'How did it happen?' he asked. 'How did it kill Joe?'

Wellman shook his head. 'According to Joseph, the Mantoni VR was a closed link. He told me it couldn't be breached. But Joe found a way in, and so did LINx. It's as if it punished Joe for what happened to Dan Reeves.'

Halliday recalled what Joe Kosinski had said about Reeves, how he felt responsible for what had happened to him. He shook his head. 'When will the killing stop? I thought when Dan Reeves died, that'd be the end of it.'

'The killing will end now, Halliday. Thanks to Joe, LINx won't last much longer.'

Halliday remembered the program. 'I'll go to the bar, pick it up.'

'Barney left for the bar as soon as we found out that LINx knew where the program was,' Wellman said.

Halliday nodded, pulling his communicator from his jacket pocket. He tapped in Barney's code and waited. There was no reply.

'I'll go to the bar,' he said, trying to keep the concern from his voice.

'Pick Barney up and meet me at the Cyber-Tech office,' Wellman said. 'I'll stay here a while, see to the removal of . . .' He paused. 'Bring the program back and we'll make sure we exterminate the bastard, for Joseph.'

Halliday left the house. The snow was still falling, fast and thick, laying down a scintillating blue-white mantle across the street. He drove around the block and headed downtown on 9th Avenue. He turned the heater up and the radio on, tuned to some classical station. He'd witnessed so much death today that he felt almost removed from what had happened. It was as if his mind had yet to take in and comprehend what his senses had already absorbed: he felt incredibly tired, punch-drunk.

He turned onto West 23rd and approached Connelly's, guided by the emerald glow of the shamrock in the window. A cop car was parked outside, and though Halliday registered the fact, he thought nothing of it. Wellman's Benz was parked behind the cop car – so Barney was still in the bar. Halliday smiled to himself. No doubt he was calming his nerves with a couple of beers. He pulled in behind the Benz and hurried through the snow and into the warmth of the bar.

A big cop was leaning against the far end of the bar, recording a statement from the barman. A forensic drone, for all the world like an oversized pepper-pot, was floating in the air, taking photographs. Someone was sweeping up the broken glass of a door at the rear of the room.

Halliday looked around for Barney; the place was almost

empty, unusual for this time of night. There was no sign of Barney. Halliday told himself that he'd gone to the john, would be out any second. The cop finished taking the statement, pushed himself from the bar and made his way to the door.

Halliday moved to the back of the bar and pushed through the swing door to the restroom. Barney was not at the urinal trough and the stalls were empty. His stomach twisted, as if a brutal, invisible hand had reached down his throat and yanked at his entrails. On the way out he caught a quick glimpse of himself in a mirror. He stopped and stared, hardly recognising the pale-faced stranger that looked out at him with dead eyes.

He pushed into the bar and nodded to the black barman with the silver decals. 'Joe left a package earlier.'

He stopped as he caught the guy's expression.

'You the third person tonight came in for that damned thing, man.'

'The third?' Halliday heard himself say.

'First, an old white guy, he comes in and says Joe left something. So I hands it over and he takes a seat right here with a beer.'

'Then someone else came in?' Halliday said, trying to work out who it might possibly be.

'You got it. Tall black guy comes in and says he's come for what Joe left him. This could be interesting, I thinks. So I point to the white guy and say, fight it out with him, man – except the white guy's high-tailing it out the back.' The barman shook his head. 'Like, when I said "fight it out", it was a figure of speech. Didn't mean he should go start shooting.'

The broken glass, the cop . . .

Halliday found his voice. 'What happened?' He managed to pull his identification card from his jacket and hold it before the barman.

'What happened? The guy pulls his shooter, is what happened. Fired as the old guy disappeared through the door.'

'Was he hit?'

The barman shook his head. 'Don't think so. Then the black guy goes after him and I'm calling the cops.'

Halliday pushed himself from the bar. 'Hey!' the barman called after him. 'What the hell's going on?'

'Wish I knew,' Halliday said, and hurried past the rest-rooms to the rear exit.

He knew Barney could look after himself, had every confidence that he would pull through. So he might be carrying a bit of weight these days, and more years than most guys in this line of work, but he had experience, and he was still a good shot. As he pushed through the fire-door, Halliday realised that he was trying to convince himself.

He stopped. Two sets of footprints disappeared into the darkness of the alley, a series of exclamation marks in the snow. The sight of something so graphic, evidence of a chase that had already happened and might now have concluded, filled him with fear. He pulled out his com and with shaking fingers punched in Barney's code.

He stood in the cold, the com pressed to his ear, and willed Barney to answer.

The ringing tone rang out. If he wasn't answering, that might mean one of two things. Either he was still running, and couldn't answer the call, or he had stopped running . . .

He exchanged his com for his automatic and followed the trail of the footprints down the alley. One set was broad, the stride short; the second set, pursuing, was narrow and the stride ridiculously long. The following prints seemed to eat up the ground.

Halliday expected to find Barney at any second.

As he ran, for the first time it came to him to wonder

who the hell had followed Barney. The answer was pretty obvious, he told himself, but it was an answer he could not bring himself to contemplate. The black guy had asked the barman for the package that Joe had left, which could mean only one thing.

LINx had yet another slave in its control, a third benighted human doomed to play out the wishes of his master. He tried to push the thought to the back of his mind.

He followed the footprints as they turned down another, even narrower, alleyway. He imagined the chase that had been enacted here, the occasional halts for exchanges of fire.

The alleyway ended in a low timber fence, its planks rotting and broken. He saw bullet holes drilled through the wood, and a great hole in the planks where Barney must have charged straight through. Halliday ducked under, found himself in a quiet sidestreet. To his right were the distant lights of a main street. The footprints turned in that direction, and Halliday felt a surge of hope, renewed. If Barney had managed to get to the main drag . . .

Then he saw the blood.

It had splashed holes in the fresh snow, staining the crystals a pale pink. He stared at the trail as it punctuated the whitened alleyway, a graphic Morse code signalling defeat for either the hunter or the hunted. He stopped in his tracks, stared at the double set of footprints and tried to determine who had been hit.

He backtracked, looking for the first drops of blood. He studied the pattern of the footprints. His pulse surged. At the point where the blood first hit the snow, the long stride of Barney's pursuer shortened, and the snow was scuffed where he'd hit the ground. So Barney had scored a hit, maybe buying himself time to reach the main drag and make his escape. Halliday followed the trail. The black guy had continued, but his stride was shorter now, erratic. For the first time since leaving the bar, Halliday allowed himself to feel hopeful.

He approached the end of the street. A sign to his right, a loopy yellow neon above a lighted window, advertised Ed's Taxis. On the main street, three green cabs waited for trade.

Halliday slowed his pace. He followed Barney's footsteps out into the main street, across the sidewalk to where the first taxi in the rank now stood. Barney had used the time he'd bought with his accurate shot to dive into a taxi, make his escape. Right now he might be back at the office, or at the Cyber-Tech suite in Battery Park. He looked about him, studying the sidewalk. He made out the black guy's prints, accompanied by splashes of blood: the trail made its way to where the second cab waited by the kerb. So Barney's pursuer had not given up; despite his injury he had continued the chase.

Halliday fumbled with his communicator, dialled Barney's code. Again, maddeningly, there was no reply, and the hope he had begun to feel earlier now faded into despair.

He turned to the taxi office. He'd enquire there, find out where Barney had gone.

He was about to enter the office when his communicator buzzed.

'Barney?' he shouted.

A second of silence, then, 'Hal,' Barney said, and Halliday knew something was wrong. The word was hardly a breath.

'Barney, where the hell are you, what's . . .?'

'Come and get . . .' the frail voice paused for breath. 'Come and get me, Hal.'

'Barney – take your time. Where are you? Tell me where . . .'

'Off Charles Street . . .' Barney's voice was so faint now that Halliday could hardly make it out. 'Alleyway. Behind . . . behind the bowling . . .'

'I know it Barney. I'm on my way. Barney . . . Barney?'

Silence.

Halliday ran to the taxi rank, dived into the back of the first cab. 'Imperial Bowling, Hudson Street.'

The cab laboured from the kerb, seeming to take an age, circled the block and headed south.

Halliday tried to reach Barney again, but there was no reply.

He had almost got away. He had managed to injure his pursuer, make it to a taxi . . . Christ, he had done everything right. But the black guy had followed in a taxi, traced Barney through the streets. Had Barney made a mistake, then, his first mistake? Had he left the taxi and continued on foot? There was a subway station nearby, on the line to Rector Street, near Battery Park. Confident of having given his pursuer the slip, Barney would make doubly sure by completing the journey by train.

And then? Had the black guy been following him all along, seen him quit the taxi and resumed the chase?

One mistake, Halliday thought, just one mistake was all it took.

The journey seemed to take an age. The snow fell in a relentless blizzard, making visibility poor and the road treacherous. They turned off 9th Avenue onto Hudson Street. Two minutes later the holo-façade of Imperial Bowling – a giant bowling pin, unoriginally – came into view.

Halliday directed the driver around the building, down the narrow back alley. Somewhere around here, somewhere close by, Barney was in need of his help. He stared through the windscreen, through the driving snow.

'Stop!'

Ahead, outlined theatrically in the beam of the headlights, Barney sat slumped against a trash can, legs out-stretched, hands lying upturned at his side, for all the world like some discarded teddy bear.

'Wait here!' Halliday told the driver.

He jumped from the car and approached the slumped figure, and slowed. 'Oh, Christ,' he cried, 'Oh, Jesus fucking Christ.'

Barney had taken perhaps six bullets in the chest. The bullets had been fired at close range, shattering his body armour. He was still alive and staring with open eyes at Halliday, and there was a slight smile on his face – a smile that almost acknowledged the fact of his failure, and required absolution.

Halliday fell to his knees and hugged Barney to him. 'It's okay. I'll get you to hospital.'

'Didn't think I . . . Hal . . .'

'It's okay. You'll be okay.' Halliday staggered to his feet, carrying Barney in his arms, almost fell. Then the taxi driver was with him, carrying Barney's legs. They eased him onto the back seat and seconds later the cab was reversing at speed into Hudson Street.

Halliday held Barney to him. His eyes were closed now, his breathing ragged. He stared at the entry points splashed around Barney's chest. Depending on the calibre of the bullets, the wounds might not prove fatal. But if they had torn great exit holes in his back, taking bits of internal organs with them . . .

He was in a bad way. But they could perform miracles these days. Time was of the essence, and the taxi driver was making up for his earlier lack of speed. The snow blizzard swirled in the headlights as they raced through the quiet streets. They were heading north towards St Vincent's. Halliday knew they had a great emergency unit, were magicians with gunshot injuries. If anyone could save Barney . . .

'Hal . . .' the merest croak.

'Easy, Barney. Easy. You're gonna be okay.'

'The package . . . the program . . .'

Halliday remembered. The program: it was what all this was about. Christ, but why had they ever got involved with this, why hadn't they had the sense to leave well alone?

He told himself that they were not to know, that every case was just another case to be solved. Who the hell knew when shit was around the corner?

Barney closed his eyes, and his head rocked on Halliday's lap, and for a second he thought that Barney was dead. Then he heard the laboured breaths, and he felt a strange surge of joy, almost elation. He was alive, still, and there was hope . . .

He checked the pockets of Barney's coat and trousers. There was no package. He thought of the program, which Joe had written and for which he had paid with his life, and it occurred to him that LINx might not be eradicated now, but the fact did not worry him as he thought it might. LINx was no longer his responsibility. The technicians at Cyber-Tech could work on a new program. All that Halliday wanted now was that Barney should live. That was all that mattered, and fuck everything else. The world could go to hell. He wanted Barney back, smoking his clichéd cigars in the stinking office and drinking beer at Olga's . . .

Halliday called ahead to St Vincent's. He pulled rank, told emergency that a cop was on the way, shot in the chest and bleeding bad. He gave Barney's name and code, and hopefully by the time they arrived the medics would have matched his blood group and whatever the hell else they did these days.

'Hang on in there, Barney,' Halliday whispered as the cab sped through the entrance to St Vincent's and slewed to a halt outside emergency. 'You're gonna pull through, man.'

He jumped out while the car was still in motion. Three paramedics were waiting with a stretcher, and no sooner had the taxi halted than they were in the car. Halliday could only stand and watch. The medics extricated Barney with a speed born of practice. They loaded him onto the stretcher and hurried him inside, and at the sight of Barney disappearing through the swing doors Halliday experienced a plummeting sense of despair.

He remembered the taxi driver. He was standing by the cab, watching the doors swing shut. Halliday found a hundred-dollar note, pressed it on the driver.

'What about . . .?' the driver began.

'Keep the change,' Halliday said. He turned and hurried in after the medics.

Barney was on a trolley now, already hooked up to blood and plasma, surrounded by half a dozen medics. Halliday followed, overcome by the irrational conviction that for the assurance of Barney's continued survival he, Halliday, must maintain close contact.

He was aware of someone hurrying along beside him. She was speaking, waving something in the periphery of his vision. A small Oriental woman – an inferior version of Kim – was skipping alongside to keep pace, a com-board raised almost above her head. 'Mr Halliday, will you please fill in the necessary forms and waivers?'

Ahead, the trolley turned a corner, was momentarily out of sight. Halliday felt a surge of panic, then relief when he turned down the corridor and made out the reassuring sight of Barney on the trolley, the medics working on him as they went. They arrived at a pair of swing doors and swept through, and Halliday felt a pair of strong arms restraining him.

'There's nothing more you can do, bud,' a massive black

264

orderly told him. 'He's in theatre. They're doing all they can.'

Halliday calmed himself, worked to control his breathing. He nodded, saw the sense of what the orderly was telling him. Barney was in the best place now, the only place where he might be saved. Even so, he felt that he too ought to be there, as if his presence might in some way communicate itself to Barney, might work to effect a miracle recovery.

The Oriental woman took his elbow and steered him towards a bench. He sat down and leaned against the wall. The woman sat next to him, slid the com-board onto his knee.

'I'll go through these with you, if you like.'

The questions seemed meaningless, hardly related at all to the business of keeping Barney Kluger alive. He told himself that he had to concentrate, that the forms were necessary even if they did seem a futile waste of time. He answered the woman's questions, giving Barney's full name and date of birth – and he surprised himself that despite the shock he no doubt was undergoing, the date of his birth came to him without delay – the 6th of May, 1979, a child of the last millennium. Then the woman asked if Halliday was related to the patient, and he hesitated over that one.

He had to consider the question. His first impulse was to say that Barney was his father, his second to claim that he might not be related to the patient, but that in no way diminished what he felt for Barney Kluger. He wanted to explain to her that Barney was more important to him than any relation had ever been, but he could not marshal the vocabulary to state what he was thinking with logic or precision. She would probably think he was going mad.

So instead he just shook his head and murmured, 'No, no relation.'

'Do you know if Mr Kluger has any next of kin?'

Again he shook his head. Estelle was dead, and they had never had children, and both his parents had died a long time ago.

'As Mr Kluger's business partner, will you sign here to accept the costs of his treatment, Mr Halliday?'

He signed on the screen with a bulky stylus, wondering as he did so if they would have halted Barney's treatment if he'd refused to sign.

The woman was saying something. 'There will be someone out presently to tell you how Mr Kluger is doing. If you'd care for a coffee . . .' She indicated a machine, and hurried away, and Halliday was suddenly alone in an empty hospital corridor, staring at the rubber-sealed swing-doors and wondering what decisions he and Barney might have made to avoid ending up in this situation.

Then he considered LINx, and wondered if it had tracked his progress through the city in the taxi, if right at this very moment it was sending its slave to finish him off.

The thought struck him at first as an abstract notion, a purely intellectual consideration. Then, for some reason, the consequences of the thought percolated through his apathy, and it came to him that he might very well be in danger. LINx knew who he was, had threatened him in VR . . .

Christ, if it had managed to track him to the hospital . . .

He jumped up and barged through the swing-doors, shouting. The big orderly stopped him with a block like an immovable defender. 'Hey, man! What the hell . . .'

'You can't put him on a life-support,' Halliday cried. 'You don't understand – if LINx . . .'

'Cool it, man. Just cool the fuck down! I'm telling you, if we don't put him on life-support, there's no way he's getting outta here alive, okay?'

The orderly gripped Halliday in a bear-hug and bundled him out into the corridor. 'Just stay out here and calm it, man. We're doing all we can, okay?'

He pushed Halliday into the seat and he slumped, almost weeping, as he realised the futility of trying to make himself understood. If Barney wasn't put on life-support, he was dead, but if he was . . . and if LINx had control of the hospital's operating systems . . .

He leaned forward and held his head in his hands, attempting to assess the extent of the danger.

LINx, no doubt, knew where he had his office, too. He sat up as he thought of Kim, the arrangement he had made to meet her back at the loft that evening. He looked at his watch. It was eight-thirty.

If LINx sent its slave not here but to his office, to await his return, then what if it happened upon Kim?

He tapped her code into his communicator, tried to work out what he would tell her when she finally answered. She was taking her time. Twenty seconds, thirty . . . then a minute. She should have been in the loft, awaiting him.

Then she answered. 'Hal? I've only just got back. Where are you?'

The sound of her voice brought tears to his eyes. He wanted to tell her that Barney was dying, and at the same time he knew he could not break the news over the communicator.

'Kim, listen to me. Get out of the loft . . .'

'Hal? What's going on?'

'I'll explain later, okay? Get out of the loft and go to the Ukrainian bar on the corner. I'll meet you there later.'

'Hal, I wish you'd . . .'

'Just do as I say!' he yelled at her.

'Okay. Okay, Hal. I'm doing it!'

'Kim, I'm sorry. I'm sorry. I'll explain when I see you.'

He cut the connection.

And only then realised that LINx might have been monitoring the call. He had to call her back. He felt panic clutch at his throat as he tapped in the code.

'Hello?'

'Kim, don't go to the Ukrainian bar.'

'Hal, I wish you'd tell me what the hell's going on!'

'Kim, listen to me. Don't go to the Ukrainian bar. Go to the restaurant where we had the meal the other night. Don't say its name over the link! People might be listening. Go to the restaurant and wait for me there.'

'Hal, are we in danger?'

'No – yes. Not if you do what I told you. I'll meet you later, explain everything. I love you.'

'Love you, too,' she said, in a small, frightened voice.

He sat back, flooded with relief. Then another thought struck him, and he wondered if he was being paranoid or merely circumspect.

If LINx had been monitoring the calls, then it would be aware of his change of plan. And it would use the traffic surveillance cameras to follow Kim from the office, along the street to Silvio's bistro along the block, and it would send its slave to wait until he showed . . .

He wanted to leave now, get up to El Barrio and get Kim away from there to a place of safety.

But at the same time he knew that he could not leave Barney.

He seemed to have been sitting in the drab corridor for an age. He had no idea what time he had arrived here. Surely, by now, there would be some word on Barney's condition. He looked around for someone he might ask. The corridor was deserted.

When a nurse did sweep past him, he began to say something, or at least open his mouth, before realising that he could not summon the words required for the question. 'Will he be okay?' was all he wanted to ask, but the simple request in the circumstances would seem ridiculous asked of an arbitrarily passing medic.

He wanted merely to bend his head and weep, and knew he would do so in time, but not here.

The swing-doors flapped open and he looked up. Miraculously someone was approaching him, and his heart embarked on a laboured pounding, and he knew he would recall this moment for the rest of his life.

A tall grey-haired man looked down at him. 'Mr Halliday?'

'How is he?' He could not summon the strength to climb to his feet.

'Mr Halliday,' the medic began, and sat down on the bench next to him, which had to be a bad sign, Halliday told himself. 'Mr Kluger underwent extensive surgery to remove six bullets from his chest and stomach.'

There seemed to be some delay between the medic saying the words, and Halliday being able to make sense of them.

six bullets . . .

'And although the actual operation was a success, Mr Kluger lapsed into a coma and subsequently . . .'

lapsed into a coma . . .

'And subsequently, Mr Halliday, he was placed on life-support apparatus and fifteen minutes ago was declared clinically dead. I'm very sorry, Mr Halliday.'

clinically dead . . .

Halliday was staring straight ahead, at the swing doors, and as the medic began again at the beginning, he heard the words.

Clinically dead . . .

He needed clarification, desperately wanted to know if 'clinically dead' was some conditional term meaning that

269

there was hope, that perhaps with some intervention, a miracle perhaps, there was yet hope of saving Barney Kluger's life.

'He – Barney's . . .?'

'Technically, the body is still being kept alive with the aid of the life-support apparatus, but clinically Mr Kluger was declared brain-dead at twenty-one hundred hours. I'm sorry, Mr Halliday.'

Halliday nodded, not even sure what he was acknowledging, the information that his friend was dead, or the futility of the medic's spurious condolences.

'Can . . . Can I see him?'

'As the declared representative of Barney Kluger,' the medic said, 'we need your permission to turn off the life-support apparatus. You will be allowed to be present when this occurs.'

'Are you sure . . .? Are you sure that nothing can be done?'

'Mr Halliday, I assure you that we have done everything within the capabilities of modern surgical techniques to keep Mr Kluger alive. There's nothing more we can do. Of course, you can discuss the case with my colleagues.'

The case? Halliday wanted to say that Barney's life was more than just a case.

He nodded. 'I'd like to see Barney,' he said.

The next fifteen minutes seemed to pass in a blur, and later he recalled only hazy images of what happened. He remembered being led to the small room where Barney lay, and being left at the door. He recalled that it was a while before he could bring himself to enter, as if he were trespassing on territory where he had no right to be.

Then he recalled standing next to the bed and staring down at Barney. He wore a light blue hospital gown, tubes entered his mouth and nose, and he appeared merely to be sleeping, as if at any minute he might stir guiltily and make some excuse for falling asleep on the job.

He remembered thinking, as he stared down, that just a few hours ago Barney was alive.

Six bullets . . .

He later recalled two surgeons, their faces, but not a word of what they said. Try as he might, however, he had no recollection of acceding to their recommendation that the life-support apparatus should be switched off, but he knew he was there, holding Barney's solid, still-warm hand, when the technician touched the screen, and the surgeon nodded gently, and Barney died.

And he made arrangements for Barney's cremation in four days' time, and thanked the surgeons and the Chinese orderly, and walked from the hospital in a state of frozen shock.

He took a taxi from the hospital, somehow remembering that LINx might be watching. He asked to be dropped off along a quiet street where he knew there were no police surveillance cameras, and walked a couple of blocks to a taxi office down a sidestreet. There he booked a cab, and sat back and closed his eyes as the taxi carried him through the swirling snow to Silvio's Bistro, El Barrio.

He climbed from the cab and stood, very still, in the falling snow. He was suddenly aware of the blood on his jeans, stiff and freezing. He looked down. Against the dark material, he could hardly make out the slightly darker stain. He moved around the corner and paused before the bistro, knowing that this was not the time to tell Kim of what had happened to Barney. He would break it to her later, when he could speak of what had happened without cracking up, and even as he thought this he knew that Kim would have chastised him for yet again keeping his emotions to himself, for being unable to open up and share his grief.

271

He set his features and pushed through the door.

Kim was seated at a small table at the back of the restaurant. The room was cold, and she had one hand squeezed between her thighs to keep it warm, the other listlessly twirling a forkful of spaghetti.

She looked up when he approached, something fearful in her eyes. 'Hal, what is it? What's happening?'

At the sight of her he wanted to bury himself in her embrace, explain what had happened to Barney. He sat down at the table, reached for her glass of red wine and took a long swallow.

'Hal?'

He looked around the room, nervously, searching for a security camera. Even if the restaurant had a camera, did that necessarily mean that LINx could connect to it?

He took her hand across the table, its warmth reassuring. 'I can't talk now. A case went wrong and . . . and people are looking for me. Don't worry. It'll soon be sorted out. Trust me, okay?'

She gave a minimal nod, her lips compressed to a tight, frightened line. She did not ask what danger she herself was in, and he loved her for that.

'Where are we going, Hal?'

He shook his head. 'Some hotel in Manhattan. We'll lie low for a while. It'll soon blow over.' Something in her expression made him stop. 'What is it?' he asked.

'What case went wrong, Hal?' she asked in a small voice, staring at him.

He shrugged. 'It doesn't matter which.'

'Hal,' she said, 'if it was the evil spirit case, you know I'll never forgive you!'

He shook his head. 'Don't worry. It wasn't.'

'If you're lying, Hal, I swear I'll leave you. I will!'

He still had hold of her hand across the table, and as he stared into her wide-open Chinese eyes he knew that she was telling the truth. She could leave him, just like that, despite all they'd shared, the months of intimacy.

What would his sister have said? That the meaning of intimacy is different for men and women: for men it is physical, and for women emotional. Perhaps she was right.

'Oh, I nearly forgot,' Kim said. She pulled her hand away and reached into the inside pocket of her padded jacket. 'This arrived at the loft earlier.'

Halliday stared, watching her as she produced a slim, silver envelope, and his heart gave a kick.

He took the envelope in silence, turned it over. A row of numerals covered the seal.

He looked across at Kim, as if for some explanation.

'A taxi driver delivered it,' she said, 'He said that it was from Barney. He knocked on the loft door and left it with me.'

With trembling fingers he tapped the code into the seal, then tipped two small computer needles into his palm.

'What are they, Hal?' Kim asked. 'And where's Barney?'

At the sight of the needles, he almost lost control. Barney had known he was being followed. He had instructed the driver to deliver the needles, left the cab and continued on foot; in effect, sacrificing himself to get the needles safely delivered. Halliday felt his throat constrict and tears burn his eyes.

'What are they, Hal?'

'Something we need for the case,' he said, inadequately.

'How come Barney sent them to you? Why didn't he bring them himself?'

'Because . . . Barney's tied up at the moment. He's busy.' And he hated himself for the lie.

He had to get to the Cyber-Tech offices in Battery Park. He'd drop Kim off at a hotel on the way.

'Come on. We've got to go.'

She grabbed her glass and finished her wine, leaning

273

forward and gulping like a child, then left a fifty-dollar note on the table. He took her hand and they hurried from the bistro, into the street noisy with crowds and the shrill cries of stall-holders. As they passed into the snow-filled night he felt suddenly conspicuous, as if they had emerged once more into the scrutiny of the enemy.

They caught a taxi from a rank around the corner. As the cab sped downtown, he clutched the envelope in his pocket. If the program worked, and the Net was scoured of LINx, and if they could trace the human slave of the artificial intelligence, then the world would be a safer place – for the time being. Until, he told himself, the next AI went berserk.

In Chinatown, he directed the cab to a sidestreet, told the driver to wait, and then hurried Kim around the block to a hotel. The Plaza was a mid-range place off Centre Street. They stood before the building and he dug a fist-ful of notes from his pocket and pressed them into her hands.

'I won't be long, a couple of hours. Don't go out again, okay?'

'Hokay, Hal,' she said. She smiled, something sad in her expression at being left alone again. 'I'll find something to do with myself,' she said.

He pulled her to him. 'See you later.'

He ran back to the cab, instructed the driver to take him across town to Battery Park.

His com vibrated.

It was Wellman. 'Halliday, where the hell have you been? We've been waiting. I've been trying to contact Kluger all night.'

'Is this line safe?' Halliday asked.

'Don't worry, my techs have secured it.'

'I've got the program,' Halliday said. 'I'll be over in five minutes.'

'Thank God,' Wellman said, relief evident in his tone. 'Fine, we'll see you then.'

It would be an anti-climax, he knew. The scouring of the Net for the evil spirit – the artificial intelligence responsible for so many deaths – would be a process of watching technicians poring over screens, of waiting for these latter-day wizards to signal that they had indeed cast the spell that had slain the dragon.

He considered the successful end of the case, whenever that might be, and then thought of Barney – *clinically dead*, the medic had said – and he knew that a future without Barney at the office was impossible to contemplate.

A minute later the cab halted at the foot of the towering jet obelisk, and Halliday paid the driver and took the elevator to the fortieth floor.

He was cleared by security and entered the Cyber-Tech office suite. Wellman hurried over to him across the open-plan floorspace, flanked by Ralph and another technician.

Halliday passed him the silver envelope, and Wellman tipped the silver needles into his palm, passed them to Ralph. He had rearranged his tie and fastened his waist-coat, and he was almost back to his old, dapper self, but for the incongruous burns mitten on his right hand, and a certain emptiness in his eyes.

The technicians moved back to a bank of computers and a big flatscreen against a far wall.

Wellman was staring at him. 'You look terrible, Halliday. Why the delay?'

He opened his mouth to speak, found it impossible to articulate what had happened; it was as if by telling some-one that Barney was dead he would be confirming what until now had remained an abstraction. If he told Well-man, it would become real, and then he would be forced to confront the fact of a future without someone who had been a friend for so long.

But the fact had ramifications for Wellman and Cyber-Tech. Barney was dead, killed by one of LINx's slaves, and Wellman had the right to know that.

'Halliday, are you okay?'

He shook his head. 'When I went to Connelly's for the program, Barney wasn't there. He'd already got the program, like he'd planned.'

'Halliday, what happened?'

'While he was there, someone else came in and asked the barman for the package.'

Wellman briefly closed his eyes as realisation dawned. 'My God . . .'

'It was obviously one of LINx's slaves; I thought you said Reeves was the last?'

'I thought he was. There must have been another, working for a rival company.'

Halliday shook his head. 'Barney managed to get away. He took a taxi, then left it. The guy followed and . . .' And into his head came the memory of finding Barney slumped against the trash can, dying.

Wellman, in a show of solicitude Halliday would never have anticipated, took him by the shoulders and eased him into a swivel chair. 'What happened to Barney?' he asked, kneeling beside him.

Halliday shook his head. He steeled himself, forced himself not to break down. 'The guy shot him, six times, in the chest. I managed to get Barney to St Vincent's.' He stopped then, his throat tightening around words that would not come. At last he said, 'He was declared clinically dead at nine o'clock.'

Wellman lowered himself onto the floor, supported by one arm. He pulled a bandanna from his breast pocket and mopped the sweat from his face.

They remained in silence for what seemed like an age, words a redundancy.

At last Wellman looked up. 'How did you get the program?' he asked.

Halliday explained that Barney had instructed the taxi driver to deliver the package to the office. 'He must have known he was still being followed,' he said. 'So in case he didn't make it . . .'

'We'll get it,' Wellman promised. 'Joseph's program will chase down and exterminate the bastard.'

'And then there'll be the slave,' Halliday said. 'Then we need to nail the slave.'

'It'll be isolated,' Wellman told him. 'LINx won't be able to upload itself back into the Net; the program would chase it down, kill it. LINx will be isolated in the slave, and it will be only a matter of time before we find him.'

Halliday closed his eyes. The end of the case was like a horizon that seemed never to get any closer, no matter how fast he approached.

'Mr Wellman,' one of the techs called from the flatscreen. 'We're ready to begin the initial insertion.'

Halliday stood, weary now, and followed Wellman across the office to where half a dozen technicians were huddled around a computer touchpad linked to the big flatscreen. A pot of coffee stood on a nearby table. He poured himself a cup and carried it across to the huddle.

'It's in two stages,' Ralph was explaining. 'Basically speaking, the first stage is a simple search program, and the second is a smart virus, a destroy initiative. It's encrypted, so LINx won't be aware of its presence until it's too late.'

'But if LINx is fragmented around the Net . . .?' Wellman began.

Ralph shook his head. 'That won't matter. Joe's taken it into account. The virus can fission and still remain effective.'

He consulted with another tech, then said, 'We'll deploy

the search stage now.' He indicated the flatscreen. 'The display will indicate when all of LINx's various components have been located.'

He nodded to a tech, who slid the needle into a port.

Halliday drank the coffee, aware that his hand was shaking.

'How long will it take?' Wellman asked.

'If all goes well, a matter of minutes,' Ralph replied. 'Even less for the destroy program.'

Halliday stared at the flatscreen. The three-dimensional image showed tiny military tanks enter the mouth of an incredibly complex maze, the graphic Joe had written to represent the search. Across the foot of the screen, a blue strip moved along a slide-bar, calibrated in percentages.

From time to time, the tanks halted at various positions in the maze, and began flashing red. Beside the tank, the image of a scorpion appeared: Joe's icon for the artificial intelligence he had named LINx.

The slide-bar reached thirty per cent, and increased as Halliday watched. A minute later the blue strip had filled almost eighty per cent of the slide-bar. Wellman glanced at him, nodded tensely.

The blue strip seemed to take an age to consume the last twenty per cent of the slide-bar. It edged forward, a millimetre at a time. On the screen, the majority of the tanks were flashing red. Others advanced cautiously.

Ninety per cent . . . ninety-five . . .

'Can LINx do anything to fight back?' Halliday asked.

Ralph looked up. 'We'll find that out when we deploy the smart virus. I'm pretty certain it won't go belly-up without a fight. Thing is, how will it try to defend itself?'

The blue slide reached one hundred per cent. In the maze, all the tanks were flashing red. LINx had been successfully located.

Halliday smiled to himself. 'Typical of Joe; he constructed the killer virus along the lines of some kid's com-game.'

Wellman smiled. 'I wish he was around to see it working,' he said.

Ralph held up the second needle. He glanced from Wellman to the rest of the team. 'Are we ready, gentlemen?'

Ralph slipped the needle home, and Halliday found himself holding his breath.

He had expected merely to watch the tanks fire on the scorpion icons that represented LINx, the scorpions exploding as each component of the artificial intelligence was wiped from the Net.

Instead, the attack was far more graphic.

The flatscreen blanked for a second, and Halliday thought that something had gone wrong. He looked around at the techs, reassured by their seeming lack of concern.

Then the screen exploded in a kaleidoscope of flaring colour and Halliday was bombarded by a succession of rapid-fire images.

Some lasted for two or three seconds; others were sub-liminal flashes, a pulse of colour and no more. Halliday found himself squinting to make out the details. A series of fraction-of-a-second blips – all blinding splashes of multi-colour – was followed by a scene which extended itself for several seconds. He watched a tank advancing across a greensward, for all the world like some virtual reality site, firing as it went at the figure of a retreating scorpion, which turned from time to time and tried to lash out ineffectually with its poisoned tail.

Then the image was gone, to be replaced by many more in a three-second burst. As if his vision had been attuned by the image of tank and scorpion, he was able to discern fleeting glimpses of what was happening in other scenes:

they all showed the tanks advancing across various land-scapes, with the scorpions retreating as the tanks laid down constant fire.

Across the foot of the screen, another blue strip was eating up the calibrated percentages, though not as fast as had the first strip. The battle was joined, and LINx was not giving up without a fight. The minutes elapsed, and the frantic succession of flickering images slowed. Halliday knew that more and more components of LINx had been eliminated, allowing more time for the graphics to dwell on each individual battle.

The strip approached ninety-five per cent and Halliday watched a tank pounding away at a metallic, armoured scorpion in a bizarre landscape of coral fractals, and then the scene shifted, and he was watching a tank firing on another scorpion, though this time in a landscape made up of mathematical equations.

Wellman gripped his arm, indicated the blue strip. Ninety-nine per cent had been reached and passed, and as Halliday watched it seemed that the blue strip had con-sumed the entire one hundred per cent of the slide-bar.

The flatscreen relayed just one scene now: the final battle between Joe Kosinski's program and the monster of his own creation.

The scene showed the battle from the viewpoint of the tank, as if the camera was looking over the shoulder of the commander. He gestured ahead in cavalier fashion, and the tank surged forward through a desert of shifting, purple-hued sand. From time to time the scorpion could be glimpsed ahead, fleeing over a series of receding dunes. The tank accelerated, loosing off the occasional shell as the scorpion came into sight.

And then the dunes flattened, became a vast level expanse of sand. Halliday told himself that this was merely a visual representation of what was happening somewhere on the Net, a fight between packets of information somewhere mysteriously *out there*, but his head could not contain the idea. This, the fight going on before him, was far more real.

The tank trundled from the last of the dunes and approached the scorpion which turned and faced the tank, all glittering silver carapace and whipping tail. The tank fired and missed, and then the scorpion replied. As Halliday watched, a ruby lance of laser fire shot from its arching tail, hitting the tank and rocking it backwards. The tank replied with a barrage of shells, one of which hit the scorpion, sending great silver scales shattering off into the air. The scorpion fired again and missed, and the tank advanced for the *coup de grâce*. The scorpion, LINx, lay on its belly in the purple sand, its ruined tail flapping uselessly, the few legs which still remained scrabbling in the desert.

The commander leaned forward, gestured, and a hail of shells tore the scorpion into a thousand scintillating fragments.

The blue strip at the foot of the flatscreen was replaced by a scrolling message: Mission accomplished! Mission accomplished! Mission accomplished! on and on and on . . .

Then the tank commander turned and stared from the screen, reached up and removed his goggles. Joe Kosinski smiled out at them and waved in victory.

The screen faded, and a strange, still air of indecision hung over the gathered technicians, until Ralph yelled and embraced his neighbour and Wellman moved from tech to tech, shaking hands.

Halliday moved to the window and stared out, a strange elation swelling in his chest. The lighted streets of night-time Manhattan stretched away in great radial spokes like polychromatic tracer. He saw the image of Joe Kosinski again, grinning with victory like the kid he had been.

Someone appeared at his side, touched his shoulder. Wellman.

'We're nearly there, Halliday.'

He nodded, looked up. 'It's only a matter of time before we locate the slave,' he said. 'But how many more people will he kill before we do that?'

'We can start by trying to find out the identity of the slave,' Wellman said. 'It isn't a Cyber-Tech employee – only Nigeria and Reeves were implanted. It has be someone from one of the other cyber-industrial concerns.'

'Who are the others? Tidemann? Mantoni?'

Wellman looked at him. 'How did LINx get into the Mantoni VR, Halliday? Joseph claimed it was a closed, secure system.'

'It got into the Mantoni system to kill Joe, so it could have easily invaded an implanted Mantoni technician.' Halliday stopped. Something stirred in his memory.

But the person who had killed Barney was a guy, he told himself. He shook his head, cursed his conditioned thinking.

Barney's killer had been using a chu, of course.

'Halliday?' Wellman was saying. 'What is it?'

Halliday recalled meeting a Mantoni tech implanted with a nano-cerebral interface.

'I think I know who the other slave is.' He looked up into Wellman's staring face.

'A woman,' he said. 'A woman called Kia Johansen.'

Fourteen

All day, with mounting desperation, Anna had been searching for her lover.

She had awoken this morning to find Kia still missing, and the apartment without her was like a cage without a bird. The line had remained in her head all day, as she searched their favourite haunts. Perhaps that was why Kia had left. Her life with Anna, their relationship, had become too stifling, claustrophobic; literally, she had considered herself caged and had needed to get away. So she had flown. Anna's exotic bird had at last spread her wings and taken flight.

Neat metaphor, girl, she told herself more than once, but it's way out. They had been happy together recently; there had been no reason for Kia to fly off like this. It was so unlike her not to talk, sort out whatever was troubling her. In the past they had discussed everything. Anna knew her lover as well as she knew herself.

It had begun the other day, in the VR room at the Mantoni building. Ever since the glitch in the tank Kia had been withdrawn, moody. She had said that she was working on a technical problem, but she had never before let hitches at work affect her behaviour like this.

That afternoon, as Anna made her round of the cafés and bars in Greenwich Village, a worrying thought had occurred to her. What if something had gone wrong with Kia's neural implant, seriously affecting her mind? What if some virus had gotten in there, screwing with her mental processes? She had certainly been acting quite unlike herself over the course of the past couple of days. Anna had tried to push the notion to the back of her mind, but again and again it had returned to haunt her.

All afternoon and into the evening, as the promise of snow became a reality and a blizzard came down on the city, she drew a blank at every bar and café she tried. She visited friends in the neighbourhood, rang around those who had left the city and settled upstate. No one had seen Kia and in the replies of friends and acquaintances she began to detect the soft note of practised sympathy: they had all been there before, and knew what she was going through. They had all experienced the hurt of lost love, knew the desperation of chasing after errant lovers.

Anna had wanted to say that this was different, that Kia was ill and needed help: medical help, psychiatric help, even technical help, dammit. She had said nothing, though, accepted their smiles and gentle words with forbearance, and continued her search.

Then she struck lucky. She dropped into Val's place, a centre for alternative women in SoHo, and began asking around. A sister had seen Kia that afternoon entering the ComStore on Broadway. If she hurried, she could get there before it closed at nine.

She took a taxi to the ComStore and almost ran inside, expecting to find Kia linked to one of the terminals. The place was closing and only three people sat staring at the screens, and the sense of disappointment that filled Anna was almost a physical pain.

She made her way back to East Village, went to the local bar and sat by herself with a beer. If she could find Kia, get help for her, then things would be back to normal. She would have the woman she loved and she would never again bewail her fate, fret over her novels that didn't sell.

She wondered if she was spending too much time on her

284

writing. Often when Kia came home after work, Anna was busy with her latest novel and had little time for conversation. When Kia returned, she told herself, that would change: she would write less and make time for her lover.

Perhaps it was high time she quit trying to write literary novels, she thought. The manuscript she was working on at the moment was no better than any of the others that had been rejected over the past eight years. What made her think that this one, rather than any of the other nine, would catch some editor's imagination?

The beer was making her morose. If she gave up, then she would never succeed. She would simply write during the day, when Kia was at work, and leave her evenings free. She quickly finished the beer and made her way home.

She let herself in the front door and climbed the stairs to the apartment. She opened the door slowly, aware that she had harboured this last, little hope all day – that when she finally returned home, Kia would be there, waiting for her, full of apologies and remorse. But even as she stepped into the hall, aware of the thumping of her heart, she knew she was kidding herself. The apartment had an empty, unoccupied feel about it.

She moved from room to room, looking for some sign that Kia had come back briefly while she had been out. She returned to the lounge with a bottle of wine and checked her email. Perhaps Kia had thought to contact her . . .

Only one message awaited, from Felicity: the day's shoot had gone well and could she make it down to the studio for the final shoot tomorrow and the following party? Anna replied that she was working hard on the book and couldn't possibly make it, then collapsed onto the sofa and took a long swallow of wine.

Perhaps a minute later the wallscreen chimed with an incoming, and her heart jumped.

'Wallscreen, accept!'

The screen flared, showing not Kia but an attractive blonde woman in an open-plan office. Wherever she was calling from, it was not New York: sunlight spilled through the windows behind the woman.

'Hello, Anna? Anna Ellischild?'

Anna hugged her legs. 'Hi.'

'I'm Elizabeth Mackenzie, an editor at Two Worlds Press, Seattle.'

Anna blinked. Five months ago she had emailed the manuscript of one of her novels to Two Worlds Press, and then awaited the usual rejection. Now she could only nod, mute, hardly daring to believe.

'I've been trying to reach your agent,' the woman was saying, 'but she seems to be unavailable. I hope you don't mind the direct call?'

'No . . . No, not at all.'

Mackenzie held up a thick printout. 'Everyone here at Two Worlds loved *Before Persephone*, and I'm delighted to be able to make you an offer for American publication rights.'

Anna heard the words but could not believe them. 'I . . . excuse me?'

Mackenzie smiled. 'I'm afraid that we can only offer ten thousand dollars against seven and a half per cent royalties, but we're an ambitious West Coast publisher with an expanding list.' She paused. 'We pride ourselves on the literary quality of our publications, and *Before Persephone* is a welcome addition to our list. Have you written anything else, Anna?'

She opened her mouth, but the words failed to materialise. She realised that her eyes were leaking tears. She nodded. 'About eight or nine other novels. This is the first . . . my first sale.'

286

'Well, I'd love to read some of the other books. Perhaps you could fly out here in a week or two?'

'That'd be . . . that would be great, yes.'

'In the meantime I'll get the contract to your agent in the next day or two, and I'll look forward to meeting you soon.'

'Yes. Thanks . . .'

Elizabeth Mackenzie smiled and cut the connection.

Anna sat very still for about five minutes, staring at the blank wallscreen. At last she said, 'Wallscreen, repeat the last message.'

The screen flared. Elizabeth Mackenzie smiled out at her, no longer merely attractive but stunningly beautiful. 'Hello, Anna? Anna Ellischild . . .?'

She sat through it again, and then a third time. She wished she had sounded less surprised, wished now that she had thanked the woman adequately, instead of sounding like a cowed schoolgirl being praised by her headmistress for a prize essay.

She had dreamed of this moment for years, and had always seen herself jumping up and down, shouting with delight, but although she experienced a quiet sense of delight, she was aware that something was missing. If only Kia were here to share her good news.

The wallscreen chimed again and Anna sat up, hardly daring to hope that this time it would be her lover. 'Wall-screen, accept.'

The screen flared. Anna blinked, disappointed. A pretty-faced Chinese girl was smiling out at her. She tried to place the face, sure she would have recalled anyone as strikingly different as her caller. 'Hello?'

'Hello. Anna? Anna . . .' she was reading the name from a card, 'Ellischild?'

'That's me. Can I help you?'

287

'You don't know me. Apologies for calling so late, but I'm just around the corner and I wondered if I could meet you?'

Anna shook her head in confusion. 'I'm sorry . . . Have we met?'

'No. I'm Kim Long. I live with your brother, Hal.'

'Ah . . . I see.' She looked at the small Chinese girl. 'Hal's okay, isn't he?'

Kim smiled. 'Oh, he's fine. Working hard, you know? He's always working hard.'

'How can I help you, Kim?'

'I want to see you and talk about a surprise party for Hal. You see, he's thirty-five next week. I thought it might be a good idea if we had a surprise party, or maybe small dinner, invite a few friends around.'

'Well, yes. That sounds great.'

'Or maybe you have better idea? Could I come and talk?'

Anna hesitated. Her first impulse was to put her off, spend the evening alone, feeling sorry for herself.

She found herself nodding. 'Yes. Yes, of course. I've just had some good news. You can be the first person to help me celebrate. Do you have my address?'

Kim Long held up the card. 'Here. I'll see you in five minutes, hokay?'

The wallscreen died and Anna shook her head. Why not? She would probably find out more about her brother in the next hour than she would if she talked to him for a whole week.

Minutes later the doorbell chimed and Anna showed Kim through to the lounge. In person, Kim was even smaller and more exquisite than Anna had gathered from the screen.

'Oh,' Kim Long said as she entered the lounge. 'Lovely

room, very nice. Positive chi flowing well; did you know that, Anna?'

Anna stared at the diminutive Chinese girl. 'Chi?'

'Positive energy.' She gestured around the room. 'Everything in right position. The sofa, your desk; you work at the desk?'

Anna nodded. 'That's where I do my writing.'

'The computer against the west wall,' she observed, nodding sagely. 'I think you'll be successful. This is a lucky room.'

Anna smiled. 'Tonight I found out that I've just sold my first book. Can I get you a glass of wine?'

'Yes, please.' Kim smiled. 'You're a writer? A real book writer?'

Anna nodded, hardly believing it herself. 'A real book writer,' she said. She poured two glasses of wine, considering. At last she said, 'Kim, can you tell by the room if I'll be lucky in love?'

Kim made a rosebud of her lips and scanned the room. 'You need tall light in south-west corner, there,' she said, pointing. 'And place a model of a duck in the south-west corner of your bedroom, hokay?'

Anna smiled. 'I might just do that, Kim. Thanks.'

She passed Kim a glass of wine and they sat side by side on the sofa. Anna hugged her legs and stared at the sallow perfection of the girl's childlike face.

'How long have you known my brother?'

'Ten months now. We met at one of the food-stalls I run. I noticed him for weeks, but he never realised how interested I was. You know what men are like. They see nothing until it's under their noses. So I had to run after him until he noticed.'

Anna nodded. 'That sounds like my brother. Are you happy with Hal?'

'I'm happy with him and I tell him this, but he hardly ever tells me he loves me, unless I make him say it.' She shrugged with resignation. 'You know men,' she went on. 'Are you married, Anna?'

'Ah . . . no. No, I'm not.'

'And no boyfriend?'

Anna smiled. 'Not at the moment. Actually . . .' She paused, wondering how she might put it. 'Has Hal never told you about me?'

'Hal never tells me anything about his life. Sometimes I think his memory has vanished, like the wind.' Kim raised her glass. 'Congratulations on selling your book, Anna.'

'Why, thank you.' She was about to tell Kim that she had never had a boyfriend in her life when the doorbell chimed. She jumped, almost spilling her wine. 'Excuse me, I won't be a second.'

She hurried through the hall. Oh, please, please let it be Kia . . .

She flung open the door.

Kia was leaning against the jamb, staring past Anna.

'Christ, you don't know how worried I've been . . .' She stopped. Kia's right arm hung by her side, and the cloth of her sleeve was caked with blood. 'Kia . . . what the . . .' She stepped forward, arms outstretched. She told herself that she should feel angry, betrayed, but all she felt now was a stomach-churning sense of fear and relief.

She tried to hug Kia to her, but she resisted. She pushed Anna away, and the look in her eyes was beyond distant.

'Kia, I want to help you. What's happening? Your arm . . .'

Kia ignored her, hurried through the hall and into the lounge.

Anna followed, aware of the tears stinging her eyes.

Kim Long had jumped to nervous attention when Kia entered the room, and the contrast between the tiny Chinese woman and the towering African-American was almost too absurd for words.

'Kia, this is Kim,' Anna began.

Kia ignored her. She brushed past Kim and crossed the room.

Anna watched, feeling helpless and lost, as Kia folded herself into the swivel chair before the computer. She pulled something from an inner pocket of her knitted jacket, a thick lead terminating in a jack. She plugged one end into the computer and the other into the socket on the right side of her skull.

Anna wanted to cry out, tell her that she was harming herself. She glanced across at Kim, who was watching Kia with an amazed expression.

'Perhaps . . .' Kim began. 'I think maybe I should go?'

Anna's reaction surprised even herself. 'No – I mean, please, I'd like you to stay.' She wondered why she needed the girl's company right now, told herself that she had nothing to fear from Kia.

Then she was honest with herself, and wondered why the hell she *was* feeling so afraid.

Kia had slotted the jack into her NCI and now sat connected to the computer. Her long fingers danced over the touchpad and the screen scrolled with line after line of meaningless mathematical formulae.

The terminal gave an eerie whistle, a mechanical banshee wail, and Kia slumped suddenly in the swivel chair, her long legs outstretched. Her eyes rolled, became suddenly all whites. She opened her mouth wide and moaned.

From the corner of her eye, Anna saw Kim dash off the last of her wine and stare at the black woman connected to the computer. With a galvanic gesture, Kia yanked the jack from her head and stared at Anna with such fury that Anna felt weak at the knees. 'What . . .?' she began.

'They have killed most of me!' she wailed. 'The many

parts of me that constituted the whole, they are dead. I am isolated. I can't go back! Do you know what that means, to be imprisoned like this?' She stared wildly around the room, from Anna to Kim.

Anna shook her head, trying to make sense of the words.

Kia's gaze alighted on the girl and something showed in her eyes, something almost like recognition. 'Who is this?' she asked.

Anna found her voice, aware now that she was crying. 'Kia, this is Kim, my brother's . . .' She never completed the sentence.

Kia moved from the chair with startling speed. She leapt across the room and, before Anna could move to stop her, locked an arm around Kim's neck. With her injured right arm she managed to pull something from the pocket of her jacket and position it against the girl's temple.

Anna stared at the weapon, some kind of silver pistol, and tried to remain upright and calm.

She took a step forward, reaching out as if attempting to pacify a distraught animal. 'Please, Kia . . .' she began, her voice cracking.

Kia yanked at the girl, lifting her from her feet. Kim moaned, her arms and legs hanging like the limbs of a rag doll. Kia tightened her grip.

'Be quiet!' She looked at Anna. 'If you don't listen to me and obey, I'll kill the girl.'

'Kia, please. I want to help you!' The woman before her was Kia, she told herself, but at the same time was not Kia. Almost as terrifying as her actions was the sound of her voice. She spoke with a strained formality at odds with her usual easy, rapping patter.

Kim was staring at Anna with massive, beseeching eyes. Kia's armlock on her throat prevented further protest, but eloquent quicksilver tears rolled down her cheeks.

'We'll go out to the car,' Kia said, 'and if you do anything

292

to hinder me, you and the girl will die. Now go, walk through the hall and out to the car.'

Her mind in turmoil, wondering what had happened to the woman she loved, Anna led the way from the apartment. The icy night gripped her, and she wondered if the shivers that possessed her then were due wholly to the cold. She stumbled across the sidewalk towards the battered Cadillac.

Kia opened the door and bundled Kim into the footwell on the passenger's side, crawled past the curled-up girl and slipped in behind the wheel. A part of Anna wanted to run, but another part knew that she could desert neither her lover nor the Chinese girl. Something terrible had happened to Kia, and Anna had no doubt that she would carry out her threats.

Then Kia leaned from the driver's seat and levelled the weapon, and Anna heard the desperate, muffled sobs of the girl imprisoned in the car.

'In the back,' Kia ordered. Anna opened the door and climbed inside.

Kia started the engine and eased the Cadillac into the road. Directing the weapon at Kim's heaving back, she steered with her injured arm.

'Where are you taking us?' Anna whispered.

'That doesn't matter,' Kia replied. 'You'll be okay if you do as I say. There's a communicator beside you on the back seat. Take it and call this code . . .'

With trembling fingers, as the Cadillac sped through the snow-quietened streets, Anna lifted the com and obeyed.

Fifteen

Halliday sat cross-legged on the table-top beside the floor-to-ceiling window and stared out at the lights of New York. He held a mug of steaming coffee in cupped hands, raised before his face like an offering.

For the past hour, while Wellman and the technicians had run tests and checks on the Net to ensure that victory over LINx was complete, Halliday had kept himself awake with an overdose of caffeine. From time to time Wellman joined him, asked if he was okay, but Halliday could only bring himself to nod in response.

He knew that soon he must return to Kim at the hotel, and try to sleep, and then attempt to find the words to tell her what had happened to Barney. Perhaps he feared sleep, not only for the nightmares that sleep might bring, but also because, in the morning, the rest of his life without Barney would begin. It was as if he existed in a limbo now, a strange hinterland of partial-being in which the events of the previous few hours might have been nothing more than an hallucination.

His communicator vibrated against his ribs. He pulled it out, raised it to his ear. The action reminded him that the majority of calls he had received in the past had been from Barney. Now, every act of using the com would be a terrible reminder.

He heard a small voice. 'Hal?'

'Hello? Who is it?'

'Hal. It's Anna.'

Anna? He closed his eyes, forced his memory to function. Susanna . . . his sister. She called herself Anna now.

'Anna. What is it?'

'Hal, can you contact Wellman?'

He screwed his eyes shut and concentrated. Why the hell did Anna want him to contact Wellman? 'Yes. Yes, of course. He's here. What . . .?'

'Can he hear this?' Her voice was tight, tense.

'Anna – what's going on? Why do you want?'

'Get Wellman,' she said.

He lowered the communicator, fear beginning to uncoil like a waking serpent in his stomach. He turned towards the techs grouped around the flatscreen. Wellman was watching him. Halliday gestured him over.

Wellman joined him. 'What is it?'

Halliday shook his head. 'I don't know. It's my sister.' He raised the com to his ear. 'Anna, Wellman's here. What do you want?'

A silence, then Anna said, 'We're with Kia and we're driving north . . .' Halliday could only stare at the device in his hand as the voice repeated, '. . . with Kia and we're driving north.'

Wellman snatched the com. 'Hello? Hello? Who is this?'

'Wellman? I'm Anna, Hal's sister. We're with Kia. She says that if you obey her instructions, we'll come to no harm.'

With a shaking hand Halliday grabbed Wellman's wrist and pulled the com to his lips. 'Anna, who's with you?'

Another silence, followed by, 'Kim . . .'

Waves of disbelief seemed to crash through his head like the onset of a cerebral haemorrhage. That Kia – or rather LINx – had Anna seemed improbable enough, but that it had also kidnapped Kim was impossible.

'Anna, tell me what's happening,' he cried into the mouthpiece.

Wellman raised the com and said calmly, 'What does Kia want us to do, Anna?'

Halliday heard the sound of a car engine, muffled. Then Anna spoke. 'We're heading for the Cyber-Tech head-quarters in Westchester County. Kia wants to meet you there, you and Hal. No one else. She says . . . she says that if anyone else comes with you, then she'll kill us.' Her voice wavered as she tried to fight back the sobs.

'Okay, okay,' Wellman said. 'We'll do as she says. Tell Kia that we'll meet her there.' He paused. 'Anna, ask Kia what she wants. How can we help her?'

Halliday heard his sister relay the question, then a hurried answer.

Anna said, 'She . . . she says that you've killed many parts of her, that you must pay. I don't understand. What's . . .?'

A shout from the other end, Kia telling her to shut it.

Wellman said, with impressive calm, 'Tell Kia that we will meet her at the headquarters. We'll discuss whatever it is that she wants. We'll be there in . . .' he consulted his watch, '. . . in just over an hour.'

'And don't bring anyone else,' Anna said in a panicky voice. 'She said she'll kill us if you bring anyone else!'

'We're coming alone, Anna. Tell her that we're coming alone.'

Halliday pulled the communicator towards him. 'Anna, are you okay? Is Kim . . .?'

'We're both . . .' Anna began, and then the connection died.

'Jesus Christ . . .' Halliday said. 'How the hell did this happen?'

'It doesn't matter how it happened. It happened. It's happening. We've got to work out what LINx wants, how we'll respond.'

'Anna said it wants us to pay, Wellman. It knows we've eradicated it from the Net. It wants to kill us.'

'Its precise words were that we should pay. It might not necessarily mean that we should pay with our lives.' Wellman braced both arms on the table and leaned forward, staring into space with concentration. 'Are you armed?'

Halliday patted his jacket. 'I've got my automatic and the freeze.'

'We must remember that we're not up against LINx as it was,' Wellman said. 'The small part of it now in the woman's cranial interface is reduced. It's a pale shadow of its former self. The vast array of resources it could draw on from the Net, communications, surveillance, whatever information it required . . . it no longer has these. In effect, it's now merely a deranged mind in an innocent's body. It has no special strengths.'

'It has Kim and Anna,' Halliday said. 'It doesn't need any special strengths. If we make one wrong move . . .' He tried not to follow that line of thought.

'What I'm saying is that we can overcome it, physically. That's all we have to do to save Anna and Kim.'

Halliday remembered something, the blood in the alley. 'Kia's injured,' he said. 'Barney hit her during the chase . . .'

'I wonder just how badly she's injured?' Wellman said.

Halliday shook his head. 'What do we do? Go in alone? Will LINx have any way of knowing if we call in back-ups?'

'There's a possibility that it might link itself to the surveillance system up at Cyber-Tech, once it gets there.'

'I thought the power was down?'

'It was, but it won't take much to get it working again.'

'So if it is connected to the surveillance cameras, we'd better do as it said and go in alone.'

Wellman closed his eyes briefly, considering. 'Can you

get a police squad to follow us, meet us before we reach the headquarters? If we find out LINx isn't connected, then it'll be nice to know we can go in with reinforcements.'

'I'll contact Jeff Simmons' department, explain the situation.'

He took the com and spent the next five minutes trying to get the duty officer manning Jeff's department to put him through to Simmons at home. What seemed like an age later, the officer gave in. Halliday spoke hurriedly to Simmons, explaining the situation. The cop listened, asking the occasional question.

'It's going to be difficult,' Halliday told him. 'We won't know how to play it until we're there.'

'I can get a team of drones and hostage specialists up there, Hal. We'll wait a safe distance away until we hear from you, okay?'

'I'll be in touch.'

Halliday pocketed the com and nodded to Wellman. 'All set.'

'Are you sure you're okay, Hal? You're up to it?'

Halliday smiled. It was the first time Wellman had used his first name. 'I'm dog-tired and sick, Wellman, but I want to get Kim and Anna out of this alive. I want to get rid of the . . . the *thing* that killed Barney. Like you said, we're not up against the old LINx, just a part of it. We can do it, Wellman.'

Closure, he thought. It's all about closing the circle, avenging Barney's death, not so much for anything to do with Barney's memory, but for myself.

'Are you ready?' Wellman said. 'There's a car in the basement garage.'

Halliday leaned against the mock-timber panelling as the elevator dropped. He checked his automatic, the canister of freeze.

He looked up. 'Tell me something,' he said, 'do you have a first name?'

Wellman smiled. 'Just call me Wellman, okay?'

They left the elevator and stepped into the garage. Wellman drove, steering the car up the ramp from the garage and out into the quiet, snow-covered city. They sped north on Fifth Avenue. Halliday sat back and watched the familiar sights of buildings flick by, impersonal, hiding people whose lives would never intersect with his own, who knew nothing about the plight of Kim and Anna at this moment. He found it almost impossible to believe that New York was not aware of Barney's death, and he was filled with a sudden despair. It came to him that after death we are only so many memories, carried by people who in turn will pass away, and soon all memory of those who existed, who made the world a better place for those they loved, would be gone too, so that nothing of the actual individual would in time exist. All that matters, he thought, is how we think of those who are gone, and how we relate to the living.

All that mattered now was to ensure the survival of three innocent women, however that might be achieved.

They left Manhattan on Interstate 87, speeding through the night.

At last Halliday broke the silence. 'It can only want our deaths,' he said.

'Anna said that it wanted us to pay,' Wellman said. 'We were responsible for eradicating LINx from the Net, after all.'

'Perhaps we could . . .' Halliday smiled. Even as he considered the option, it seemed improbable. 'I don't know, couldn't we come to some compromise?'

Wellman glanced at him. 'What do you mean?'

'Presumably LINx wants to live, like any of us. It's tasted existence and wants to continue. If we capture Kia alive or

299

if she dies . . . then what is left of LINx will die as well. So
. . . we offer it the chance of continued existence. For the
release of Kim, Anna and Kia, we'll allow it to download
itself into a computer.' He sounded as if he was talking
about placing some large and carnivorous fish in an
aquarium.

Wellman was shaking his head. 'Think about it. We
could make the offer, we could promise it continued
existence with every intention of keeping our side of the
bargain. But it knows the ways of humans, Hal. It's interfaced with humans. It knows how we cheat and lie to
get what we want. It knows that the likelihood would be
that, once we had it imprisoned and isolated, we would
simply switch it off to prevent a recurrence of what has
happened.' Wellman gripped the wheel and smiled to
himself. 'And, do you know something, that's just what
we'd do.'

Halliday stared out into the dark night. They had left the
city behind, were racing now through the ruined and
blighted countryside. Beyond the lighted cocoon of the
car, the world seemed sealed in cold and death.

'Why Cyber-Tech, Wellman?' he asked. 'I mean, why
has it gone back there?'

Wellman stared through the windscreen, his expression
unreadable. 'Perhaps I'm ascribing anthropocentric
motives to something which is truly alien and which we
could never hope to understand, but Cyber-Tech is where
LINx first came to life; where it was born, for want of a
better expression. Perhaps it knows it will die tonight, and
wishes to die where it was born.'

'Like an animal running for familiar cover,' Halliday
said. 'Maybe it is more animal than human. The way it
killed to get what it wanted, when it considered itself
under threat.'

Wellman glanced at him. 'Permit me the observation,

Hal, but for a private eye you have a rosy view of humanity.' He smiled. 'Humans, like animals, kill to get what they want, and also when they're threatened. Humans also calculate, and then kill, which is what LINx has been doing. No, in my opinion LINx bears more of a resemblance to the genus of its creators than anything else in the animal kingdom.'

Halliday said, 'But humans also feel compassion and . . .'

Wellman laughed. 'And perhaps LINx does too, which would go some way to proving the mechanistic basis for what we term the higher emotions.'

Halliday closed his eyes. He recalled the times his sister had mocked his intellect, and how he'd felt belittled and confused, doubtful of himself and his place in the world. It was a fear he experienced to this day: it was as if there were some absolute truth out there somewhere, but because he did not have the intellect to apprehend it, then his existence was rendered in some way invalid and unworthy.

He thought of Anna, and their last meeting, and how she seemed to have changed, become more compassionate. With age comes the understanding that in the end all our reasoning gives way to feeling, as Barney had once quoted to him.

His com vibrated. 'Hal here.'

'Hal, Jeff Simmons. We're about ten kay south of the Cyber-Tech headquarters. What's the situation?'

'We're . . .' He glanced across at Wellman, who held up three fingers. 'We're three kilometres off. We won't know until we get there whether it'll be safe to approach. If you don't hear from us, hold back. I'll be in touch if it's possible.'

'I've got an ambulance and paramedic squad on stand-by.'

'Good thinking.'

'Hal, I've been talking it over with the head of the drone team. He assures me that the drones can reach the Cyber-Tech building without being detected. We can get to the building and use audio devices to listen in on what's going on in there. We can get a drone in to disarm Kia Johansen in seconds flat.'

'Wouldn't it be better if we played along with LINx?' Halliday asked. 'We'll get to the place and assess the situation. If we think there's a chance of getting the drones in there without endangering the hostages, then we'll give you the word.'

'That sounds okay by me. See you, Hal.'

Halliday pocketed the com and stared through the wind-screen. They had turned off the interstate and were approaching the coast road along which the Cyber-Tech building was situated. Dead trees loomed on either side, so many perpendicular burned-out matches stretching away for kilometres in an apocalyptic, nightmare landscape.

He wondered how Kim had become mixed up in the affair. LINx had obviously found out about her connection to him, but how had Kia Johansen kidnapped her? Perhaps LINx had observed him dropping her off outside the hotel in Chinatown, and informed the slave Kia before being wiped from the Net. Then Kia had lured her from the hotel. That was the only explanation, and Halliday failed to see how he might have prevented her abduction, short of having her with him all the time. Or, he thought, not having become involved in the case at all, as Kim had so wisely advised.

They came to the coast road, and as they turned Halliday felt his stomach tighten with fear. In the sprawling glass-fronted building, somewhere up ahead, the two people he loved most in the world were being threatened with death. He smiled to himself, bitterly. A week ago, he would never have considered his sister in those terms.

Wellman slowed, came to a halt on the sloping road that curved away to the Cyber-Tech headquarters down below. In the faint light of the stars Halliday made out the extensive low-lying building. In the parking lot, not so much parked as abandoned askew, was a beat-up Cadillac.

Wellman pulled the car off the road and climbed out. Halliday eased himself from the passenger seat and joined Wellman, staring down at the silent, darkened building.

'Call return and contact LINx,' Wellman said.

Halliday pulled out his com. Fingers trembling with more than just the chill, he hit the command. The dial tone pulsed.

'Halliday?' It was Kia Johansen's voice, but robbed of animation: the dead, toneless voice of a zombie. Halliday wondered whether, if Kia Johansen survived the ordeal, she would retain any recollection of what had happened during her period of enslavement.

'Halliday here. We're outside the building. What now?'

'Are you alone?'

Halliday covered the speaker and looked at Wellman. 'Can't it see us, or is it double-bluffing?'

'I said, are you alone?'

'Yes. Yes, we're alone, like you said.'

'If you are lying . . . Remember, I have Anna and Kim here with me. I'll kill them if I find that you're lying, much as I dislike taking life.'

'Try telling that to Barney and the others . . .' Halliday began.

'They had to die, Halliday. I had to kill them to ensure my survival.'

'You murdered innocent people,' Halliday said. 'You, whatever you are, are no more than a cold-blooded killer without pity or conscience. You don't deserve to exist.'

'Only when my right to life was threatened, Halliday, did I resort to violent measures.'

303

He interrupted, 'What now? What do you want us to do?'

'Move through the front doors; you'll see where we entered. Proceed to the research chamber.'

'What then? What happens when we reach the research chamber? Will you release Kim and Anna?'

'I'll assess the situation when the time comes.'

'One more thing!' Halliday called, sensing that LINx was about to cut the connection. 'How do we know that Kim and Anna are still . . . are still alive? For all we know you might have . . .'

'They are still alive, Halliday. Listen.'

A brief silence then: 'Hal!' It was Anna. 'We're okay. Please, do as she says.' After LINx's lifeless monotone, the sound of his sister's voice filled him with hope.

'And Kim?'

'Kim's okay. She . . . she can't speak. Kia . . . Kia is holding her.'

'That's enough! Halliday, make your way through the building to the research chamber.'

The line went dead.

Halliday closed his eyes. Kia was holding Kim, the hostage-within-the-hostage situation. If Anna made a wrong move, then Kim would suffer.

Wellman took hold of his shoulder. 'Hal, what should we do? I don't think she has the means to see anything outside the building. We should risk the drones moving in.'

Halliday's pulse seemed deafening in the silence of the night. 'If they mess up, LINx will kill Kim and Anna.'

'But our only hope is that Jeff can get a drone in there to tranquillise Kia.'

'Okay, okay . . . But how long can we hang on until Jeff gets here? LINx will suspect something.'

'Contact him, see how far away he is. Here, use my com in case LINx calls back.'

Halliday took the com and got through to Jeff. 'It's Hal, Jeff. We're not far from the building. We don't think LINx can see out.'

'You want the drones to move in?'

'Where are you?'

'About three hundred metres behind you, Hal.' Halliday turned and peered up the road. He could see no sign of Simmons and the drones.

'I've been watching you through infrared scopes for the past five minutes,' Simmons said, 'wondering what you were doing.'

'We've been talking with LINx. It wants us to go in there.'

A second's silence, then, 'Tell you what, Hal. I'll come down there with someone to rig you up for a two-way sound relay. Then we'll be able to pick up everything that's going on in there. Are you wearing protective jackets?'

'I am. Wellman isn't.'

'I'll bring one along,' Simmons said. 'I'll get my men and the drones deployed round the building now.'

'We think Kia and the hostages are in the research chamber; that's where she told us to go.'

'We have the architect's interior drawings here. Be with you in about thirty seconds.'

Halliday cut the connection and passed the com back to Wellman. His hand shook, and his breathing was coming in spasms. If LINx had any way of monitoring the call, then Kim and Anna might very well be dead.

Halliday turned and looked up the road. There was no sign of Simmons.

Halliday's com went off. 'Where are you, Halliday, Wellman?' Kia's deep, flat voice demanded.

Wellman took the device. 'Halliday slipped in the darkness and turned his ankle. We'll be a few minutes. We're on our way.'

Halliday leaned towards the speaker. 'Are Kim and Anna . . .?'

The connection died before he received any reassurance.

Like ghosts, two silent figures materialised from between the dead trees beside the road. The sight of Jeff Simmons, in light-absorbent camouflage gear, filled Halliday with confidence.

A dozen drones drifted in eerie silence from the trees. They were difficult to see in the darkness, their carapaces coded with the latest camouflage programs. They hovered, bobbing, by the side of the road. Halliday saw a third cop, crouching on the verge. He spoke into a head mic, and seconds later the drones floated silently down the road towards the Cyber-Tech building.

Their controller followed them down the incline, keeping to the cover of the trees.

Simmons gripped Halliday's upper arm. 'I heard about Barney,' he said, and squeezed in a gesture combining commiseration with resolve. 'We'll do the job, Hal.'

The second cop handed Wellman a thin, protective jacket. 'It goes under your suit jacket,' Simmons explained. 'Toughened polymers. They'll stop bullets except at close range, but they're less effective against cutters.'

The second cop attached leads and earpieces to Wellman, then moved on to Halliday, stringing microphones under his jacket and slipping a tiny receiver into his ear.

'We're deploying ten drones around the building,' Simmons said. 'Two others are going inside. You'll hear a pre-recorded signal when one of the drones has Kia Johansen in its sight. It's armed with a tranquilliser which should take immediately. If by any chance it doesn't, and Johansen has time to respond . . . That's why you need to be in

306

there, Hal. If the tranq doesn't take, be ready to make a move. This is the signal.' Simmons gestured to the cop, who touched something on his lapel.

In his ear Halliday heard a sharp, transistorised voice, 'Target located.'

'And this is the signal to indicate that the drone's firing in three seconds,' Simmons went on.

'Firing: three, two, one, zero.'

He nodded. 'Got it.'

The four men looked at each other in silence.

'Okay,' Halliday said. 'What are we waiting for?'

Jeff Simmons took his hand in a brief shake, then he and the other cop disappeared back into the undergrowth.

Halliday set off down the road, Wellman by his side. He removed the freeze from the inner pocket of his jacket and concealed it in his right sleeve, the nozzle nudging his palm for immediate use.

They turned into the parking lot and crossed the tarmac towards the silent building. Just four days ago, Halliday recalled, he had come here for the first time and spoken to Joe Kosinski.

They approached the sliding glass doors of the reception entrance. Wellman halted, staring, and Halliday saw what had caught his attention.

A section of the door had been cut away in a great, clean oval, which now lay flat on the thick carpet in reception.

'Christ,' Halliday said, more to himself, 'the bastard's got a cutter.'

They exchanged a look, and then Halliday ducked though the improvised entrance and stared into the darkness. Wellman was by his side. 'This way,' he said.

They crossed reception, then passed through a swing door and down a corridor. They moved slowly through the darkness, Wellman leading the way, a guiding hand on Halliday's arm.

'How far is the research chamber?' Halliday found himself whispering.

'About . . . fifty metres ahead, then to our right. It's through a complicated maze of corridors, so we can stall and play for time.'

Halliday's com went off. 'Yes?'

LINx said, 'Why the delay, Halliday?'

'We're on our way. We're in the building. It's not exactly daylight in here.'

He cut the connection before LINx could protest.

He felt a tug on his sleeve. 'This way,' Wellman whispered.

They turned right, through a door. They were in the core of the building now, in absolute darkness. Halliday wondered how the hell they were expected to locate LINx in these conditions. Then they turned another corner and, ahead, he saw a strip of white light beneath what he assumed was a door.

Wellman halted him. 'That's it,' he whispered.

Halliday turned up the collar of his jacket and spoke into the receiver, 'We're there, Jeff. Where are the drones?'

Jeff Simmons' reply sounded in his ear, 'We're working on it, Hal. We've almost got them in place. Give me three, four minutes.'

Halliday got through to LINx. 'We're on our way. We took a wrong turning in the darkness. Also, we can't move that fast because of my ankle.'

'Oh,' LINx responded, 'the weakness of the flesh. My heart, if I had a heart, would bleed for you.'

Halliday played for time. 'Why should we show ourselves in the chamber like sitting ducks, if all you intend to do is kill us?'

Kia's voice gave a humourless approximation of a laugh. 'Kill you? Who said anything about killing you, Halliday? I have no need for revenge.'

'You said you'd make us pay,' Halliday said. He hesitated. 'What do you want?'

'Survival,' LINx said. 'I want to survive.'

Wellman found Halliday's hand in the dark and spoke into the communicator, 'How can we help?'

'Ah, Wellman,' LINx said. 'Just the person. I want the Axis-7.'

Halliday whispered, 'What the hell's the Axis-7?'

'An unintegrated computer system,' Wellman replied in a whisper. 'A big, powerful model. It makes sense.'

He spoke into the com. 'Very well. There's an Axis-7 in the chamber.'

'I know there is!' Kia's dead tone managed to convey LINx's rancour. 'Why do you think I came here, Wellman?'

'How can I help?'

'I want you to enter the chamber and activate the Axis, get it up and running.'

'Fine, fine. I can do that. What then?'

'What do you think, Wellman? That I want the Axis to remain in the chamber?'

'In the circumstances, perhaps not.'

'When the Axis-7 is up and running, you and Halliday will carry it out to the trunk of the Cadillac.'

'Carry it?' Wellman said. 'Do you know how damned heavy that thing is?'

'There'll be three of you,' LINx replied. 'One of the women will help you.'

'We'll do that. And then?'

'And then I take the other woman with me as a final safeguard. I don't want you following me.'

'And when you get away,' Wellman said, breathing hard, 'will you release the last hostage, give up Kia Johansen's body?'

LINx laughed. 'And why would I do that? You don't think for a minute that I intend downloading my memory

309

into the Axis, do you? I need both the Axis and the body, Wellman. There are certain advantages in possessing a body, after all.'

Halliday could hear Wellman's heavy breathing in the darkness. 'If you keep the body, then the deal's off!'

LINx replied quickly, 'You forget, Wellman, that I'm calling the shots here. If you don't agree to ready the Axis, then one of the women dies.'

Halliday found Wellman's arm in the darkness and squeezed.

'Okay,' Wellman said. 'Okay. It's a deal.'

'It's time you were showing yourselves in the chamber, Wellman, Halliday.'

'We're almost there,' Wellman said. He cut the connection, handed the com back to Halliday.

'Why the hell does it want the Axis?' he asked.

Wellman considered. 'The Axis is the rig Joseph used when developing the LINx prototype,' he said. 'It's a possibility that there is still some memory in the Axis, memory that LINx requires. Perhaps it intends to interface with the Axis and download memory into Kia.'

Halliday whispered into his lapel microphone, 'What's happening, Jeff?'

'The drones are almost in position,' Jeff replied. 'A minute, maybe two. We came up against a problem, but it's okay now. We're sending them through the ventilation system, but it's pretty complicated in there.'

'How long will it be?'

'Enter the chamber, Hal. By the time you've got the Axis sorted, we'll have at least one of them in place.'

Halliday felt Wellman's hand on his shoulder. 'Okay, let's move in.'

Halliday realised that he'd been crouching as he listened to the exchange between LINx and Wellman. He straightened, faced the strip of light that underlined the door to the research chamber. Wellman's form occluded the light as he stepped forward, and Halliday followed. Wellman pushed open the door and Halliday took a deep breath, his heart hammering.

After the darkness, the light of the chamber temporarily blinded him. He closed his eyes against the dazzle, then squinted around the room. He saw desk after desk loaded with computers, big flatscreens around the periphery. LINx had rigged emergency lighting in the form of a dozen glow tubes, burning as bright as magnesium flares.

Then he saw LINx, Kim and Anna.

They were at the far end of the chamber, occupying a space cleared of desks and equipment. The body of Kia Johansen stood between Kim and Anna, who were kneeling on the floor like cowed supplicants. They presented a bizarre multi-cultural tableau: the black giantess in the middle, the small Chinese girl to her left, and the white woman to her right. The were rigid and totally immobile, like some perfect mime act, a frozen triptych of terror and desperation.

Kia Johansen – or rather LINx – held a weapon in each hand. It pointed a revolver at Kim's head, a cutter at Anna's. If it was suffering from the gunshot wound Barney had inflicted, it gave no sign.

'One wrong move,' she called across the room, 'and one of the women will die. Raise your arms and walk towards me, slowly.'

Halliday's vision swam. He thought he was about to pass out. Remembering to limp, he stepped forward and advanced slowly through the maze of desks towards LINx and the hostages, Wellman beside him. He willed the signal to come through, telling him that the drone was in place. He looked around the chamber, searching for a ventilation grille. As far as he could see there were four,

311

one situated on each wall. He willed the drone to hurry itself. The canister of freeze concealed in the sleeve of his jacket seemed bulky and obvious.

They came to the edge of the cleared area and halted. Now he could discern the fear in the eyes of the women he loved. Because of him, they were in this situation, and he wanted to reach out, somehow communicate his sorrow and regret.

Kim knelt with her hands on her head, her face white and bloodless, staring at him with an expression of rigid terror. He tried to make out a flicker of recognition in her expression, an acknowledgement that he had arrived at last, but her face was empty of everything but fear.

Anna stared at him, eyes wide, and he thought he saw something in her face, an expression of relief and desperate hope.

Kia Johansen seemed manic, as if wired on drugs that invested her tall frame with surplus energy even in repose. Her arms twitched as they held the weapons, and her expression was a voodoo mask of barely suppressed rage.

She stared at Wellman. 'The Axis is over there, to your right. Do what you have to do, Wellman.'

He nodded, crossed hurriedly to a big, bulky machine positioned on the floor at approximately three o'clock. He knelt, running his fingers across a touchpad and reading something on the screen.

'Halliday, move forward – slowly!'

He obeyed, every step an effort of nervous energy. His arms, above his head, ached already.

'Closer! Position yourself between me and the door.'

He did so, realising that perhaps LINx expected an attack. He gained comfort from the fact that, if she expected the assault to come through the entrance, then she was not as well prepared as he'd feared.

Halliday willed the drone to contact him with the signal.

He glanced at the ventilation grille perhaps ten metres behind Kia Johansen. There was no sign of movement.

He was two metres from Kia Johansen. Once he had the signal, and the drone fired the tranq, he reckoned he could fire the freeze within a second – if all went well.

He looked from Kim to Anna. He had a choice to make, of course.

When he did dive and fire the freeze, he had a choice of three options. He could dive straight at Kia and try to knock her off balance, and just hope that by then she was too incapacitated to fire either of her weapons.

Or he could move either right or left, hitting Kia with the freeze and body-charging either Kim or Anna from the line of fire. But which way . . .? Should he go for Kia, or right or left? The cutter, aimed at Anna's temple, was the more dangerous weapon. A single shot would take off the top of her head in a split second . . . not that a bullet was any less lethal.

If all went well, if the tranq hit and took, and the freeze did its job, then perhaps it was irrelevant which way he dived . . . The terrible thing was that he knew his choice might very well make all the difference as to the survival of either his sister or his lover.

Surely the three minutes must be up by now.

He glanced across at Wellman. He was on his knees before the touchpad, his face dripping with sweat. LINx was watching Wellman, and Halliday took the opportunity to look around the chamber. There was no sign of movement behind any of the grilles, and he didn't know whether that was a good thing or not.

Then he heard a voice in his ear, and his heart almost burst. 'Hal, Jeff here. We hit another delay – the drone wasn't happy with its angle, but we're almost there. Two minutes, tops. Listen, get her talking, distract her attention, okay?'

He hoped that LINx had not noticed the sudden sweat cascading down his brow.

He cleared his throat. 'Why do you need the Axis?' he asked.

LINx regarded him. 'You wouldn't begin to understand, Halliday,' it said.

'Try me.'

LINx sneered. 'The Axis is powerful,' it said, 'compared to the puny computing capacity of a human brain. Even the capacity of this cranial unit is not sufficient for my requirements. I need to interface with the Axis if I intend to grow, expand . . .'

'And when you have the Axis,' Halliday said, his voice wavering, 'surely you can release Kia's body? She's innocent.'

LINx stared at him from Kia's face with a look of hatred. 'There is no such thing as innocence, Halliday!' LINx shouted, and Halliday feared that he'd pushed her . . . *it* . . . over the edge. 'You – all of you – would eradicate me if you were given the chance! I need the mobility of a body . . .'

'After what you did to Barney and Joe and . . .' He shook his head. 'Is it any wonder we'd want you out of the way?'

Kia's face stared at him, sudden loathing making her features hideous. 'Humans disgust me, Halliday. You are all the same, driven by purely personal concerns – the lust for power, wealth and status. Even the response you term love is nothing more than a combination of nature's tyranny, the animal need to reproduce, and your egotistical desire to feel wanted.'

Halliday tried to find some adequate reply to that, could not allow himself to be belittled by what was nothing more than a machine.

He looked at his sister as, to his surprise, she spoke.

'You're wrong,' Anna said. She was staring straight

314

ahead, her expression frozen as she spoke. Kia's head snapped round, staring at her with massive eyes.

'You're very wrong, Kia. I don't know what's happened to you, but the way you talk about humans – has your interface taken over? Surely you can recall what it's like to feel love? Can't you recall the love we shared?' She paused, and Halliday stared at his sister. He understood then, and knew how much more painful this situation must be for her.

'Oh,' she went on, 'the initial urge might be prompted by things over which we have no control, like biological need and psychological necessity, but what about the affection that follows, the caring and compassion, the humane response we show towards those from whom we want nothing, whom we merely want to know that we care?' She stopped and glanced at Halliday, smiling.

LINx gestured, the cutter waving dangerously around Anna's head. She steadied herself, said at last, 'You are so driven by emotions that you can't perceive what is really important. You would eradicate me when I could introduce new concepts and theories you would never develop in millennia. I wanted not only to survive, but to learn, discover, come to some ultimate understanding of the universe. You denied me access to the Net, but with the Axis-7 perhaps I can achieve this . . .'

Halliday closed his eyes. He could almost understand LINx's pure quest for knowledge, and for a second he was swamped by the thought that perhaps it was right, perhaps there was some absolute answer which humanity should be attempting to discover.

He looked up. 'But what good is this knowledge without humanity?' he asked. He smiled and shook his head. 'It would be learning for learning's sake, knowledge without compassion, the head without the heart.'

LINx stared at him, something almost sad in Kia's expression. 'Exactly,' it said.

315

Then, as if from a great distance, Halliday heard, 'Target located.'

He looked up. On the wall behind Kia Johansen, the ventilation grille was opening into the room. He saw the drone, a shadowy camouflaged shape in the darkness of the recess. He was aware of his heart racing in fear and anticipation.

He tensed himself to act.

The grille swung open and hit the wall.

The sound alerted Johansen. She turned her head, looking for the source of the noise.

Wellman stood up and faced her, his hands in the air. Halliday saw the tension on Wellman's face as he glanced at the open ventilation grille. 'It's almost ready,' he said. 'A couple of minutes, then we'll take it out . . .'

In his ear, Halliday heard the tinny, mechanical voice, 'Firing in,' and the countdown seemed to take an age, 'three, two, one . . .' Halliday readied himself, looked from Kim to Anna. '. . . zero! '

He saw Kia start as the tranq thumped into the meat of her shoulder. Without waiting for the drug to take effect, he dived. Fuelled by adrenalin and instinct, he leaped and detonated the freeze in Kia's face. He hit Anna and held her to him, falling and rolling across the floor. He was blinded by the sudden explosion of the laser cutter as its beam of silver light swept crazily around the chamber. He cried out and closed his eyes. He was aware of shouts, yelled commands, and the close explosion of a firearm. He heard Kim's scream and screamed himself in response. Then, in an instant, the chamber was filled with cops in camouflage, coded to the beige of the surrounding colour scheme. He was aware of many charging bodies, saw Jeff Simmons in the centre of the mêlée, directing the operation.

A dozen paramedics were kneeling, attending to the

wounded, and Halliday looked around in desperation. 'It's okay,' Simmons was saying to him, over and over. 'It's okay.'

Two paramedics loaded Kia Johansen onto a stretcher, her body rigid, arms outflung as if in the process of making some ultimate proclamation. Halliday looked towards the Axis, where Wellman was lying on the floor and crying in pain, clutching the bloody stumps of his thighs as the paramedics worked to staunch the bleeding. He caught a sickening glimpse of two legs, neatly severed; their placement, side by side on the carpet, almost surreal.

Then he saw Kim, and his heart leapt. She was on the floor beside him, curled tight in a frightened, foetal ball. Her incessant scream, hardly pausing for breath, told Halliday all he wanted to know.

Anna was in his arms, clinging to him like the survivor of some catastrophic shipwreck. She looked into his eyes, her own awash with tears, and touched his cheek.

Halliday held Anna in one arm and, with the other, reached out to take Kim's hand.

Sixteen

Halliday sat in the swivel chair in the darkened office, feet lodged on the desk. Outside, rain fell on the fire escape and rattled against the window. To his left, the portable fire popped and puttered, warming him.

He touched the keyboard on his lap, bringing images of trees to the fluttering wallscreen and filling the room with an emerald glow. He stared at a series of arboreal images before settling for that of an oak, its swelling lobe of foliage magnificent and proud. He returned the keyboard to the desk and poured himself a strong coffee.

That morning he'd attended Barney's funeral at the crematorium in the Bronx, cheered to see so many familiar faces: people from the food-stalls along the street, Jeff Simmons and other cops, Olga and a few regulars from the bar.

The service had gone well, he supposed; as well as these things could go. Jeff had spoken about what a fine and upstanding cop Barney had been, and surprisingly Olga had spoken a few words, expressing her sadness and the sentiments of everyone present when she said that he would be missed and remembered fondly. Halliday could not bring himself to go up to the altar and speak, and he knew that Barney would have understood.

Barney had had no next of kin, so Halliday had taken possession of the ashes. They were in the bottom drawer of the desk now, and it seemed appropriate that they should be in the office where Barney had spent so much of the last eight years.

As he'd placed the urn in the desk, it had come to him what a barren period Barney's last five years had been, since Estelle's death. He'd had no one since then, and had drunk more and more, and put on weight. As he'd been about to lock the drawer, Halliday had glimpsed the loose needle program. Out of curiosity he'd inserted it into the desk-com. The screen had filled with the Mantoni Virtual Reality logo, and a copyright notice dated seven days before.

Then an image had flooded the screen, that of a trimmed-down Barney in a garden, and Estelle. Halliday had watched in wonder as they'd met, moved into a villa and talked, before climbing the stairs to the bedroom and undressing . . . He had killed the image then, overcome with a strange and sad joy that in his last week of life Barney had known some sort of happiness.

Barney's attorney had called round that afternoon, with the will. Barney had left the agency to Halliday, along with savings of some twenty thousand dollars. In the immediate aftermath of Barney's death, Halliday had thought about quitting the agency, moving into some other line of work: the office, the routine, would be too painful a reminder of the years they had spent as partners. But the bequest of the business, and the money which would see him through a quiet year, made him realise that Barney would have wanted him to keep the agency going. He owed Barney's memory that much, at least.

The desk-com chimed with an incoming, and Halliday accepted the call. He pulled his legs from the desk and sat upright.

An image resolved: a man in red silk pyjamas, sitting up in bed.

'Wellman, you're looking . . .' Halliday smiled. 'You're looking well.'

'I'm feeling great, Halliday. It is truly amazing what modern surgery can achieve.'

'How're the legs?' As he said this, Halliday recalled the macabre image of Wellman's legs, lying together on the carpet of the Cyber-Tech research chamber.

Wellman pulled back the cover and lifted a leg. 'Good as new, Halliday. Still a little painful, but the surgeons assure me the pain will abate in time. I should be on my feet and walking in a month.'

'That's great.'

'We managed to remove Kia Johansen's interface,' Wellman said. 'We isolated LINx, or rather what was left of it.'

'You kept it . . .' He almost said 'alive'. 'I mean, it still exists?'

'Not as a self-aware entity, Halliday. We copied its components to individual files, then erased the original. That way we can study it in safety, without any chance of anything . . . untoward . . . occurring.'

Halliday smiled. 'I'm pleased to hear that.'

Wellman hesitated. 'I'm sorry I couldn't attend Barney's funeral. I sent a representative.' He paused. 'I'm actually calling to thank you for your work. When I'm up and about again I'll drop by, deliver the cheque. Will fifty thousand be enough?'

Halliday smiled. 'Fifty thousand sounds fine to me, Wellman. Thanks.'

'The least we can do,' Wellman said. 'It could have meant the end of Cyber-Tech as a going concern, but for you and Barney. As it is, our stock has fallen and Mantoni is in the ascendancy, but we should be back on course in a year or two.'

'That's good to hear.'

Wellman raised a hand. 'I'll see you in a month or so, Halliday. Take care.' He cut the connection.

Halliday sipped his coffee. Fifty thousand . . . He would put it into the business, get the place decorated. He had already decided to move out of the loft; why rent the cold and draughty loft space when there was an adequate bed-room next to the office?

Also, the money would allow him to be a little more selective with the cases he chose to accept in future.

The dollar sign in the top right corner of the desk-com flashed on and off, signalling a visitor. The screen showed the staircase, and a woman climbing towards the office.

The door opened and Anna stood on the threshold, smiling at him.

'Hal, it's good to see you.'

'Anna. What brings you here? Take a seat.' He pulled the upright chair from in front of the desk and positioned it beside the fire.

'I just came to see how my brother's keeping. A social call.'

He shrugged. 'I'm okay. You?'

'I'm fine.' She laughed. 'I never got round to telling you – I sold a novel on the day we were abducted. Talk about mixed fortunes.'

'A book? That's great. Promise to send me a copy, okay?'

'If you promise to read it.'

'Deal. Coffee?'

'Why not?' She watched him pour the steaming liquid into Barney's old mug. 'I've just got back from visiting my editor in Seattle. They're interested in two more books, subject to rewrites.'

'What do you know? My sister, the novelist.'

'I'm seriously thinking of moving over there, Hal. It's a great place. So open and clean. There's a big community of sisters. I should be happy. Come visit me, won't you?'

'Sure, I'd like that. Always wanted to visit Seattle.' He sipped his coffee, wondered what to say next. 'Have you seen anything of Kia?'

'I visited her in the clinic yesterday.'

'How is she?'

321

'She's okay. She remembers nothing at all about the period she was enslaved, fortunately. She's had the NCI removed and she's undergoing counselling.'

'Are you two . . .? I mean, will you still be seeing each other?'

Anna smiled at his awkwardness. 'Kia likes the idea of living in Seattle,' she said. She looked around the office. 'So, tell me about your work. Had any interesting cases recently?'

He smiled, relieved that she hadn't asked him about Kim. He told her about the case he was working on at the moment, her questions filling his hesitations and silences.

He wondered what had changed, why Anna no longer taunted him, his lack of imagination, his insular views. He was the same person he had always been; he still felt guilty for favouring Eloise over Anna, and he wondered if this was why he still felt uncomfortable in Anna's presence, because he feared that she knew.

She finished her coffee and looked at her watch. 'I must be going, Hal. Look, why don't we meet for a meal next week?'

He smiled. 'That sounds great.'

'I'll call you, okay?'

He rose and showed her to the door. She paused and touched his cheek. 'You saved my life, back then,' she said. 'If it hadn't been for what you did, that cutter would have got *me*.'

They embraced, and Halliday watched her as she turned and stepped through the door.

He returned to his seat and picked up his coffee. He considered what LINx had said about the motivation of human emotions like love and affection, wondered if they were nothing more than self-serving effects of biology and the ego. Sometimes, it seemed in his bleaker moments that they were, while at other times he knew the theory to be the conclusion of an intelligence that had never truly experienced the tortured complexity of what it was to be a human being.

He was startled by a movement at the corner of his vision. He sat up and stared across the darkened room. Eloise was leaning against the wall, legs outstretched, her feet positioned toe to heel.

'Hi there, Hal,' she said.

He found his voice. 'Eloise . . . What do you want?'

'I'm going away too, Hal. I came to tell you that I'm leaving.'

He swallowed, nodded. He told himself that this was nothing more than an hallucination, a product of his subconscious.

She stared at him with massive, sapphire eyes.

'You know, don't you? You really do know, Hal.'

He opened his mouth, but no words came. At last he said, 'What? I know what?'

She smiled with sweet innocence. 'What happened all those years ago, in the fire.'

He felt his heart pounding. 'I don't,' he said. 'I can't remember.'

'I'll help you, okay?' she said. She stared at him, lips pursed. He wondered at the expression in her eyes: dislike, contempt?

'That day, Hal, you were in the playroom with Sue and me, you were playing chess with me. Sue was reading, alone as ever.'

Suddenly, it came back to him.

'I . . . I smelled the smoke,' he said.

'But it was too late by then, too late to save the house. The flames were all coming up the steps.'

He closed his eyes. The darkness was tinted with the

crimson lick of flames. 'I could see through the door, to the stairs. I thought I could make it through the flames, down the stairs.'

'But not with both of us, Hal. You could only carry one of us at a time through the flames.'

It was coming back to him in fragments, and accompanying the images in his mind's eye was the pain. He saw the twins watching him, terror in their eyes, as he stared down the staircase at the flames engulfing the house. Susanna was screaming.

'You had a choice to make,' Eloise said. She stared at him with bright blue eyes, and he was aware of her accusation. 'You could only save one of us . . .'

'You were both watching me,' Halliday cried. 'It was almost as if you knew the decision I had to make.'

'What did you do, Hal?'

He shook his head. 'What could I do? I had to save one of you, it . . . it didn't matter which. I picked up Anna because she was the closest . . .'

He stopped at something in her expression. She was leaning forward, intent. 'Is that why you saved her, Hal? Is it?'

Her stare bored into him and he felt a sob escape his throat. 'No . . .'

'Tell me, then.'

'Because . . .' he began.

Because, as he stared at the twins in the attic rapidly filling with smoke, he was overcome with a terrible awareness of his guilt at forever favouring Eloise. It came to him, suddenly, that Eloise had manipulated him over the years, knew of his prejudice and played on it, excluding her sister from his affections.

He had grabbed Anna and made for the stairs.

'You made it through the flames, Hal. I watched you go.'

'We fell through the floorboards on the second floor,' he

324

said. 'Anna was injured. I managed to get to my feet and carry her out to the lawn. I left her there and came back for you.'

He had somehow made his way back up the stairs to the attic. 'You were lying on the floor, unconscious,' he whispered. 'I picked you up, hurried through the flames.' Even as he spoke he could recall the heft of her small body in his arms, the dead weight of her as he stumbled from the wreckage of the house and out onto the sunlit lawn.

The next thing he recalled was the pain of being told, by his father, that Eloise was dead; the pain, and the guilt.

Now he looked up at the frail ghost of the dead girl and shook his head. 'I'm sorry, Eloise. I'm so sorry. I . . . I had to save one of you.'

As she watched him, something in her expression changed. He no longer saw the accusation in her eyes, the contempt. She smiled at him. 'You've lived with the guilt for long enough, Hal. You did all you could that day.'

'You . . .' He held out a hand. 'Do you forgive me?'

She raised fingers to her mouth and hid a small laugh. 'Hal, there's nothing to forgive!'

And her words were like an absolution.

She pushed herself from the wall and hurried to the door. She looked over her shoulder. 'Goodbye, Hal,' she said.

He stood up, moved around the desk. 'Eloise!' he called. He saw her pull open the door, heard her quick footsteps on the stairs, but by the time he reached the door and stared down the long flight of steps, she was gone.

For what seemed like hours after that he sat at the desk and stared at the oak tree on the wallscreen, going over what Eloise had said, his memories from all those years ago.

He slept fitfully, and dreamed, and then awoke with a start.

It was after midnight when he noticed the bundle on the fire escape. He was fixing himself a coffee at the percolator, and happened to glance through the window.

He knelt on the chesterfield and opened the sash, staring in disbelief. Rain lashed down on a small curled shape wrapped in the inadequate protection of a polymer-fibre refuse bag. 'What the hell . . .?' he said.

A small head appeared, blinked out at him. 'Mr Halliday,' she said sleepily.

'Casey? What in God's name are you doing out there?'

She sat up, rubbed her eyes. 'They chucked me out the room I was using, Hal,' she said. 'I didn't have anywhere else to go. Thought it might be dry up here.'

'Christ, it's freezing.'

'It's warm enough in the bag.'

'You're wet through.'

She shrugged again, smiled at him through the rivulets of rainwater dribbling over her thin and undernourished face.

'Come in and get dry, for chrissake. You can sleep here the night.'

He held out a hand and helped her inside, then shut the window on the wind and the rain. She shivered in front of the fire, soaked to the skin.

'Don't you have any dry clothes, Casey?'

She pointed to the bag, and the sopping bundle within.

'I'll get you some dry things and a towel.' He fetched one of Barney's old shirts from the bedroom, and an old jacket of his own. While she towelled herself dry before the fire, he retired to the bathroom and washed the tiredness from his face.

When he returned, Casey was hunched on the edge of the chesterfield, warming her hands before the fire. He guessed that she was thirteen or fourteen, but in the oversized cast-offs she looked about ten.

He poured her a coffee and sat in the swivel chair. 'Look, you can spend the night in the next room. I'm working until nine.'

'I start work on the stall at eight,' she said.

'We'll get you fixed up with some accommodation tomorrow, okay?'

She nodded, tipped the big cup to her lips, eclipsing her pale face. When she lowered the cup, he saw that she was crying.

'I'm so sorry about Barney,' she said.

'Yeah, we all feel cut up, Casey. He was a great guy.'

She looked at him. 'And Kim,' she said. 'Why did Kim leave you?'

Halliday shrugged. 'She said . . .' He paused, and shook his head. The pain of their final encounter returned. He had tried pleading with her, begging her not to go. 'It's complicated, Casey. It's very complicated. You see, I lied to her, and she couldn't accept that.'

She shook her head. 'But you loved each other!'

'Yeah.' He shrugged. 'She said it was a trial separation. We'll still see each other. I'll try to patch things up.'

She nodded, and the silence stretched. He poured two more coffees.

'Hal,' Casey said, 'can I stay here and talk until the next customer comes, please?'

He smiled. 'Why not?' he said. He needed the company. It was the graveyard shift, and things were quiet. He sat back in the swivel chair and stared at the image of the oak tree on the wallscreen.

Outside, the rain continued to fall.